ACROSS

A BROKEN

SHORE

ACROSS A BROKEN SHORE

AMY TRUEBLOOD

flux®

Mendota Heights, Minnesota

First Edition
First Printing, 2019

Book design by Sarah Taplin
Cover design by Sarah Taplin
Cover images by Pixabay, Willard/iStockphoto, Ysbrand Cosijn/iStockphoto, Massonstock/iStockphoto

Flux, an imprint of North Star Editions, Inc.

This is a work of fiction. Names, characters, places, and incidents are either the product of the author's imagination or are used fictitiously, and any resemblance to actual persons living or dead, business establishments, events, or locales is entirely coincidental. Cover models used for illustrative purposes only and may not endorse or represent the book's subject.

Library of Congress Cataloging-in-Publication Data
Names: Trueblood, Amy, author.
Title: Across a broken shore / Amy Trueblood.
Description: First edition. | Mendota Heights, MN : Flux, an imprint of
   North Star Editions, Inc., [2019] | Summary: "In 1936 San Francisco,
   eighteen-year-old Willa MacCarthy is bound for the convent. But when she discovers
   her love of medicine, she will defy her family and work with a female doctor to care
   for those building the Golden Gate Bridge"—Provided by publisher.
Identifiers: LCCN 2019015457 (print) | LCCN 2019018169 (ebook) | ISBN
   9781635830439 (ebook) | ISBN 9781635830422 (pbk.)
Subjects: | CYAC: Physicians—Fiction. | Sex role—Fiction. | Family life—California—
   San Francisco—Fiction. | Irish Americans—Fiction. | Catholics—Fiction. | Golden
   Gate Bridge (San Francisco, Calif.)—Design and construction—Fiction. | San
   Francisco (Calif.)—History—20th century—Fiction.
Classification: LCC PZ7.1.T765 (ebook) | LCC PZ7.1.T765 Acr 2019 (print) |
   DDC [Fic]—dc23
LC record available at https://lccn.loc.gov/2019015457

Flux
North Star Editions, Inc.
2297 Waters Drive
Mendota Heights, MN 55120
www.fluxnow.com

Printed in the United States of America

For Joan Price Trueblood, who taught her
five children that words matter, strength is a gift,
and love is the most powerful force of all.

*"The secret to happiness is a love
for our chosen profession."*

Dr. Lucy M. Field Wanzer

*First woman to graduate from the UCSF School of Medicine
(then known as the Medical Department of the
University of California) in 1876.*

CHAPTER ONE

MacCarthy Residence
San Francisco, California
October 6, 1936

It only took a stitch, maybe two, before I drew blood.

Mam circled my chair like a hawk ferreting out its prey. Stalking. Waiting. She'd spent countless hours in the parlor with me, explaining how to properly hold a needle to darn socks or reattach buttons. The knots in my shoulders tightened. The pad of my finger bloomed red. I welcomed the sting. It was the perfect distraction from Mam's stare.

"Keep trying, Wilhelmina."

She ran a hand over her ink-black hair stretched tight against her scalp. The low hiss escaping her mouth resembled our old teapot coming to boil on the stove.

"Place the needle against the button just below the collar." The tinge of sadness that always filled her voice forced me to sink lower in my chair.

As I was about to place the needle against the fabric again, low voices filled the apartment. Da and Father O'Sullivan entered, discussing last Sunday's sermon about Wall Street and the current economic state of the country. It was a favorite topic of Father O'Sullivan, who continually railed on about the Depression and the greediness of mankind.

When the men found Mam and me in the parlor their conversation stopped. Father O'Sullivan scrubbed a hand through his shorn gray hair and pulled at the thick white collar at his neck. I turned my head, pretending to focus on my task. No matter the time or place, Father O'Sullivan's stern gaze warned he could sense the smallest sin even if you tried to hide it.

"Always nice to see a young lady learning to sew. In the convent, Willa will be expected to do her own mending. Be self-sufficient. It is not a life of relaxation but a dedication of every moment to God. You should be very proud that she's about to sacrifice her life to the church."

"We certainly are," Da said in reverence.

"Willa knows the importance of her decision," Mam added. "How her purpose is for the greater good."

I focused on the task in front of me, trying to picture my life in the convent. The joy it would bring my parents. I'd always been a good and faithful daughter. Found solace in the familiar prayers and routine of Mass. It would be easy to settle into the life of a nun, I reminded myself on a regular basis, especially since the topic always brought a rare glimmer of light to my parents' eyes.

Since graduating from school in June, I'd done everything in my power to forget where my future was headed. To Mam and Da, having a daughter in the convent brought them a sense of pride and acknowledgment. They spoke as if submitting me to the spiritual community was a gift to God they were all too willing to make at my expense. The thought of being alone in that cold, quiet building for the rest of my life chilled my bones quicker than a sharp fall breeze.

I stabbed the needle through the cloth over and over. Each time I pulled the thread through the cloth, I lost the stitch. Halfway through my third attempt to add the button, a deep, keening wail rose from the pub. The terrifying sound rattled the walls like the small earthquakes that frequently shook our tiny apartment.

"Was that Paddy?" I asked.

Da and Father O'Sullivan froze in place. Mam locked eyes with me. Her lips went so tight I thought they might shatter.

"Don't you dare, young lady. Your da can go and see what's happening downstairs."

Before she could reach out and stop me, I jumped from the chair and escaped out the door. I hopped down the first step and took the rest of the stairs two at a time. Once through the solid oak door connecting the first-floor lobby to the pub, I batted my way through a foggy haze of cigarette smoke in desperate search of my brother, Paddy.

The room buzzed with early evening revelry. The twang of the fiddle beat against my ears as the folk band played yet another rendition of "Molly Malone" to a crowd of ironworkers fresh off their shift at the half-built bridge spanning the Golden Gate.

I raced through the maze of bar stools and tables. Swirls of dancing men and women spun around me, their limbs loose from pints of ale and good music. With each step, my saddle shoes popped up from the floor, the wood planks sticky from the beer, whiskey, and bourbon spilled over the course of a long day.

More than a few drunk men tipped their hats in my direction. "Good day, Willa," they murmured as I rushed to the end of the mahogany bar. Once there, I found Nick, one of my four brothers, holding a blood-soaked cloth over Paddy's hand.

"What happened?" I asked doing my best to keep the quiver from my voice.

Da rushed past me. His face twisted as I stood amid the noise of clinking glasses and voices raised in song. Weeks past my eighteenth birthday, and my father still squirmed like he was being poked with a hot iron every time I stepped inside our family-owned bar. A place he considered respectable for everyone but his only daughter.

"Willa, go back upstairs," Da snapped. "You still have matters to discuss with your mother and Father O'Sullivan. We'll take care of this."

The tick in Da's cheek, and the trickle of sweat tumbling down Nick's ginger-tinged hairline, said they had no idea how to handle the situation.

A dozen blinking eyes watched from the rickety wood stools.

"Mind yer own business or get out," Da barked in their direction. The men bowed their heads, favoring drink over the commotion happening next to the bar.

Blood continued to seep through the cloth as Paddy wobbled on his feet. Da peeked under the thin rag he used to wipe up the suds from an overpour. He took a deep gulp, his face whiter than the sour milk Mam used in her soda bread.

"Looks like the tips of two of his fingers are gone." He spoke more in the direction of Nick than me.

Blood pounded in my ears, its beat louder than the strum of the nearby guitar. Why weren't they doing anything to help him?

"Hurts," Paddy mumbled in between rough gasps.

Da reached over the bar and popped the cork out of a bottle of whiskey. He shoved the bottle to Paddy's lips, watching him take several deep swallows.

"Told you he was no good with a knife," Nick grumbled. "But no, you said 'Sure, go on and have the lad chop up the vegetables for the soup.'"

My gaze moved to a spot behind the bar. Blood pooled on

the countertop and dotted mounds of chopped onion turned a ghastly shade of pink.

"Willa, leave now," Nick ordered.

Paddy reached out his free hand and squeezed my wrist. Da and Nick could glance at the door as much as they wanted but I wasn't leaving Paddy's side.

"I'm not going anywhere," I reassured Paddy.

"Dammit! This is the last thing we need." Da swept a shaky hand through his copper hair, a dash of white sprouting above his ears. The entire MacCarthy family—with the red hair, deep brown eyes, and sprinkling of freckles across the nose—was the spitting image of our Da and his long line of Irish ancestors.

Paddy continued to gulp the whiskey. Small rivers of the brown liquid slid down over his lips and neck.

"Da, alcohol won't fix his hand," I said over the strains of the banjo as the band worked its way into a stirring version of "Rocky Road to Dublin."

I turned back to Paddy. His skin was clammy. His pupils widened with each of his strangled gasps. If we didn't act quick, he was going to faint.

"We need to get him to a doctor!" Ignoring their frantic pacing and graying pallor, I pulled another rag off the bar, tore the cloth in half, and moved to Paddy's side.

I'd never admit this to anyone except God, but Paddy was my saving grace in this family. Just a year younger than Nick, Paddy was the only one who didn't give me a murderous stare when he caught me with my medical books. The one who taught me how to hide them under the loose floorboard in my room so Mam wouldn't catch me with them. What good was all my reading if I couldn't help him now?

"What are you doing, Will?" Paddy's words began to slur and it wasn't because of the whiskey.

"Taking care of you. Once I get the cloth around your fingers, you have to put pressure on them to stop the bleeding. Can you do that?"

He gave me a slow nod. Da and Nick's mouths dropped into wide Os as I secured the cloth, made a tight knot, and then another, securing the tourniquet at the base of his fingers.

Da gulped and double blinked as I finished. "That's enough now, Wilhelmina. You get back upstairs. Nick can take him over to Doc Maloy. He'll know what to do."

"Fine," Nick said. "Take him around front while I grab the car."

Da's chin dipped. I didn't like the way his mouth trembled. "The twins were begging to help out around here so I sent them to pick up two more barrels of wheat ale. Heaven knows when those two will return."

A chill danced down my spine like the ripple of the bow across the fiddle's strings. Sean and Michael were as goofy as the Marx Brothers and had about as much sense as our neighbor's old poodle. I could stand here and let them grumble all day but then Paddy would bleed to death.

"We can't wait for them." I slid under Paddy's shoulder, doing my best to balance his swaying body.

Da and Nick thought of me as a silly young girl with barely a sensible thought in her head. Every time they talked of politics or local news at the table, they spoke over my contributions even though I was the only one in our home who read the *San Francisco Chronicle* from cover to cover every morning. In the past I'd kept quiet, but I couldn't allow them to ignore me this time. I had to act before Paddy collapsed.

"Nick, let's go." I moved quickly, too afraid that if I stopped, Da would order me back upstairs again.

We pulled Paddy out the door and down Geary Street. As we moved along the uneven sidewalks, the ding of the streetcar filled the air as the evening sounds of the Richmond District came to life. A misty sheen clung to my skin. October was usually a warm month, but today the temperature dipped lower than normal. The fog began its slow stroll toward the city. Its thick tendrils swooped in like an apparition and quickly swallowed the sky.

At one point along the sidewalk, Nick had to stop and slap Paddy's face to keep him from passing out.

"Can't walk anymore," Paddy protested.

"We're almost there," I reassured him.

I reminded Paddy to hold pressure on the cloth that was now close to the color of cooked beets. Every time Nick looked down, he took a deep swallow. The last thing we needed was him losing his lunch here on the sidewalk.

"We should hurry," I said. "Those fingers need to be cleaned and stitched up before he loses any more blood."

"You learn that from that block of a book you're poring over every night while Mam and Da think you're saying your prayers?"

"That book is called *Gray's Anatomy* for your information. It's full of all sorts of interesting facts about the body," I said ignoring Nick's prickly tone.

"Whatever you're reading, it won't matter once you're at the convent," Nick grumbled. "Can't see the nuns taking kindly to you hiding that tome under your postulant skirts."

"I bet you don't even know about half the wonders of the human body," I shot back not wanting to talk about the turn my life would take in five short months.

"Are we close?" Paddy moaned. "I'm tired of listening to you crows snipe at each other."

"Almost there." I hitched myself up higher to better balance Paddy's weight. The shift made him moan again as we dragged him farther down the street. Nick and I kept our heads bent, doing our best to avoid the curious looks pointed in our direction.

"All right," Nick played along. "What don't I know?"

He was always quick to ignore me when I spouted out medical facts, but the quivering in his lower lip made me speak faster. "Blood accounts for about eight percent of a human's weight. The average Joe like you has twelve pints pumping through his veins."

Nick stumbled and all the color drained from his cheeks. As the oldest boy in the MacCarthy clan he was supposed to be the toughest, but even the slightest injury, bruise, or deep cut made his hulking body shiver.

Lucky for him we turned the corner at 19th Avenue or I would have told him bile is almost the same color as the stew Mam served every Sunday evening.

Nick stumbled to a halt. "Where's Doc Maloy's sign?"

I ignored him and dragged Paddy the last few steps. His weight grew heavier by the minute. He was complaining of nausea now. We didn't have a minute to spare.

After two quick raps on the white door, it swung open. A woman hovered in the threshold. Her short gold hair curled around her ears. Small drops of what looked like dried blood coated the sleeves of her white coat.

"Can I help you?" she asked.

"Doc Maloy here?" Nick leaned in and surveyed the open room cluttered with a few wood chairs, a worn green velvet sofa, and a narrow wood desk covered in books, bottles, and paperwork. It wasn't luxurious by any means, but the wood-paneled walls and antique pictures made it seem like you were in someone's front parlor, not a physician's office.

"The doctor retired a few months back." The lines around her mouth drooped when she caught sight of Paddy's blood-stained hand. "Is this man hurt? Please, bring him inside."

"Is there someone replacing the doc?" Nick stayed in the doorway.

"You're looking at his replacement. I'm Doctor Katherine Winston."

In Nick's moment of hesitation, I dragged Paddy around him and inside the office.

Doctor Winston raced to an open room a few feet away and we quickly followed.

"Set him down on the exam table," she instructed.

"You . . . You're a doctor?" Nick stuttered as he helped me set Paddy onto the long table in the center of the room.

A small tick at her lips warned this wasn't the first time she'd seen shock on a man's face. My heart sped up as she moved to a nearby table and picked up a stethoscope. I'd heard of lady doctors before but had never been in the presence of one.

"Your friend here is losing blood fast. May I get started?"

Before Nick could utter a word, I said, "Yes, please help our brother."

CHAPTER TWO

Two fingertips laid across the dirty bar rag settled in my lap. The pieces sat in a clean row, lined up like diced sausages. The moment Doctor Winston unwrapped Paddy's hand and pulled away the entire cloth it was clear both tips were severed an inch above the second and third knuckles.

After she'd taken the rag away and placed it on a side table, morbid curiosity had me reaching for the blood-stained cloth. I couldn't stop staring at the purple discoloration creeping up the edges of the skin. How the rounded fingertips, once attached to my brother, were still caked with small bits of potato and carrot.

Doctor Winston rushed about the exam room, which wasn't much bigger than a closet. "My apologies. My nurse quit last week, and I was just getting ready to close for the day when you knocked." She set out a row of shiny silver instruments on a steel cart beside the table. "Tell me your names and how this happened to your brother."

"Paddy, er, Patrick MacCarthy," Nick gulped, eyeing the sharp edges of the instruments. "I'm Nick and this is our kid sister, Wilhelmina."

"Willa," I said under my breath.

Doctor Winston opened a door in an old wooden hutch and pulled out a brown glass bottle, which she set next to her instruments. "Willa, in there," she pointed to a battered china cabinet behind me, "is a stack of clean dressings. Would you please bring me a few?"

I wrapped the severed fingers in the cloth and slid it into the pocket of my dress.

"I'm going to be honest," she started. "After looking at the wound, your brother should really go to the hospital."

"No!" Paddy jerked up from the exam table, finally showing some signs of life. "No hospital. Can't afford it. I've had friends go in and be held for several days, even weeks. Da needs me at the pub." He gripped Nick's fingers with his good hand. "Please."

Nick tapped his foot. Several nervous beats passed without a word from him.

"Do what you need to do, Doc," I said.

She gave a firm nod in my direction even as Nick mumbled under his breath about me keeping quiet.

"You've lost a lot of blood, Paddy. And the stitching," Doctor Winston chewed on her lower lip. "It may not be pretty."

Paddy let go of Nick and sunk back against the table. Color drained from his cheeks. Sweat covered his brow. Watching him deteriorate so quickly made my heart practically burst from my chest.

"Please help him," I said again in a frantic rush.

"I trust you, Doc." The words slid past Paddy's lips in a moan. His arms and legs went limp before his eyelids inched down.

"He's unconscious." Doctor Winston felt his pulse once more. "If we're going to do this, I need to act fast."

She filled a syringe with what I guessed was some type of painkiller and slid the needle into the crook of Paddy's arm. "This will keep him asleep while I stitch him up."

Nick dropped his hands firmly onto Paddy's shoulders. He bent his head and began to pray. I joined him until the dark thoughts spinning in my head became too much. For years now I'd hidden in my room and pored over those medical texts until the wee hours of the morning. It felt like a sin to do nothing while Paddy laid still as a corpse on the table.

"Can I do anything to help?" I asked.

"You can hold his hand. Talk to him. Let him know he's going to be all right. I firmly believe even if a patient is unconscious, some part of the brain still processes sound and touch."

Once I was in place next to her, I leaned in to get a better view of Paddy's hand. After dabbing at the area with clean gauze, Doctor Winston irrigated the wounds with a clear liquid that faintly reeked of bleach.

"Is that an antiseptic?" I asked.

"Yes, it's Dakin's Solution. With this kind of trauma, I like to use it for its sanitizing power."

This time I leaned in much too close and she gave me a look that said I was invading her space, but curiosity kept me frozen in place. Even under my steady gaze, she continued cleaning the ravaged skin, talking in a calm, measured tone.

"First, I'm going to excise some of the muscle, flesh, and bone from the fingers." Nick took a deep gulp. "Then I'm going to tie off the arteries. Once I'm sure he's stopped bleeding, I'll pull over the remaining skin, stitch the wounds, and use a heavy bandage to keep infection at bay."

There wasn't any hesitation in her movements. Her hands flew over the skin in sharp, methodical strokes. With Paddy's hand laid out flat, she went to work with a steel needle and black synthetic thread stitching the mangled skin around his pointer and middle finger. She placed one quick stitch after the other until they formed an x-pattern. After knotting off the first stump, she moved to the next. Mam would have been impressed with her handiwork.

A flicker of warmth moved over her face as I did my best not to lean in much closer. "I take it you applied the tourniquet to the fingers?"

"Yes, that's correct," I replied, my gaze not moving from her effortless motion. It was as if her fingers and the needle were one instrument working together to save my brother. Adrenaline pumped through my veins. I should have been worried about Paddy, but her skill told me he was in good hands.

"Smart thinking on your part. I like how you secured the knot at the base of the fingers. Taking that action likely stopped most of the bleeding. Do you have any nurse's training?"

Nick shot me a strained look.

Nurse's training? No. The only training I was headed toward was a life of endless Mass and hours spent praying for the forgiveness of the world's sins.

"No ma'am" I whispered. "I've been reading *Stedman's Medical Dictionary* and a few other medical books."

The feel of Paddy's fingers in my pocket weighed me down. All I'd wanted since I discovered that *Gray's Anatomy* in the trash bins behind our apartment two years ago was to be a physician. From the first pages, I was entranced by the skeletal drawings of the human body. The cross-section diagrams of the heart and lungs. In the dim light of my bedside lamp, I pored over the details in a sketch of the connection of the thoracic vertebrae. One evening I was so entirely swept up in the pages, I didn't hear Mam creep into my bedroom. The look of shock and horror on her face was akin to something out of a Bella Lugosi picture show. She chastised me for choosing the book over saying my prayers and swept out of the room with my dreams tucked under her arm.

When she left for Mass the following morning, I tore her and Da's bedroom apart. When I couldn't find the book, I returned to the trash bins. After an hour of searching through discarded bottles and sodden newspapers, I discovered it beneath a mound of coffee grounds.

I learned an important lesson that day. If I wanted to study medicine, it would have to be done in secret. My parents would never allow me to become a doctor, but that didn't mean I had to stop learning.

Nick swayed on his feet as the doctor made one final stitch. He swiveled his head away while my focus remained intent on her work. How many times would I get to see a procedure like this in person?

When Doctor Winston finished, she wrapped clean dressings around Paddy's hand. "I'm afraid that's all I can do now."

She moved to the side of the exam table and tapped Paddy's cheeks. Slowly his eyes fluttered open. With Nick's help, she sat him up. He blinked several times and then slammed back against the table, his cheeks paler than the sky on a February morning.

"I was afraid of that," she clucked her tongue. "Do you by any chance have a car?"

"Yes ma'am we do, but it's with our other brothers right now. We need it to run our business." Nick eyed a bloody spot on the planked floor. "Willa and me had to walk Paddy here."

Quietly I cursed Da for letting the twins run amok in the city while Paddy laid too still on the exam room table.

"Your brother's lost too much blood. Walking is out of the question. He really should go to the hospital," she said.

Nick's lips pinched together the way Da's did when he only had funds to pay for one kind of ale for the pub. A trip to the hospital meant money and we barely had enough to keep the pub doors open and food on our table. Everyone was pitching in to keep the family afloat.

My twin brothers, Sean and Michael, were only a year older than me. Every day since graduation they'd stood over at the Bay Bridge, and now at The Gate, waiting for a lad to get sick or scared so a job would open up. They had their union cards, and worked every once in a while on President Roosevelt's Works Progress Administration projects, but even the WPA jobs didn't add anything steady to our family's income. At least with me delivered into the church's hands soon, there'd be one less mouth to feed.

In the moment of Nick's hesitation, Doctor Winston leaned over and patted his mitt-sized hand. "Could he stay here with me for a while? I'll keep a watch on his vitals. Hopefully, he can return home in a few hours," she said.

"But didn't you say you were done for the day?" I asked.

"My apartment is upstairs. I don't mind staying until your brother is stable and ready to go home."

"Fine by me. I'll let our da know." Nick slid his hands along his pants trying to wipe Paddy's blood off his fingers. "Wilhelmina, let's go and leave the doc and Paddy in peace."

My gaze swept over the room, memorizing the scene. The medical texts with the fancy gold lettering on the spines stacked up shoulder-high along the tables. The rows of colored bottles nestled next to each other. How the steel instruments glimmered in the orange-tinted light streaming in through the windows. When

I was left to do nothing but kneel and pray in front of a crucifix in my small cell of a room at the convent, I would recall this day and dream about all the important work she was doing here.

After Doctor Winston reassured me twice that Paddy would be all right, I followed Nick out to the sidewalk. Folks filled the streetcars or hustled down the sidewalk, anxious to get home from work. In vacant lots, men curled up into tight balls trying to find warm spots to sleep for the night. A breeze tugged at my hair and blouse as I raced behind Nick trying to keep up with his long strides. When we crossed 21st Avenue, a businessman bumped into my side. The juicy squish in my pocket reminded me what was hidden there.

"Nick," I sped up to catch him. "I still have Paddy's fingers." I slid out the dark purple-stained cloth. "Think the doctor may want to dispose of them?"

His skin took on a greenish tinge. "I need to get back to the pub," he grumbled. "You drop those off and then head straight home. It'll be dark soon and Mam will be expecting you to help with dinner."

"Of course." I turned on my heel and rushed back to the office.

I gave two sharp knocks on the door and when it swung open a knowing smile lifted Doctor Winston's lips.

CHAPTER THREE

The Office of Doctor Katherine Winston
San Francisco, California
October 6, 1936

Piece by piece Doctor Winston dropped the used dressings into a steel bucket underneath the exam table. She pointed at my pocket. Spots of blood seeped through the fabric. "I'll take those fingers now."

I fumbled for a moment until I slid the soaked gauze into her hand. She carried the dressing like a precious gift to a side table cluttered with open books and half-full beakers of yellow liquid. Once the fingers were free, she slid one under a microscope. Her jaw ticked as she examined the skin.

"One day there will be a way to reattach severed limbs. Until then, we can study these to see how quickly necrosis sets in without blood flow." She waved me in closer. "Necrosis is . . . "

"The morphological changes indicative of cell death caused by enzymatic degradation," I said. "Without blood circulation, the skin begins dying."

A knowing smile lifted her lips. "*Gray's Anatomy*?" she asked.

"Yes," I breathed out.

"Very good. Use every chance you have to study the body, Willa. When I was in medical school the professors consistently doubted my skill. They pushed me harder than the men. I had to study more. Excel at testing to get through the rigorous training."

Paddy snored in the exam room only feet away. I moved to the door, needing to see the steady rise and fall of his chest.

"The injection I gave him earlier will take care of most of the pain for now." She clicked the microscope's knob and took another look. "Have you ever thought about medicine as a career?"

"Medical school is nothing but a dream." I studied the planked floor for more blood stains. The least I could do was help her mop up, considering she hadn't requested payment.

"Is money an issue?" She stopped and huffed out a deep breath. "My apologies. That's none of my business."

"Church is the issue," I said. "Five generations of MacCarthy women have given their life to God. My parents expect the same from me as I'm the only girl." Dread mixed with a tinge of sadness crept up my throat. "It's been the plan for me since I was young. Our parish priest is expecting me to report in February. If I backed out, it would embarrass my parents. Bring shame to our name. I could never do that to them."

She swept by me and gently touched Paddy's wrist. "His pulse is back to normal. That's good."

I stepped in closer. "Could you teach me how to do that?"

She replaced her hand with mine. "Your pointer and third finger go between the bone and tendon over the radial artery. Never use your thumb, as it has a pulse of its own."

For thirty seconds we counted each beat. The thrum of Paddy's life coursing beneath my fingertips sent a sharp thrill of joy through me. I let my mind wander for a moment to what it would be like to be a doctor. To have this life every single day.

Doctor Winston placed her stethoscope over Paddy's heart. He shifted but didn't wake. "You remind me a lot of myself when I was young. I grew up in a tiny town on the California and Oregon border. My little brother, Jasper, died of pneumonia the summer I turned fourteen. I was always maddened by the thought that the town doctor couldn't do anything to save him."

"Is that what made you want to study medicine?" I asked.

"It was a thought, but my parents always wanted me to be a teacher." She patted my hand. "I, too, understand parental expectations."

She moved around the table and slid her hand over Paddy's forehead. "No sign of fever. That's good too."

"May I?"

The knots in my shoulders relaxed as she guided my hand over his cool skin. She handed me her stethoscope and pointed where to place the circular metal pad on his chest. The steady *thump, thump* of his heart brought a smile to my lips.

"I do understand your parents' commitment to the church, but we need smart, strong-willed girls like you in medicine. You certainly have an instinct for it."

Doctor Winston stepped back from the table. The edges of her doctor's coat flailed out around her waist. Even with her hands covered in blood, she still managed to look regal.

"Your first thought today was to stop your brother's bleeding. You knew exactly where to place the tourniquet." She took the stethoscope back and placed it on the side table. "From that interaction with your oldest brother, I can tell you're not one to go along with the usual train of thought or defer to an adult. I suspect it was you who insisted Paddy be brought here for medical care, and then you pushed through that door even though the only physician here was female."

She smiled and laid a hand on my arm. "That is the instinct

every physician should have, Willa. To act when someone is injured. To push past all obstacles to ensure your patient has care."

She pointed to a document that hung over the exam room door. "I will apply dietetic measures for the benefit of the sick according to my ability and judgment; I will keep them from harm and injustice," she said, a self-satisfied grin lifting her lips. "That's part of the Hippocratic Oath every physician must abide by. On your own, you followed those rules without realizing it."

The clock near the door chimed six times.

"Oh my goodness," I gasped. "I must get home to help my mam with dinner." I rushed to the door and stopped half way through. "Thank you, Doctor Winston. For everything."

"You're welcome back any time. If you're interested, I could use an extra set of hands around here. I can't pay much, but I can teach you more about medicine."

"Not sure I have time. There's my chores at home. Daily Mass. Weekly Confession," I said. "And people I know, they may see me here."

Doctor Winston crossed her arms over her chest. The corner of her mouth ticked like Mam's did when she was trying to figure out how to get the truth out of me.

"Tell me one thing, Willa. Why did you put the fingers into your pocket instead of setting them back on the counter? Could it have been you wanted a reason to return without your brother?"

Her words kept me in place. My mind thrummed as quickly as my heart.

"I don't know," was all I offered.

Was Doctor Winston right? Had I kept the fingers as an excuse to return? I wasn't sure, but some force was certainly drawing me back here.

"As far as people seeing you, I can assure you that won't be an issue. The minute people learned I was a female physician, this office got very quiet. The majority of my patients are women and families who have no real means." In my moment of pause, she patted my shoulder. "I am a firm believer that if you want something bad enough, there are ways to make it happen. Think about it. That's all I ask."

My head was lighter than a county fair balloon as I rushed out the door. Since I watched Doctor Winston slide the stethoscope over Paddy's heart, something deep inside my soul awakened. It was as if witnessing her work opened a locked door in my mind I never knew existed.

CHAPTER FOUR

St. Monica Catholic Church
San Francisco, California
October 11, 1936

Mam claimed the minute she stepped inside the vestibule of St. Monica she was encircled in the warm embrace of God. Every time I dipped my fingers into the holy water and made the sign of the cross, I waited to feel what she described. Peace. Serenity. Anything at all. Unfortunately, all that enveloped my body was the cold sweat of dread.

Even though I'd secured my hat with at least four pins, it shifted over my forehead as I walked down the crimson-colored aisle toward our regular pew. Being a nun was a noble pursuit, my brothers often reminded me. Before I graduated, girls in my school were already talking about joining the church. They discussed the "divine touch" or "the calling"— a deep churning need to serve the Lord. Since the day my parents sat me down at twelve years old and explained what they expected my path to be, I waited for a sign from God. A settling in my stomach that said church was the correct path for me. Not once in the last six years had I felt anything except worry that this life would never bring me happiness, but I held out hope. Every night before I went to bed I said my prayers, convinced my faith would show me the way.

Father O'Sullivan stepped out from the sacristy and approached the altar. The church was silent save for the click of his shoes across the marble floor. Two young altar boys quickly trailed behind him, their white robes fluttering around their shoes.

A low hum floated out from the organ as morning light streamed through the stained-glass windows. Blasts of orange, red, and green moved over the floor in a gorgeous prismatic dance. Music was a constant part of the Mass and recently the congregation had raised enough funds to install a new set of pipes.

Father O'Sullivan turned his back to the congregation and began the Mass. I settled onto the creaky wood pew next to Mam. Her dark brown hat shifted against her hair as she bent her head in prayer, whispering along with the priest in Latin. My father settled in on the other side of her with Nick and Paddy. Today was the first time Paddy had ventured outside since the accident last week. With all the rest, the pink in his cheeks was finally returning.

Sean and Michael sat on the other side of me at the end of the pew. Out of the watchful eyes of our mam, it was the perfect spot to take a snooze during the sermon and make a quick getaway when the final prayer was past the priest's lips.

Two rows in front of us, I spotted the silky golden hair of my best friend, Cara. The arch of her shoulders and dip of her chin said she'd slid the latest issue of *Photoplay* in between the pages of her hymnal.

When we were kids Paddy nicknamed her "firecracker" because you never knew when she might go off. The moment a male classmate teased her about her tiny stature, she'd toss back an equally demeaning comment usually about his anatomy or lack thereof. I marveled at how she never withered under anyone's gaze. Her two older sisters had already taken their church vows, so all the pressure was off her. I envied how she was free to choose the path for her own life.

Together at school we'd talked about our futures. Hers always included traveling to some exotic place we'd learned about through International Club. Not long after I discovered the copy of *Gray's Anatomy*, I told her about my interest in medicine. Like the true pal she was, she'd gotten her own library card and regularly checked out books for me knowing the lengths I had to go to hide my secret from my parents.

As if she could feel the heat of my gaze, she turned and gave me a wink. I coughed and forced down a laugh. Mam was already rattled this morning thanks to Sean and Michael wandering in drunk late last night. Hearing my snicker would only make things worse.

With two sharps notes, the organist began a new song and Cara rose from her seat. She mounted the marble steps and took her spot in front of the altar. Latin streamed from her lips. The familiar sounds of "Ave Maria" floated along the air and up into the rafters.

On the third verse, I let my mind wander back to the sights and smells of Doctor Winston's office. The gleam of the instruments. How the sharp scent of alcohol tickled my nose. I glanced down the pew at Paddy. His head hung low, while his lips moved along with the chorus. The white bandages on his hand were a stark contrast against his black pants.

I knew the real reason he refused to leave the house. Unlike my other brothers, Paddy had a thing for looking his best. He understood fashion and refused to go in public unless his shirt was starched and he could see his own reflection in the shine of his shoes. When we strolled down the street, he always had to stop in front of the window of Marbury's. Black derbys. Brown blocked fedoras. Gray Homburgs. No matter the style, his feet tapped with joy as he marveled at the hats on display. Twice over the last few days, I'd caught him wrestling with a button on his shirt. It wasn't pain, but vanity, that kept him inside.

Though he'd protested this morning, I checked his stitches before rewrapping his hand. My books told me to look for fever or red patches around the wound. When I found neither, I breathed a sigh of relief there was no infection.

Before I could leave the room, Paddy reached for my hand. MacCarthy men were terrible at expressing their feelings, but Paddy always managed to tell me how he felt through a smile or gentle squeeze.

"At least I can still pour a pint," he joked, but the twinge in his voice warned he was still mourning the loss of his fingers.

As Father O'Sullivan read from the Gospel, I turned my attention to the front pews. In a long line sat a row of nuns. Their ebony-colored habits swallowed most of their heads. Did they comb their hair anymore? Did they even have hair under there?

On instinct, I felt for a curl around my ear. I'd always hated my cherry-colored hair but somehow the thought of never feeling the warm summer sun on my head twisted my stomach. And I'd never been interested in clothing like Paddy, but the idea of wearing a floor-length black dress for the rest of my life brought a prickling heat to my eyes.

Father O'Sullivan's droning voice filled the sanctuary, but all I heard was the frantic pounding of my heart. I wanted the church to bring me serenity. On my knees in front of my bed every evening, I prayed for it. But the only time I was at peace was when I was caught inside the world of my medical texts. It was easy to lose myself in the illustrations of the human brain or skeletal system. Even now, I couldn't look at the two men in the pew in front of me without thinking about the connection of the mastoid process to the C-1 vertebrae as they bent their heads in prayer. Or how the priest's phalanges moved in a fluid motion as he poured the wine into a silver chalice on the altar.

A quick tap on my leg pulled me out of my thoughts. Mam pursed her thin lips and shook her head like she knew I was day-dreaming. I didn't know why she was bothering me when Sean and Michael snored quietly at the end of the pew.

The rest of the Mass dragged on until it was time for Communion. We made one long thin line as we migrated toward the altar. I did my best to look penitent until a low scrape of feet caught my attention.

Across the aisle, Mrs. Boyle clung to the arm of a young man. His thick hand circled her upper arm. The dazzling smile she gave him was blinding. She'd run the local boardinghouse on Fillmore Street for as long as I could remember, but I'd never seen a single tenant help her along.

As if they could feel the heat of my stare, they both looked in my direction. Mrs. Boyle gave me a small wave. The young man's feet stuttered along the tile. His face was thin like most men these days, but his deep, ocean-colored eyes were a stark contrast to his hair, which was a shade paler than the wheat ale Da served in the pub. For years I'd been gaga over matinee idol Clark Gable, but this fellow was a hundred times more handsome.

A poke from behind sent me forward.

"Where's your head, Willy? Move along before Mam sees you staring at that fella across the aisle."

I didn't bother to turn and look at Paddy, his voice full of glee.

At the long railing facing the altar, I knelt and waited for Father O'Sullivan to place the Eucharist on my tongue. When he reached me, a flicker of darkness in his eyes sent a shiver down my spine. Due to Paddy's accident, I'd missed our meeting and hadn't bothered to reschedule even at the constant prodding of my mother. I bent my head and pretended I didn't see the look of disappointment as he moved down the row of worshippers.

When Mass ended, I made a beeline for the exit. With every step, a surge of freedom washed over me. I tapped my fingers into the holy water, crossed myself, and burst through the doors. Sucking in a deep breath, and allowing the cool ocean air fill every inch of my lungs, I stepped out into the sun and straightened the brim of my hat, shading my eyes from the late morning rays.

"How's Paddy?" Cara stopped only inches behind me, the tips of her pointed-toe shoes scraping along the sidewalk. The heels brought her barely up to my chin.

"Healing," I said.

She moved in closer, her bright blue eyes narrowed. "I heard you saved his life."

"Who told you that?"

She huffed out a laugh. "We live in one of the most tight-knit communities in San Francisco, Willa. You can't sneeze without a neighbor calling 'bless you' out a nearby window."

"It wasn't that dramatic. He was bleeding and I made sure he saw a doc. That's all."

Her mouth puckered like she knew that was only part of the story.

"It was a lady doctor," I added.

Her eyes quickly brightened. "Really? A woman with real medical school training?"

"Yes. She was quite extraordinary."

At the lift in my voice she inched in closer. "Oh, really?"

"She fixed him up and then we went on our way."

The white ribbon on her hat flapped about as she shook her head. "There's more to the story than what you're saying."

"There's not."

I usually told Cara everything, but for some reason I held the fact that the doctor offered me a job tight to my chest. Acknowledging I wasn't brave enough to take advantage of the opportunity would only make me feel worse.

Cara tilted her head. Her way of trying to determine if I was lying. When I refused to flinch, she inched in closer. "I have more books stashed for you at the house. It's rather fun to check out the ones with all the grotesque pictures. The librarian looks at me like I'm some sort of mad scientist."

Only Cara would find a probing stare amusing.

Sean and Michael rushed by us on the street. Their hoots and hollers filled the air as did Da's voice as he called at them not to be late for Sunday dinner.

Cara's gaze followed them down Geary Street. "Heard anything else about the bridge lately? Have your brothers been hired on yet?"

From her bedroom window, Cara could see the construction slowly come together. Besides boys, and music, the bridge was her favorite topic. She talked endlessly about the barges dragging in steel, or the men hanging from the suspender ropes painting the bridge an odd shade of orange.

"That bridge is quite a sight, ain't it?" a male voice said behind us.

Mrs. Boyle's tenant leaned against the stucco wall of the church. The collar of his blue work shirt wilted along his sharp collarbone. He pulled down on the edge of his brown hat and flicked his cigarette to the curb.

He walked toward us and Cara let loose the high-pitched giggle she saved for attractive boys.

"It's all right," I said focusing on the sky and not his steady gaze.

Parishioners continued to file out of the church as the sharp sounds of the organ filled the city air.

"Do you know why it's painted orange?" He stepped in closer. Too close. If my brothers caught the way he stared at me like I was a cold pint of ale on a hot summer day, there'd be trouble. Still, my feet stayed planted to the sidewalk.

"So it stands out in the fog?" The words shot out of my mouth in a brazen way and there was no time to reel them back.

"No, but a good guess. The paint acts like a shield from the salty air. It keeps the steel from breaking down in this horrible thing you all call weather." There was something sweet, almost boyish, about the way he bounced on his toes as he spoke.

"I take it you don't like the dreary mist and the way our city is swallowed up by the foggy ghosts almost every day?" Cara's voice trilled.

He shoved his hands into his pockets and kicked at the uneven sidewalk. "No, Miss. I'm more of an open desert sort of fella. I like the sun beating against my skin." Even though Cara continued to stare at him, his focus remained on me.

"Will," Paddy moved in, nudging Cara away with his hip. The man took two steps back at the warning tone in my brother's voice. "Mam's looking for you, and Father O'Sullivan is attached to her side. If you don't want to have that talk about the meeting you've been avoiding, may I suggest we get out of here?"

Cara returned his hip bump. At one time I thought she had a crush on Paddy, but over the years I'd learned she just loved to get under people's skin. Nestle down deep like a splinter and poke around in irritation. I chalked it up to being picked on regularly by her older siblings. A fact I understood all too well.

"She doesn't always need a protector, Patrick," she teased. Out of all our family and friends, Cara was the only one who called him by his given name. Another way she loved to irritate him.

"Yes, she does." Paddy followed her hungry gaze to Mrs. Boyle's tenant. "And by the looks of things, so do you."

Cara opened her mouth to reply but stopped when her mother called for her.

"See you later, Willa." She bounced off completely unruffled by Paddy's tone. Another thing I envied about her.

I clutched my handbag to my side as a peal of bells rang out like a warning that my time as a young, free girl was waning. The man tipped his hat in my direction. Before I could ask his name, Paddy yanked me down the street.

It was hard to keep up with his long stride in the stiff, black-strap Oxfords Mam insisted I wear with the old indigo-colored dress that was too long for my liking. On the streets, gals were wearing pants and dresses that skimmed at spots below their kneecaps, but according to Mam only questionable women dressed in that type of fashion.

When we reached the corner, Paddy stopped short. He pushed his cap back and shook his head when he caught me staring at his hand.

"What's spinning inside that head of yours?"

"I can't stop thinking about the woman doctor. How she seemed so in command of every step of your care."

"You thinking about taking her up on her offer?"

"You heard that?"

"Yes. You thought I was snoozing on that table in the exam room, but I heard every word. The lady doc is right. You got a head for the medicine thing." He sucked in a deep breath. "Without you, I might not be standing here right now."

"That's not true, Paddy. Nick would have taken you to the doc in plenty of time."

"No matter, you tied up my hand so I stopped bleeding. I know Mam and Da wouldn't approve, but you're smarter than us lot of boys put together." His eyes narrowed. "You should take that job."

When we reached the corner, the flush in Paddy's cheeks was gone. I led him down the street until I found a bench outside the butcher shop. Once we were seated, I placed my hand on his forehead like I'd seen Doctor Winston do. His skin was cool to the touch and a relieved sigh left my lips.

"You've overdone it today."

He reached for my hand and set it back in my lap. The dressing on his hand scratched against my palm. No matter how hard I tried, I couldn't get that day with Doctor Winston out of my head. The calm that swept over her as Paddy bled all over her exam table. The way she kept her composure even as he went unconscious. On that day she'd saved him, but she'd also shown me that a woman could handle a dire situation just as easily as a man.

"Paddy, could you help me figure out a way to go back to Doctor Winston's office? Maybe cover for me when I'm gone?"

His cheeks bunched into a wide smile. "You know I'd do anything for you, Willy."

"You sure? If Mam and Da found out, we could be in a whole lot of trouble. They might ship me right off to the convent, and I don't even want to think about the punishment Da would put you through at the pub. You may be cleaning toilets for a long time."

"Toilets or no toilets, you mean the world to me."

He swallowed a laugh and his face quickly sobered. "I'm glad you're taking this chance. Someone in this family has to make a name for themselves. Nick and I are stuck with the pub, and Sean and Michael have just enough dumb luck to get jobs over at The Gate one day. You've got something special in that head of yours and it shouldn't go to waste. Besides, I owe you."

"We don't keep score in this family, Paddy MacCarthy."

"No, we don't, but we do make sure that we follow God's plan. There's no hiding from the bitter taste of truth, Will. For you, that's working with the lady doc."

He laid his head back against the bench and took a full breath. This time my heart wasn't heavy. Paddy was healing, and I had Doctor Winston to thank for that small miracle. If I took this chance, learned from her, maybe I could do the same thing for someone else's brother one day. It was a sin lying to my parents, my brothers, my priest, but for the first time in my life I understood this was a risk I had to take.

CHAPTER FIVE

MacCarthy Residence
San Francisco, California
October 12, 1936

"Will. Willa!"

My bed shook like we were having an earthquake. I scrubbed the sleep from my eyes. Paddy leaned over my bed. The sweat on his brow shimmered in the dim moonlight seeping in through my window.

"Paddy, what's wrong?"

He sunk onto the edge of my bed. His shoulders rolled in and his body vibrated with pain.

"I don't know. My hand is throbbing."

I swiped the lamp from my side table and looked at the new dressing I'd applied before he went to bed.

"The wound doesn't appear to be bleeding."

"Maybe it's all in my head. Sorry for waking you." He moved to stand and pain pinched every part of his face.

"We need to get you back to the doctor."

I dressed quickly and led him to the front door. Once his jacket was propped around his shoulders, I walked him down the stairs. There was no use in waking our parents. They'd only ask questions and keep us from getting to Doctor Winston's office.

A small prayer slid past my lips as Paddy clung to the sleeves of my coat. The night was warm and a full moon lit the cracked concrete path along Geary Street. The silence of the city carried a morbid feel. The shadows crept in closer as if warning of dark things to come. I held onto Paddy tighter, cursing our father. It would have been easier to slide him into the car, but Da refused to teach me how to drive.

"Stop looking at me like that!" he growled.

"I'm not looking at anything."

"Oh, yes you are. Those eyebrows of yours are pinched so tight I'm worried they might leap off your face." He squeezed my hand. "I'm not gonna die, Will."

Typical Paddy. Trying to comfort me when he was the one that was sick.

Once we reached the office, I sat Paddy on the curb. "The doc lives upstairs. Wait here and I'll go get her."

I raced up the steps and rapped twice on the door. When nothing happened, I knocked four more times until the door flew open.

"Willa?"

A floral bathrobe covered Doctor Winston's thin frame. Her golden curls formed a frizzy cloud around her face. Her apartment was nothing but a cave-like room with a small kitchenette and a sparse seating area.

"Please Doctor Winston, can you help us? Something's wrong with Paddy. His face is ash gray and he keeps telling me he's in terrible pain."

"Give me a minute to get dressed."

I flew back down the stairs. Paddy's eyes were closed and my hand flew to his neck. The thump of his steady pulse fluttered under my touch, but the purple-tinge on his remaining fingers made my head spin with worry. I tried to stay strong for him, but my resolve was crumbling.

Dressed in her white coat, Doctor Winston rushed past us.

She flipped on the lights inside and helped Paddy to the exam room. Once he was on the table, she listened to his heart with her stethoscope.

"Sounds normal." Her gaze flew over his body and stopped at his bandaged hand.

"When was this dressing last changed?" she asked.

"I did it about an hour ago, before he went to bed," I said.

She loosened the white gauzy material. The tinge of his skin turned pink and Paddy sucked in a full, deep breath.

"It's all right, Mr. MacCarthy. The dressing was wrapped too tightly and it cut off the blood flow in your hand. Let me fix it and you can be on your way."

She may as well have dropped an anvil on my heart. Here I was reading all these books, thinking I was so smart, but I'd made Paddy worse. *I'd made him sick.* Why did I even give myself a sliver of hope I could understand medicine? Perhaps my place *was* in the convent where the only harm I could do would be to the other postulants' ears when they heard me sing in vespers.

"I'm sorry, Paddy," I choked out.

Doctor Winston set Paddy's hand across his lap. She leaned in to examine the wound.

"Healing nicely," she whispered. "Your sister is taking good care of you."

"No, I'm not," I said quietly.

"Yes, you are," he winked in my direction.

She laid a new dressing across his hand and weaved it between his injured fingers.

"My first year in medical school I was working with a professor on how to take a patient's vitals—blood pressure, pulse. He instructed me to draw the man's blood. Time and time again, I slid the needle into the patient's arm unable to find a vein. In his frustration, the professor ordered me from the room. The snickers from the male students rang like a bell in my head."

Once Paddy's hand was covered, she secured the dressing. "It would have been easy to run away that day in embarrassment. To convince myself I wasn't meant to be a physician. All I had to do was walk out the door and never look back."

"What made you stay?" I asked.

"Somehow I knew I wouldn't be the only one who couldn't hit a vein. I was right. Student after student joined me in the hallway. Finally, the professor called us back inside and taught us techniques like using a tourniquet to bring a vein to the surface of the skin."

"I would have hated to be that volunteer. More like a pin cushion than a patient," Paddy said.

A smile lit her weary face. "He was a good sport all considering. Medicine is like any other profession. It takes time to learn the right techniques to get the job done. Today, your sister simply wrapped your hand too tight. My guess is she'll never make that mistake again."

Paddy bobbed his head. "She's right. Now you know better."

"I could teach you more things, Willa. All you have to do is come and work with me."

My brother trusted me to take care of him. To make sure he'd recover, but all I'd done was hurt him. I'd already let my family down in so many ways, and here I was doing it again.

"No. I proved today I'm not cut out for this. I don't have the right instincts."

"That's a load of baloney," Paddy argued. "You gotta do it. I see how you watch the doc here. It's like nothing or no one else in the world exists. Give it a chance."

He reached for the dressing and unraveled her work. "Sorry, Doc, but I think Willy here needs to practice."

She laughed and helped untie the white cloth. "You are quite persistent, Mr. MacCarthy."

"My mam told me when Willa was born it was my job to look after her." He wiped his free hand over his mouth. "I'm sure this is *not* what she had in mind, but it's right all the same." He waved me forward. "Get to work now."

"Paddy, I can't. Mam and Da wouldn't approve, and there's no use in starting something I'll never get to finish. It'd break my heart."

"Just like the doc says, you only need practice. You can't tell me your heart doesn't gallop at the opportunity to learn from the doc. I see how you pore over those books at home. The way your eyes narrow and your lips twitch when you're learning something fascinating. You got a fire inside for this kind of work, and I refuse to let it be snuffed out."

"But if Mam and Da found out, they'd send me straight off to the convent without a single thought."

"You let me worry about that. What I want you to do is to focus on learning all about medicine. Can't have you cutting off my circulation again can we?"

A part of me wanted to slap away the grin on his face, but I couldn't refuse him. The smell of the room, shine of the instruments, did set my heart racing.

With two tentative steps, I planted myself in front of Paddy. My hands shook as Doctor Winston guided them in a steady pattern.

Over and over, she looped the gauze in between the dips in his fingers. Her words measured, pointed, as she taught me a technique I hoped would be the first of many.

CHAPTER SIX

MacCarthy Residence
San Francisco, California
October 19, 1936

I sat on the edge of my bed, the patchwork quilt wrinkling beneath me. Between my fingers, I squeezed *Gray's Anatomy* hoping to find strength in the battered edges and yellowed pages of my beloved textbook. Since the evening we returned from Doctor Winston's clinic, I'd been plotting how to get back to her office. The thundering of my heart warned that once I put the plan in motion and started on this path of deceit there would be no turning back.

A shuffle of footsteps in the hall forced me to shove the book back into its regular spot underneath the floorboards. Heaven knows what Mam would do if she caught me with it again.

Paddy knocked once on my bedroom door and pushed it open. He looked sharp in his starched blue wool pants and matching coat. The brim of his black fedora sat at a perfect angle just above his red brows.

"Grab your things. We're off to work." His voice boomed between the thin walls as he gave a quick wink in my direction. Subtlety was not in Paddy's nature.

Last night after dinner, I explained to Mam and Da that as a lead-up to entering the convent, I wanted to participate in Christian service by volunteering at the local soup kitchen. Of course, Paddy would have to join me as an escort.

Amid Mam's protests, Da remained quiet. His solemn gaze

moved between me and Paddy's bandaged hand. He'd caught us coming back home the night after we'd been to the clinic. After we explained ourselves, he'd shooed us back to bed saying there was no reason why he should worry Mam. Now, with him staring me down like a rabbit caught in the crosshairs, I wasn't quite sure what he'd do.

"Let them go, Mary," he sighed. "Better not to have them underfoot all day."

Mam relented but only after we promised that Paddy would be back in enough time to help with the evening pub crowd, and I committed to saying a few extra rosaries.

Paddy tapped the toe of his black polished wingtip against the wood floor. "Come on, Willy. Let's get outta here before Mam changes her mind."

Once my coat was over my shoulders, I popped on my favorite hat with the dark blue ribbon around the crown.

His stare moved over the wide brim. "It's October. Time to put away the summer-weight felt."

"Ugh, Paddy. This is no time to argue over my poor fashion choices."

We rushed out the door, tossing a quick goodbye to Mam, who was scrubbing the last of the breakfast dishes. Her echo of a reply followed us out into the street.

The sun was like a small child waking for the day. Its rays stretched out like thin arms, ebbing in and out of the wispy clouds hovering over the city. A sweep of a warm fall breeze danced across my shoulders. Paddy grabbed my hand and pushed through the crowd. The gauze dressing around his missing fingertips scratched against my palm. He glanced down where our hands met.

"Just think, Will. One day a lad like me might wander into

your practice and you'll help him like the doc saved me. Doesn't that fill you with a sense of joy? Purpose?"

"It fills me with nausea," I whispered under my breath.

The idea of helping someone like Paddy was a wonderful thought, but a small part of me warned not to get too attached to the idea. A day spent in Doctor Winston's office did not suddenly open the door to a future in medicine.

The sour scent of antiseptic hit me first. The office was empty save for a small family settled on the lumpy green couch in the center of the room. A small girl huddled next to an older boy. The two sat close to a man with broad shoulders and a wiry black beard. Even at our entrance, their solemn eyes never moved from the exam room and the faint, muffled wails sliding out from underneath the door.

I nodded to the family. "I'm going to ask if I can help them."

A knowing smile slid over Paddy's lips. He tipped his hat and escaped out the door.

I didn't get more than two steps toward the family when the small girl jumped off the couch.

"Are ya here to see the lady doc?" she asked, her long dark lashes fluttering.

"No, I'm here to *help* the lady doc." The words slid across my lips easier than I expected.

Her eyes lit up and she pried herself from the careful grip of her brother. He gave his head a quick shake and she ignored him. A girl after my own heart.

The man's stare never faltered from the exam room door and the sharp wails.

"My mam's supposed to have a baby." She took tentative steps toward me. "But she hasn't felt it kick in a while."

"Don't you worry. Doctor Winston is the best. She'll take good care of her," I said.

"It's hard for her to sleep on the cold ground. Sometimes when I wake at night her whole body is a quivering."

Cold ground?

I bent down until we were eye-to-eye. "I'm Willa. What's your name?"

Her dirty cheeks bunched up into a smile. "I'm Maeve." She pointed to the boy sitting on the couch. "That's my big brother, Simon." Her mouth pinched. "He's always telling me what to do."

"I understand. I have four older brothers."

Her eyes widened. She inched a step closer.

"Maeve, can you tell me where you live?"

Her voice dropped to a whisper. "Can you keep a secret?"

I bobbed my head once.

"Maeve!" Her older brother, who couldn't have been more than twelve, stomped toward us. "Leave the lady alone."

She rolled her eyes. "See what I mean."

I swallowed down a laugh as her brother pointed a finger in her direction and ordered her back to the couch.

Another sharp wail burst from the exam room. Maeve let out a small cough. I gave her back a quick, comforting pat.

"Is my mam gonna be all right?" she asked.

"Of course. Why don't you go sit back with your brother and let me find out what's going on?"

She shuffled back to the couch, her brother helping her onto the overstuffed cushions. I knocked once on the exam room door. Anatomical drawings of the brain, spine, and heart greeted me when it swung open.

"Miss MacCarthy?" Doctor Winston's hair was a disheveled blonde cloud drooping down around her ears.

Had she forgotten her offer? Perhaps it was wrong for me to show up unannounced. Maybe her invitation to teach me was simply out of kindness. I hesitated and kicked my foot against the plank floor. The whimper of the patient filled my ears.

I squared my shoulders and planted my feet. "You said you could use some assistance?"

"Of course." She swept a hand over her furrowed brow. "Please, come in."

She took the small woman's hand in her own. "Mrs. Cleery came to see me only an hour ago complaining of pain in her lower abdomen." She pointed to the woman's round belly stretched wide with child. "I've done a full examination and asked her a few preliminary questions such as how long she has been pregnant, if she feels regular movement, and what her recent diet has been like." Doctor Winston stumbled over the word diet.

"It seems she's been giving what little food she and her husband can provide to their children and has felt no movement as of late. I've checked and there is a heartbeat. Now I'm explaining that while she has a duty to her family outside the womb, she must also care about the child *inside* her womb. She is early into her third trimester and it's important for her to stay vigilant about her health."

A small moan slid past Mrs. Cleery's lips again.

"Here comes another false contraction, Louise. Like I mentioned before, this does not mean you are in active labor. You need to breathe through them."

The woman let out a low hiss. Her face twisted in torment. Her moans brought back dark memories of a day I wanted to forget. I stayed in place unable to move, barely breathing, as she writhed on the table.

"Willa," Doctor Winston gave my shoulder a rough tap and pointed to the opposite side of the table. As I flanked the other side of the woman, she clamped down on my hand. Instinct had me closing my eyes in prayer, but I stopped when Doctor Winston started to count through the pain. With each round of contractions, the woman's grip loosened. We counted and talked for over an hour until the waves of pain subsided.

Doctor Winston walked Louise out of the room and into the arms of her waiting family. As her children embraced her, the doc pulled the man aside. In muted whispers, she gave instructions for Louise's care. When the doc reached into her pocket and tried to press something into the man's hand he turned away. She continued to speak. Her tones hushed yet comforting until he finally took the wad of bills she offered.

The sounds of the city barged into the small office and faded as he shuffled his family out the door.

"Well, nothing like jumping in feet first." She rushed back to the exam room and removed instruments from the side table dumping them into a basin reeking of rubbing alcohol.

"I had all these plans of easing you in slowly, but it's better this way. This job is never the same on any given day. While my focus is on obstetrics, people come in for any number of problems. Some issues I can care for like a general practitioner. Others must be sent to another physician or hospital."

"Obstetrics is caring for the private areas of females, right?"

The tick of her lips told me I was wrong. I wanted to shrivel out of sight on the spot.

"Close. Gynecology is the care of women's reproductive

anatomy. Obstetrics is treatment of women during the childbirth process."

She gave my hand a reassuring pat. "Don't be afraid to ask questions. Make mistakes. It's all a part of learning." Her lips thinned. "I understand religion is important to you, but in this office, action must take precedent over prayer. Is that understood?"

Her words shook me. My life was a basic routine of home and church. The two constantly intertwined. But here, the only thing that mattered was the patient. Her unwavering gaze told me I needed to obey that rule if I wanted to learn from her.

"Yes, ma'am."

She gave a brief nod and rushed back to the sink with more instruments. "Being a physician isn't easy, especially for a woman. You will need to make sacrifices." She turned the gold band on her ring finger. "My husband, while a good man, isn't too keen on me being the only breadwinner. He's gone south to try and find work."

Her story explained why I hadn't seen her husband the night I'd wrapped Paddy's hand too tight. I'd stood and watched her in awe never thinking that she was hurting like so many other people in the city.

She plunged her hands into a bowl near the sink and scrubbed between her fingers. "These are hard times. People like Mr. Cleery might not like taking a handout, but if it means keeping his family well, he must consider what's best. There's no room for pride when your family is starving."

She moved back to the open office and patted at her pockets. Her gaze darted around the room and landed on a nearby desk. "Ah, there it is." She pulled an engraved silver pen from in-between two empty beakers.

"That's beautiful," I said.

"It was a wedding gift from my husband, Jack." She twirled the pen in her fingers. "He said I needed something to remind me of him when I was busy in my whirlwind of work."

Her far-off gaze reminded me of the way my mam looked when she talked about the night she met my da at a church social. How she believed God had guided her there so they would cross paths.

Doctor Winston ran an elegant finger along the engraving. "This is our wedding date. It was a thoughtful present. I love it, but I always seem to misplace it."

Her eyes clouded over for a moment before she pointed to a battered wood table in a far corner of the room. "Until we have another patient, I'd like you to put those texts back onto the bookshelves in alphabetical order. When that task is completed, I want to walk you through the steps of the sterilization process. It is one of the most critical parts of this office. Soiled instruments mean infection. I must assure my patients they will get the best care here."

She looked at me with confidence. Trust. I understood that if I wanted to do this job right, earn her respect, I had to be honest.

"Before I start, I need to tell you something," I said.

She shoved her hand into the pockets of her white coat and waited.

"I'm very interested in learning about medicine, but my parents would never approve. Just in the course of coming here today, I've told several lies. I will have to continue to lie if I want to learn from you."

She stepped forward and gripped my shoulders. "Thank you for being honest. In this practice, we must learn to trust one another. I will not judge you for the choices you make to be here. Patients come through that door worried about themselves or their families. I do my best to reassure them. Prove to them that hope has wings. No matter if you work with me for a week, or a few months, I'd be honored if you'd allow me to do the same thing for you."

Heat burned behind my eyes. I wanted to embrace her, but we'd only known each other a short time so I hoped my warm smile would show my immense gratitude.

She stepped back, yet her narrowed gaze never left my face. "From the moment you walked into the exam room today, I've watched you struggle. But, you've also trusted your own judgment and instincts. That's good too. Just promise me if this all gets too difficult, you'll let me know."

"I promise," I said.

She gave me a quick nod. "Then let's get started."

In between pregnant women, children with croup, and a trickle of complaints about headaches, the late morning flew by. No words could describe the joy I felt each time Doctor Winston waved me in closer to assist in a procedure. How with a solid and firm voice she taught me to wrap an arm in gauze or hold a crying child during their examination. It was hard not to bow my head in prayer each time and thank God for giving me this day, but I promised to focus on the work and that was what I intended to do.

When we had a lull, I reshelved the stacks of books strewn across the tables. With each one, I took a rag and wiped away the dust covering the spines. Having clean instruments wasn't the only way to prevent infection. Dirt of any kind in an open wound could be a problem, too, according to the medical texts I'd memorized over the last several years.

Doctor Winston busied herself in the exam room cleaning instruments and quietly humming under her breath. The last patient, a malnourished child, forced the doctor's body to hang low like a branch buckling under the weight of a stiff winter wind.

I considered what she'd said about sacrifice and wondered how odd it must be to walk up the steps behind the office and into a quiet apartment alone each night. Silence was the one thing I could not bear for too long. Maybe it was growing up in a house full of loud-mouthed brothers, or the constant traffic of family and friends in and out of our apartment, but noise was a calming companion for me.

A sharp knock pulled me out of my thoughts. Doctor Winston open the door and a man stepped inside. He bowed slightly and tucked his black fedora under his arm. His thick dark hair was clipped tight around his ears. A pair of wire spectacles perched perilously close to the end of his nose. The gold pocket watch at his waist bobbed as he spoke in hushed tones.

Curious, I pretended to dust a shelf closer to their discussion. They exchanged words like "blood," "saloon," and "death." The man slid a piece of paper into her hand. Doctor Winston gave a stiff nod and opened the door for him to exit.

"Willa, grab my doctor's bag in the cabinet where I keep the dressings."

She pulled her sky-blue coat off a nearby peg. She hesitated a moment and then plucked my coat off another peg. "That was a colleague of mine, Doctor Owens. He can't cover his shift over at the field hospital near the bridge. He's asked that I step in for him and you are going to join me. Nothing like a bit of out-of-office training."

Coming here to assist her was one thing. Following her to The Gate was another risk entirely.

Sensing my hesitation, she stepped closer and shoved my coat into my hands. "Willa, being a doctor isn't always about practicing inside a cozy office. Sometimes people out in the world need our help, and we must be willing to go outside our sphere of comfort. That's all part of the work."

She shrugged on her coat. "Can you be fearless? Can you walk out to The Gate with me despite your worries? You can refuse and I won't think less of you."

Her eyes burned with a dedication that made my head spin. Up to this point, my agreeing to come here had been somewhat of a lark. A chance to spend a day seeing if the want in my heart was worth the amount of lying and deceit I'd have to serve up regularly to my family.

Why had I spent all those hours huddled under my bedcovers, gazing at the illustrations of the human body, learning about disease, if I never planned on using what I'd learned? I'd dreamt of this moment for so long. I couldn't let it all slip away because I was too afraid of what would happen if I got caught.

I slid on my coat and rushed over to the cabinet. Pushing aside the dressings, I grabbed her black leather bag. It hung heavy in my hand. The weight felt right. Like my fingers were meant to curl around the handle and carry the burden of the task facing us.

CHAPTER SEVEN

Golden Gate Bridge Field Hospital
San Francisco, California
October 19, 1936

The sun beat against my head. I should have been wearing my hat, but it was still on a hook back at the office. I'd rushed out so quickly, determined to prove how brave I was, I'd completely forgotten my sense of propriety. Good thing Mam wasn't here to see me.

Doctor Winston slid behind the wheel of her automobile and we took off through the Richmond District. I didn't mean to stare, but I'd only ever seen a man drive a car. She looked smart navigating the sleek black Chrysler down Geary Street.

Other cars bumbled down the road beside us. Men and women hustled along the sidewalk trying to catch the streetcar. In the distance, I swore I heard the peal of bells from St. Monica. It was hard not to think of it as a warning sign. As if God was acknowledging my deceit.

"What exactly is a field hospital?" I asked needing to bat away my guilt.

"It's usually a small building or tent set up for basic care. Mostly it's a place to triage minor cuts and abrasions as the bosses want the men back on the worksite as quickly as possible. In rare cases, doctors diagnose patients with more serious issues and send them on to hospitals."

"Do they do surgeries?"

"No, I'd guess not in this situation. During the Great War, field hospitals treated those wounded during battle. Surgery was often required. My suspicion is the hospital at the bridge will be used for general triage. Only a few cots and basic instruments. But as Doctor Owens just reminded me, the brave men working on the bridge deserve our help no matter the environment."

A chill skipped down my spine. In quiet whispers at the dinner table, Sean and Michael told us about the conditions at The Gate. The treacherous heights. The way the wind and mist turned the steel slick. How one false move could send a man plunging to his death.

Last week when I was delivering a message to Da in the pub, I'd overheard a drunk foreman talk about safety at the bridge. He said the bigshots who ran the site expected one death per every million dollars spent. He'd slurred on that it meant that at least thirty-five men would go to their grave before the bridge was completed.

Doctor Winston sped down Geary until we reached 25th Avenue. She made a turn in the direction of the Sea Cliff neighborhood and then turned again onto El Camino Del Mar. The car raced north until the Marin hills spread out in front of us like sparkling green jewels. I couldn't quell my gasp at the monstrous structure stretched out across the strait. The bridge was a splash of orange paint across a stark blue sky. Its suspension cables dipped and looped like waves rolling across the ocean. Platforms below formed what would be the road carrying passengers across the wide expanse of the Golden Gate. Each separated piece reminded me of a smiling child who'd lost several teeth.

We drove along until we came to a gate separating the road from the bridge's construction perimeter. Doctor Winston waved the paper Doctor Owens gave her in the direction of a broad-shouldered guard with a menacing stare.

As he read the note, his lips tucked into a frown. "Ma'am, you sure about this?"

"Yes, now please do not detain us any longer. We have a shift to cover."

The man poked his head inside the automobile. "Who's she?"

"My assistant," she replied easily.

I couldn't help but smile at her confidence as she spoke to the grim-faced man. *Her assistant.* My heart warmed with pride at the words.

"Now, which way to the field hospital?" she asked.

He jabbed a finger toward a primitive dirt road inches inside the gate. Before he could say another word, she put the car in gear and took off.

The car bumped along until we reached a parking area above the massive brick structure called Fort Point. In school, we'd learned the building was erected before the Civil War to defend the narrow entrance to San Francisco harbor. The newspapers said they wanted to knock it down as it would be a nuisance during construction, but the leaders of the bridge project decided to build around it and use it to store materials.

I followed Doctor Winston down a winding path leading toward the water. With each step, I cursed myself for wearing my worn rounded-toe Oxfords that caught on every loose rock along the way. We rushed past heavy work equipment and men in hard hats. I kept pace with her, doing my best to ignore the startled looks from the workers. Under my breath, I whispered a prayer that I didn't run into my brothers who always hovered near the fences hoping a union foreman would single them out and put them to work.

When we reached a small wood building that looked more like an oversized fishing shack than a hospital, Doctor Winston yanked on its thin metal door. A row of white-sheeted cots covered the narrow space. In one corner, a row of silver instruments lined what resembled a battered wood dining table. Rolls of bandages and clear bottles with dark brown cork stoppers lined the shelves. Two nurses in stiff white uniforms and matching caps moved among the occupied cots offering men glasses of water and checking bloody dressings. I hovered in the doorway. The sights and smells of the cramped space quickly shook my confidence.

A gentleman with snow white hair and a sour lemon expression charged toward us. "Unless you are nurses, there is no reason for you ladies to be in my hospital."

"I take it you are Doctor Fairchild?" Doctor Winston said.

The man's left eyebrow arched. "Yes and who are you?"

A small wry smile danced over her lips. "My name is Doctor Katherine Winston. Doctor Owens sends his regrets as he will not be able to cover his shift today. I'm here to fill in for him and Miss MacCarthy will assist me."

"Well," he pulled at the immaculate curlicues on his handlebar mustache. "It would have been nice if he'd availed me of this situation."

"Oh, he would have, but it was an emergency of an important nature." She flitted past him and headed in the direction of the occupied cots. "Where should we get started?"

Doctor Fairchild smoothed down the collar on his coat and followed quickly behind her. "I'm not sure how much Doctor Owens told you about the hospital."

"Why don't you start by telling us the hospital's purpose and what kind of injuries you regularly treat," she said.

"Fine," he grumbled. "Safety is of utmost importance on the bridge. The lead man on this project is Chief Engineer Joseph Strauss. One of his first tasks was having this field hospital erected. Since the earliest days, when the risk was at its highest with the towers being built on both shores, and the eventual spinning of the cables, safety engineers demanded all workers wear Bullard hardhats like those worn by coal miners. The men who work at incredible heights are also required to be tied into safety lines."

A nurse stopped and was about to ask a question when he shooed her away like he would a fly.

"As more proof of the commitment to safety, a few months ago engineers recommended that over $130,000 be spent to manufacture a trapeze-style net to hang under the roadway construction. This adherence to safety protocols has paid off. In the first forty-six months of this project, we've not had a single death. In fact, last week was the first time we've had a serious injury."

He continued to walk down the row of occupied cots and stop every few steps to check each nurse's work.

"What happened?" Doctor Winston prodded Doctor Fairchild.

"A fella was jumping from stringer to stringer on the back-span over near the Marin tower. He missed his footing on a beam and fell. The net wasn't properly anchored over the rocks on the craggy hillside. When he landed it didn't fully absorb the force of his fall and he broke four vertebrae in his back."

He worked his way down the end of the row, stopping at a bank of tables covered in stacks of paperwork. "Your job will be to care for whatever comes in that door. Mostly we see broken bones or slight head injuries from drift pins or tools being accidentally dropped from men working high up on the towers. We've had a few others impaled on equipment."

A young nurse a few beds away called for his assistance. "Start with that gentleman in the corner who is complaining of a headache."

He shoved his hand into his pockets, his pinched expression wearing on my nerves.

"A few rules before I go. First, you must keep meticulous paperwork on each patient you treat. Management requires it for risk issues. Second, while we act like a working hospital, we cannot care for those who are critically injured. If there is a case that requires quick attention, I must be notified immediately. It is upon me as head of this field hospital to assess the injury and send for an ambulance if needed. Last," his eyes flicked in my direction and then darted to Doctor Winston's left hand. "There is to be no male and female fraternization. I'm not running a social club here. We need to take care of the ill and then send them on for further care or back to work. Is that understood, ladies?"

I waited on Doctor Winston to bark out a heated reply. Instead, she gave a brief nod and allowed him to stalk away.

For the next several hours I trailed Doctor Winston from cot to cot. We gave out aspirin and sauerkraut juice for suspected hangovers, set two broken wrists, and stitched up one small laceration. With each patient, she walked me through the steps of care directing me on what to do. I'd read the *American Red Cross First Aid Textbook* on how to treat injuries at least a dozen times, but it still shook me when a man grabbed my wrist while crying out in pain.

As we were working on a fella who complained of dizziness, a young nurse stopped next to the cot. "I apologize for interrupting, but by any chance have you seen a thin silver watch with a diamond-shaped face lying about?"

"No, I'm sorry, I haven't," I said.

A glimmer of tears shined in her eyes. "It was my grandmother's. I could have sworn I set it down on one of the tables next to these cots when I was cleaning one of the worker's cuts. I've looked for over an hour now and I can't find it."

"What's your name?" I asked.

"I'm Francis Abbott. Call me Francie."

"Francie, I promise if I see it, I'll return it to you promptly."

She swiped a hand over her tear-stained cheek. A dark curl clung to her forehead. "Thank you." Her desperate gaze flicked to each of the bedside tables in the row as she walked away.

The day's shadows crept across the cold concrete floor. After I assisted Doctor Winston on one final laceration, she let me know we could leave for the day. I followed her to a set of metal basins. Before we could dip our hands into the water, the tumble of a loud male voice filled the once quiet room.

"Nurse!" A man in khaki overalls beelined in our direction. The tip of his hard hat hid his brows. Dirt and a fine sheen of orange paint covered his fingertips and the top parts of his forearms.

"Name's Seamus Moran. I got a pal I need ya to take a look at outside," he said.

"Why don't you bring him in to be examined?" Doctor Winston asked.

He leaned in and lowered his shoulder. "He's a worker here, but he's not exactly steady on his feet at the moment if you know what I mean."

"No matter, bring him in," she replied.

He yanked the hard hat off his head. "All right, but if I do will you get a doc to look at him?"

"She is a doctor," I said with a little bit too much edge to my voice.

His eyes widened. "Beg your pardon, ma'am."

He turned on his heel and returned a minute later dragging another wide-shouldered male. Blood poured from a cut on his forehead. By the stutter of his steps, and pitch of his body, it was clear he'd had one too many pints.

"Benny, the doc here is gonna treat yer head. Be a good lad now and give her a moment to take a look."

A two-inch gash sliced into his scalp turning his blond hair a disheartening shade of pink. Once his pal laid him onto the cot, the man's eyes inched closed.

"Willa, please go get some bandages. On that far shelf near the door, there's a glass bottle marked Mercurochrome. Bring that too."

The hem of her black wide-legged pants pooled onto the ground as she leaned in closer. Blood spilled down the man's head in a bright red gush. It skipped over his eyes, danced down his right cheek, and with a final thrust plunged off the edge of his whiskered chin.

The room tilted. The edges of my vision turned a fuzzy shade of white.

Doctor Winston plopped a firm hand on my shoulder. "Willa, stay with me. It's all right. Head wounds bleed heavily. You've seen worse with your brother."

Her reassuring smile sent me stumbling across the room to a bank of shelves loaded with clean dressings. My head thrummed with a steady pound. Doubt settled deep in my bones like the chill of winter fog. It was ridiculous to think because I'd read a few textbooks I could help the doctor. She'd had years of training and I was a silly young woman with only a high school education. Why had she even considered bringing me here?

The door swung open again as a few more workers entered the room. I could walk out the same door. There'd be no shame in admitting this wasn't the right job for me. I'd told myself this would only be for the day. It wasn't like I'd promised Doctor Winston I'd stay.

I rushed to grab what she requested and returned with her items. Doctor Winston reached for my hand and yanked me forward like she knew what I was contemplating.

"His pulse is steady." She moved her hand to check his pupils and Benny's eyes flew open.

"What's this?" he screamed. "I'll not have a woman I don't know touching me!"

"Sir, I'm trying to help you."

Benny's arms flailed out in a frantic windmill and landed a blow across her cheek. She stumbled back and I caught her before she crashed to the ground.

"Benny, no!" Seamus pressed him down into the cot. "Stop lad! We need to get you fixed up. This lady doc is going to help."

"Doctor Winston, are you all right?" I asked.

She pressed her hand to her face and blinked several times. "Yes," she finally breathed out. "I'll be fine."

I would have been worried about her state if I hadn't seen the fierce determination burning in her eyes.

The jarring screech of a high-pitched whistle marked the day's end. Nurses and doctors began to clean up around us. Benny continued to thrash and yell obscenities that made my cheeks heat. With all the ruckus, I thought for sure Doctor Fairchild would appear, but he was nowhere in sight, thank goodness. I could only imagine what he'd say if he saw the bruise blooming on Doctor Winston's cheek.

The door swung open again and a face I'd seen before stalked in our direction.

"Enough!" The man yanked off his hard hat and sank down on the edge of the cot. "If you want to keep yer job, I suggest ya settle down."

The young man I'd seen at church pressed Benny's shoulders into the sheets and held on until he stopped twisting and thrashing.

"That's enough now, Sam," Seamus insisted.

I double-blinked as I took in his sharp cheekbones and ocean-colored eyes. He gave me a tight nod like he did that day outside of St. Monica.

Doctor Winston went to work examining the severity of the cut on Benny's head. I pressed a white cloth into her hand. She doused it with the reddish-brown liquid from the bottle and placed it over the wound. Benny screamed and his back arched off the cot. Sam gritted his teeth and held on as if restraining a bucking horse.

"Can't you give him anything for the pain?" he asked.

"I'm Doctor Winston. And what is your name, sir?"

"Sam Butler," he replied.

"Are you friends? Brothers?"

"He's my cousin."

"We are still studying head injuries, Mr. Butler. I've read some papers about issues with the brain after a blow to the head. I cannot give him anything until I assess the severity of the wound."

Doctor Winston waved me in closer while she continued to dab at the deep cut. "Willa, as I mentioned before, we must consider treating the whole body, not just the wound."

Sam's eyes shifted in my direction at the mention of my name.

"The laceration looks to be quite deep." She took a lamp from the bedside table to get a clearer view while she prodded the edges of the wound.

"Sir, can you tell me your full name?" Doctor Winston asked.

His thrashing slowed as Sam forced down his shoulders. "Answer her, Ben. She's trying to help you."

"Benjamin William Butler. My friends call me Benny." He snapped his jaw tight, delivering a searing stare at Sam.

"And how many fingers am I holding up, Mr. Butler?"

"Three," he said on an exhale.

"Excellent," the doctor murmured. "No hesitation."

She directed me to compress the wound as she searched inside her bag.

"I can tell from your breath, you've had quite a bit to drink today." She pulled out a pair of silver shears. "Do you think you can remain still? I'll need to cut away a bit of your hair in order to stitch up that cut."

Benny mumbled something resembling yes.

Chunks of hair fell to the ground around my shoes. With precision, Doctor Winston trimmed a path down the scalp, revealing a clear view of the jagged wound. She handed me the scissors and asked for the needle and suture thread.

"Now that I know your head wound isn't too severe, I can give you something for the pain."

"Lady, I've been through a hell of a lot worse. Start your stitchin'," he slurred.

She bent down, bobbed back up, moving back and forth trying to get into a comfortable position.

"Seamus, go see if you can find the doc a chair. I have a feeling it's gonna take her a while to put Benny back together," Sam snapped.

"He's not Humpty Dumpty," Seamus bristled.

"Is that so? Last time I looked he was just as stupid as that egg falling off the wall." Sam said before turning his venom onto Benny. "There are at least five dozen men out at that fence who would give anything to be working up on those platforms. And you ruin it for yourself by drinking. I have half a mind to march up to Superintendent Scarpetti and tell him what you've done."

"Come on, Sam. We know you won't rat out your own family," Seamus said.

"Maybe not, but what if his stupidity injured one of the men up there? He's just lucky that piece of rebar sliced open his head rather than someone else's or there'd be hell to pay from the rest of the crew."

Benny thrashed on the cot. His cheeks went gray. I took two steps back. This was nothing like my textbooks.

"Willa, pay attention!" Doctor Winston ordered. "I need you to compress the wound again before I can start suturing."

Out of instinct and raw fear, I grabbed a clean dressing and staunched the blood flow. It soaked through the gauze and stained my fingers a deep crimson. The edges of Benny's eyes pinched together. His breaths came in ragged heaves. He arched up and spewed the contents of his stomach all over my shoes and the lower part of my skirt.

"Oh, Jesus, Mary, and Joseph," Sam hissed. "Are you all right, Miss?"

The stench made my stomach roil but I continued to press down on the wound. Every inch of me wanted to bow my head in prayer. To ask God for help. Slowly, under my own touch, the regular pump of blood slowed. Benny's breathing returned to a normal rhythm. The urge in my veins to flee vanished. Doctor Winston needed me and I wasn't about to abandon her.

"Miss, did you hear me? I asked if you are all right?"

Those stunning cobalt eyes locked on me.

"I'm fine," I managed to reply, although my tongue felt twice its size and I was sure he could hear the tremble in my voice.

Doctor Winston slid into the chair Seamus located. "Bad head injuries cause dizziness and nausea. But in this case, I'd guess it's more about the few pints he's had today. I'll call for someone to come clean that up."

She waved over a nurse and handed me another clean dressing. "Focus now, Willa. Move up to the top part of the scalp and continue to apply pressure."

In between his moans and hisses, Benny managed to stay still. Doctor Winston worked the stitches back into the scalp. Without her asking, I slid a clean dressing into her hand. Once it was soaked, she'd toss it into a nearby steel basin and I'd hand her a new one. We worked in quiet unison as the men watched our every move.

Sam shifted on the cot readjusting his tight hold on Benny's shoulders. Every once in a while, he'd let out his own hiss when Benny started to thrash again.

In between stitches, Doctor Winston spoke in low tones, explaining where she was placing the needle and how to work the thread into a skillful knot. When my pressure wasn't steady enough, or I'd placed gauze in the wrong place, she'd redirect my position. Her tone was never harsh but measured and clear like she trusted me to follow her lead.

Sam's stare burned into me but I kept my focus on her technique. I couldn't be distracted. Each experience with Doctor Winston was another lesson on how challenging the work of a physician could be.

She placed the final stitch and dabbed at the skin with more antiseptic. After covering the wound with a clean dressing, she turned her attention to Sam.

"Your cousin must stay off the bridge for a day or two. Again, head injuries are tricky. He doesn't need to be up there if he gets dizzy. Also, the cut needs to be kept as clean as possible. If infection sets in, he must go to a hospital."

"I ain't going to no hospital," Benny slurred.

"You have my word that he'll behave and do his best to stay clean," Sam replied.

Doctor Winston searched through her bag. She pulled out a white card and slid it in Sam's direction, her bloody thumbprint staining a corner. "He'll need to come to my office in a week so I can look at the wound again and remove the stitches." She reached for another dressing and wiped off her hands. The dark blood tattooed the skin around her nails and knuckles. "Can you make sure that happens? Perhaps you know someone older who can talk some sense into him?"

"I'm twenty ma'am, and let me assure you the only one who can get Benny to listen is me. I promise, even if I have to toss him into a wheelbarrow and push him through the district, he'll be there."

Twenty? He was the same age as the twins, but he managed to carry himself like he had a brain in his head.

"Doctor Winston," I said in warning as Doctor Fairchild appeared and marched in our direction.

"We are closing up for the evening." He glanced for a long minute at Doctor Winston's cheek before turning his focus on Benny. "Does this man need to be sent to the hospital?"

"No," Seamus stepped to the edge of the cot. "I can see him home. We live in the same boardinghouse."

"I've got him," Sam shot back.

"Maybe you need a little breather, friend. Why don't you see these ladies home?" He slid a tree-trunk sized arm under Benny and walked him out of the hospital.

Doctor Winston turned to Doctor Fairchild. "It's been illuminating, sir. Are you in need of more physicians here? I'd be more than happy to return another day and help again."

"We have enough staff at the moment," he spit out.

"Surely you could use another well-trained doc," Sam said. "Us lads up on the bridge would be grateful to know we have another person capable of caring for us down here."

His voice bordered on stern and Doctor Fairchild begrudgingly agreed.

Once we'd gathered our things, we left the building. We didn't get more than a few steps outside when Sam caught up to us. He reached into his pocket and thrust a few coins in Doctor Winston's direction. "This is all I have with me, but Benny's due to get paid at the end of the week. I'll see to it that you get the full amount for your services."

Doctor Winston waved away his offering. "From what I understand, the care here is free. Just assure me your cousin will not return to work for a few days."

"You have my word. Now, please let me escort you both back

to your car. There can be quite a few hooligans around here who would have no greater pleasure than bothering two fine ladies such as yourselves."

"Thank you, sir." Doctor Winston said before charging up the path.

Every inch of my body protested as I moved. I'd never stood on my feet for six hours and my aching back warned I'd be sore tomorrow.

"How long have you been practicing, Doctor Winston?" he asked.

"Close to eight years, Mr. Butler."

"Please call me Sam." His gaze darted in my direction as if the offer was for me too.

"Have you always practiced in this area?"

"I've lived and practiced in the Richmond District for the last several years."

Her blue coat flailed around her as the wind picked up. Wisps of golden hair trailed behind. Whether it was a screeching patient, or an overbearing physician, I was struck by her ability to stay calm in a heated situation. In my house, my mother always deferred to my father and brothers even though on occasion the twist of her lips said she wanted to speak up.

"And you, Miss?"

The last line out of Sam's mouth caught my attention.

"I'm sorry. Did you ask me something?"

His eyes danced in amusement. "I asked how long you've been working for the doc?"

I waited for Doctor Winston to speak up but she was already ten paces ahead. "This was my first day."

"Really? The way you two acted in there I was sure you'd been together a while. Do you have college training like her?"

"No. She saw I had an interest in medicine and offered to teach me a thing or two."

Unable to handle the intensity of his gaze, I swept my hand across the edges of my skirt. How was I going to explain the mud caked to the hem? It wasn't like there were mounds of dirt lying around the soup kitchen.

"Well, you sure seem to have a head for it," he prattled on. "Most gals I know would faint at the sight of blood. And they'd definitely not wanna get their clothes covered in it." He leveled his gaze at a dark crimson stain on the hem of my skirt. He was enough of a gentleman not to mention how I stunk of vomit too.

I heaved in a sigh. Yet another thing I'd have to explain to my family.

"What's your job on the bridge?" I asked, growing increasingly uncomfortable at the way his smile made my heart thump in a rapid staccato beat.

"I'm an ironworker. Have a buddy in the union who got me a special permit to work on the bridge. For the last couple of months, I've been piecing the roadway together."

"The director of the field hospital told us about all the safety measures. I'm curious, does it make you feel safer when you're up there?"

"Yes and no. A few lads think having all those rules in place keeps them from having a bit of fun, which makes them unnecessarily reckless. On a job like this though, fear is what keeps you smart *and* alive."

Dread washed over me like a fall rainstorm. My brothers wanted to work on that bridge. What if they were like that man who fell and broke his back? My parents had enough pain in their past. The last thing they needed was one of the twins getting hurt or even worse.

Another breeze blew across the water. I couldn't help but revel in its warmth knowing soon enough the air would have an icy bite. We reached the top of the hill and Doctor Winston already had the car running.

"Tell the doc thanks again for taking care of Benny." He tipped his cap, turned, and took a few steps before rounding back to me. "Perhaps our paths will cross again, Willa."

Goosebumps dimpled my arms at the sound of my name on his lips. I silently cursed my foolishness. This was not the time to act like a silly young girl, especially not with Doctor Winston watching.

"I'm not sure that will be the case, Mr. Butler. Thank you again for your assistance today. Both the doctor and I appreciate it."

I raced to the car and settled myself in the seat. Sam gave a brief wave goodbye. I hadn't meant my words to be harsh, but I already had enough problems in my life with lying to my parents and working with the doc. Standing there in the fading afternoon light with his wry quirk of a smile, Sam Butler was another piece of trouble I didn't need.

CHAPTER EIGHT

The Reilly Residence
San Francisco, California
October 19, 1936

No matter the time of year, Sea Cliff was beautiful. The neighbor-hood, only a few blocks from where I lived, was awash in houses with grassy lawns, wide porches, and welcoming entrances. While many parts of San Francisco were caught deep in the grip of the Depression, Sea Cliff managed to sidestep the dark shroud hang-ing over the city.

Cara's bright blue house with the large white door sat on a quiet street a block in from the main road. For years before the crash, Mr. Reilly warned everyone who would listen about the hazards of the stock market. Something he boasted about a little too much at church socials. Still, I'd never heard Cara once com-plain about not having enough food, and she often had a new dress for church on Sunday. They'd even had enough money a year ago to build a new room onto the back of the house for community gatherings and dances.

At the corner, I hid behind a towering eucalyptus tree. Thankfully, it was Monday. Soon all four-foot-ten of Mrs. Reilly would be out the door, pocketbook tucked under her little arm, as she headed to the ladies' six o'clock Bible study at church.

I inhaled the scent of salt off the ocean, desperate to smell anything besides the rot currently soiling my shoes and skirt. In my current state I couldn't go home, and Cara was the only one besides Paddy I trusted with my secret.

The minute Mrs. Reilly appeared in a yellow dress and scurried off in the direction of 25th Avenue, I raced onto Cara's front porch. I knocked several times. The sounds of the phonograph floated out the second-floor window. The enchanting voice of Cara's favorite singer, Billie Holiday, tangled with the soft sway of the branches in the trees.

On my third attempt, the door flew open. Cara's big blue eyes bulged. The wrinkle of her nose said I smelled even worse than I thought. "What in blazes happened to you?"

"Are you alone?"

"Yes, why?"

I pushed past her and mounted the stairs until I landed in the large confines of her bedroom. A sense of peace washed over me when I stepped over the threshold. The room held a sense of warmth I could never bring to my own space at home. Maybe it was more just a reflection of Cara: bright and welcoming.

The phonograph clicked in a measured tone as the needle reached the end of the record. Cara raced past me and slid the handle back onto its resting place. "Dad made me use part of my salary to pay for a new needle last week," she huffed.

"How are things settling in at his office? Has he given you any other job than fixing coffee?" I asked.

"Yes," she groaned. "Now I'm in the back doing all his filing. It's a thousand times worse."

When Cara refused to go to the local women's college, her parents told her the only other choice she had was to work at her father's law firm. She'd only been there a few months, but by the way she grumbled you would have thought she'd been toiling away for years.

"I love 'Summertime.' Billie's voice is breathtaking. Will you play it again?" I asked.

"Oh no." She shook a tiny finger in my direction. "You can't barge into my house without an explanation, looking and smelling like you've been rummaging around the trash bins outside the pub."

"I promise I will as soon as I wash off the stench. Can I borrow a dress?"

She marched to her wardrobe and tossed a pale pink skirt and matching top at me. "That'll barely fit, but it'll do for now. Go take a bath, I can't stand the smell of you. Wash off your shoes too. They reek. Afterward, you can tell me what's going on."

Once the tub was full, I sunk down into the water, letting the heat penetrate deep into my bones. The tension left my shoulders and images of the field hospital filled my head. The creak of the steel cots. The faces of the men carved deep with worry.

Sam's bright eyes flickered across my memory. He'd been so worked up about his cousin, but beneath his chastising tone there was a sweetness to the way he reassured Doctor Winston that Benny would be all right. At first, his words may have been tinged with anger, but the way his shoulders shook as the blood pumped from his cousin's head said they were as close as brothers.

I sank deeper into the bubbles rippling around me like sea foam. From the minute Doctor Winston first set a toe inside the field hospital, she'd controlled the scene. She never flinched at the tension and sense of loathing wafting off Doctor Fairchild. I couldn't help but smile at the way she trusted me. It was the first time in my life an adult regarded me with an air of respect. At home I was always young Willa. A thing to be talked around, and about, but never actually addressed.

At the dinner table, Mam and Da planned my life. When I would talk to the priest. How I would first meet the Mother Superior. The day I would enter the convent and eventually take my vows.

I'd become a spectator in my own life until today. The scene with Benny was terrifying. When I found the strength to push away the fear, to step beside Doctor Winston and do what was needed, a sense of purpose and peace unfurled within me.

Convinced the lavender soap had finally washed away my stench, I dressed and headed back to Cara's room. Fred Astaire's "Pick Yourself Up" filled the air. Cara sang along. Her voice was just as good or better than most female songbirds on the radio.

"That song was only released a short time ago. How do you already have the words memorized?"

"It's my business to know the words," she said. "Singing is not only about understanding the melody, but about delivering the lyrics in an emotional way so you reach the listener."

"How did you learn that? It's not like old Mrs. Gleason at school knew anything about melody. She could barely direct the Glee Club and play that old piano in the music room."

"Don't you try to distract me with music talk, Willa. You need to tell me what you're hiding." She plopped down on the bed. The fancy pink silk bedcovers fluttered beneath her.

A part of me walked into this house knowing I could never lie to Cara. As little girls, we'd held onto one another when we were learning to walk. We'd outwitted my bossy brothers and stood up to the meanest girls in school. She was the closest thing I'd ever have to a sister. Plus, she had a wicked temper. When I was eight,

I tried to tell her the drab gray pinafore her mother bought for Easter Sunday Mass was pretty. She knew I was fibbing through my teeth and didn't talk to me for a week. That was the first, and last, time I wasn't honest with my best friend.

I put out my pinkie finger and she leaned forward and looped hers around it. "Solemnly swear that what I'm about to share is part of our secret circle."

She rolled her eyes. "We are not ten."

"Swear," I repeated.

"Fine," she moaned. "I swear."

I sat beside her. Like she'd promised, there was a stack of library books waiting for me on her bedside table. I snatched the bright red book off the top of the pile.

"Ooh. I've been waiting ages to read the latest edition of *Preventive Medicine*."

"Willa." She yanked the book out of my hands. "Enough with the secrecy."

I jumped to my feet and began to pace, trying to put together everything that happened today.

"Hey," she reached out a hand and stopped me. "What is going on? You're shaking like a leaf."

"The doctor who took care of Paddy offered me a chance to come and work with her. Today was my first day, and as you can tell by my prior scent, it wasn't easy." I said it so quickly I wasn't sure she heard me until her perfectly penciled brows jumped to her hairline.

"Okay," she huffed. "Tell me every single detail."

I filled her in on the day we took Paddy to first see Doctor Winston. How later I'd wrapped his hand too tight. Her smile grew wider as I talked about following Doctor Winston to the hospital beside The Gate.

"He vomited right on you and you didn't run away?" She reached forward and flipped over my wrist and ran her fingers over the scar just below the bend in my elbow. A wound I'd earned when I was ten after falling out of a tree while playing with my brothers in Golden Gate Park.

"What are you doing?"

"Just making sure it's really you and not some re-creation like we saw in that *Bride of Frankenstein* film last year. I still have nightmares about that Boris Karloff fella."

I slid her hand away. My mind still spun over the events of the day. How I was going to lie to my parents once I got home. "Don't make fun. I'm worried enough as it is."

"I'm sorry, Willa. This doesn't sound like you." She opened her mouth and quickly snapped it shut.

"Go on and say what you want. We've always been honest with each other. No need to stop now."

"Don't get me wrong, I know how you adore medicine. But for so long you've walked the straight and narrow. Always putting your family's wishes before your own." She chewed on the corner of her lip. "Just now when you were talking about the lady doc, I heard real happiness in your voice, but I worry you're getting yourself into something so deep you won't be able to climb out once your parents send you to the convent."

I stayed quiet and played with a loose thread on her bedcover.

"You're still going to the convent, right?" She took in a long breath. "Or have you changed your mind?"

"Of course not. I would never do that to my parents."

She narrowed those big blue eyes. "I see what you're doing.

You are not responsible for what happened to your sister, you hear me? It was an accident."

Heat pricked at my eyes. "I made a promise, Cara."

"Your mother's miscarriage was not your fault, Wilhelmina MacCarthy." She did her best to hide the creak in her voice but it still shook me. "Just because at twelve you made a solemn promise to be a nun, does not mean you have to keep it now no matter how often your parents tell you it is family tradition. And please, do not worry about what this little community will say if you back out of going to the convent. This is 1936, not 1836. People need to mind their own business. Young women have a choice to be anything they want these days. Look at Mary Sue Potter. The day after graduation she jumped on a train to go to college in Boston and study law. And Joan Brewer, she and her sister drove down to Los Angeles a month ago to try and make it in the pictures."

She yanked me to the phonograph and shoved a new record into my hand. "I understand your parents. Your mam especially has had a rough go these past years, but you shouldn't be caged in by their old-school beliefs. Or a long ago promise you should have never made."

Her eyes narrowed into a familiar stare. It was the same look of pity mixed with outrage she only leveled at me when this topic came up.

The shrieking of the telephone echoed through her room. Cara rushed out into the hallway and caught it on the third ring. Her whisper was too low for me to hear the conversation. I moved back to the stack of records, thumbing through her growing pile. As I moved past Bing Crosby and Fred Astaire, a piece of paper slid out and wafted to the ground. My throat tightened as I read the advertisement:

Auditions open for chorus positions in "On Your Toes." The latest thrilling musical from Rogers and Hart now performing at the world-renowned Imperial Theater, New York City.

The phone clunked down on the receiver, and I quickly placed the paper back among the stack. I slid out another record and placed it onto the phonograph. The first notes of Cole Porter's "You're the Top" eased out of the speakers.

"That was Paddy. He said he went by the doctor's office and she told him she'd dropped you here. He grumbled about you making him late for his shift at the pub but said he'd swing by close to seven to walk you home." She reached for my hand and pretended to foxtrot with me. For years she'd been trying to teach me to dance, but I could never keep any of the steps straight.

"About working with the doc," she said sashaying around me. "I'm the last one to tell you what to do—you get enough of that at home. Please, just tell me you'll keep your mind open. The world is a big place and San Francisco is only one small corner."

She continued to swing her hips and move. Everything about her was carefree. I couldn't figure out how she did it. Allowing an easy smile to cross her lips when she, too, was hiding a deep dark secret from the most important people in her life.

CHAPTER NINE

The Richmond District
San Francisco, California
October 19, 1936

For the entire walk home, Paddy never took a breath. Questions rolled off his tongue so quickly I had to remind him his lungs needed oxygen. When we reached the hill at the top of 25th Avenue he pulled me to an abrupt stop.

"Now, explain to me why you're wearing Cara's clothes?"

I waved him forward, skirting around businessmen and women dragging along small children. He was way past late for his shift, and he'd certainly get an earful from Da.

As we moved along, I explained about the patients and the blood and bodily fluids that spilled all over my skirt at the field hospital. How Cara promised to sneak my clothes into her laundry and return them so Mam would never know.

He grabbed my arm and yanked me apart from the bustling crowd. "You went to the bridge?"

I could only nod knowing what he'd say next.

"Willa, going to the doc's office is one thing, but if you'd run into the twins . . . "

"Paddy, I get it. But when Doctor Winston asked me to go, I couldn't refuse. You should have seen it. She showed me how to take a patient's vitals. The correct procedure for placing sutures."

Cara was right. There was joy in my voice.

Paddy scrubbed a hand over his pinched brow. "It sounds

great, Will. Just promise me you'll be careful. There's a big difference between working within the confines of an office and being out at that site with so many people to see you."

"You have my word. I won't take any unnecessary risks."

When I asked about where he'd been all day he ignored my question, intent on getting us home. The sounds of the pub floated down the street toward us. A chill raced over my shoulders even though a warm fall breeze swept across my ears. I'd never told a bold-face lie to my parents. I was always too afraid I'd have to confess it to Father O'Sullivan a few days later in that cold dark box at St. Monica.

"I need you to create a diversion so I can get inside without Mam seeing me in this outfit. The thought of having to lie about one more thing today is making me nauseous."

"Okay," he said. "Once we're through the door, I'll distract her with a complaint about my hand explaining that's what's keeping me from my shift at the pub. You get into the washroom before she can see you. And Will, wash your hands again. There's still blood underneath your nails."

Paddy led the way up the stairs. Music from inside the pub beat in time with the nervous thud of my heart. The door to the apartment creaked open and the smell of boiling meat and vegetables filled the air. My stomach growled. I'd been too busy watching and learning from Doctor Winston that I'd completely forgotten to eat lunch.

Paddy moved toward the kitchen while I dashed through the parlor. "Mam, it smells good. What are we having?"

I grabbed the first dress I could find in my wardrobe and raced into the washroom. My hands shook on the edges of the porcelain basin, proving I wasn't cut out for a life of deceit.

"Wilhelmina." Mam tapped on the door. "You all right in there?"

"Yes," I said scrubbing my hands underneath the faucet in hopes it would drown out the quiver in my voice.

"You rushed by so quickly, but I noticed you're wearing different clothes than this morning. Are you on your monthly? Did you stain your skirt?" she whispered just loud enough for me to hear. So much for Paddy's diversion.

I wanted to open the door, wrap her in my arms, and spill out everything that happened today. But sadly, I knew deep in my bones she'd never understand.

"No, I'm not bleeding. Things are fine, Mam." I bit my lip, praying she wouldn't press about the clothes.

"How was the soup kitchen? Did you see Father O'Sullivan? Did he say anything about meeting with Mother Superior?"

I struggled with a reply. Up to this point, I'd been a good daughter. Believed my parents knew what was right for me. Done my best to try and accept my place in this world. But today, my existence shifted. I'd breathed in Doctor Winston's world. Placed my hand into the blood and skin of a man and held on. When it mattered, I didn't faint. Didn't flinch. The burning embers of want were unleashed as Benny thrashed in protest. As I held onto that blood-stained gauze, I'd tried to ignore their pull, but the flames refused to be snuffed out. The truth was I wanted them to rise and grow.

"He said he was still waiting on details." The lie trickled out of my mouth easily. Guilt wound around my chest like a snake crushing my lungs.

"Well, then there's nothing else to do for now. Your da

begrudgingly agreed to let one of Nick's friends man the pub for a half hour so we can all have dinner together. Hurry along now."

"I'll be right out," I said.

My fingers trembled as they pushed the pearl-like buttons through the small holes in my dress. Doctor Winston had warned me this life wouldn't be easy, and she was right in more ways than one. My sinning had begun and there was no going back.

The tinny sound of forks scraping against plates filled our small dining room. My brothers reached over one another in a mad frenzy. Food dribbled out of their mouths as they scrambled for thin slices of meat and helpings of potatoes. In between bites, Da asked Nick about the count in the till and how many pints he'd poured that day. Once Nick answered, Da scrubbed at his copper beard. His mouth twitched as if counting the numbers. The Depression had hit everyone hard, but men still found coins for a pint even when their children were starving.

"Conall O'Malley got up on The Gate today," Michael said knocking Sean's hand out of the way as he reached for the green beans. They'd clipped each other's hair again and it was hard not to laugh at the bald spots stamped across their scalps. Last week they'd worked on a one-day project digging roads for the WPA, but now they were without jobs again, which meant trouble.

More than once I'd heard whispers about them getting drunk and causing a ruckus at local dance halls like the Hibernian and the KRB. Mothers warned their daughters away from the likes of the youngest MacCarthy boys. When I heard those conversations, I was never brave enough to speak up, but I did manage to shoot those mothers an evil stare.

Sean and Michael could be a handful. I think that's what kept Da from giving them regular work at the pub. While they annoyed me most of the time, I had to admit they were also a welcome relief to the frequent dour tone of our home. Their boisterous laughter, and propensity for telling inappropriate jokes, often lightened the mood. While Mam often chastised them, I think she let them get away with their bawdy behavior because deep down she understood our house needed light every now and then.

"More and more men with their union cards show up every day at the bridge. We wait patiently, but it's hard not to feel like we're all a bunch of cows getting looked over to see which is the best side of beef," Sean whined.

The twins both stood in excess of six feet and carried at least two hundred and fifteen pounds. Together they were hard to miss in a crowd, but now that the bridge was rumored to be a year from completion the need for skilled laborers was more important than brute strength.

"Me and Michael did our best to stand out, look strong, but he ended up picking Conall because he needed someone with welding experience," Sean added.

The unnaturally deep timbre of Sean's voice practically carried out in the street. I chalked it up to his current addiction to Dashiell Hammett. A ratty copy of *The Maltese Falcon* took up permanent residence in his back pocket. I was sure he'd dragged Michael over to the Alexandria Theater at least ten times to watch *The Thin Man*. I'd even heard him brag to the gals he knew that he'd visited 891 Post Street where Hammett once lived and was supposedly the fictional home of his favorite detective, Sam Spade.

Mam patted Sean's hand. "Chin up, love. I keep saying the Rosary for you lads. I know God will find a spot for you and your brother soon." She rubbed the tarnished crucifix dangling from a thin chain around her neck.

"I dunno, Mam," Michael said. He plucked his wire-rimmed glasses off the edge of his nose and wiped them with the hem of his shirt. "Superintendent Scarpetti hires fewer and fewer men each week." He pulled a small notebook from his pocket and ran a finger down a dog-eared page. "According to some of the men I've talked to, the last suspender ropes will be hung in a couple of weeks. They're making record time with laying the roadway. I heard a few men say they'll close the gap by early next month." He scrubbed a hand over the soup dribbling down his chin. "You know, Sean and I could help more around the pub, especially now that Paddy's at the soup kitchen with Willa."

Sean bobbed his head. "Think we did all right grabbing those barrels of ale last time."

"Nick and I have the pub under control, even if Paddy here can't show up on time," Da grumbled.

Paddy gave me a gentle kick under the table and I shot him an apologetic smile.

"You boys need to focus on getting work at the bridge. Now tell me, whose job did Conall take?" Da asked around a slurp of soup.

"Cyrus Browne's," Michael said.

"Isn't that the Protestant fella you and Sean went to school with?" Nick asked.

"That's the one." Sean swiped the last bit of bread off Michael's plate. He slathered it with butter and chomped into it with a huge bite.

"Seeeeean!" Mam dragged out his name in one long breath and shoved a cloth in his direction.

"Did he find a better job elsewhere?" Paddy wiped at the

corners of his mouth with a napkin. Out of all my brothers, he was the only one who had manners.

The table went quiet. Da continued to slurp his soup in between beats of silence. Michael and Sean swapped a hesitant look that could only mean trouble.

"Well, go on. Your brother asked a question," Da barked in the twin's direction.

"He left the city," Sean said finding something very interesting on his plate filled with nothing but crumbs.

"And," Paddy nudged him.

"He went with Molly Gallagher."

Mam's fork clattered against her plate and took a dive straight onto the floor. "No! You must have heard wrong. Molly was to go to the convent with your sister. Her mother told me so last week at our sewing circle."

Molly graduated with the twins and was known in our circles for being quite the beauty with her caramel brown hair and bright green eyes. At one time, I think both Sean and Michael had a crush on her.

"They took off in the night two days ago," Sean mumbled.

Mam dabbed at the thin tight lines around her mouth. "Why would a sweet girl like that do such a thing?"

That same look I didn't like from the twins, the one that said they'd rather eat lard than speak, raced across their faces.

"Now's not the time to be skittish." Nick crossed his thick arms over his chest. "Tell Mam what you know."

Sean opened his mouth, but Michael spoke first. "We only heard rumors, but some of the lads from school said she was in a family way."

A half gurgle, half choke spilled from Mam's lips. Her cheeks went pale, and of course, her focus landed on me.

"This is why we don't let you go to dances without a chaperone. Why you'll never wear a skirt that goes higher than your calves. These are desperate times and girls like you are not thinking straight!" Mam reached for her glass of water and took a deep gulp. "The sooner we get you to the convent, the less time there is for trouble." With a trembling hand, she set down the glass and fled the table.

"A Protestant! A child!" Her choked mumbles spilled out from the kitchen.

Paddy looked down at his napkin while the heated stares of every other MacCarthy male landed on me. Words of protest punched against my lips. When a female we knew got into trouble, all of a sudden every girl within earshot was assumed to make the same mistake.

I'd known for a long time that Molly and Cyrus had a thing. When no one was watching, they'd slip out during dances at the KRB. One time in the heat of summer last year, I went outside to get some air and caught them kissing in the alley. Molly begged me to keep quiet. I did because the light in her eyes, and pink flush against her cheeks, screamed she was in love.

Not every girl was desperate to get out of San Francisco. Many of us followed the rules. Kept our legs crossed even when the boys touched us, wanted us, in more carnal ways. I couldn't fault Molly for her choices, but I'd never fall into that trap. Mam didn't need to worry about me and boys. What she should have been afraid of was the lure of college and medicine.

"Willa," Nick tapped at the table to get my attention. "Maybe you should go in and see if Mam needs a hand with the dishes."

Every inch of me wanted to tell him he had two fine arms and legs. That he was perfectly capable of going to help. All of my brothers were. Instead, I pushed back my chair. There was a time and place to speak up, but this was not it. After talking with Cara today, I'd made up my mind. For as long as I could, I'd work with Doctor Winston. The appeal of her teaching was too much to deny. If I wanted to slip away each day, I needed to keep them happy. Content in believing I was following all the house rules.

I inched around the table, gathering plates and glasses until the weight sagged down my arms. Da watched me struggle and gave a small smile at my effort. It was the first sign of affection I'd had from him in months.

In the kitchen, Mam stood in front of the sink. A bloom of white bubbles rose from the water. Even though the faucet was on full blast, it didn't mask her sniffles. I went to work beside her, hoping my presence might give her some comfort. Together, we scrubbed glasses and dishes covered in thick gravy.

"Some people might say I'm overreacting about Molly," she shook her head, tears tumbling down her cheeks. "But pregnancy is not a game. You have to take care of yourself. Eat right. Sleep right." Her voice shook with the kind of pain I never wanted to feel.

"I'm sorry, Mam. I wish I could change things."

For a brief flash, she looked at me like she really saw me. Then, like a lit candle held out in the wind, that light was gone.

"Water under the bridge," she said.

I was so used to her stern tone that when she spoke quietly I imagined her splintering into a thousand shards of glass. "I'm just glad you're being a good girl. Keeping your promises," she whispered.

Promises. The word plunged into me like a sharp knife. It was if by sending me to the convent, she was pinning all her hopes and dreams on me. It was a heavy weight I'd never recognized until I'd stumbled into Doctor Winston's office and considered there could be more to my life.

Her hands dove deeper into the sink. This time she went to work on a handful of silverware. Every inch of me screamed to pull her close. To whisper another apology, but my feet stayed firmly in place.

No matter what I said, or promised, life for Mam and Da would always be haunted by the child they'd lost.

CHAPTER TEN

Golden Gate Bridge Field Hospital
San Francisco, California
October 23, 1936

Four days later we were called back to the field hospital. This time it wasn't fear that filled my chest but a sense of anticipation of what patients we might see today. As we walked down the narrow path, I kept my head bent praying I'd be as lucky as last time and avoid my brothers.

As soon as we swept through the door, Francie, the young nurse who'd misplaced her watch, rushed in our direction. A chin-high pile of papers filled her arms.

"I'm so glad you're here. We could really use your help today."

She waved us to a corner of the room. "As you might have read in the papers, we had our first fatality two days ago. One of the derrick pins got loose on a crane near midspan. It dismantled a support leg and the whole thing toppled over. It knocked a tag line man into the net. He's going to live, but another fella, he got hit across the head and shoulders and didn't make it."

Her eyes widened when she spied Doctor Fairchild headed in our direction. "I better go."

Doctor Fairchild greeted us like a different man this time. "Thank you for returning today." He glanced in the direction Francie headed. "I suppose you've heard about the accident."

"Yes, it's a tragedy," Doctor Winston said.

"It's too bad. Was hoping we might get through this entire

project without a single fatality." He reached out and shook Doctor Winston's hand. "Again, I'm grateful you both are here. Please, let me know if you need any assistance today."

Doctor Winston smiled graciously while he shuffled off to see a waiting patient.

"Why does he seem so different today? He's acting practically human," I said.

She reached for a stack of files waiting for us on a nearby table. The slightest purple tint of a bruise colored her cheek where Benny had struck her. Looking at it still made my blood boil.

"My guess is he received a call from a friend of mine over at the university."

"What friend?" I asked taking the overflow of files from her hands.

"My old mentor, Doctor Briar is quite influential in the California State Medical Society. I'd guess that Doctor Owens told him about my agreeing to fill in for him here. Word travels fast in the medical community."

Most men would gloat in this situation, but in the short time I'd worked with her I'd learned that wasn't Doctor Winston's style. When men wandered into her office their reaction was always the same: a wide-eyed stare, accompanied by a curse under their breath, followed by a sharp turn out the door. In every single instance, she shrugged and moved on to the next patient, which was usually a wealthy woman's maid or a down-on-her-luck mother looking for care for her child. No matter the patient, Doctor Winston always treated them with respect.

My gut clenched. When my mother had been sick those years ago, I expected there to be tenderness from the physician considering what she'd been through, what she'd lost. Instead, as soon as her bleeding stopped, he shuffled her out the door as if he couldn't wait to get another patient in her empty bed.

"Willa," Doctor Winston tapped my shoulder. "You all right?"

"Yes, ma'am." I scrubbed away the heat burning the corner of my eyes. "Do we have a patient waiting?"

"This way."

I trailed behind her to a cot at the end of the room. A breeze whipped through the door and fluttered the sheets on a nearby bed. It was usually warm this time in October, but today the wind's icy bite, and the dark clouds looming over the water, held the promise of a storm.

Doctor Winston sat next to a cot occupied by a man tucked deep into the sheets. As I checked his pulse and used her stethoscope to listen to his heartbeat, she asked her regular line of questions. Even with two blankets on top of him, he shivered.

"What's your name?" she asked.

The man's thick dark brows knotted. That familiar look of curiosity mixed with worry pinched his eyes. "Lorenzo Minetti," he answered.

"And what do you do on the bridge, sir?"

"Can't you tell?" He waved to the orange sheen coloring the tops of his cheeks, arms, and fingertips.

"Painter?" I guessed.

"Yes, Miss." He shivered again, his lips tinged a faint blue.

"You seem to be very cold, Mr. Minetti." Doctor Winston pressed a hand to his forehead.

"It's hell out there," he gulped. "It's impossible to work in some of these conditions. Certain days the rough wind makes it hard to stand upright. And the rain," he shook his head. "It comes in so sharp it beats against your hard hat like bullets."

He leaned in. "The other morning heavy mist covered the deck. I dangled in that bosun chair for hours doing my best to get the paint to stick to the wet cables. My partner left two days ago complaining of a headache. He ain't returned to work yet. You don't think I caught whatever he had?"

"Let me finish examining you. Continue with your story," she said.

"The foreman called us down to a warm-up shack convinced we should let the late morning sun dry out the cables. Once I was on the ground, I moved over a narrow walkway and hit a wire. Turned my foot and teetered on the edge of a rail. The net below pitched in another gust. Thought for sure I'd go in. A steel worker nearby started cursing at me. Made me so mad, I caught my balance and walked the rest of the rail to the shack. When we got inside, I shook his hand."

"You shook his hand even though he cursed at you?" she asked.

"Yes, it's an old trick amongst us bridge men. Get the fella mad so he stops being scared. Sounds crude I know, but it works." He shivered again. "Don't wanna be part of the 'Halfway To Hell' club or the bridge's next victim like that fella who got crushed to bits the other day."

"What's the 'Halfway To Hell' club?" I asked.

"That's what they call the gents who fall into the net and live to tell the tale."

Doctor Winston ordered me to take his temperature while she continued to examine him. A few minutes later she pulled the thermometer from his mouth. "Looks like you're headed home, Mr. Minetti. Temperature is one hundred and two."

A low hiss left his mouth.

"Is there a problem?" she asked.

"Eight for eight or out the gate," he grumbled.

"Excuse me?" she said.

"It means you put in eight hours of work for eight hours of pay. I'll be fined for anything less." He scrubbed an orange-tinted hand over his chapped lips. "How long do you think I'll have to be out?"

"That doesn't seem right that they'd dock your pay," she said.

"The foreman is a tough bloke. He's always threating to give our jobs to other union fellas if we don't carry our weight."

She patted at her pockets. I reached across the bedside table and retrieved the silver pen she was always misplacing. "I'll mark in your file that you need rest. The doctor in charge will inform your boss that you are to stay home and rest for at least two days. That should cover you."

He gave Doctor Winston a wide gap-toothed smile. "Thank you, ma'am . . . I mean doc. Got three little boys at home. Need to make sure they stay fed."

She patted his hand. "I understand, sir."

We only saw two more patients for the rest of our shift, both of whom had the same symptoms as Mr. Minetti. We were about to call it a day, when the door blew open. Rain coming down in a hard slant pounded against the roof.

Mr. Minetti was right. It did sound like bullets.

A tall, thin body draped in an oil-skin parka raced inside. "Hello, ladies."

The temperature was quickly dropping and Sam was soaked to the bone.

"Been coming in last couple of days to see if you're here."

He plucked the hard hat from his head. I took an uncomfortable gulp. His eyes were the color of the dark sea outside. Raindrops drizzled over his narrow cheekbones and plunged off the cleft in his chin.

Just looking at him felt like sinning.

"Wanted to let you both know Benny is following orders. Today is his first day back."

"That's good news," Doctor Winston said. "And what about you? Any fever or chills?" She glanced at the bed Mr. Minetti once occupied.

He scrubbed a hand over his eyes and swiped back his sopping wet hair. "No, feeling fit as a fiddle." He spoke to her, but his eyes stayed on me. "And you Miss Willa, are you doing well?"

"I'm fine." I turned away doing my best to ignore the flutter in my chest. Even soaking wet, he was beautiful. "Doctor Winston, weren't you saying something about leaving for the day?" I couldn't turn back and risk Sam seeing the heat blooming at my cheeks.

"Yes," she began when an ear-splitting screech stopped her.

"What in heaven was that?" I asked.

Sam didn't hesitate. He raced out the door, and we chased after him.

"Stop, thief!" Francie sprinted past us up the dirt path headed in the direction of the access road.

Ahead of her, a boy sped up the hill. His dark hair clung to his head as the rain poured from the sky in thick sheets. Francie followed in quick pursuit until her foot hit a small hole and she went down into a puddle face first.

"Willa, I'm going back in to grab my bag. Go check on her," Doctor Winston ordered.

I bolted up the steep hill. My feet sucked and popped in and out of mud holes. Sam stayed beside me. His hand hovered close to my hip like he expected me to take a fall too.

The boy reached the top of the hill and spun around. I knew that face. He shook his head at me like a warning not to follow.

When we reached Francie, I slid down beside her. Before I could stop him, Sam took off in the direction of the boy.

"Mr. Butler, don't," I called out, but my voice was lost in a deafening roar of thunder.

"My ankle. It's broken," Francie sobbed. "I heard it snap." Her once white uniform was awash in thick brown mud and dirty rain water.

"Are you hurt anywhere else?" I asked.

"No." Her voice shook as she sat up. "I was dumb. Never should have chased after him, but I saw him take Nurse Mayhew's pocketbook and I couldn't let him get away."

Doctor Winston sunk down beside us. The edges of her navy pants floated in the growing mud puddle.

"She says it's her ankle. Should we try to splint it here?"

"Let's get her back inside where I can get a better look," she said.

Her gaze darted around the inclined path. "Where is Mr. Butler?"

"He took off after the boy."

"Boy?"

Francie bobbed her head. "I've seen him nosing around here the last couple of weeks. Thought he was scrounging for food. Now I understand why he took off when I offered him the Hershey bar I always keep in my pocketbook. He wasn't looking for food; he was here to steal!" The tears on her cheeks mixed with the flow of rain from the sky.

Doctor Winston and I helped Francie back to the hospital. Once inside, she showed me how to wrap the ankle. Halfway through the splinting process, Sam swept in the door.

Francie's cheeks brightened for the first time since we brought her inside. "Did you catch him?"

"No. Chased him as far as the hills above Baker Beach. That bugger was fast. Lost him in all the brush."

She sagged back against the pillows. "I'll never get my grandmother's watch back."

I handed her a handkerchief and she sniffled into the embroidered cloth while Doctor Winston finished treating her ankle.

The knowledge that I knew the boy, Simon, stayed lodged in my throat. His little sister Maeve's words about their mother sleeping on the hard ground kept me silent. He shouldn't get away with stealing, but a deep prickle in my chest warned there was much more to the story. Like Sean's favorite detective, Sam Spade, I'd hunt him down and get to the truth.

CHAPTER ELEVEN

Golden Gate Bridge Field Hospital
San Francisco, California
October 23, 1936

After the downpour, the sun dug its way out from behind the clouds. Doctor Winston offered to drive me back to the office but I made an excuse about wanting to take a walk and clear my head. After grumbling about me not wearing the right shoes, and the blocks it would take to get home, she relented.

"What are you up to?" Sam hovered behind me as I waved to the doctor until she disappeared down the access road.

"Mr. Butler, you're still here?" I tugged my coat around my shoulders. The edges of my cotton blouse clung to my rain-soaked skin.

His eyes narrowed. "Seen that look before. That's the face of a woman who is hatching a plan."

"I have no idea what you are talking about."

Deep down I understood this game we were playing. I'd done it a dozen times with my brothers. They thought they could see inside my head as if I was completely transparent. Lucky for me, they frequently underestimated what I was doing. When we'd played hide-and-seek as children, I was always the last one discovered. They were the transparent ones. Always searching in the same spots. Not clever enough to think about the small cupboard below the stairs in the lobby or the hidden nook inside my parents' closet.

The biting wind roared off the ocean. I flipped up the collar on my coat. If I was going to put my plan in motion, I had to get rid of him.

"Good to see you again, Mr. Butler."

I swept up the hill. Once I reached the summit, I turned toward the military installation, the Presidio, which was farther to the east. Another few steps ahead, I found a small access road and banked my way up and around the narrow path. I waited in the shadows. Sam paced for a few minutes. His gaze darted in the direction I'd walked and then back to the access road. Why wouldn't he leave?

For a few more agonizing minutes he stood in place before he tucked his hard hat under his arm and stalked back in the direction of the Presidio.

Once I was convinced he was gone, I took off in the direction Simon ran. I walked for what I guessed was a half-mile through rain-drenched puddles headed toward Baker Beach. My head spun with several different questions. Why was Simon stealing? Did his parents know? What would I say when I found him? Accusing him of thievery without proof wasn't the right approach.

Cold water and bits of rock and sand soaked my socks and toes, making it difficult to pick my way along the rubble-strewn road toward the beach. My sodden clothes clung to every inch of me. Ignoring the bite of the breeze, I shook off my coat and allowed the flow of wind to dry my blouse and skirt. Yet another outfit caked in mud.

I walked for at least another quarter mile. The sun made its slow dip toward the horizon. A chill prickled along my arms. Yet again, I'd be late to meet Paddy. What excuse would we devise this time for Mam and Da? Knots bunched at my neck again as I considered the mountain of lies I'd already told.

I glanced at the trail in front of me, questioning if I should give up when I spied a set of footprints. They twisted and turned down a steep path. Ahead, the rough surf pounded against the beach. Several men with their pants rolled to the knee waded into the waves. Fishing poles settled tightly in their grip as their lines disappeared into the sea-foam-stained water.

Following the footprints, I moved along the narrowing trail. The scent of burning wood prickled at my nose. A puff of gray smoke became a beacon leading me further into a copse of low-hanging trees and coastal brush. My shoes became weights as they continued to fill with dirt and sand. My damp coat hung heavy in my arms as I walked toward what I guessed was a campfire.

The trees bunched together in a tight fist. An overhang of greenery tore at my hair and neck. I flung back the tangle of branches and kicked away small shrubs until I stumbled into a wide clearing. The thud in my chest from the hike was nothing compared to the heartbreaking scene laid out before me.

Twenty brown canvas tents littered the clearing. The scent of rotting meat, human waste, and body odor coated the air. Men dressed in worn overalls and wrinkled shirts scrubbed worry from their red-rimmed eyes. Mothers bustled around open fires, stoking the flames in hopes of warming their small children from the late afternoon chill.

I'd heard my brothers talk about these villages called "Hoovervilles." Over the past few years they'd popped up across the country. They'd earned the name thanks to our last president, Herbert Hoover, whom many blamed for the market crash. I didn't believe them when they talked about how homeless families gathered in these places when they had nowhere else to go. There was no denying it now as the small community spread out before me in living color.

Is this what Maeve meant about her mother sleeping on the hard ground?

I sunk back into the shadows. Walking into the village, confronting Simon, wasn't me. I never argued. My shins had permanent bruises from where Paddy kicked me under the table when I refused to speak up at dinnertime. My family told me when to eat, when to sleep, when to pray. What did I think I'd accomplish by coming here? The minute I approached Mrs. Cleery, what would I say? Mentioning her son was a thief probably wasn't the best place to begin.

No. I wouldn't run away, but I needed a plan. Taking a few steps back, I stumbled into a solid wall of body. Before a scream could part my lips, a voice whispered, "Thought you told the doc you were headed home?"

"Let go of me!" I shook out of Sam's grasp. "Who do you think you are, stalking behind me like some jungle cat?"

"It wasn't hard to figure out what you were planning. I saw how you looked at that boy. You know him."

"That still doesn't excuse you from traipsing after me like some hooligan!" Harsher words bubbled at my lips, but I swallowed them down.

He wiped a hand over his hardened mouth. "Do you know what you're getting yourself into? Do you have a plan? These people are living a hard life. How do you think they're going to react when you barge into their world looking pink-cheeked and well-fed? You are a living, breathing reminder of all the things they do not have."

The fire inside me quickly extinguished. He was right. Marching into the camp was akin to entering an unknown neighborhood and banging on people's doors asking if they needed help. It was the last way to earn anybody's trust.

"Tell me, how do you know the boy?" he asked.

Wet leaves clung to his hair like barnacles in the sea below us. On instinct, I rose on tip-toe and brushed the sticky evergreen pieces from his light hair. He caught my hand in his. The mixture of hunger and aggravation in his eyes was too much and I staggered back.

"He's been to the office." My voice wobbled in a way I didn't like. "Doctor Winston took care of his pregnant mother a few days ago."

"Okay, so what is your plan?"

"If anyone stops me, I'll tell them I know Mrs. Cleery. That I'm here to check on her condition." I did my best to act confident even though I had no idea if I was brave enough to push on.

"Fine," he huffed. "But you aren't going in alone."

He swept a hand forward, encouraging me to take the lead. I stood frozen in the mud-covered spot at a complete loss for words. Surely, I hadn't heard him right. Every inch of me expected him to be as stern as my brothers. To order me back home. To tell me to act like a good and proper girl. Instead, his bright blue eyes narrowed into a gaze filled with confidence and respect. I was trying hard to keep my distance from him, but his genuine kindness and concern continued to draw me in.

"Let's hurry, Willa. It will be dark soon."

His words shook me out of my trance. This was no time to be caught up in a girlish fantasy. I snapped back my shoulders and prayed I wasn't making a mistake. One foot in front of the other,

I moved into the clearing and toward the closest tent. A woman stoking a fire double-blinked as if I was some sort of ghost. I asked about Simon and his family. She shook her head. When I prattled on about my worries regarding Mrs. Cleery and the baby, she hesitated. The narrow line of her cheekbones and her cracked, bleeding lips dug into my soul. I pulled an apple I'd taken from the field hospital out of my pocket. A bright smile lit her face and she greedily wrenched it from my hand. After two large bites, juice dribbling down the edge of her chin, she poked a ragged, dirt-covered fingernail in the direction of a tent on the far side of the clearing.

"Well done," Sam whispered.

The stern look I gave him forced him to step back. He could act like a protector, but if people were going to trust me here he couldn't seem like my chaperone.

We trudged past families of every configuration. Mothers. Fathers. Grandparents. Children sat on discarded apple crates, their bellies swollen with hunger. Old men, shoulders hung deep with worry, paged through soggy old newspapers. Emaciated dogs dug through piles of tin cans and trash in a desperate attempt to find scraps.

Outside a dark brown tent, I spied Simon. When he caught sight of me he took off toward the edge of the clearing. Sam sprinted after him and caught the edge of his shirt before he could escape. He dragged him into the trees and I followed. Simon struggled under Sam's tight hold screaming obscenities that made me blush.

"Enough!" Sam snapped. "Calm down and watch your mouth around the lady." He wrapped his arms tighter against a thrashing

Simon. I'd seen Sam hold down Benny. There was no way Simon was getting away this time.

"We're not here to get you in trouble." I approached like he was a feral animal—lowered voice and slow, steady steps. "We just need you to give back what you stole. Don't you think your mam would be upset if she knew what you were doing?"

"No," he spit out, still thrashing in Sam's arms. "She and Maeve have had a few good meals in the last day or two thanks to my thieving. It's what I got to do now that my da is . . ." He bit his lip and sagged in Sam's arms.

I bent down in front of him. "Where is your da, Simon?"

He turned into Sam's chest. "He went down south to find work. What little money he left us is already gone," he mumbled through gasping sobs.

In my hurry to hunt him down it never dawned on me to ask why he was stealing. My parents and brothers whispered about those on the streets who were desperate for food and shelter. The stories became so frequent I began to ignore them. But standing in front of Simon, seeing pain no child should have to experience, it hit me how naïve I'd been about the world.

A white-hot flash of shame washed over me. All this time I'd been caught up in my own selfish worries about the convent that I never considered the greater tragedies happening in my own city.

Simon pulled out a green embroidered pocketbook from behind a nearby rock. "I'm sorry," he said shoving it into Sam's hand.

"That's the right choice, pal."

Simon curled in on himself like a beaten animal. "Please don't tell my mam. She's already upset and worried about so many things."

"What about the watch you took?" I asked.

"Sold it to a buttoned-up bloke on the street yesterday for two dollars."

"You'll have to pay it back somehow," I said. "And you'll need to apologize to Nurse Abbott. She'll be very sad to know her grandmother's watch is gone."

"Yes, ma'am." He glanced at the hard hat tucked under Sam's arm. "Do you think they'd hire me over at the bridge? I'm a real good learner. Could be a help up on those platforms. Then I could pay the lady back."

Sam patted the top of Simon's head. "Wish that was possible. They have strict rules about who they hire. Plus, I imagine your mother would much rather have you in school."

Simon shrugged. "Not going. Mam teaches me reading and how to do my letters. She says that's enough to get a job one day."

"Not even men my age who are big and strong are being hired," Sam said. "There's not enough work to go around."

Simon's thin shoulders sagged again.

"Let's head back to the tent and check on your mam," I said.

Mrs. Cleery stood next to a small fire, stirring the contents cooking in a cast iron pot. Maeve sat beside the fire. When she caught sight of me, her sunshine smile filled me with light.

"I was hoping I'd see you again," she chirped. A deep cough I didn't like rattled her chest.

"Hello," I said to Mrs. Cleery. "I'm Willa. We met at Doctor Winston's office. I wanted to come and check on you." Her sunken eyes and trembling hands made me regret giving the apple to the woman near the clearing.

"Thank you, Miss."

"You're welcome. How are you feeling?"

She pressed a hand to her swollen belly. "No contractions

since that day." Her thick Irish brogue reminded me of the men who filled the pub day after day.

"That's good news. Have you been eating like the doctor instructed?"

"A bit yesterday."

The edge to her voice warned she wasn't being honest. Her shoulders quivered, and I understood why Simon had taken such drastic measures to feed his family. My brothers, my family, were my world. Stealing wasn't right, but I couldn't condemn him. If faced with the same difficult choice, I might resort to stealing too.

"Where are you from in Ireland?" Sam asked.

Mrs. Cleery blinked in his direction.

"My apologies," I said. "This is an acquaintance of mine, Mr. Butler. He insisted in accompanying me here."

The tension in her face relaxed. "That's good, Miss. A young lady such as yourself might not be safe traipsing in and out of here alone."

Her eyes darted around the edges of the clearing and back to Simon. He wasn't more than twelve. If there was trouble, how could he protect his mother and sister?

I bit back the sob scratching in my throat. A few weeks ago, I would have allowed myself to cry, but turning into a blubbering girl would not help me earn this family's trust. Doctor Winston would remain stoic in this situation, and I could do the same.

"We're from County Wexford. Mam and Da grew up there." Simon planted his feet and puffed out his chest. "Maeve and me were born there. We've only be in the States 'bout a year."

Maeve slid back behind her mother. Her chest heaved up and down and another wet cough burst from her lips.

I bent down and pressed my hand to her forehead. No fever.

"Are you feeling all right?" I asked.

She inched in and gave a small nod.

"Miss, my friend Bea lives a couple of tents away. She's been complaining of a stomachache for the last few days. Was wondering if you'd mind checking on her?" Mrs. Cleery asked.

"I'm not a doctor. Will she trust me?"

"No matter, just give her a look over. Maybe tell her to go see the lady doc if she needs it." She moved in closer, glancing over her shoulder at the other tents. "The doc mentioned she was open to seeing folks like us for free."

"I'll see what I can do. Where is she again?"

"Simon can show you."

Maeve wrapped her tiny arms around me. It hurt to feel the bones protruding from her back. I reached into my pocketbook and pulled out a few coins. Mrs. Cleery shook her head. "Please," I curled them into her hand. "Doctor Winston said you need to eat. Do it for the baby. For the children."

Her lips thinned. "Just this once. We are not a charity case." She glanced at Simon. "Their da will be sending us money soon."

Simon stalked ten steps ahead of us, shoving aside brush and smacking every tree branch he could touch. The pounding roar of the waves thudded behind us as we moved higher up an embankment.

"We don't need handouts," Simon huffed in my direction. "My da will have a job soon. He'll send money. Then we won't have to live in this place anymore."

"Listen, Simon," Sam stopped and placed his hands on the boy's shoulders. "Being a man doesn't mean you and your family need to starve. I bet when your da left he told you to look out for them. Protect them. Right?"

"Yes, sir." He crossed his arms over his chest. "And I been doing just that."

"That's honorable. Now to keep them safe, you need to ensure they stay healthy. There's no shame in taking a few dollars here and there to help. Done it myself a time or two."

"You?" Simon's eyes widened. "You've taken a handout? But you're so big and strong."

We continued to traipse through the brush. I hung back, letting them have their boy talk. The more Simon learned to trust, the more he'd allow me to help.

"I've been on my own since I was fourteen," Sam said. "Me and my cousin, Benny, been traveling around the entire United States together. Working wherever we could get hired."

"Fourteen?" Simon gasped. "That's only two years older than me! Weren't you scared?"

"At certain times, yes. But we had to learn to be brave. Kind of like what you're doing now."

Simon's stride straightened. The crease in his brows faded. Sam kept talking. I enjoyed the melodic sound of his confident voice. The way he was at ease with Simon. How he engaged him in conversation while trying to teach him too. Their quick affection for each other reminded me of earlier times I'd spent with my da.

When I was small, he'd take me on a ferry across the bay to have picnics. The two of us would stand on the deck and pretend to be explorers discovering new lands. He'd called it his special daughter time. An ache radiated across my chest. He'd opened the pub a few years ago, and I started spending more time with Cara, but that had nothing to do with why our special outings ended.

"Simon, can you tell me how long your sister's been breathing that roughly?"

"'Bout a month. Mam's been giving her boiled water with honey she borrowed from a neighbor in the tent next door. But she stopped asking for it about a week ago when the old woman screamed at her over how expensive it was."

"It's important your sister comes back to see Doctor Winston. Tell your Mam."

"All right, Miss. I promise."

He stopped in front of a small dark green tent. "This is where Ms. Bea lives. Gotta warn you though, she can be a bit ornery with folks she doesn't know."

I pointed to a spot with fallen logs and large chunks of driftwood. "Sam, why don't you and Simon continue your conversation over there."

Once they were gone, I called inside the tent. "Hello, Ms. Bea. My name is Willa MacCarthy. Mrs. Cleery sent me to check on you."

A knobby hand emerged from the tent followed by a stooped woman with round cheeks and a small rosebud mouth. "That Mrs. Cleery, God love her, is always getting into my business."

She shuffled past me toward a circle of stones. Her wrinkled hands yanked a small metal pan off the rack hovering over a makeshift firepit.

"Coffee?" she asked through a voice cracked by years of age.

"No, thank you."

She reached for the pan, but her fingers couldn't circle the handle. It slid from her grip and clanked onto the rock-strewn ground.

"Let me help."

She shooed me away with a fling of her hand.

"I got this, girl."

She bent slowly and her bones creaked in protest. In my head, I listed the elements Doctor Winston taught me to look for when evaluating a patient. Physical appearance. Mobility. Speech. It would be tricky, but I needed to get close enough to evaluate her better.

She reached for the pan again. I helped her guide it to a small bag nearby filled with less than a handful of ground coffee. Her pulse hummed a steady beat under my fingertips.

"Don't think you're so clever," she huffed. "Know when I'm being doctored." She sunk down on a nearby log. "I might as well sit still so you can get a better look at me."

In this setting it was impossible to do a proper examination, but I did my best. When I finished, her eyes narrowed. "Bit young to be a doctor. How old are you?"

"Eighteen. Right now, I'm learning from a doctor over on Geary Street." I pulled Doctor Winston's card from my coat pocket. "You seem in fine shape except for what appears to be arthritis in your fingers. That's why you're having a hard time gripping the pan."

"Ain't nothing," she moved to stand. "Last time I looked, being aged wasn't a sickness."

"Oh, I'm not saying you're sick. You're just . . ."

"Old?" she finished. "Girly," she chuckled. "You *are* new at this. Might ask that doc to teach you a little about bedside manner."

"Bedside manner?"

"Yes," she shuffled back to the firepit and sunk back down. "You know, how to talk and treat patients without insulting them."

I couldn't help but laugh at the way she delivered the words. They weren't sharp as much as annoyed.

"I know what bedside manner is, but I'm curious how you know the term."

She tossed pieces of driftwood into the firepit. After digging through her pockets, she found a match and struck it against a nearby rock. Flames sprung to life under the charred rack.

"Was a nurse back in the Great War. A bit long in the tooth to be working in France, but they needed hands and mine were good and steady back then. Took care of lots of sick boys. Some from California, Nebraska, and New York. It was a real tragedy."

"My apologies. I should have asked a little more about your background."

She gave me a crooked smile. "Dear, we all gotta start somewhere."

The fire crackled. Flames danced beneath the smoke and wood as she placed the cast iron pot back onto the rack.

Her eyes moved from the growing fire and landed on Simon hovering close by. He twisted his hands and took several deep gulps.

"What is it lad?" she asked.

"Code green," he said quickly. "We gotta get the lady doc outta here."

I was surprised how quickly she jumped to her feet. "Nice meeting you." She kicked sand and dirt into the pit, suffocating the flames, and disappeared back into her tent.

Sam appeared at my arm. "Military police from the Presidio are on the other side of the embankment. Simon says they've rousted them out of this area once already. People were arrested. Best that you not be found here."

"But what about Mrs. Cleery? Maeve?"

"We know what to do. Where to hide," Simon interrupted. "It's best you leave now, Miss."

He started off toward the trees, stopped, and sprinted back.

"Thanks for the talk, Sam." He jutted out his hand in his direction.

Sam shook it with a firm grip. "Might be back soon to check on you. Keep up the good work with your family, and no more thieving."

"Yes, sir. I promise." He turned to go but I caught his shoulder.

"You're a good son and brother, Simon. And from now on, you need to call me Willa."

"From now on? Does that mean you'll be coming back?

I patted his shoulder. "You can count on it."

He gave a small whoop and raced back into the trees.

A look of concern flashed over Sam's face.

"What's the matter?"

"Like Mrs. Cleery said, you shouldn't be wandering around here alone." He shifted back on his feet and lowered his chin. "But something tells me that now you've seen these folks, you'll keep coming back."

"You're learning quickly, Mr. Butler."

I brushed past him and trudged down a small path until my feet sunk into the cool sand of Baker Beach.

CHAPTER TWELVE

Baker Beach
San Francisco, California
October 23, 1936

The movement of the tide higher up the shore warned it was getting late. Once again, I'd get an earful from Paddy about how bad I was at keeping track of the time. A sick twist in my gut had me considering what lie I'd have to tell my parents this time to convince them I was being a good girl.

Every few steps, my gaze flitted to the hidden area above the shore. Would Simon make it back to his family in time? Why would the military bother those people if they had nowhere else to go? Too many questions tumbled through my head without any answers.

Sam stayed quiet beside me. I enjoyed the silence until the tension between us made every step uncomfortable.

"What's on your mind?" he finally asked.

"I don't understand why the military police would make such a fuss. Those folks are down on their luck. No different than any-where else in the city."

"They don't see it that way. This is government land. They worry the fires might burn down the brush. That the trash will pile up. How crime may spread with folks drinking and living in such close quarters."

"All our families came to this shore searching for a better life just like them. It's not right to roust them out of the only homes they have."

Sam stopped and plucked a smooth round rock from the sand. His muscles flexed as he dragged his arm back and tossed the stone far out into the roaring sea.

"How is Benny really doing?" I asked.

He stayed quiet, toeing at bits of shell on the beach.

"Your silence can only mean one thing. He's drinking again."

The edges of his eyes crinkled. "How would you know such a thing?"

"My family owns a pub. Since Prohibition was repealed, I've seen many men like him behave badly."

"Which pub?"

"The Dublin Crown."

He shoved his hands into his pockets and dipped his chin.

"I take it you've been there before?"

"Only to pull out a friend or two after a long night."

His gaze moved back to the ocean's churning waves. The edges of his light hair ruffled in the wind. He was a hard man to figure out. One minute he was firm with Simon, and the next he was gentle like he could understand the young boy's pain.

"You did a good job comforting Simon. Do you have any brothers or sisters?"

"No. Benny is my only living relative."

"Well, it's a good thing you came along today," I admitted. "I'm not sure he would have listened to me."

His focus stayed on the dark, unforgiving sea. "It's hard to be that young and have so much responsibility heaped upon you," he said. "That kind of thing makes a child grow up much too fast."

The painful weight in his voice chilled me. I wanted to press for more, but he faced forward and marched down the beach.

At the end of the shore, we climbed up a winding path until we reached its crest. The bridge was a bright orange giant rising from the sea. A pinch of fading sunlight bounced off the cables in a spark of silver.

Sam followed my line of sight. "That's one of the reasons I came to San Francisco. To work on that bridge."

He nodded to a row of oversized rocks farther back from the shore. He sunk down onto a flat smooth boulder. I straightened my mud-encrusted skirt and sat beside him. Once I was settled, he pointed to the bridge.

"Strauss has been working on this project since 1919. After he got the city to approve the plan, it stalled due to the market crash. The big shots in town knew it was important to get the bridge built. They asked the government for money, but they refused. Word spread via the papers, and the citizens of San Francisco did an amazing thing. They put up their homes and businesses as collateral so they could get funding for the bridge."

His eyes fixed on the suspension cables bucking in the breeze. The once pinched lines around his mouth eased down.

"How do you know all those details?" I asked.

He kicked out his long legs and ran a hand over the hint of blond whiskers shadowing the space over his lips and chin. "I may look like quite the roustabout, but I can read a newspaper."

My cheeks flamed. "I never meant to suggest . . ."

He chuckled. "It's all right. You're not accusing me of anything I haven't heard before."

We sat in silence with nothing but the crash of the waves keeping us company. This was my favorite time of year. The summer fog faded away. The warm days of fall would soon succumb to the cool grasp of winter. I took a deep breath and tilted my chin to the skies.

"How come I didn't see you at church last Sunday?" I asked.

His eyes darkened and he nodded to the path. "Perhaps I should be getting you home. A young girl like you shouldn't be out late."

His tone spoke volumes. He thought I was a child.

"I've been out of school a few months now. In February, I'll be joining the Sisters of the Sacred Spirit. For a year, I'll learn their rules. Then, once I take my final vows, I will be trained as a teacher."

He inched back on the rock. "You're going to be a nun?"

"Yes. Is that so hard to imagine?"

"But you're so good with the doctoring, I thought . . ."

"You thought what?"

"The world is changing at a fast clip. I assumed you'd be going to college. Studying to be a physician."

The way he looked at me with such confidence made me wish I had another life. One where all my family's hopes and dreams didn't rest on me. Where I was free to choose my own path. My own passions.

I let my eyes close and imagined myself sitting among other students in a room at the local college. Turning a textbook on biology, anatomy, or chemistry over in my hands. I could practically feel the weight of the book pressed against my fingers; the sharp edges of the pages poking into my skin. While being a physician was a nice dream, it could never be my reality. On a cold morning six years ago my path was set in stone.

I jumped to my feet and glanced at the winding path up to the road. "Excuse me, I've spent too long here."

My footsteps pounded along the rocky slope as I made my way back to the street. Dirt spit up and covered the tips of my shoes. Another thing I would have to hide from my mam.

"Willa, wait!"

Sam jogged toward me. When he was only inches away he curled his fingers around my hand. Heat rippled up my arm in waves like the sea below us.

"My apologies. I did not mean to offend you."

"You didn't say anything wrong," I said shaking away his warm grip. "I must go. My family will wonder where I am."

"Please, let me walk you back."

"I've lived here all my life, Sam. There's no reason why I can't walk the several blocks home."

A wicked grin lifted his lips. I was giving him another brush-off. Why was he smiling like he'd won a prize?

"It's about time you used my first name. Guess we're finally friends."

That same heat that always flooded my cheeks reappeared. "Well," I huffed. "It's really not anything to cheer."

He laughed and tucked his chin. "Let me see you home." The determined set of his jaw warned there was no use in arguing.

"Fine, but just out of the Presidio to 25th Avenue."

"Why?"

"Because I have brothers who would much rather get into my business then attend to their own."

I picked up my steps and Sam kept pace.

"That fella you were with at church? Was he your brother?"

"Yes, that's Paddy. He tends to be very protective." I let out a small laugh. "Well, they're all that way."

"All?" His eyebrows shot to his hairline.

"There are four MacCarthy boys in total."

"That must be . . ." he hesitated. "Nice. I mean, to have such a big family."

"For them maybe. They wrestle and jab at each other nonstop. That's when they're not stuffing their faces morning, noon, and night. It's really quite annoying."

"And the short little gal that was with you at the church, is she your sister?"

Sister. Just hearing the word stung my heart.

"No, but I wish she was. That's my best pal, Cara."

Once we arrived at 25th Avenue and Clement, we were surrounded by folks racing their way home. The distant hum of the streetcars shook the ground below our feet. Ocean air filled my lungs, and my heart kept pace with the pulse of my beloved city.

"Family's nice but they tie you down," he said. "It's good to be free. To be able to head in whatever direction I want without people stopping me. Making my own decision to travel north or south with nothing but the whisper of the wind for guidance."

I'd never known anything but the incessant weight of family expectation. It sounded exciting to be able to steer your life in whichever direction instinct called. To not have your path predetermined, but to allow fate to take charge.

Even though it was close to six o' clock, wooden stands along the sidewalk still brimmed with a fall harvest of vegetables carted in from the nearby farms in Santa Rosa. In front of the apothecary, Mr. Richardson slid a fresh coat of glue over the latest advertisement for Wrigley's Spearmint Gum, ensuring it would stick to the brick wall. At this end of the district, people could afford fresh vegetables and an ice-cold beverage, but in other parts of the city many businesses were shuttered thanks to the poor financial times.

When we reached the corner, I stopped. "I can make my way from here."

"It was a real pleasure seeing you again." He chewed on his lip. "Is there any way I can convince you not to go back to the camp alone?"

"There are families, children, who need care. I'll keep returning as long as there's a need."

"There's no use in arguing is there? You're like one of those steel ships crossing the water beneath the bridge. Pointed in a specific direction with not even the stiffest swell holding you back."

"I'll consider that a compliment."

"That's how it's supposed to be taken, Willa."

It was hard to ignore the flutter in my chest as he said my name as if it were a sweet melody.

Like he understood the power of that single word, a small smile covered his lips. He turned and disappeared into the crowd shuffling down the busy street.

With my brothers I had a retort for every situation, but with Sam Butler all logical thought dissolved from my brain the minute he spoke. I didn't like it one bit.

CHAPTER THIRTEEN

The Richmond District
San Francisco, California
October 23, 1936

"Where have you been?"

Paddy dragged me into the lobby of our building. I couldn't help but smile at the strength in his grip. A strange thrum filled my veins. Even though he'd lost those fingertips, his hold was as tight as ever. Doctor Winston had done that for him. Saved his life. Made it possible for him to still be here with me.

"Everyone is in an uproar that you're not at Confession, especially since the soup kitchen closed an hour ago. I made up an excuse. Said you went to the Salvation Army to help hand out clothes to the homeless."

He did his best to brush away the thick mud caked to the hem of my skirt. The twitch of his eye warned I was a mess. "Go and get changed. Then we'll head to St. Monica."

Quicker than a wink, I slid into a clean blouse and skirt. Paddy met me on the street and we rushed in the direction of the church.

"You missed the big news this morning. Sean and Michael got hired over at the bridge. Apparently, a few fellas got the flu real bad and can't return to work. They said they're gonna get hooked up on those cables in some sort of chair and work all day slathering the bridge in bright orange."

"That's good news." The words scraped across my tongue like broken glass. With them working on the bridge, there was an even greater chance they'd catch me at the hospital. Now I had to pray each and every day that neither of them got hurt and needed medical care.

"It is for Nick. Michael will stop pestering him every few minutes about working behind the bar, and Sean won't bore him anymore with his Sam Spade impressions. Personally, I'd be happy to give my shifts over to them."

"You don't like working at the pub?"

He tried to hide the tick in his cheek. "It's not that. It's a little hard right now with my hand still healing."

The thick lines around his mouth tightened. He wanted to say more, but I understood Paddy better than anyone. If he wasn't ready to share what was spinning through his head, there was no point in pushing.

Steps from the church, I slid my hand over my mouth and cheeks worrying my face might be covered in dirt after poking through the brush over at the camp. If Mam noticed a single hair out of place, I wasn't sure I'd be capable of telling her one more lie.

"I think you may have gotten a reprieve with Mam and Da," he said on an exhale.

"What do you mean?"

"This morning I heard them whispering in the kitchen. The archbishop ordered Father O'Sullivan to start visiting small cities farther down the coast. There are places where people are working in the middle of nowhere, traveling with their families, living like vagabonds, and searching for work in the fields. They pick crops and do about anything to sustain their families. Because of all the traveling there's no place to worship, so the church is sending out a few priests to attend to their spiritual needs."

A small light of hope filled my chest. Maybe the break I'd

been praying for was finally coming true. "With him gone, he can't coordinate my delivery to the convent. Maybe they'll have to wait until he returns. Did they say how long he'd be away?"

Paddy's lips pinched together. "The diocese is sending someone to replace him. Father O'Sullivan has assured Mam and Da things won't change for you."

A heavy sigh slid past my lips. My small light of hope quickly flickered out. "How is that a reprieve, Paddy?"

He slid an arm across my shoulders. The brim of his fedora tipped over his brows. His fitted chocolate-brown suit matched the color of his eyes. "With O'Sullivan gone, he can't tell them you're missing Mass and Confession. This new priest won't know you from Eve, and he'll have his hands full with our parish."

"Guess you're right," I said, although my footsteps slowed as we got closer to church.

Paddy waved at people we knew along Geary. Some faces I recognized from the pub, others were kids from school. I admired his natural way with people. How he could draw out someone's life story with a gentle smile. The quiet way he'd listen as someone at the pub told him their tale of woe. No matter who was talking, Paddy gave them his full attention. Made them feel special.

"You gonna tell me why you're so late today?" he asked.

I explained that I'd gone to the field hospital with the doctor again. How she'd taught me to care for broken bones and wounds that required many stitches. I went on to tell him about Simon stealing the watch. How my heart collapsed at the sight of the camp. The quick way it bloomed back to life the minute Simon referred to me as the "lady doc."

Paddy pulled a piece of gnarled branch from my hair and placed it in my hand. His tight mouth held an unsaid warning.

Each day, I risked someone discovering my secret. It should have scared me. But as I clutched the loose piece of branch, I knew my need to help the people at the camp was stronger than the fear of my lies being revealed.

The Confessional box wasn't much larger than a phone booth and stunk of incense and sweat. My legs wobbled on the kneeler. With a click, the small-screened window in front of me slid open. I made the sign of the cross. "Bless me father for I have sinned. It's been a little while since my last confession."

"Go on." With only a few words, Father O'Sullivan managed to make me feel ten years old again.

The small Confessional used to scare Cara. Her mother would bribe her with candy or an ice cream to get her to enter the small box. Up until a few weeks ago, it had been a comfort to me. A place to shake off every worry, every misstep, by sharing my mistakes with God. But now my sins were graver. Each word spoken, a betrayal to my parents.

"I've sinned multiple times over the past few days." I gulped as the acid churned in my stomach. "Taken the Lord's name in vain. Been disrespectful to my parents."

"And do you feel repentant?" His low voice boomed around the tight walls.

"Yes, but . . ." I hesitated. When you confessed there needed to be a part of you that never wanted to sin again. Problem was, I'd go on lying and disrespecting my parents as long as I worked for Doctor Winston.

"Yes, I do," I whispered, doing my best to sound confident even though every part of me was riddled with guilt.

"That's all I need to hear, my child," he replied. "Say five 'Hail Marys' and four 'Our Fathers' and your sins will be forgiven."

He whispered a short absolution blessing. Before the last word slid past his lips, I was out the door.

Gulping down bits of warm air, I made my way to the front pew. Mam trained her eyes on me. Did she see the sin in my eyes? The dirt still lingering in my hair?

She didn't move as I took my place on the kneeler beside her. This was the moment where I should have said my prayers, repented for my sins, but instead I watched Mam close her eyes. The kneeler shook as Paddy settled down beside me. He, too, bent his head in prayer. The lines around his mouth relaxed.

He belonged here. So did Mam. How had this become a peaceful place for them when to me St. Monica was a cage? Four solid walls boxing me in. The oxygen in the air thinner with every breath. My entire life I'd witnessed people lean their heads into their hands. Their shoulders easing as they found solace in their faith and prayers. Now I understood. That sense of peace is what surrounded me the moment I stepped inside Doctor Winston's office.

The line dwindled in front of the Confessional. Father O'Sullivan appeared a few minutes later, and Mam scurried to catch him. I turned for the exit, but Paddy grabbed me before I could make a getaway.

"Act calm, smile, and say as few words as possible," he said.

Mam pulled Father O'Sullivan toward us. The hem of his black cassock fluttered over the top of his shoes.

"Willa. Patrick. Good to see you." He bowed slightly, not a single gray hair on his head moved out of place.

His gaze lingered on me a minute too long. Our time in the

Confessional was supposed to be anonymous, but I was sure Father O'Sullivan recognized every single voice in his parish.

"I recently heard about your move, and I must say it makes me very uneasy," Mam said.

"While you are not the only one with concerns, Mrs. MacCarthy, my duty is to follow the orders of the diocese and the archbishop. There are other penitent souls in this world who need my care. I must go wherever they direct me."

"Of course, we would never question the diocese's decision," Mam insisted.

"While I am dismayed that Willa never rescheduled our meeting." His disapproving tone made me glance at the exit. My brain and body screamed to flee. "Father Murphy will be arriving next week. I will make sure he is aware of all the happenings in the congregation, including Willa's intentions to join the Sisters of the Sacred Spirit. Give him time to settle in, and then you can meet to discuss next steps."

How could they talk about my future so nonchalantly? Blood pounded louder than a steel banjo in my ears. It was almost impossible to swallow over the knot in my throat.

"Excuse me."

I dashed to the end of the aisle, made the sign of the cross, and flew out the door not bothering to say my own repentant prayers. If God was watching over us like Father O'Sullivan said, then he'd know my prayers would be hollow.

Outside the church, I sank down onto the concrete steps and dropped my head in my hands.

"What's troubling you dear?" Mrs. Boyle's cane thumped across the steps toward me.

"I'm fine. Just a bit tired," I gulped.

Her lips pursed and she pointed to the spot next to me. I reached out a hand to help her sit.

"No matter our age, there always seems to be struggles." She offered me a bright smile.

"How is everything going at your boardinghouse? Full as usual?"

"With the state of the world, things have been a little hard as of late. But with the bridge still being built, I've been lucky enough to have most of my rooms rented."

"I met one of your tenants the other day. Sam Butler."

Her eyes brightened. "He's a good one that boy. Too bad he's not Catholic."

"But he was here with you at church a few weeks ago," I sputtered.

"Like I said, he's a good boy. That day I was having issues with my lumbago and couldn't walk so well. He offered to attend Mass with me. Make sure I got around all right. Shows real character of a Protestant man to step into a Catholic church to help an old woman."

The blood in my veins turned to ice. A Protestant? That explained why he'd avoided my question earlier. He'd said he was a wanderer. I'd taken that to mean he moved from place to place not having a regular spot to worship. It shouldn't have bothered me that he wasn't Catholic, but the dull ache in my chest reminded me that no matter how much time we spent together we had completely separate paths.

"Getting ready to enter the convent?' she asked. "It'll be soon now."

"February." My head pounded as I realized the days were drawing closer.

"My sister, Helen took her vows when she was not much older than you. She was terrified. In fact, I remember quite a few evenings her sobs kept me awake."

"Was she afraid to go?" I asked.

Mrs. Boyle ran a shaky hand down the hem of her calico-style dress. "I believe she was. The day she left, I remember her offering me her Bible. She touched my cheek and whispered several things in my ear. 'Be good to our parents. Finish school.' But what I recall most vividly was her urge for me to live a fruitful life. To experience every part of the world for both of us."

A small sigh escaped her lips. "Several years later after I'd married, she contracted pneumonia and died at the convent. Not a day goes by, I don't think about her. How she adored red lipstick and the scent of lilac perfume. But she also loved God. At first, I think she was miserable at the convent, but she eventually found her place. She was certainly proud of the honor she'd brought our family. It was something my parents talked about until the day they died."

She patted my knee. "You're doing the same thing for your folks."

Honor and respect. Two things I was certainly not showing my parents as I continued to lie every single day.

Her legs wobbled and I reached for her hand to help her up. "I best be headed back to the boardinghouse. Those young men can get into trouble when I'm not there to mother them. Should I say hello to Sam for you?"

"Sam? Who's Sam?"

It was just my luck that Mam appeared at the exact wrong time.

"Oh, he's one of my boarders." Mrs. Boyle must have seen the panic in my eyes. "I was inquiring if your sons might know him. He's working over at the bridge."

"No, I'm sure they don't. I've seen those men in the pub." Mam's nose wrinkled like she'd smelled rotten fish. "They are not the sort my sons would befriend."

I swallowed a laugh. Sean and Michael were no saints. Mam knew that but would never admit it out loud.

Paddy appeared at Mam's shoulder. He hunched forward and gurgled out a rough breath.

"Paddy, are you not feeling well again?" Mam pulled him in and patted his shoulders. When he caught my eye, his lips slid into a devilish grin. Paddy to the rescue once again.

"We should get him home to rest," I insisted.

"Good seeing you again, Mrs. Boyle." I gave a quick wave and shuffled Paddy down the street.

The conversation with Mrs. Boyle burrowed deep into my bones. My parents had been through so much. They were counting on me to keep my promise to the church. Each day my heart was splintering into small pieces. As much as I adored working with Doctor Winston, I loved my family more.

Mrs. Boyle's story was like a bright signal from a lighthouse keeping ships from the shore. It was a warning that my lies would catch up with me soon if I didn't make a choice.

CHAPTER FOURTEEN

The Office of Doctor Katherine Winston
San Francisco, California
October 26, 1936

The sounds of the city swept around me as I left Paddy at the corner of 20th Avenue and headed for Doctor Winston's office. He'd brushed off my inquiries again when I asked where he was headed. When I pushed for an answer, his lips pinched as he mumbled something about wandering around Union Square.

Motorcars tooted their horns and rumbled down Geary. The clang of the streetcar's bell rang in my ears. Merchants whistled under their breaths as they opened their shops for the day.

Two steps in front of me a man teetered on his feet. He was like so many fellows I'd seen at the pub. Stumbling home after a long day of drink, except it was eight in the morning. I continued to follow his wobbly frame down the sidewalk. A voice in my head warned something was wrong.

He turned onto 19th Avenue and wandered past the office. I should have stopped. Left him alone, but Doctor Winston's instructive voice reminding me to keep my eyes open, to watch for signs of a patient in distress, pushed me on.

The man stumbled forward a few steps more and then turned into an abandoned lot. The land was empty save for a group of homeless men huddled around a makeshift fire. My heart knocked in my chest. It was a warning that it was wrong for a young woman like me to continue on. To follow a stranger into a dangerous place my brothers often warned me about.

The man took two more steps and collapsed to the ground. He wasn't much older than Paddy. His thick chest hitched up and down like a buoy bouncing out on the sea.

"Sir, what's wrong?" His unflinching stare burned through me.

"Can you tell me if you're experiencing any pain?" I asked.

He mumbled incoherently. None of his speech made sense but there was no scent of alcohol on his breath. I began to ask another question when his arm shot out and clenched my hand. His eyes rolled back in his head while his legs twitched and thumped against the ground.

I inhaled a slow breath, pushing away the fear clawing at my chest. Closing my eyes, I pictured the dozens of medical texts I'd read. My mind clicked through each one until I recalled reading about the same symptoms. The erratic movement of the extremities. Confusion. Loss of consciousness. My confidence strengthened as I unraveled the diagnosis.

"Miss, you shouldn't be here." An older man with a black derby tapped me on the shoulder. "This is no place for a young woman." His eyes went wide as the young man continued to twitch in front of us.

"This man is in distress. Run back down the street to the office of Dr. Katherine Winston. Ask her to come quickly." He hesitated, his gaze flicking between me and the group of homeless men now staring in our direction.

"Go now!" I ordered.

The older gentleman hustled away.

The young man's body continued to arch off the ground and shake. A pink-tinged froth bubbled from his mouth.

I shook out the contents of my pocketbook until I found the item I needed. The pencil shook in my hand as I wrapped it in a handkerchief and shoved it lengthwise into the man's mouth, careful not to get my fingers caught in his clenched jaw.

The man's fit continued as Doctor Winston swept into the lot. She knelt on the other side of him and held down his right shoulder while I continued to press onto his left.

Her gaze darted to the pencil clenched between his teeth. "Well done," she said.

The gentleman with the black derby hovered behind her. "Thank you. You may be on your way now," she said. He grimaced and steadied his feet. "I *am* a physician, sir. I can assure you the situation is under control." The edges of his mouth tightened. He let out a huff and stomped away.

Doctor Winston and I continued to hold down the young man to ensure he didn't harm himself. After what felt like two dozen heartbeats, his twitching stopped.

"Sir, I'm Doctor Winston. Do you know where you are?" She swiped a hand over a patch of dark brown hair clinging to his damp forehead.

"19th Avenue," he said. "I felt the spell comin' on and tried to get some place where no one would see me."

"Have you had an epileptic fit before?" I asked.

"A what?" He rubbed a shaky hand along the dark whiskers at his chin.

"An epileptic fit is when the body loses control of the extremities. We still do not understand what causes it," I said.

The man popped a brow in my direction. "That so?" he snapped. "All I can tell you, Miss, is since I been about ten years old I've been getting these fits. Scares the livin' daylights out of everyone around me when it happens."

"People shouldn't fault you for that. You can't control it," I said.

"Don't matter. No one gonna hire a fella who scares off the customers." He stood, shoved the tail end of his shirt back into his pants, and moved in the direction of the street.

"Wait, sir," Doctor Winston said. "Please come to my office. It's not far from here. Allow me to do a thorough exam. I can give you a few tips on what you need to do when you feel a fit coming on."

"That's all right. Almost twenty-two years old now. Been living with it long enough." The sneer in his voice made my blood boil. He marched down the street without even saying thank you.

Doctor Winston brushed off her pants and rose slowly. She took in several breaths, glancing at all the homeless men. Their deep coughs and moans of hunger surrounded us. Her fingers wound around my arm and she dragged me back to the street.

"Willa." The snap in her voice set my teeth on edge. It was the same tone my mother used almost every time she spoke to me. "What were you thinking? Do you have no care for your own personal safety?"

"Of course I do. But that man, some part of me sensed he was in trouble, and I followed that instinct. Didn't you tell me we should always be intent on patient care? That we should be willing to go outside our sphere of comfort if someone is in need?"

"Yes," she sighed. "But that's when we are aware of the task in front of us. It's dangerous to blindly follow someone, even if you think they may need care. We cannot save everyone." Her voice remained firm, but the lines around her eyes softened. "I love that you are eager to help. Anxious to learn. But that does not mean you can be reckless. Do you understand me?"

My throat scratched with a dozen apologies, but all I could muster was a short, defeated nod.

"I'm not angry with you," she said stopping at the office door. "Despite how careless you were, you performed like a true professional today. You should hold your head high. Be confident in the knowledge that this is most certainly the right path for you."

All morning I couldn't keep the grin from my face. Ever since I'd talked to Mrs. Boyle, I'd worried that I'd made the wrong decision in choosing to work with the doctor. But today, on my own, I'd helped that man. As he twitched on the ground, a sense of purpose filled my bones. My mind focused and forced me to do the job. With that one act, my dedication to Doctor Winston was solidified.

Now as I stood with a wailing baby boy squirming in my arms, I understood this was where I was meant to be. Doctor Winston moved around the small room while the child's mother explained her sorrow over having no milk. Doctor Winston consoled her and explained about diet and hydration, encouraging her to bring the child to her chest to suckle. The woman did as instructed. When the child started to nurse, the diaper loosened and a warm stream from between his legs doused both me and the doctor. I tried to act professional until a burst of laughter escaped Doctor Winston's lips. I couldn't help but join in.

She grabbed a cloth from a nearby table and tossed it in my direction. "Now that's what I call a baptism," she joked. Her laugh reminded me that while she'd been firm with me before, she still believed in me. Wanted me here.

The poor woman was mortified, but between her cackles, Doctor Winston assured her this had happened many times before.

Once the woman had success with nursing, Doctor Winston led her to the door giving her more instructions.

We continued to work until the last of the patients were seen. There was still another hour in the day so I returned to the exam room to begin cleaning. Doctor Winston joined me a minute later.

"While I didn't appreciate the shower," she smiled brightly, "it's nice to laugh once in a while. To be reminded that the human body is a miracle that never quite does what you expect."

She began to hum as she dropped soiled instruments into the metal basin on the counter.

"Something on your mind?" she asked.

"Why do you ask?"

She pointed to my hands. "You're scrubbing that clamp so hard, I think you might rub off all the steel."

"I don't mean to be disrespectful," I said loosening my grip on the gleaming steel tool. "But why did you let that man who had the fit speak to you in such a gruff manner this morning?"

"What man?"

She feigned ignorance, but she knew what I was saying. With the doctor at the field hospital, with Benny, even earlier with the gentleman in the black derby, she'd ignored the stares. The quiet jabs. The subtle hints that she'd never be better than a male doctor no matter where she'd studied or how many years of experience were under her belt.

"You know which man," I pressed.

She anxiously readjusted the stethoscope around her neck. "I told you this would not be an easy undertaking, Willa. Medicine has always been, and will continue to be, a man's world. In my medical class ten percent of the students were female. We were far ahead of many universities at the time, but it did not stop our male counterparts, or the professors, from constantly harassing us. Warning us our time was better spent at home caring for children and a husband. Some women dropped out under the pressure, but I refused."

She ran a hand over her frizzy curls. "At one point, I had a professor tell me I was wasting my 'precious birthing years' by taking up space in his classroom." She sighed and shoved her hands into her pockets.

"Did you reply?"

"I told him when he grew female anatomy he could lecture me about the aging of my ovaries and uterus." A wicked smile ticked at her lips. "The entire gallery went pin drop silent. I thought for sure he'd order me from the room."

She turned and busied herself with cleaning a set of nearby instruments.

"Did he?" I said, offering her a clean cloth to dry the scalpel in her hand.

"No," she chuckled. "He paused for a minute, scanned the entire gathering of students, and then said, 'valid point.' The red pulsing at his cheeks warned I'd embarrassed him though. It was the longest class I can ever remember. I was convinced once it was over he'd lecture me about female decorum, even send me to the dean, but he didn't. In fact, a week later he drew me aside and offered to mentor me through the remaining two years of my studies."

"Mentor?" I repeated, stunned by the revelation.

"He told me it would take gumption to make it in medicine and that day I'd proven I could elbow my way through an uncomfortable situation. And while my sharp tongue might get me in trouble, my tenacity would prove to be helpful in dealing with difficult patients. He said he saw potential in me. There'd never been a man in my life who'd shown me that level of respect before. It almost knocked me off my feet."

Her chest hitched once, then twice. "When you rushed in here with your brothers, I saw the same light in you. That professor warned me I'd have to fight every prejudice if I wanted to practice. Said the best way to do that was not through argument but expert care. He told me that every day I'd have to prove I was capable and competent in my practice of medicine."

"Is that why you don't argue with the men?"

"It's not necessary. My skill and education do the speaking for me."

She swiped at her tired eyes and opened the exam room door. Leaning against the frame, her weary shoulders eased down from her ears. "A young man and his mother just came in the door. Bring him in. I don't like the sound of that cough."

With a quick pat on my shoulder, she moved back to the exam table. It was hard not to race to her side and give her an embrace. To say thank you for her honesty about a world that would push and challenge me at every turn. Up until now I'd felt powerless in my own life. But today with the man on the sidewalk, she'd held back. Allowed me to discover my strength as a woman and a healer. I was sure that was a debt I could never repay.

CHAPTER FIFTEEN

Baker Beach
San Francisco, California
October 30, 1936

Paddy pointed to the old rag doll peeking out of the canvas bag slung over my shoulder.

"Do I want to know?" he asked, tugging at the red yarn used for its hair.

"It's for a little girl at the Hooverville."

"Willa," he grumbled. "Be careful."

Without answering, I pulled him in for a quick hug and then waved him on at the corner of 25th Avenue. He crossed the street and headed back in the direction of home. A part of me was curious and wanted to see where he headed. I still hadn't gotten a straight answer out of him about where he spent his time. Unfortunately, I lost him in the crowd once he crossed 24th Avenue.

When I reached the camp, the early morning sounds of the ocean greeted me. Waves pounded against the shore. Seagulls wafted on the wind before bulleting down into the waves for their post-dawn meal.

My heart knocked in a solid rhythm as I passed tents and wood lean-tos. Paddy's warning echoed in my ears. I stopped in front of Simon and Maeve's tent and called inside. A few moments later Simon greeted me, the line of his shoulders rigid. His young mouth much too tight for his age.

"Why are you here?" he snapped.

"I said I'd be back to check on you. Wanted to make sure you were all right after the military swept in here."

"It's been a week, doc. Sam's already been back twice," he grumbled. "And with those soldiers, it's always the same thing. They order us to leave and then they go on their way."

"Remember, I said you should call me Willa. I'm not a doctor." I tousled his thick hair, my fingers scrubbing between the knots. When I pulled my hand away he scratched around his ears and the back of his scalp.

"Whatever you say." He kicked at a loose rock, sending it across the field.

"Simon, would you mind stepping in a bit closer?"

He did as I asked and remained still while I ran my fingers through his hair starting at his center part.

"Somethin' wrong?" he asked.

"How long has your head been itching?"

"Blimey, since I seen ya last week I guess."

"Is Maeve scratching too?"

He gave a firm nod.

"Is your mother here?"

"Nah." He parted his feet. His stance defensive. "She went into town to see if anyone was hiring at the seamstress shops."

"You said Sam's been back here twice?" I asked.

He fought it, but a reluctant smile brightened his face. "Yes. We went down to the water. Tossed a few stones into the waves. He told me I could talk to him while my da was gone. That it was okay to miss him."

He swiped a hand over his red eyes. "He sure likes to talk about you. Thinks you're a real fine lady."

Heat quickly warmed my cheeks, and I turned back to the tent. The sounds of a hacking cough floated outside. "Maeve still not feeling well?"

He bowed his head. "She seems to be getting worse."

"May I go inside and see her?"

"I dunno."

"Please," I pleaded.

"Just for a minute. My mam wouldn't be happy to know you're looking at her while she's gone." He yanked back the tent flaps and waved me inside.

A small candle flickered in the corner, giving off the slightest glimmer of light. Old potato sacks and a battered suitcase sat in a corner. Across from two cots there were a few ragged blankets, some tattered books, and a single cast iron pan.

Maeve lay on a cot in the center of the space. A threadbare pink blanket covered her tiny frame. With each cough, her body lifted off the small bed.

"Hello Maeve." Her large round eyes flickered in my direction.

I dug out the doll from my bag. I'd always loved her crooked black thread smile. The bright blue buttons used for her eyes. She may have not been the most gorgeous doll, but she was a gift from my grandmother, which made her priceless to me.

I sat on the edge of the cot and nestled the doll beside Maeve.

"This is Annie. She was my favorite toy when I was about your age. Do you think you could keep an eye on her for a while? It'd mean a lot to me." A smile brightened her thin face. While she examined the doll, I did a quick assessment. Her cheeks sunk lower into her face. The bones around the top part of her chest protruded slightly from the skin.

"May I hold your arm?" I asked.

Her head barely bobbed forward. My fingers circled her petite wrist. Her skin was cold, but her pulse hummed nicely beneath my fingertips.

"Maeve, can you cough for me?"

I placed my hand over her chest and she did as I asked. Her lungs cracked and sighed under my touch.

"One more thing. Can I look at your pretty hair?"

Slowly she arched up into a sitting position. Within her blonde strands, I found the same white nits that were in Simon's hair.

I gave her shoulder a quick pat and helped her lie back down.

"Nice job. I'm going to head back outside." I stood and pulled an apple from my bag. "When you're ready, why don't you eat this? It'll make your tummy stop grumbling." The light in her eyes made my heart ache. "Don't eat it too quickly. Slow, small bites. Promise?"

"Promise," she replied in a voice so sweet I imagined it was what an angel sounded like.

Once I was back outside, Simon looked directly at my bag. "Brought one for you too." I plucked out another apple and dropped it into his outstretched hand.

"Thank you, Doc. I mean Willa."

"You're welcome."

He bit into the skin hungrily and I guided him to sit on a crate near the fire.

"Do you remember much about your trip from Ireland?"

"Most of it," he said around another big bite. "The ship was packed with lots of folks like us. Poor. Hungry. At first, Da told us

144

it would be an adventure. How sailing out on the high seas made us like pirates. It only took a day for the tossing and turning of the boat to make us all real sick."

His cheeks lost all color. "The stench was the worst. People were retching all over the deck because the toilets didn't work." He bit down on his trembling lip. "Da kept our spirits up, telling us about how great America would be. How he'd get a good job as soon as we landed. That one day we'd have a big house with a yard and a dog." His gaze darted around the shantytown. "It was all a lie."

While I wanted to tell him things would look up, that his da would find a job, I couldn't bear to give him false hope. I'd seen the weariness in the men's eyes at the pub. The ones who'd lost all sense of self. Who couldn't even look themselves in the mirror knowing they were failing their families. They'd not only come to the pub to drown their sorrows, but to hide from the reality of their lives.

If my family hadn't left Ireland when they did so many years ago, we could have been like the Cleerys. Homeless. Desperate. Instead, my grandmother and grandfather came to San Francisco during a time of plenty with my da and his older sister in tow. Grandfather found a job as a longshoreman thanks to the other Irish immigrants in the community. Soon, they were living in our same apartment. They had food on the table and a roof over their heads all because people in the neighborhood reached out to help. When the time came, my grandparents helped others arriving. Even though they'd passed on, people like them continued their cycle of courage and grace that made San Francisco one of the most influential cities in America. One had to only look at all the immigrants working on the bridge to realize their contributions to progress.

The thing that made my blood boil was that many of those people who were terrible to the Cleerys had parents or grandparents who were once new to these shores. How was it possible that they'd forgotten their history, their families' sacrifices, so quickly? It was shameful how they'd scrubbed away their past when that was what tethered them to this great nation in the first place.

"Simon, as you're the man of the family now, I need you to do two things for me." He rolled back his thin shoulders and sat up a bit straighter. "I need you to tell your mam to bring you and Maeve into the office as soon as possible. I think the doctor should check you both over, especially Maeve. Her cough is troubling me."

"I told Mam what you said last time, but I can't guarantee she'll listen."

I grabbed his icy hand. "Simon, it's important."

He glanced at the place where our fingers met. For an instant, he looked like the small boy he should be until the sounds of Maeve's coughs floated out toward us.

"I promise," he said quietly.

A horn bellowed far across the sea.

"One other thing." I reached into my pocketbook and pulled out a pencil and piece of paper. After quickly scratching down an address, I shoved the paper into his hand. "This is the address of a local soup kitchen. Take your mam and Maeve there today. Once the sun goes down, it'll get cold. Having a warm dinner in your belly will get you all through the night."

He clutched the paper and gave a stiff nod. "I'll do it, Miss."

"I have to run now. Doctor Winston is expecting me."

He dipped his head and focused on the rock-strewn ground. "Will you come back soon?"

"Of course I will. We're friends now, right?"

He shrugged. "Not that it means much to me, but Maeve likes seeing you."

It was wrong that a twelve-year-old boy had to carry the weight of the world on his shoulders.

"I promise I'll be back. Next time I might even bring cookies."

The tight line of his shoulders returned but he couldn't hide the smile ticking at the corners of his mouth.

I walked up the narrow path away from the beach still thinking about Ms. Bea. On my way out of the camp, I stopped at her tent. While her knobby fingers still bent at odd angles, she insisted I didn't need to fuss over her.

A freighter crept across the dark water below. Its bow arched up and down, creating a brilliant splash of white across the sapphire water. Work at the bridge was in full swing. I glanced at the suspender cables. Where were Sean and Michael? Were they covered in orange paint? How high were they? The wind blustered all week and I worried about them getting knocked about.

I raced past the bridge access road and picked up my pace knowing I'd be late to the office again. A black car whooshed past me and skidded to an abrupt halt.

"Willa!" Sam jumped from the passenger side door. He tore his hard hat from his head and ran toward me.

"Sam, what's going on?"

"I've been looking for you everywhere. When I couldn't find

you at the field hospital I went to the camp. Simon told me you were headed back this way."

"Slow down. What's wrong?"

"It's Benny. He was working in a secluded spot with me and my pal Carlo so we could keep an eye on him. He was messing around. The last car on the supply train had a beam sticking out and it hit him. He fell down and cut his ear real bad. Think his arm might be broken too."

"Why are you standing here talking to me? Get him down to the field hospital."

"We can't. He screams in pain every time we move him."

"He needs a doctor, Sam."

His eyes darted to the bridge and then back to the car.

"What aren't you telling me?"

"He's drunk. If we take him to the field hospital, he'll lose his job for sure."

The plea in his voice shook my bones.

"Where is he now?" I asked.

"We were at a far corner of the bridge when it happened. We dragged him behind a warming shack. I promise, no one will bother you if you come and help."

I shaded my eyes, taking in the towering sight before me. The thought of standing up on that bridge with nothing but a half-built road standing between me and the black water swirling below shot ice through my veins. I was still far from knowing anything beyond what I'd learned in my short time with Doctor Winston, and what I'd read in my medical texts. She'd told me not to be reckless, but if Doctor Winston was standing next to me I know what she'd do.

"All right. Let's go."

Sam and the driver, Carlo, marched me toward the bridge. A stiff breeze batted at the hairs on my neck. Sea air mixed with the scent of steel and grime wafted off the men.

We climbed a small grass berm and walked across a rocky path toward the mass of towering steel. The tools on the men's belts clanked in an odd symphony. They stopped at the bottom of a set of rickety wood stairs. A large white sign fixed into the dirt stated smoking and chewing tobacco was prohibited. Farther up the path, another sign warned that the wearing of masks by riveters, buckle-ups, and burners inside the towers was compulsory. Each sign was a forewarning that I shouldn't be in this area. I fought off the black thoughts and pressed on behind them.

The elevator outside the South Tower was more like an upright steel coffin. Below us the water sparkled. I focused on the ships flitting across the waves. As quickly as we lifted, the steel cage shuddered and we came to an abrupt halt. I staggered back and Sam caught me around the waist.

"You all right?" he breathed against my ear.

I shouldn't have felt safe within his tight hold, but I did.

Only a few steps outside the elevator I stumbled to a stop. Laid out before me was the full length of the bridge. Orange-red latticework stretched out toward the Marin Tower. Beams and girders ran across the floor vertically, laterally, horizontally, and diagonally with only a half-inch of space in between.

"Miss, we need to hurry." Carlo encouraged me forward, but I couldn't move. "It's all right. In the next month or so the whole road will be complete." A look of pride washed over his face. "It takes a lot of work to build the floor. The bridge men have to connect and rivet the latticework all while balancing themselves on girders not much bigger than the span of their foot. There aren't any handrails or walkways out here. All day long the men look at nothing but the drop to the water more than two hundred feet below."

A layer of mist covered every surface in a thick wet sheet. Wind swirled off the water like the crack of a whip. The sick painter we'd taken care of, Mr. Minetti, described the frantic scene perfectly. How *did* anyone get work done up here?

My heart thrummed like a beating drum, but I was here, caught up in the chaos of the bridge, and there was no turning back.

"You're safe up here. Sam and I won't let nothing happen to you." Carlo nodded in the direction we needed to go. I followed him and Sam to the side of a small building, which was nothing more than a four-sided, wood lean-to. Behind the shack, Benny lay flat on his back. His right arm was bent as if some force had twisted it completely backward. Blood dripped from his left ear, leaving a deep red pool on the ground. Doctor Winston's stitches, which he'd never had removed from his scalp, mocked me.

Carlo knelt next to him. "Ben, the doc's here now. She'll fix you up."

Hadn't he listened? I was *not* a doctor.

Benny turned to face me, recognition flashed in his eyes. "Not her," he grinded out through clenched teeth. "She'll make it worse."

He was right. One false move and I could cost him his arm. What was I thinking? I couldn't treat this man. I'd only worked for Doctor Winston for a few weeks. That was hardly enough time to care for a patient—properly assess his wounds.

A bone-chilling moan slid past Benny's lips. I had two choices:

run away or splint his arm. When that man seized on the ground, I'd taken care of him just fine. Even Doctor Winston had praised me. If I could help him with his fit, why couldn't I use my knowledge to splint Benny's arm?

My hands shook. The hem of my skirt wobbled along with my knees. It wasn't fear that made my legs knock. The bridge itself bucked beneath my feet.

Sam must have seen the terror in my eyes. He placed his palms against my cheeks. His gentle touch slowed my racing pulse. "It's all right. The bridge is supposed to sway. We had an earthquake out here one day. Engineers showed up after and tracked the aftershocks. It rocked thirty feet in each direction without any structural problems. Mr. Strauss and his engineers have it all planned out."

He searched my eyes for a long beat. The steady hold of his gaze promised he'd keep me safe, protect me. The bridge continued to move, but I didn't feel anything but the warmth of his hands against my skin and the steady beat of my heart.

"Willa, listen to me. I watched how the doc trusted you in the tent with Benny. You *can* help him."

"What if I hurt him more?" The words scratched against my dry throat.

"Trust what you know. What you've read in those books of yours."

The books.

I shucked the canvas bag off my shoulder. My fingers flew over several spines until I found the book I needed.

"Carlo, I need two boards about a foot long, a lot of newspaper, and cloth. Bandanas. Handkerchiefs. Whatever you can bring. I also need you to find two men strong enough to hold him down." He nodded and took off in the direction of the center of the bridge.

I shoved the book at Sam. "Page 160. Slowly read me the steps listed."

Sam laid out the book. His lips moved while he scanned the pages.

"She's outta her bloomin' head if she thinks she's gonna touch me," Benny roared, his arm flipping about. His jaw wrenched tight as another bellow left his lips.

"Ben, you are in a world of trouble. You lie still and listen to Willa. If you're too loud, cause a commotion, you're gonna draw attention to yourself and get fired for sure."

Like he didn't hear a word Sam said, he roared and continued to move against the concrete floor.

"Stop thrashing," I ordered. "You may have a severe break. If you keep moving, there's a chance you'll cause more damage. Now stay still." The determined pitch of my own voice, forceful, resolute, should have sounded foreign, but I'd heard Doctor Winston speak in the same tone and it always seemed to make the patients listen.

Carlo rushed back toward us with the armful of supplies I requested. "Most men are on their break, but I found these two fellas near midspan. Thought they could help."

The men came into view. All rational thought left my head. The wind no longer screeched in my ears. The motion of the bridge stopped. As if I'd been punched, all breath raced from my lungs.

"What in the blazes are you doing here, Willa?" Sean double-blinked like he wasn't quite sure I was only standing a few feet away.

"What is happening?" Michael took a deep gulp when his eyes landed on Benny.

"Do you know these men?" Sam asked doing his best to hold down Benny as he thrashed and moaned again.

I dropped my head unable to handle the twins' probing stares. "This is Sean and Michael MacCarthy," I said. "My brothers."

"Oh!" Sam's eyes widened. "Nice to meet you."

"Who the hell are you?" Sean barked.

"I'm Willa's friend," Sam said. "I've asked her to come and help my cousin here who's hurt."

Michael propped his hands on his hips. "How is our sister supposed to help? She's just a little girl."

"She's not a little girl," Sam snapped. "I've watched her work with a prominent lady doctor. She knows about medicine. Caring for the sick. Your sister is actually quite brilliant."

"Is that right?" Sean growled.

"Enough!" The force of my voice sent them all skittering back. "This man is hurt and you two are going to help us take care of him."

Sam waved the twins forward. They took tentative steps toward us, moving slower than turtles on a log. "Kneel on either side of him. Hold down his shoulder," Sam said.

"Wilhelmina," Michael's nose wrinkled. "Do you know what you're doing? This man is clearly drunk." He pulled a small notebook from the front pocket of his khaki work overalls. "The plan is to lay fifty feet of concrete today. Sean and I are expected to finish the painting on the areas near the center of the bridge. We can't help, and you shouldn't be here. If one of the foremen catches you, there'll be hell to pay."

"Do as Sam instructed." They stayed frozen until I pointed at Benny's shoulders. "Now!"

The boys moved into position, grumbling protests under their breath.

Sam's solid, steady gaze never left my face. "Should I keep reading? Tell me what to do next," he said.

"First, I need to examine him."

Cuts and abrasions covered most of Benny's left arm but none of them were concerning.

"Benny, can you tell me what happened?" I asked.

He continued to thrash. "If you want to stop hurting, you gotta tell her about the accident," Sam said.

"Was walking the platform. Making sure concrete was poured right," he groaned. "Materials train was loading everything in. It got loose. Before I could move, a beam crashed right into me. Lower arm, wrist, and ear all hurt." The bitter scent of bourbon polluted the air around us.

The odd angle of the arm and swelling indicated that perhaps both the radius and ulna bones could be broken. While the wind continued to whip across the platform, the sweat at his brow worried me. He could go into shock at any moment.

"Benny, I'm most concerned about your arm. We're going to have to splint it and then get you to the hospital." He moved like he wanted to sit up. The whites of his eyes spread wide and then he crashed backward.

Sean and Michael gasped.

"What's happening?" Sam asked.

"Is he dying, Will?" Sean's face went from pale white to green in seconds. Heavens, why were all the MacCarthy men so squeamish?

"No. The pain caused him to pass out. I'm worried he may be going into shock. We need to splint the arm quickly."

"You sure you know how to do that?" Michael took a deep swallow. His look of worry sent a shiver through my bones.

"Willa," Sam patted my hand. "What do you need from us?"

"Give me a minute."

I gently slid Benny's hand across his chest. His pulse was elevated but his breathing was normal. I pressed my own handkerchief to his ear, trying to staunch the flow of blood. As I worked, I ordered Sam and the twins to tie the cloth into what resembled three pieces of long rope.

"I wish I had a stethoscope." I took Benny's pulse again, praying I was counting the beats right.

"You can do this, Willa. I believe in you."

Sam's look of confidence gave me the courage to get to work. The laceration on the ear would need a few stitches, but for now I needed to focus on Benny's arm.

"Sean, Michael, Carlo, please hold him still," I said.

As soon as the men held him down, Benny's eyes popped open. In his disoriented state, he started to thrash again.

"Stop! If the bone punctures the skin you may never use your arm again," I said.

The twins gulped and shifted their position but didn't utter a word. Sam's mouth twitched into a tight line.

I nodded at Sam. "Start reading please."

"Fracture of forearm and wrist," he began. "Start with patient's hand extended, palm toward chest, thumb up."

The clang of machines in the distance kept time with my thrumming heart. Sunbeams broke through the clouds and gave the bridge a celestial glow. The sudden burst of angelic light forced me to focus on Benny and what needed to be done.

"Benny, this may hurt but it's necessary to apply the splint."

"Fine," he gritted out.

I tried not to gag at the putrid, raw scent of his alcohol-tainted breath floating directly into my face.

"Secure two boards long enough to extend from elbow, reaching to fingertips." Sam clenched the stiff pages. "Pad each board well on the side used next to the arm."

"Boys, I need someone to hold the boards for me." I pointed to the wood pieces they'd located and showed them how to wrap them in the newspaper until they were adequately padded.

"Keep going, Sam," I said doing my best to keep my tone steady as I checked Benny's pulse.

"Apply padded splint to outer side from elbow to beyond injured wrist. Other board should be placed to inner surface and extend to fingertips," he read. "More soft padding allows for less danger of circulation issues."

A low throbbing in the back of my neck grew. *Circulation issues.* Paddy's ash gray face flashed across my mind. No. I couldn't worry about that now.

"Sam, hold the arm as we place the boards," I said.

Benny let out a cry as Sam gently lifted his arm. "Boys, Carlo, I need you to put the boards vertically against each side of the arm." My brothers slid the boards into place. "Sam, hold them tight on both sides."

Sam did as I instructed. Benny let out a sharp gasp. His eyes rolled back in his head and he went unconscious again. Carlo hissed but I ignored him. There was no stopping if I wanted to get Benny to the hospital as soon as possible.

"Michael. Sean. Grab me every single piece of cotton rope we fashioned. While Sam holds the boards in place, we are going to tie them around the arm."

"Willa," Sean sputtered. "You sure?"

"Yes. The cotton ropes need to be tied firm enough to hold the arm but not too tight as to cut off his circulation. Do you understand?"

"Curculation?" Michael said, dragging a hand through his hair.

"Circulation. It's the blood supply to his lower arm and wrist. We need to make sure we don't hinder it in any way."

His face paled like Sean's. He reached for my hand and bowed his head. His prayers were barely audible above the frenetic din of the bridge. Doctor Winston warned that I shouldn't allow prayer to get in the way of caring for the patient, but at this point I needed all the grace God could spare.

At the end, we both whispered "amen" and Michael motioned for us to start.

"On the count of three. Sam, you ready?" I said.

Our eyes locked and a stillness washed over me. The look wasn't fear. Or trepidation. It was confidence mixed with respect. A look I'd always wanted from my family but never received.

"One. Two. Three," I counted.

With a quick shift, Benny's arm went up. The crudely engineered ropes were wrapped in succession around the boards. When the splints were secured against the arm, we knotted off the ties.

"What next?" Sam breathed out.

"Lift his arm high up on his chest so his fingers are above his heart. I'm going to bandage the cut on his ear."

I grabbed a piece of leftover cloth. Under my breath, I cursed that I didn't have any antiseptic to clean the wound. At least I could stop the bleeding. I placed the cloth to the ear. Blood oozed across my hands and sunk its way deep below my fingernails. I tore a thin strip into the dressing, my bloody fingerprints staining the white cotton. I wrapped the material around Benny's head twice before securing it against his ear with a knot to keep it in place.

My brothers stood inches away. Their open mouths could have caught flies if there were any buzzing around.

"Sean and Michael, you're going to assist Benny to the elevator. Carlo is going to lead you to his car. He and Sam are going to take Benny to St. Mary's."

I kneeled over Benny and took his pulse. The beat thrummed strong and steady. I patted his cheeks once, twice. His eyes fluttered open. "The splint is on. We are going to take you down in the elevator now."

I showed my brothers how to steady him under the armpits and made for the elevator with Sam and Carlo on my heels. Once we descended, we scooted far out of the way of the field hospital and up to the edge of the work perimeter. While we waited for Carlo's car, I continued to check Benny's pulse and pain levels. The fact he hadn't fainted again was a good sign.

Once Carlo arrived, Sam loaded Benny into the back seat of the dark sedan.

Michael pulled me to the side with Sean quickly following. "I'm not sure what just happened up on that platform, but we are not done talking about this," Michael huffed.

"Yes, Willa. Do Mam and Da know you're doing this? Working for some lady doc?" Sean spoke as if he and Michael were innocent as angels.

"Do Mam and Da know you and Michael have been skimming

money from the till to go to Barber's Dance Hall almost every night? Or that you have magazines with half-naked ladies hidden in your room?"

Their Adam's apples bobbed in a deep gulp. Sam turned away, hiding his smile.

"How about the fact that late at night the two of you go down to the pub and practice pouring drinks all in the hope Da will trust you with the bar one day?"

Both their heads drooped in defeat.

"Let's make a deal. I'll keep your secrets, if you keep mine," I said.

They could easily head straight home and tell our parents of my deceit. In a matter of a few sentences, they could destroy my whole world. A world I lived for now.

The twins leaned into each other. Heated whispers floated between them. Michael's mouth formed into a thin sharp line. Sean's words became more insistent until they broke apart.

"We'll keep quiet as long as you promise to come clean to Mam and Da before you go to the convent. Lying is a sin," Sean snapped.

"Ha. That's novel coming from the likes of you two," I shot back.

Michael shoved his glasses up the bridge of his nose. "That's the deal. Take it or leave it."

"Fine. If you want to keep your jobs, I suggest you head back before anyone misses you."

They grumbled and cursed under their breath. I pointed a sharp finger at the worksite and they stalked back to the bridge.

"Sam, let's go," Carlo shouted out the car window.

"Keep him still in the back seat," I said. "Don't let Carlo drive fast or take any sharp turns. That arm must stay immobilized." I glanced back in the direction of the net swaying under the bridge. "Will you get in trouble for leaving work?"

"Nah. Laid my part of the concrete for the day. Carlo's the lead on my crew and a good friend. We'll be back to work on the next patch tomorrow."

Carlo called for Sam again.

"Best be on your way now," I said. "Be sure to tell the doctors that Benny's ear needs to be cleaned or he'll get an infection. And that arm it needs to stay steady, and . . ."

He gripped my hand, threading his fingers through mine. I could fight it all I wanted but there was something calming about the way he understood what I needed before I did. The twins were beyond angry. Benny was bleeding in the back seat of the rumbling car. My nerves were far beyond frayed, but his calm touch steadied me. A low thrum in my temples warned we were a bad idea. That we were too different to ever work. None of that mattered anyway. As soon as the bridge was finished, he'd be on to another city.

"You did well today, Willa. Don't you worry. We'll take good care of him."

"This can't happen again. Sam, he's dangerous up there. One of these days he could hurt another man. That could be my brothers. Or you."

He dragged both hands down his face. "I know he gets a little out of control, but he's promised he'll stop."

"When? After he kills himself or someone else? He's out of control. I bet he wouldn't let you bring him back to have his stitches removed even after you promised."

His silence was all the confirmation I needed.

"Either you make him quit drinking, or the next time he makes a mess of things I'll speak up."

He edged in closer so we were toe-to-toe. "You have my solemn promise." His gaze moved to my lips and remained there for one beat and then two more.

Carlo laid on the horn again sending us both a step back.

"Thank you for your help up there. I couldn't have done it without you."

"Willa MacCarthy, I don't think there's a thing you can't do once you set your mind to it."

He leaned in and swept a loose lock of hair behind my ear. A flurry like a whirlwind filled my chest. Carlo gunned the engine again. Sam gave me one of his irresistible grins and then dashed to the car.

I kept fighting it, but he continued to wind me into his world. My heart was a willing follower, but my mind warned that path would end in nothing but heartbreak.

CHAPTER SIXTEEN

Two sharp raps was all it took. The door swung open and I rushed inside.

"Willa? What in the devil is going on?" Why are your fingers covered in blood?" Doctor Winston grabbed my hands and examined them.

"I'm not bleeding, but I did help someone who was."

She rushed me to the sink and plopped a bar of soap in my hands. "Good thing I didn't schedule any appointments until after lunch today."

Benny's blood clung to my fingertips and the underside of my nails. A thick, sticky reminder that what I'd done should remain a mark on me for all time.

As I rubbed my skin, Doctor Winston handed me a cloth. "It's best to use a bit of rubbing alcohol for the more difficult stains." She shook liquid out of a green glass bottle and went to work on my nailbeds, which matched the crimson stains on my fingertips.

"Would you like to tell me what happened?" she asked working my skin raw.

The words hovered on my lips. I imagined how angry, even disappointed, she'd be when she'd discovered what I'd done. She'd warned me to be smart. To not do anything outside the office, and I'd ignored her wishes. The magnitude of my decision weighed me down like a wet heavy blanket. What if I splinted the arm wrong? Caused infection because I hadn't cleaned the ear wound properly?

"Whatever it is Willa, you can trust me."

I turned away unable to look at her and admit what I'd done. "I've been going to a camp, more like a Hooverville, near Baker Beach." The words spilled out of my mouth too quickly. "That day, the child who stole the pocketbook from the field hospital, it was Mrs. Cleery's boy, Simon. At first, I only wanted to get Francie's watch back, and the money he'd taken, but then I saw Maeve and the rest of the starving folks, and I know you warned me not to be reckless . . ."

It was impossible to put into words the pull the shantytown had on me. I went to sleep thinking about the people in need and woke up with a desire to do all I could to help. It was why over the past weeks I'd continued to lie to my parents, my brothers, my priest, about where I was going and what I was doing with my time. A sense of guilt or remorse should have filled my bones, but instead I was steadfast with purpose.

"Today, I went back to the camp and checked on the Cleerys. After I was finished, Mr. Butler, Sam, he caught me on my way back here. He told me his cousin Benny got hurt again. Said no one could know or Benny would lose his job. They brought him down to a small spot on the bridge behind a warming shack and away from the bosses.

"Sam asked me to examine him. I insisted they take him to the field hospital, but Sam said Benny was too injured to move." Tears spilled down my cheeks. "If you need me to leave, I understand. I wanted to do what was right, but I had no business tending to him alone."

Before I could take another jagged breath, Doctor Winston circled me in her arms. It was the first real embrace I'd had from an adult in a long time. My mam did her best, but it'd been years since she'd shown me any affection.

She patted my back, and I breathed in the tinge of formaldehyde clinging to her skin. "You didn't have a choice." She pulled back, her eyes sharp as knives. "What did I tell you when we first met?"

Using the back of my hand, I swiped away my tears. "If a patient is in need, it's our duty to care for him."

"That's right. Now tell me what happened to Benny. I need every detail."

I went on to explain about the accident and Benny's crushed wrist and forearm. The way the men loaded him into the car for his trip to St. Mary's. I didn't tell her about my brothers. If I didn't say it out loud, then I didn't have to think about it, at least for a while.

"I'll go and check on him tomorrow. I'm sure he will be fine," she said.

"But what if I splinted the wrist wrong? And his ear had a chunk of skin missing. I dressed the wound but didn't have any antiseptic."

"Did you use a board splint?" she asked.

"Yes. I didn't have any cloth, so I wrapped the boards in newspaper."

"And the ties?" she asked.

"Knotted together bandanas and cotton handkerchiefs."

That look of pride my father often gave to my brothers, the one I always wanted to receive but never did, bloomed across her pink cheeks.

"Did you do anything I hadn't already taught you, or you'd read about in one of those textbooks you carry around? In any way did you put that man in danger? Did you try to set his arm?"

"No, I left that to the doctors."

"That's right." She led me back to the sink, scrubbing at my fingertips again. "I'm sure with your religious background you're familiar with the story of the Good Samaritan."

"Of course," I said.

She turned off the water and handed me a towel. "If you had walked away from that scene, you would have regretted it your whole life."

Her eyes narrowed and she chewed on her lower lip like she had something more to say. "I'm not your mother. It's not my place to say what you can't do outside this office, but I caution you about visiting that shantytown alone. It's dangerous for a young woman like you." Her shoulders sank on her next exhale. "But in all honesty, I'd have done the same thing."

With a huff, she marched out of the room. When she returned, a small black leather bag dangled from her fingertips. "This was my first doctor's bag. It's filled with gauze and a few medicines. I'd like you to have it, but you must promise you'll only visit the shantytown during the day."

The small brass lock had a high shine. The leather-bound handles barely showed any wear. If I didn't know better, I'd guess it was brand new.

"I promise, but I can't take the bag," I said.

She ignored my protests and pushed it into my chest. "Willa, you have an inherent sense to help those in need. That's not a curse, it's a gift. Today, you did not overstep your bounds. You did your duty."

I clenched the bag between my fingers. "But what if I did more harm than good?"

"That's always the risk. But to not help at all, well, that is a much greater sin." She shoved her hands into the pockets of her black linen pants. "Now, I've closed the office this morning because we are going on an excursion. Are you up to it?"

"An excursion?"

She walked to the wood rack and grabbed her coat. "Yes. Leave the bag. You can collect it later. We need to be on our way."

Before I set the bag down, I ran a hand over the smooth leather. It was too generous of a gift, but it confirmed how much she believed in me.

"Willa, hurry! We need to catch the B streetcar."

I chased her out the door and matched her wide strides down Geary Street.

On the streetcar, Doctor Winston was quiet. Her always busy hands remained still in her lap. We continued to bounce along, our backsides bumping up and down on the wooden bench.

"Where are we going?" I finally asked.

"You'll see in a few minutes more."

The Geary streetcar rumbled down the tracks past 16th Avenue, and I still had no idea where we were headed.

"Could you give me a hint?" I prodded.

The edges of her lips lifted. "I like that about you, Willa. You're very curious." She slid her hands down her linen pants and kicked out her step-in pumps with the satin ribbon on the toe.

"We've talked a bit about medical school, but you've never asked about other aspects of my life."

I twisted the fabric of my skirt between my fingers. "With my four brothers always skulking around, I don't get much privacy. I don't like it when folks pry into my business, so I never thought to ask about yours."

The streetcar came to a jarring halt. Women clutched their pocketbooks to their chest as they climbed aboard, anticipating hours of shopping at the department stores downtown. Men scurried up the steps and quickly grabbed a looped leather strap above their heads before the streetcar rumbled down the track once more.

"After my brother passed, my parents had one simple wish. They wanted me to get an education. Perhaps be a teacher for a short while before I got married and had babies."

Bodies shifted next to us as the streetcar shot down the track. "I did as they asked, but teaching never felt right to me. When I was twenty, I moved to San Francisco and worked for a while in a telegraph office. There were many days I wandered the city searching for what I wanted to do next. One lazy morning as I was drinking my tea I read in the *San Francisco Chronicle* that a handful of women had graduated from the Medical Department at the University of California. It was as if lightning struck me in my chair right there and then. I left my house and went up to the university and applied."

She patted a hand through the blonde waves bouncing at her neck. "After I'd been at the university for a year I met my husband, Jack. He was a real looker with bright green eyes and hair darker than coal. What I loved about him was he was a free-thinking man. When he was quite young, he marched alongside his mother to help ladies get the vote. He'd listened to me talk for hours about losing my brother. I told him about Doctor Lucy Wanzer, the first woman to graduate from Toland Medical School, which is now the university, and a well-known local physician, Doctor Emma Sutro Merritt."

"Sutro? Like in that family who owns the fancy Cliff House?" I asked.

"Yes, one in the same. Rumors say her father was unhappy when she became a doctor. Despite the times, she went on to practice at Children's Hospital for twenty years. I believe she is retired now. Much like Doctor Wanzer, she inspired the next generation of female physicians."

The streetcar halted as more passengers wiggled their way into the few spaces available on the car.

"Doctor Wanzer had an office farther up Geary. She worked every day until she passed in 1930." Her voice rose over the clang of the bell. "I heard her speak at a medical meeting two years before she died. Her dedication to the San Francisco community, and to her patients, was awe-inspiring. I knew then, despite the rigors of medical school, I'd chosen the right path even if my parents did not approve."

I couldn't help but wonder if Doctor Winston's parents gave her the same judgmental looks my parents frequently gave me.

A gentleman close by cleared his throat. The tight line of his shoulders warned he didn't care much for our conversation.

"When I first came to practice in the Richmond District, only the poor and the wealthy families who needed medical attention for their staff were my patients." Doctor Winston ignored the man's disapproving glare. "Word spread over time about my quality of care. Eventually, Doctor Maloy, whose wife was a former patient, offered to sell me his practice. As you can imagine, that did not go over so well with those previously in his care."

As the tracks hummed beneath us, I fell under the spell of her words. How she spoke about her struggles so effortlessly. I could only hope to be as brave as she proved to be time and again.

"Willa!"

A voice flew toward me from the back of the car. Bodies parted until Cara, dressed in a bright orange dress with pale pink flowers, appeared with her mother.

"I thought that was you. Where are you going?"

She stopped short when her gaze landed on Doctor Winston. We locked eyes, but even with a quick shake of my head there was no getting out of the situation once her mother spotted me.

The streetcar bounced along but all I heard was Paddy's warning about not doing anything outside the office with Doctor Winston. This was the moment his warnings became real. It was the nightmare that kept me up at night—my secret being discovered.

"Hello, Willa," Mrs. Reilly brightened at the sight of me. "Cara and I are on our way to do some shopping, then we're headed over to the KRB to talk to a few musicians about the kitchen racket at our place a week from Sunday. I assume you and your family will be attending?" The streetcar shook on the rails and Mrs. Reilly bumbled about the car trying to find a steady place to hold on.

Doctor Winston jumped to her feet. "Ma'am, please take my seat."

"Thank you, Miss . . ."

"Winston."

Mrs. Reilly plopped down onto the seat, her little brown hat sliding down her forehead.

"Uh, uh, Mrs. Winston." I gulped down the words. She'd earned the term doctor and it burned not to use it. "This is my best friend, Cara and her mother, Mrs. June Reilly."

Doctor Winston gave both their hands a firm shake.

"And how do you know our lovely, Willa?" Mrs. Reilly asked.

Doctor Winston opened her mouth once, twice, searching for something to say.

The bell chimed again. The car screeched to a halt and more people piled into the tight space. We raced along the track again, and I was sure every single passenger could hear the erratic hammering of my heart.

"If I may ask," Doctor Winston found her voice. "What is a kitchen racket?"

I glanced up at the roof grateful she'd rerouted the conversation. It was the perfect topic as Mrs. Reilly loved to talk about her parties.

"It's a local get-together where we have food and drink at a local parishioner's home," Mrs. Reilly said. "We serve dinner. Have local musicians play. That's why Cara and I are headed down to the KRB."

Doctor Winston's brows knitted together.

"KRB is Knights of the Red Branch," I said. "It's a local Irish-American gathering spot over on Mission Street. They have meetings and dances."

Mrs. Reilly's gaze traveled down the length of Doctor Winston and her right eyebrow twitched. Doctor Winston dressed like a modern woman in dark slacks and a blouse. Since I'd known her, I'd never seen her wear a hat.

Never one to let a subject go, Mrs. Reilly pressed on. "How are you and Willa acquainted?"

My mind spun with all the things I wondered Mrs. Reilly might buy about my acquaintance with this woman in the community she didn't know.

What felt like one hundred heartbeats passed until Cara said, "Didn't you tell me you met at the library, Will? Checking out some of the same books? Your mam is always going on about how much time you spend there."

I loved Cara. In the toughest spots, in the hardest moments, she always protected me even if it meant lying through her teeth.

"Yes," Doctor Winston chimed in. "We both enjoy Agatha Christie's mysteries."

"Mysteries? Well, that's good to hear." Mrs. Reilly leaned forward, her mouth puckering. "Your mother was a little concerned you were spending too much time looking at those medical books."

Doctor Winston turned away quickly, but not before I saw the grin sweep over her lips.

"Oh yes, Willa is always pestering me about those mysteries. What's that other detective in the series? The French one?" Cara said, laying it on a bit thick.

The French one? What was she talking about?

"Hercule Poirot," Doctor Winston swooped in saving me.

The streetcar came to a grinding halt at 10th Avenue close to Golden Gate Park.

"This is our stop. We're headed to the Academy of Sciences to broaden our minds beyond reading." Doctor Winston nodded to Mrs. Reilly. "It was a pleasure to meet you."

Mrs. Reilly's little body bobbed up and down as she shook Doctor Winston's hand.

"I'll see you both soon" I said.

Cara switched places with me as I moved to follow Doctor

Winston. She gave my hand a quick apologetic squeeze before I could get away.

"We'll expect you and your family around five for the racket," Mrs. Reilly called.

I gave them both a wave and raced to the exit.

As the streetcar trundled down the tracks, I collapsed onto the curb. My web of deceit was growing wider. It was troubling how easily I'd been able to lie to Mrs. Reilly.

"Willa, I'm sorry," Doctor Winston sighed. "I wanted to do something nice for you today but it seems I've only added to your troubles."

"No, I wanted to come along. Anyway, Cara is very good at spinning tales. By next Sunday I'm sure Mrs. Reilly will have forgotten all about it."

Again, another lie slipped past my lips. Mrs. Reilly loved gossip. The first chance she had, I'm sure she'd tell my mam about today's encounter.

I brushed out the wrinkles on my skirt and stood. "Where are you really taking me? And please don't say a museum."

Her cheeks lifted into a devilish grin. "First, we have to grab the Number 1 bus across the park. Hold onto your curiosity a little while longer."

CHAPTER SEVENTEEN

The University of California Medical Hospital
San Francisco, California
October 30, 1936

Doctor Winston bounced on her toes as soon as we stepped off the bus. Without a single word, she practically skipped down the sidewalk until we reached Irving Street. Even though I couldn't get my mind off the incident on the streetcar, it was hard not to get caught up in her jubilant mood.

"That's where we are headed." She pointed to a cluster of multistory buildings at the top of the hill. Arm-in-arm we made our ascent. At the bottom of the hill the climb didn't appear too steep, but this was San Francisco. I should have known better. Every hill was pitched so high it was as if oxygen was being sucked from your lungs with each step.

Once we reached the top, Doctor Winston swung out her arms at the breathtaking view that spilled out in front of us. "I love how on a clear day you can see all of Golden Gate Park, past the Richmond District, and all the way out to the bridge. This is truly my favorite place in the city." She giddily spun me around. "And so is this." She pointed to the buildings before us. "Welcome to the University of California Hospital and Medical School."

She rushed me through a wrought iron gate and toward the bank of tightly nestled buildings. We walked up a winding path and a flight of concrete stairs. Every few feet a man would call out "Kat" in our direction. It wasn't until I'd heard it for the fourth time, and Doctor Winston inclined her head, I realized they were addressing her.

"Kat?"

"Yes, it was my nickname while I was here." The almost permanent wrinkle in her forehead relaxed. "This place did have difficult moments, but happy ones too."

We banked around a building and into a tight alcove. It opened to a small alley with a stone-lined path that wound to a set of three steps leading to a heavy brown door.

"I'm bringing you in this secret entrance so as not to upset the front desk nurse. She'd question why we are here. Ask where we were headed. Today we'll bend the rules. We've got much to see and not a lot of time."

The clock inside chimed eleven times. It seemed a lifetime ago I'd leaned over Benny. I hoped the doctor at St. Mary's had set his forearm and wrist correctly.

Doctor Winston stared at my rumpled clothes. "Here, take this." She pulled a stethoscope from her pocket and looped it around my neck. "Now you look official. Let's go."

We traveled down a long maze of corridors. The scent of antiseptic and smoke tickled my nose. Our shoes clicked on the white tiled floor as we rushed along. Every few steps I stopped, trying to get a look inside a classroom or a ward filled with beds.

I'd only been in a hospital one other time. I tried to shake the memory of St. Mary's from my head. The cries of the babies in the ward. Even at twelve, I was old enough to understand the cruelty of having Mam in a place where everyone else had a baby except her.

"Kat!" A squat man with twinkling blue eyes and not a single strand of hair on his head rushed toward us. He skidded to a stop only inches from our feet and quickly pumped Doctor Winston's hand up and down. "It's wonderful to see you," he gushed.

"Willa, this is Calum Miller. He and I were in the same graduating class."

"Yes, our class was a real humdinger. Quite a few lads were smitten with our Kat."

"Oh, I'm not quite sure that's accurate, Cal."

Was Doctor Winston blushing?

"I seem to remember the other female students and myself being razzed quite a bit by the fellas in the class."

He popped a thick hand over his lips. "Too true," he winked at me like we were old chums. "There was a time when we were all working in the dissecting lab and—"

"That may not be the best story to tell a young lady," Doctor Winston interrupted. Her cheeks most certainly went pink this time.

"Oh my goodness, you're right," he chuckled.

"No, please. I'd love to hear about Doctor Winston's time here," I insisted.

He glanced at her for permission. When she offered a shrug, he plowed on.

"Some of the professors and lads weren't too keen on having women in our class. They liked to pull pranks on them quite often. In the dissecting lab, the men decided to position one of the male cadavers in," he tapped his fingers to his lips, "shall we say a compromising position. Kat was the first in the door that day. Our girl here, she didn't bat an eye. Went right about her business shifting the man's personal parts back into position before resuming her work."

Now I was the one with flushed cheeks.

"Things are a tad easier on the women today." His eyes narrowed on the stethoscope around my neck. "Is that why you're here? Is Kat showing you around before you begin your term?"

"No," I sputtered. "I'm—" I stopped speaking as I wasn't quite sure why she'd brought me here.

"Willa is helping me in the clinic. I'm trying to convince her we need more females in the profession."

"Quite right. But none of those women will live up to Kat here," he said. "Which reminds me, I heard you're speaking at the next San Francisco County Medical Association meeting. What's the topic?"

"Updates and current research in obstetrical care."

"Brilliant," he clapped his hands in front of him. "I'll be there."

"It was wonderful to see you, Cal, but I have more places to show Willa before we head back to the office."

"Of course. Don't be a stranger around here, Kat." He gave us both a bow and shuffled off down the hallway.

A wide smile lit up her face as she guided me through several more rooms. She insisted we move quickly, but I forced her to slow down, begging her to tell me about the research she'd done when she was a student. We passed another crowded classroom. I stopped short, wanting to hear the lecture. She even gave me a moment to examine the morgue. Out of respect for the dead, I remained quiet this time.

Halfway down another corridor, we passed two female residents. Their heads bent together in conversation as they stood at a nearby desk piled high with patient charts. My gaze lingered on the way they held their shoulders in a firm line. How sharp they looked in their calf-length white coats. Even the rapid-fire exchange of their conversation was fascinating.

Could that be me one day? Working with a colleague to discover the illness of a worrisome patient? Moving in and out of the wards with a confident stride?

I was only allowed to linger on the thought for a moment when Doctor Winston directed me through another thick door.

A whoosh of air left my lungs. I stepped inside a wide oval space that was larger than the gym at my old high school. Rows and rows of seats angled down toward the center of the room. A single steel table propped up on a pedestal shone like a brand-new nickel. A dome light wider than an open umbrella hung over the table.

From an early age I'd learned to be quiet in a church, but this room demanded a new kind of reverence. I was afraid to speak, much less breathe.

Doctor Winston hurried down the steps and pointed to a long row of wood chairs in the front of the operating theater. "This is where I sat almost every day for three years." She moved down the row and stopped at the fourth chair in. The seat creaked as she rested her full weight into it. She patted the spot next to her. "Join me."

Blood hummed in my ears as I took the seat beside her. If I wasn't sitting so close to Doctor Winston, I would have pinched myself to see if this was real.

"It was here I discovered my true love of medicine. The gleam of the scalpel. Harsh glare of the lights." Doctor Winston's solid voice bounced off the sterile white walls surrounding us. "The first day I walked in I was sure my heart would shove its way out of my chest. I was one of only five girls in a class of fifty." She turned and pointed to the far back row. "All four of them sat up there trying to stay out of sight." She shook her head. "Not me. I wanted those men to see me front and center. Understand I wasn't here on a lark. That I intended to be a serious student. For those first months, male students tried to bump me from this chair. Often times they'd use intimidation. Stare. Taunt me under their breath. I refused to be cowed by them. Those men," a small laugh trickled from her lips, "would soon be the ones asking me for help with their studies. In fact, Cal was the first one who approached with his tail between his legs."

"Of course they did. You're fearless. And brave. And smart," I said.

The enormity of the room swallowed me. I tried to picture myself ensconced in one of the thick wood chairs. A pencil clenched between my fingers while I furiously took notes during an important lecture. Try as I might, I couldn't conjure the scene. Perhaps I'd imagined myself alone in a small cell at the convent for so long I couldn't picture any other future. Or maybe I hadn't allowed myself to imagine another life for fear of disappointment.

The door to the theater creaked open.

"Returning to old haunts, are we?"

A man with thinning hair the color of fresh snow sauntered down the stairs. His two-tone oxfords clacked against each step. The hem of his white coat billowed out behind him. When he reached us, he pulled at the thick ivory whiskers on his chin.

I swallowed a laugh creeping up my throat. His smile and demeanor reminded me a little too much of the Santa Claus depicted on the cover of *The Saturday Evening Post*.

"You know how it is. Some places pull you back." Doctor Winston nodded in the man's direction, a grin lifting her lips. "Did Cal tattle on me?"

"Perhaps." He shot out a thick, doughy hand in her direction.

"Good to see you, Katherine. We missed you at the last medical society meeting. Practice too busy to associate with us old gents now?"

"Oh, Doctor Briar," her laugh knocked about the open room, "you are *not* an old gent."

"Tell that to my aching back," he mused before turning his attention to me.

"Who do we have here? Future student?"

"I hope one day." She winked at me. "This is Willa MacCarthy. She's been helping me at the office since my last nurse took off for the bright lights of New York."

"Willa, it's a pleasure." His firm grip snapped the bones in my hand to attention. "Always love to meet someone with an interest in medicine." He released my aching fingers and rounded on Doctor Winston. "I assume you've told her our history. How you challenged my male parts."

"That was you?" I gasped.

Their combined laughter boomed through the room. "Yes, can't say I'm too proud of that moment. But even an old dog can learn new tricks. Wouldn't you agree, Katherine?"

"Of course!"

Her shoulders shook with laughter. I was so used to Doctor Winston's firm instruction. The way she pressed me to do everything once, twice, until I got it right. It was as if once we stepped inside the hospital, a low burning light within her was set aflame. Even though she'd struggled here, it gave her a sense of joy that even deliberate, measured Katherine Winston couldn't hide.

He patted her shoulder and walked toward the operating platform. "Women only make up five percent of our medical student body. It's fallen in the past year or two due to our poor financial times, but I'd like to see it rise again. We need good people like Doctor Winston to keep us honest. To remind us there needs to be care and attention for *all* our patients." An understanding nod passed between them I didn't quite understand.

He took the three steps up to the platform and ran his hand over the gleaming steel table. "I'm a slow learner, but I do believe one day this theater will be filled with half men, half women. Medicine is changing quickly and we need as many intelligent, caring souls as possible to fill this room."

His warm brown gaze landed on me. "Tell me Willa, what is your favorite thing about medicine?"

My head emptied. This brilliant physician was asking me a pointed question and my mind went blank. All those hours I'd spent poring over medical texts, reading them cover-to-cover at least a dozen times, and I couldn't come up with a single thing.

"She's very adept at clinical diagnosis," Doctor Winston swooped in.

"I can take it from here," I said with a firm voice. For once in my life I would be brave enough to speak up for myself, rather than allowing others to talk over me. "Yes, I do enjoy clinical diagnosis. A few days ago, a man was acting unusual near the office. Using my knowledge, I determined he was having an epileptic fit. I made sure he was safe from harm. Placed a pencil between his teeth so he wouldn't bite his tongue and waited until the tremors ceased."

Doctor Briar narrowed his eyes. "How did you know to care for him that way? Did Doctor Winston teach you, young lady?"

"No, sir. For a few years now I've been reading medical texts I borrow from the library. I've read both *Gray's Anatomy* and *Gould's Pocket Medical Dictionary*."

"That's all good and well," he paused, "if you want to be a

nurse. But to be a physician there's much more training. Do you believe you're up to the task?" His lips dissolved into a thin, firm line. "Can you go toe-to-toe with the men in this theater? Under the pressure of the lights, and with your hand sunk deep into a living, breathing body, do you believe you can perform under pressure? Do what is necessary to save a patient?"

We were having a simple conversation, but his questions felt like a test I needed to pass. A test I desperately wanted to pass.

"My brain fires in the same way a man's does. Whether I am standing in this room, or within the confines of Doctor Winston's office, I'm equally capable of caring for a patient, sir."

The edges of his ears flamed. A tick flared in his jaw. Had I offended him? I looked to Doctor Winston but she refused to meet my gaze. I'd had one opportunity to impress this important man and I'd ruined it.

A small titter filled the room. Doctor Briar propped his hands on his hips and his shoulders began to shake until a laugh burst from his lips echoing through the wide-open theater.

"She most assuredly reminds me of you, Katherine. Fearless. Obstinate. Bright mind." His sunshine smile landed on me. "When the time comes, Miss MacCarthy, I think you will do well here."

A bell chimed overhead. "That's for me. A physician's work is never done." He bobbled down the steps and stopped next to Doctor Winston. "Not giving you a hard time over at the hospital near the bridge are they?"

She crossed her arms over her chest. "I figured that was your work. No, Doctor Fairchild is acting very professional."

"As it should be. If you don't mind before I go, can we speak for a minute in private?" He waved a hand around the room. "Feel free to wander about Miss MacCarthy."

I eyed the platform and ascended the steps. While Doctor Briar wanted to speak in private, he did nothing to lower his voice.

"Thank you for taking over for Doctor Owens at the field hospital. He spent quite a few hours with the young woman." The tone of his voice dipped. "Poor thing had already lost too much blood by the time he got to her."

"I offered to help him whenever he needs assistance," Doctor Winston said. "There are not enough of us willing to make house calls in those unfortunate situations."

"Too true. Most times we get notified too late, but we still need to be vigilant about caring for those poor souls."

Their conversation became muted whispers. My cue to stop eavesdropping.

I made my way toward the steel table. Once my feet hit the top of the platform, I closed my eyes and imagined the room filled with students. Doctor Briar in a starched white coat lecturing about diseases of the liver or lungs.

The bell chimed again. "You better go," Doctor Winston said.

"Don't miss our next gathering. We could use a level-head when the gents start to argue over the latest findings in the journals."

"As for you, Miss MacCarthy." I stepped back down the stairs and his vise-like grip clamped onto my hand again. "I hope to see you in this theater one day as a student."

The bell chimed once more. For an older man, he moved up the stairs and out the door quite briskly.

The room went quiet. As the silence swallowed me, the elation of meeting Doctor Briar flitted away. This room, this building, was like dangling a piece of candy in front of a small child. It was a wish, a dream, that could never be fulfilled. Even if I found the strength to admit to my parents I wanted to be a physician, I could never afford the schooling.

I sunk into the closest chair. "Why did you bring me here?" I asked.

"I wanted to show you what this life could be. What *your* future could be."

The room was warm, but a chill tunneled deep into my bones. She trusted me, believed in me, but I still wasn't being entirely truthful with her. Since the moment she'd treated Paddy, I'd wanted to confess about my mam. The devastating event that changed my life so many years ago. Every time I opened my mouth to tell her, flashes of my parents flew through my mind. The hunched set of their shoulders. The caverns of blueish-black carved beneath their eyes. If I was being honest, I didn't want her to know my sins. A measure of relief came with walking into her office every day and forgetting the world outside, and I didn't want that to end.

"This life will never be mine," I finally said, my voice creaking like the old wood chairs.

"I've watched you these past weeks, Willa. You have a gift for medicine. Your instincts, your ability to assess a patient, are better than most physicians I know."

"You don't understand."

She knelt in front of me. Small tendrils of golden hair curled around her ears. "Explain it to me. You're a modern girl. Why can't you have this life?"

Heat burned behind my eyes. I blinked back tears and smoothed out the line of my skirt, unable to meet her gaze. "Entering the convent has been a family conversation since I was six and dressed in a lacy white First Communion dress. Voices around me murmured how I would wear another white dress when I took my vows of service to the church." The echo of my voice in the room sounded distant, broken. "And even if there was some way I could have this life, I could never pay for it. For a brief time I've allowed myself to believe this could be my future, but seeing the reality of it now, understanding my parents would never approve, it makes being here a heartbreaking experience."

"I know how much you love your family," she said. "That day in the office with Paddy and Nick, your adoration and concern was obvious. But Willa, tradition cannot go on endlessly. The world changes and we must evolve with it. I understand that money may be an obstacle, but more and more female patients want women physicians to tend to them. Like Doctor Briar said, we are needed."

Her words had merit. Even though I protested, I knew I couldn't walk away right now no matter the worries about money or my family.

"For now, we'd best be on our way if we want to see the rest of our patients today," she said.

I followed her up the steps. The weight of our conversation, and my secrets, sunk low in my gut. Before I could think twice, I swung around and took one last look at the theater. The pale walls. The shine of the table. The echo of Doctor Briar's words.

There was a struggle building inside of me. I was both the daughter who wanted to respect her parents, and a woman who craved her own life. Only the stronger of the two would win out. At this point, I had no idea which version would win.

CHAPTER EIGHTEEN

MacCarthy Residence
San Francisco, California
November 8, 1936

Paddy squirmed in front of the bathroom mirror. His wound healed well over the last month, but with only three usable fingers on his left hand it was impossible to get his tie straight.

"Let me help," I pleaded.

"No, Willy. I'm a grown man, dammit." He continued to fumble with the knot. "One day," he lowered his voice, "you're not gonna be here. I gotta learn how to do this on my own."

I stepped out of the bathroom unable to watch him struggle. He was like the rest of the MacCarthy men. Stubborn as an old mule.

Mam appeared at the end of the hall. Her eyes lingered on my face. Since the day I'd encountered Mrs. Reilly, I'd walked around her as if tacks littered the floor. Waiting on the moment she'd ask why I was on a streetcar with some woman she didn't know. Why I wasn't at the soup kitchen like I'd promised. Every time she said my name, called me into the kitchen, my pulse raced like I'd sprinted at top speed down Geary.

Unexpectedly, a hint of a smile formed at her lips. The flash of happiness I'd long waited to see flickered across her eyes for only a moment, and then like a slamming door it disappeared.

"That dress is a little close to the kneecaps don't you think?"

I brushed my hand over the pink ruffled hem.

"I may be getting a bit taller, but it still hangs fine," I said.

"That emerald green dress with the wide sash is pretty. I'll go into your room and get it."

I stepped into her path. "It's dirty," I insisted.

"Well, what about the yellow one with the daisies on the collar?"

"Spilled soup on that one last week," I inched closer to my door.

"All right," she relented. "That is a pretty color on you."

Every part of me itched to tell her the truth. That I couldn't wear any of the dresses she mentioned because they either reeked of rubbing alcohol, or were covered in patches of blood.

"My babies have all grown up too fast." Her voice hitched on the word baby. Her hand moved out like she wanted to reach for me and then it fell back to her side. She swallowed what sounded like a small sob and called to Paddy. "We're waiting on you, son."

He appeared in the doorway, the knot in his tie off-center. "We'll meet you outside in a minute, Mam."

That forced smile that always made my heart ache flashed over her face before she disappeared down the hallway.

I reached for Paddy's tie before he could bat away my hands. "I wish that one day she could actually deliver a real smile."

Paddy's lips puckered as I yanked on the silk material.

"Careful, Willy. It's my favorite tie." He tried to push me away but I held on. "Ease up on her. She's been through a lot."

"I know better than anyone what she's been through, Paddy."

He reached for my hands and tried to stop me again.

"Let me finish," I said.

"No." This time he held onto my hands. "You need to stop blaming yourself."

"How can I when every time she and Da look at me it's like they're seeing a ghost?"

He grumbled under his breath about moving on but allowed me to go back to work unraveling the tie. We'd had this conversation many times. He'd tell me my parents loved me. That they'd moved on.

He could say the words as much as he wanted, but I knew the truth. I saw it in every interaction I had with my parents. The only time they showed any real emotion is when they talked about the convent. About how Da's sister and his aunt had brought the family great prominence as nuns. The joy the women professed about serving the Lord. How I, too, would feel the same peace. I never quite understood it, but somehow having family join the church brought great respect in our neighborhood. My parents were insistent that tradition continue with me.

Paddy's mouth worked into a thin line as I started the knot. "I overheard the twins whispering about you and an accident on the bridge. I had to intervene and tell them to keep their traps shut."

My hands froze.

"Why didn't you tell me about going up on the bridge deck?" he asked. "According to them, you handled the situation like a real doc."

He must have heard them wrong. After the lecture they gave me at the car, and their recent cold-shoulders, I was confident they'd tell Mam and Da the truth in spite of our deal.

"I didn't want you to worry. None of that matters now anyway. Nick will find out soon enough and he'll tell Mam and Da. After that, they'll shuffle me off to the sisters quicker than you can say 'Kiss the Blarney Stone.'"

"That's not going to happen. I warned the boys that if they

said a word I'd tell Mam they've been gambling over at Tom Pennebaker's place. You know how much she hates those dice games."

"Those two can never keep a secret," I said, looping the tie through the circle and cinching it up Paddy's neck.

"They'll stay quiet," Paddy insisted. "Mam may be getting older, but they're still terrified of her wrath. Plus, I told them they could work my shift next Tuesday. I've got someplace I gotta be."

"Speaking of places to be, where have you been going during the day when I help Doctor Winston? And don't say some nonsense about Union Square or the beach. I haven't seen a hint of sand on those precious wingtips of yours."

"I've been here and there. Nowhere important." I didn't like how he looked away and scratched the whiskers at his chin. We'd never kept secrets from each other. Well, until now.

Once the tie was secured at his neck, he reached for my hands again. His grip was surprisingly tight. Soon he wouldn't have to wear that bandage anymore.

"I think I should warn you the new young priest, Father Murphy, is supposed to make an appearance today."

"Young?" I stepped away from his grip and examined the tie one last time. Paddy would rip it away if it didn't lay perfectly against his shirt.

"Yes, he's fresh from the seminary. St. Monica is his first assignment. Mam was none too happy to learn that fact."

"Why wasn't he at Mass today? It would have been refreshing not to listen to Father O'Sullivan drone on about all of us needing salvation."

"Apparently, Father O'Sullivan wanted to have this one last Mass to himself. So much for sacrifice and obedience."

He laughed and swiped a hand over his head. "Don't you wish our hair wasn't the same color as a newly minted penny?"

"Why? You want to look like a Protestant?" I meant to tease him, but the words sent a flare through me as I thought of Sam.

"Sure, why not? It'd be better than blending in with the rest of the MacCarthy lot."

Once his tie was finished, I picked at the lint on his shoulders. "I have a story to tell you." His eyes instantly brightened. "Now don't get all riled up. It's not too exciting."

I laughed as he poked at my sides until I gave in.

"Doctor Winston took me to the university medical school. She showed me the operating theater. Introduced me to a professor who is the dean, Doctor Briar."

"She did what?" His voice trilled around us.

"Be quiet!" I placed my hand over his mouth and he quickly swatted it away.

"Was it as exciting as you thought it would be?" he asked.

"It was more, but I still feel guilty. Doing all this behind Mam's and Da's backs. It's eating at me."

"Come on Willy, don't tell me you aren't enjoying this. You practically bounce through the door every evening. I hear you humming as you wash your face at night. You are loving the work."

"That's true," I confessed. "But the lying, it's getting more complicated. Every day I feel like I'm balancing on a knife's edge. One wrong move and everything, including my heart, will be sliced to pieces."

"I know. Mam keeps asking me all these questions about the soup kitchen. It's getting harder to make things up."

"Where are you going during the day?" I pressed again.

He squeezed my fingers, ignoring my question. "I refuse to let you stop working with the doc. It's important."

I stayed quiet and gnawed on my lower lip.

"What aren't you telling me?" he asked.

"That day when Doctor Winston took me up to the hospital, we ran into Cara and her mother on the streetcar. Mrs. Reilly asked all sorts of questions about who Doctor Winston was. Where I was traveling. It's chilling how easily I can lie."

"I told you that might happen," he grumbled. "But it's important you push on, Will. You are headed in the right direction."

"But Paddy, I'm supposed to report to the convent in four months. I used to be resigned to the fact that this was going to be my life. Now, I don't think I can do it."

"We can figure it out, I promise. But you have to keep up the fibbing. I know it's hard, but what you're doing now, finding your own path, it's important."

"What about you?" I couldn't help but glance at his hand. "You all right with pouring pints and listening to old stories about Ireland for the rest of your days?"

He chuffed me under the chin. "You're not the only one with plans, sister dear."

What did that mean? Did it have something to do with what he did all day long?

"Children!" Mam's voice crashed through our small apartment. "We are still waiting. You know how bitter Mrs. Reilly gets if we are late with the stew and soda bread."

Before I could get more details from Paddy about his "plans," he pulled me down the hallway and out the door.

The Reilly's Sunday afternoon parties were a ritual in our part of the Richmond District. After they'd built the extra room off the back of their house, they started inviting folks to bring a covered dish and enjoy whatever musician or band they could wrangle up for the day. What began as a small get-together swelled as the bands got bigger and people started offering a small donation to help other parish families who were struggling financially. If we'd had a good week at the pub, Da would often put a dollar or two into the black hat passed around the gathering.

The minute I was in the front door, Cara grabbed my hand and dragged me out to the wide-open room in the back of the house. Bright yellow linens covered a long bank of tables along the wall. Small desserts and covered dishes sat along a smaller table near the door. In a far corner, musicians pulled their instruments from black cases.

"Batt Scanlan is playing tonight," Cara said.

"How did your mother manage that? I thought he was only teaching over in the Mission District?"

"You know my mother. When she sets her mind to something there's no stopping her. I swear she could find the most poisonous spider and convince it to spin a beautiful web for her."

I tracked Mrs. Reilly through the room. Every time she stepped close to Mam, I rushed over and interrupted their conversation. My ruse could end here tonight if Mrs. Reilly decided to tell her about our encounter on the streetcar.

Cara rattled on telling me about the latest debacle at her father's office.

"A new young lawyer joined the practice a month ago. Every time I walk by him, he figures out a way to touch me. On Friday, he brushed past me and I accidentally poured hot coffee on a certain part of his anatomy. Don't think his hands will be doing any more wandering."

Her smirk was infectious but it wasn't enough to wash away the sick twist in my stomach. Between her work, and my time with Doctor Winston, we'd not had a moment alone since I spied that flier in between her stack of records. I couldn't stop thinking about what was rushing around inside that head of hers. Since we'd left school, she'd done nothing but moan about the molasses-slow pace of her father's office. The thought of her all the way across the country in New York made my head throb, but what would it matter once I was ensconced inside the walls of the convent? I'd perhaps get a glimpse of her when I took my final vows, but there'd be no more late-night revels at the dance hall or secret conversations at Mr. Langford's soda shop.

As usual, Sean and Michael lingered near the food table gobbling up every morsel they could touch. A few feet away, Nick's red brows narrowed as he talked with the Reilly's neighbor, Mr. Lofton, about the struggling economy's effect on the pub.

The music started and couples walked to the center of the room. Da moved toward me and held out his hand. His smile made me blink, as if I was gazing at the sun breaking through the murky city fog. It had been too long since he looked at me that way.

"You are a good girl, Wilhelmina." He spun me around once as the tune picked up speed. "Always looking out for your brothers. Mam and I may not say it, but we notice."

He was covering for Mam. Over the last several years, I couldn't remember a time when she'd look at me without some sense of sadness in her eyes. Da was stern, but he'd tried his best to smooth things over between us. A task that, no matter his effort, had never taken hold.

Within his circle of warmth, I felt safe. Loved. I held onto the moment with a firm grasp knowing that when he discovered my lies all of this would fade from existence.

"Your mam, you must be patient with her. I know you may be frustrated with how she is so very focused on the church, but you need to remember it is her faith that has gotten her through difficult times." He gulped. "It's gotten both of us through tough days. But that commitment does not mean we don't also recognize that being devoted to a religion takes a period of reflection and adjustment. If you need more—"

Paddy tapped his shoulder. "Da, maybe it's time you find Mam and take her for a spin?"

Da glanced at me for a long moment. What had he been trying to tell me? His gaze flicked to Paddy's bandaged hand. He hesitated and his lips twitched as if he wanted to say more. The tempo of the song picked up speed. He shook his head, turned abruptly, and went in search of Mam. When he found her, they moved into the growing crowd.

The way their eyes locked as they clung to each other fascinated me. It was if no one else existed. I couldn't help but wonder what it would feel like to be so in love that the world disappeared when you were in that person's arms.

An ache squeezed my chest. Locked away in the convent, I would never know that kind of affection. Never have someone look at me like I was the only one in the world who mattered. Was Da trying to tell me that he understood my worry? My fear about dedicating my life to the church? I wanted to smack Paddy for interrupting our conversation, but he was too focused on steering me back toward Cara and away from our parents.

"See that young fellow with dark brown hair chatting with Mrs. Boyle near the refreshment table?" he asked.

The man looked like every other lad on the street save for the black suit and white band at his collar. I sucked in a quick breath. "Is that who I think it is?"

"Yes, that's Father Murphy," he said.

I grabbed Cara's hand. The smell of lavender soap wafted off her skin. "Come outside and distract me for a bit. If Mam sees the new priest, she'll drag him over here in a second. Once he gets a good look at me, there'll be no more fibbing about heading to Confession every week. No more working for Doctor Winston."

She squeezed my hand. "Well, we can't let that happen."

I grabbed our coats hanging on a nearby peg, hooked her arm through mine, and marched us out the door.

A crisp November breeze whooshed across the yard, and I slid on my pink wool coat. I kicked at the grass with the tip of my pointed-toe pumps and made my way to the old swing Cara's dad gifted to her on her seventh birthday. I plopped down on the worn rectangle-shaped seat. The weathered rope scraped against my palms.

As children, Cara and I spent hours trading turns on the swing. We'd stare at the sky and guess what shapes we could see in the clouds. Cara always saw the faint outline of her favorite singers or film stars like Clarke Gable or Bing Crosby. I imagined shapes like a microscope or the last line of a math equation. Even then we were so different, but we managed to balance each other out. She forced me to do something bold, like buying a dress my mother wouldn't approve of, and I convinced her to be practical when she wanted to stay out past curfew.

"There are a few new faces here," she said, giving me a gentle push on the swing. Her own dark green coat flitted around her knees. "One fella that just came in while you were dancing with your da looks real familiar. He's a gem with fair hair and blue eyes."

The lilt in her voice said the new fella was a real looker. Sam's bright blue eyes flashed through my head. I quickly pushed the thought away. I should have told Cara about Sam but I wasn't sure what was happening between us. And I knew Cara. She'd pester me endlessly about him, and I couldn't bear to think about all the ways we were different. How I would feel when he disappeared out of my life as soon as the bridge was finished.

The ropes shuddered under my hands as she pushed me higher. My gaze kept moving back to the house and Mrs. Reilly. "Did your mom suspect anything after I saw you two on the street-car?" I asked.

"She prattled on about how Doctor Winston dressed, but once we got to the KRB she dropped it."

"You don't think she'll say anything to my mam, do you?"

"Between Mr. Scanlan playing, and the new priest making the rounds, the last thing on her mind tonight is you." She glanced back at the house. I didn't like the ways her eyes crinkled like she wasn't quite sure what her mother would do.

The temperature dropped by the minute, and I swore I could see white puffs of my own breath.

"Something else eating at you?" she prodded.

I stayed quiet, too afraid to ask the question that had been on my mind since I discovered the Broadway flier in her room.

"This isn't church, Will. Say what you need to. There's no judgment here."

When I didn't say a word, she held onto the ropes until the swing stopped.

"Spill it."

"Are you leaving San Francisco?"

The question dragged across my throat like sharp fingernails. I focused on the blanket of stars beginning to glimmer in the night sky, not wanting to see the answer in her eyes.

The swing creaked below me. Leaves rustled in the trees overhead.

"What makes you ask that?" Her words came out too calculated. Forced.

"When I was in your room that day after I first went to the field hospital, I found a flier near your stack of records. It was an advertisement for auditions for a Broadway show in New York City."

For the first time since I'd known her, Cara was at a loss for words. I jumped off the swing and placed my hands on her trembling shoulders. "Now it's your turn to spill it."

Her head dipped down. "I'm miserable. My parents keep insisting I go to that dull office every day. They act like they think I don't know their plan."

"Their plan?"

"Every time a new lawyer comes into the practice, like that louse from the other day, they hope I'll fall in love and get married. With both my sisters at the convent, they're focused on me doing one thing: providing grandbabies."

She huffed and threw her hands into the air. "I'm eighteen years old for heaven's sake. The farthest I've ever been from San Francisco is that quick trip we took to Los Angeles on the train when my grandfather passed two years ago."

She walked in a circle, her tiny feet barely making an indent in the grass. "God gave me this voice. I know he'd want me to do something with it even if it means disappointing my folks."

I reached out to stop her frantic pacing. "Aren't you the one who told me young women have a choice now to be anything they want?"

"Yes." She sighed. "I need to find strength and tell them I'm going with or without their blessing. I'm leaving two days after Christmas. I already bought a train ticket. I'm sure they'll regret paying me a salary now."

"So close to the new year?" It was hard not to tear up when I thought about her leaving me behind.

"Yes, they're starting auditions for the chorus the second week of January. I want to spend some time getting settled."

"Where will you live?"

"I wired the stage manager a few weeks ago. He connected me with a few chorus girls who need a roommate."

"New Year's Eve in Times Square?" I sighed imagining the glittering lights I'd only seen in pictures. The raucous crowd singing "Auld Lang Syne" at midnight.

She bounced on her toes in anticipation. "Can you imagine it? I'll get to see that shiny ball drop."

"I'll miss you," I said gulping back a sob. "But if you feel like this is right for you, then you need to go."

She clasped my hands, her tiny fingers wrapping around mine. "What about you?"

"What about me?"

"The doctor? Your future?"

The guitar inside the house came to a crescendo as the hoots and hollers rose to a feverish pitch.

"I haven't decided what I'll do yet. It's too complicated. If I do what I want, I risk losing my family."

"But if you don't do what you want, you risk losing a life and a career that was meant to be. Can you really picture yourself in that long black dress for the rest of your life? Them chopping off all that gorgeous red hair of yours?" She shivered, but it had nothing to do with the breeze whipping across the yard. "I still can't figure out how my sisters did it."

The door clacked open behind us. "Cara Jean, what in the devil are you doing out here?" Mrs. Reilly huffed from the top of the steps. "You know I need help inside with our guests."

"Willa and I are catching up."

"You girls can go two minutes without swapping gossip. Come inside, please."

"I better go. Will you be okay out here?" She glanced back to the house. "My mother said the new priest couldn't stay too long. Maybe he's left by now."

"I need a minute. I'll be in soon."

The band moved right into an upbeat version of "You Are My Lucky Star."

"Oooh, this is a good one!" She spun on her heel and rushed back inside.

The fiddle screeched across the strings as dancers inside shifted and moved in time to the beat. I found my spot back on the swing. Stars shimmered overhead as the last gasp of the day faded into the horizon. I wanted to stop time. Have Cara stay here with me. Not run off to a new and exciting life in New York City and leave me behind. A part of me should have been envious. Cara was a symbol of the life I couldn't have, but the resentment never came. Deep down I understood New York was supposed to be her home.

The lyrics to the song inside promised hope and love, none of which would be a possibility for me once I took those vows to be a bride of Christ. A dark, sinking feeling closed in around me. Like the bay was rising up from its shore threatening to swallow me in one massive wave.

"Would you like a push?"

A deep, familiar voice melted around me. In the fading early evening light Sam's eyes were the deep-blue color of the sea. The wide set of his shoulders pulled across the tight fit of his button-front shirt.

"What are you doing here?" I stuttered jumping off the swing.

"Mrs. Boyle invited me and some of the other lads from the boardinghouse." An easy grin flashed over his lips. He leaned in so we were only a breath apart. "She made me promise not to mention I was a Protestant."

If he thought he'd get a laugh out of me, he was wrong. Being Protestant in a room full of Catholic men was not a joking matter, especially to my da and brothers.

"Around here, that sort of comment will not earn you a laugh," I said.

He shrugged. "Never really cared much for religion."

"Why not? Everyone needs something to believe in."

"It's never been part of my life. Do I think there is some sort of guiding order to the world? Yes. I've seen it in the bright yellow color of the sunflowers in Texas. In the quarter-sized snowflakes in Montana. Just not sure some celestial being is in charge of it all."

I stepped away, grateful no one inside could hear him. If they did, it would cause quite the scene.

"I'm sorry," he said. "My words have upset you, but there's no point in lying about what I believe. I've seen enough of the world to know that we alone are in charge of our own destiny. There's no need for family or friends to guide our way. Only our own head and heart."

"So you have no interest in having a family? You don't mind always being alone?"

He scrubbed a hand over his chin. "At this point, no."

His words chilled me. My life was rich because of the people who filled it.

He pointed to the swing. "Push?" he asked again.

"No, thank you. I'm not a child."

"Well, that's certainly true."

On the streetcar, I often caught men staring at me, but the look on Sam's face was different. It wasn't hungry or bold. The light in his eyes was kinder, softer, like he was gazing on a beautiful flower for the first time. My heart wrestled with his ever-changing personality. His shrill stance on independence. The way he seemed to pull me in and push me away all at the same time.

He toed his way around the wide tree in the yard. The too-short length of his pants and the way his shirt barely tucked into the waist said the clothes didn't belong to him. He followed my gaze to the way the cuffs on his sleeves barely reached his wrists.

"Guess you can tell I'm not a regular at these kitchen rackets. I can barely walk in these shoes. They're two sizes too small, but Mrs. Boyle said if I wanted to blend in I had to dress this way."

I found my way back to the swing as the sounds of the fiddle and guitar filled the air around us. The crowd inside pushed the tables to the edges of the narrow rectangular room. Before the second chorus began, the room was packed with couples dancing in time to the music.

"Why are you here?" I asked again.

He took another turn around the tree. Before I could stop him, he gave the swing a slight push.

"Sorry, I couldn't resist." He chuckled and it was hard not to smile.

"You didn't answer my question," I replied, swinging out my feet in a pumping motion. He moved around the tree once more. His solid wall of a body stopped behind me and offered another push. The heat of his palms burned through the back of my coat.

"I came here hoping to see you." The words jutted out of his mouth in a low tangle—determined yet somehow hesitant. "Mrs. Boyle told me you might be here. I wanted to tell you Benny is doing well. His arm is healing nicely."

"That's good news," I said, scraping my feet along the dirt. When I came to a halt, I hopped off the swing. "And the drinking?"

"Not a drop. Moved him into my room so I can keep an eye on him."

The band's revelry slowed into a moody melody. He stepped in my direction. When he was only an inch away he held out his hand. "May I have this dance?"

With my brothers, my parents, only steps away I should have refused but I was tired of being afraid. Of my choices disappointing every single person in my life.

"Willa, dance with me."

The creak of his voice stirred a longing inside me. We were too different. Wrong for each other. Every fiber of my being screamed it was a mistake but I still took his hand. He slid his arm around my waist. We began to sway in time to the harmony floating around us. I wanted to relax in his arms, but the fear of prying eyes kept my shoulders rigid. I guided us into the shadows behind the tree. In the fading purple light, we rocked together with the melody. His hands tightened around my waist and my bones melted into the weight of him.

"I can't stop thinking about you," he whispered. "The way you smell like sunflowers blooming in the desert. How your hair is brighter and more beautiful than the sun fading in the western sky. But mostly, I can't stop dreaming about the confident way you ordered your brothers around the platform. How secure you were in the knowledge that you could help Benny."

A low, trembling laugh escaped my lips. "I'm not sure you're talking about me. On that platform, I was petrified. I'm shocked I moved at all."

"No." He pulled back. The intensity flaring from his eyes made my knees knock. "I've seen men put two-inch fishing hooks through their fingers in Alaska. Pull their shoulders outta place while they tried to rope steer in Arizona. None of them could pull it together under the strain like you did." He held our hands up and threaded his fingers through mine slowly, one at a time. The scrape of his skin against mine offered a delicious electric shock.

"If I ever got injured, you're the only one I'd want caring for me."

He brushed his hand across my cheekbone. The pulse in his fingertips matched the steady thrum of my heart. He pulled me tighter to his chest. I closed my eyes, waiting for the press of his lips. His breath inched in closer until the loud thwack of the screen door shoved us apart.

"Willa?" Paddy's footsteps thumped toward us. I pressed my fingertip to Sam's lips and shook my head.

"Here," I said, wandering around the side of the tree.

Paddy wasn't alone. Sean and Michael flanked his sides.

"Who were you talking to?" Sean's eyes flitted around the backyard.

"I wasn't speaking to anyone."

"Come on Will, we heard a deep male voice as soon as we were out the door." Michael shoved up his glasses.

Sam stepped out of the shadows. The boys' masks of concern turned hard.

"What are you doing here?" Sean's voice vibrated with anger. Michael moved beside him, fists clenched at his sides.

"Who is this?" Paddy stepped in front of the twins, too aware of their quick tempers.

"This is Sam Butler. He's a friend. The boys know him from the bridge."

Paddy narrowed his eyes. "We've met somewhere before haven't we?"

Sam stepped forward and reached out his hand to Paddy. "Outside the church a while back."

Paddy's shoulders relaxed as he shook his hand. "So you're a new member of the parish."

"No," Sean crossed his thick arms over his chest. "He's a Protestant. Staying over at old lady Boyle's place."

"Mrs. Boyle," I snapped at him. "Show some respect."

Michael's jaw tightened. "This is no place for you," he spit out.

The twins could bluster and billow like old crows, but I refused to let them intimidate someone who didn't deserve their wrath.

"Sam can stay as long as he wants."

"Willa," Paddy hedged. "If Mam and Da knew."

"Knew what? That I made a new friend who is Protestant? God forbid I step a toe outside our designated circle."

The boys double-blinked. I was shocked by my tone too, but every inch of me was tired of being railroaded into a life I didn't want. Spoken about like I wasn't only steps away.

"Go inside. I'll be along in a minute," I said.

Sean opened his mouth, and I swung out a hand to stop him. "I said I'll be inside soon."

Paddy tried to hide his smile as he steered the twins back to the door.

"Well, that was something." Sam chuckled. "Another reason why I'm glad I'm a rambler. Family is much too complicated."

"Family keeps you grounded. Steady. Reminds you of the important things in life," I shot back. My brothers may be a nuisance, always telling me what to do, getting into my business, but they also were a safe place for me. Men like Sam would come and go, but my brothers would always be here for me.

"It's probably best you leave. The gate over there will lead you back to the street."

"I'm sorry. Seems I always say the wrong things. Please, let me make it up to you."

Before I could say a word, he dashed around the corner of the house and returned with a brown box in hand. "My apologies for not doing it up in fancy ribbon and paper." He thrust the box in my direction. It hovered in the air between us.

"It doesn't feel right to accept a gift. We hardly know each other."

"Please Willa, you need this." His gentle plea raised the hairs on my arms.

The fiddle and guitar inside weaved together in a perfect

204

melody. If I stayed outside much longer, the boys would make a return visit and I didn't want Sam to deal with them again.

I slid the package away from his outstretched fingers and wiggled off the lid. Inside sat a crimson velvet box. My hand hovered over the ornate design embossed on the lid. Two snakes entwined around a winged mast. The same design I'd heard Doctor Winston call a caduceus. The symbol for medicine.

"Go on, take it out," he urged.

I inched open the lid. I blinked twice making sure I wasn't seeing things. The angled ear pieces led to black tubing curved in a figure-eight shape. The circular diaphragm gleamed bright silver.

"A stethoscope?"

"On the bridge you said you wished you had one. Now you do." He bounced on his toes, his sweet grin returning.

It was an expensive and beautiful instrument. Too expensive.

I slammed the lid shut and thrust the box into Sam's chest. "I can't take it."

"Why not?"

"Because it's too much."

Taking the gift felt like making a promise to use it. A promise I wasn't sure I could keep.

"There are no strings attached if that's what you're thinking." His beautiful mouth tightened. "Please, it's been a long time since I wanted to be selfless. Do something kind for another person simply because it was the right thing to do. I saw the stethoscope in the window at the apothecary and every element in my body screamed it was meant to be yours."

No words came as he placed the box back into my hands. I didn't know what to say. So few people in my life wanted to know my hopes and dreams, much less go out of their way to support them. In his determined eyes, I saw a reflection of what my life could be. How it could have purpose and meaning. A growing part of me wanted him to be a part of that life.

"Don't think of it as a gift, but one person's investment in your future."

His earnest tone, and the way his eyes said he'd be heartbroken if I didn't accept it, had me curling my fingers around the box. "Again, it's too generous, but thank you."

The door creaked behind us and I shoved the box into the inside pocket of my coat. Paddy stood on the threshold watching us. His shadowy form was a reminder of the life I had inside and the people who were expecting so much of me.

"Will, Mam and Da are looking for you."

I waved a hand at him. "Be there in a minute."

Sam waited until Paddy disappeared back through the door. "I'll go. The last thing I want to do is cause more trouble." He hesitated, toeing a patch of dirt. "Meet me tomorrow at Baker Beach? We can check on Simon and his sister."

"I'm at the clinic all day. Besides, aren't you supposed to be working?"

"We can meet during lunch. Say around noon?"

"What's the point? In February I'll be off to the convent, and you'll be on your way to another city once the bridge is finished."

"People can live a lifetime in a few months, Willa."

It was hard to refuse him when he looked at me like I hung the moon. I couldn't argue with his logic. If I was going to spend the rest of my days dedicating my life to the church, what did a few months of fun matter?

"I'll try, but don't be upset if I can't get away."

"I'll wait all the same."

The band started up again with an upbeat version of "Stack of Barley."

He grabbed my waist and spun me in a quick circle. Before my momentum stopped, he planted a kiss on my cheek and disappeared out the gate.

The fiddle picked up tempo and the combined sounds of hoots and hollers filtered out into the empty yard. I pressed my hand to my face, unable to shake the tingle of where his lips stung my cheek.

CHAPTER NINETEEN

The Office of Doctor Katherine Winston
San Francisco, California
November 9, 1936

Two cases of bronchitis, one bloody nose, and countless prenatal checkups later, the clock finally chimed noon.

Doctor Winston scurried around in a frenzy. Her loose curls billowed out around her cheeks. The air reeked of alcohol as she placed instruments into the silver disinfectant bin beside the sink.

"I've got a bit of leftovers from last night's dinner. Would you like to come up to the apartment and join me for lunch? We can talk more about your schooling. Perhaps how we can find you some money. Work things out with the dean?"

There'd been tension between us ever since our conversation at the university. She'd been so kind to me, but she'd never understand that even if by some small miracle my family agreed to let me be a doctor, they would never agree to a handout for my education. The MacCarthys were a much too proud lot.

"I'm not very hungry. Think I'll head out for a bit of fresh air if you don't mind?"

"That's fine," she said. "We don't have another patient until one o'clock."

I wiped the remaining alcohol off my hands and headed for the door. Once outside, I slid on my coat and rushed west on Geary.

All morning I'd been telling myself that it was a bad idea to continue whatever was happening between Sam and me, but I

208

couldn't get the scent of his soap-tinged skin, and the heat of his kiss, off my mind. I shook my head reminding myself the point of our meeting: to check on Simon and Maeve.

Streetcars clicked along the tracks. Motorcars blared their deep horns. Crowds rushed around me eager to get to their meal, home, or place of business. At the corner, I surged forward with the masses until a hand gripped my shoulder and yanked me back.

"Let go," I snarled.

Benny pulled me from the crowd. "I'm sorry, Miss. Was hoping to catch you at the doc's office." He pointed to his head. "Finally ready to have my stitches removed. I saw you scurry out. Been chasing you for a block now. Guess you didn't hear me calling your name."

His blond hair clung to his forehead with sweat even though the November chill kept the air icy. The edges of his shoulders twitched in rhythm with his shaking hands.

"You're about two weeks late on the stitches, Mr. Butler." He swayed on his feet. "You don't look well. How is your arm?"

"Well, that's a fine how do you do."

He tried his best to joke but there was no warmth in his voice. With his free hand, he gingerly plucked the gray cap from his head. The white sling draped across his chest slowed his movement.

"The arm and wrist are healing well. The doc came to the hospital after the accident. She looked me over and said you did a real fine job." He waved to a café a few shops away. "As a thank you, can I buy you a cup of coffee?"

"I was just on my way to—"

"Meet my cousin. I know. I wanted to talk to you first." He scratched his fingers over the stubble on his chin. "Think there are some things you should know about Sam."

Red gingham tablecloths brightened the dingy café. A waitress in a white uniform swept past us with an armful of plates. Benny pointed to a small table and pulled out my chair. For all his bluster, I was surprised he had manners at all.

We both ordered a small coffee. After the waitress disappeared into the kitchen, he leaned in to speak over the frantic lunchtime crowd. "First, I must apologize. Every time you've seen me I've been drunk."

"And bleeding," I added.

He gave a simple nod and sat back once the waitress delivered our drinks. His hand shook as he lifted the cup to his lips. His skin resembled paper-thin parchment. Deep circles around his eyes were the color of a day-old bruise. His chest hitched as strangled breaths left his mouth in sharp puffs. Delirium tremens. The body fighting back against its need for alcohol. The way it was described in my medical texts was nothing compared to seeing the brutal signs of withdrawal in person.

"Sam talks about you a lot." Benny looked away from my gaze like he knew I was examining him. "He thinks you and that lady doc are some kind of angels sent down to help all of us men at the bridge."

"I am no angel," I said quickly.

"No matter, when Sam gets something in his head it's impossible to shake it loose."

The men at the table behind us argued about the recent abdication of the king of England to marry an American divorcée named Wallis Simpson. Their voices carried across the small room as they argued about the sin of divorce, and I had to lean in to catch Benny's next words.

"Me and Sam, we're ramblers. Never stay in one spot too long. It's best we don't get tied down to one city." He scrubbed his good hand over his mouth. "Or one person."

His steady stare made me feel like a cell under the doctor's microscope.

"What are you getting at?"

"Sam, he's had it rough. His pa was killed in the Great War, and his ma, well her health was never too good. People in their small town knew it. Men tried to take advantage of her. Sam spent most of his time protecting her until the day she passed." He leaned back in his chair and stared at me for a long minute. "My cousin fancies himself a protector of the meek. There's been far too many times where we've had to skedaddle out of a city because Sam's tried to defend a lady's honor. Do you see what I'm getting at?"

His assessing eyes became too intense for my liking.

"I'll spell it out for you," he huffed. "In every city, there's a new girl. Penny in Chicago. Nelly in Portland. Julia in Alaska. He almost got his jaw broke saving her from some drunk fella in a bar." His voice pitched up over the murmur of the crowd, which earned us a few stares.

The grumble of the men arguing behind us disappeared. The clank of the silverware against plates no longer rang in my ears. Sam never saw me as special. I was simply another girl in another town. The coffee made a sickening slosh in my stomach.

"I feel like I owe it to you to be honest because you've taken such good care of me." He gulped down the last bit of his coffee. "When you see Sam next time, and there will be a next time, don't encourage him. Once the bridge is done, we'll be on to another city. No use in getting attached to someone who has no intention of staying."

My mouth flopped open like a fish. No words came to mind. I'd been so naïve. Sam told me about his life. His traveling. I'd never expected him to stay in San Francisco, but he seemed so kind that I missed the signs that he was nothing more than a wolf in sheep's clothing.

I gripped the cup and took a slow sip, hoping to ease the sudden chill in the room. He must have seen me as a challenge. A girl to compromise before she went into the convent. Did he laugh behind my back at what a child I'd been to believe he wanted to help me and the people at Baker Beach? My precious stethoscope nothing more than a tool to lure me into his deceitful web? He'd tried to convince me a few months together would be fun, but I knew better. Time spent with Sam Butler would offer nothing but devastation.

I jumped up from the table and pulled a few coins from my pocketbook. "Thank you for the coffee. Be sure to head back to Doctor Winston's office and have those stitches removed."

"I promise I will." He slid the coins back. "Please, the coffee's on me." He moved his trembling hands back to his lap. "I am sorry, Miss MacCarthy. Better you know the truth now before it's too late."

I gathered my hat and coat and pushed in the chair. "Good luck to you, Mr. Butler."

Motorcars and buses filled the street. The clank and jarring grind of gears exploded in my ears. I once found comfort in the Richmond District. The people who owned the shops were family friends. Part of my parish. Part of my world. But everything in my life felt tainted now, like no matter where I went there wasn't a place for me.

CHAPTER TWENTY

The Dublin Crown
San Francisco, California
November 28, 1936

The worst and best time of the year for the pub was the holidays. Folks who were out of work wanted to drown their sorrows. Those with holiday bonuses weighing down their pockets wanted to celebrate. Often the two did not mix.

Nick whined about the troubles every year. Since Mam delivered his lunch, he'd complained nonstop about the growing crowds at the pub.

"Those bridge men spend their dough quicker than they should," he grumbled around bites of day-old stew. "I need some help."

For close to three weeks I'd managed to push away thoughts of Sam. But now flashes of him wrestling down an injured Benny filled my head. He'd seemed so kind. So sweet. How had I not seen what a louse he was?

"Paddy is off to Mass. Yet again," Da grumbled. "And we're letting the twins sleep as they've had a rough week at the bridge. Mam and me already promised Father Murphy we'd help set up the Christmas decorations at St. Monica this afternoon. You are on your own at the pub until I get back."

"What about Willa? Soup kitchen is closed today and she's got two working hands."

"You know how I feel about her being in the pub."

Surprisingly, Da reached for my fingers and gave them a small squeeze. I returned his affection, basking in the fading moment. Since our dance at the racket, a small door had opened between us that I didn't quite understand.

"She can stay behind the bar and pour pints," Nick pressed.

My hand went cold as Da released me. "Nick," he said in a low warning tone.

They continued to exchange tense glances, making the tea and toast in my stomach churn.

"I am sitting right here you know." I threw down my napkin and shoved back my chair. "Have you ever thought about talking to me instead of around me?"

Mam stopped halfway into the kitchen. Da and Nick gave me wide-eyed stares.

"Willa," Mam said in a hush. "Mind your manners."

"Fine." Da gave in. "I guess she's old enough to help now. But you must keep an eye on her at all times. Don't like the wandering hands of some of those lads."

Several hours later I made my way down the apartment stairs. A wall of thick gray smoke greeted me as I pushed through the pub's entrance. The dingy haze was worse than the fog rolling in from the ocean. At least that wall, with its mist and chill, dissipated. In the pub, the smoke only grew thicker. It curled and danced toward the ceiling. Its ashy scent saturated my hair and clothes.

I was half-tempted to run out of the house after Mam and Da left, but good old-fashioned guilt had me walking through the pub in Nick's direction. Two steps near the bar a man wearing an old brown fedora grabbed my arm. His eyes were glassy. The tilt of his shoulders warned he was two pints of ale past drunk.

"You look familiar. I know you," he slurred.

"My da owns this pub," I said ripping his fingers away from my skin.

He scrubbed at his dirty chin. "Nah, I seen you over at the hospital near the bridge. What's a pretty girl like you doing over there?"

"You're wrong sir."

"No, Missy. You were there. Helping that lady doc. Saw it with my own two eyes."

"Mistaken identity," I said quickly and swept past the table. My heart pounded in time with the staccato beat of the band's guitar. The last thing I needed was some drunk patron causing a scene and revealing my lies to the entire crowd.

As soon as I came around the bar, Nick locked eyes on me.

"Da was right about keeping an eye on you. That fellow bothering you?" I shook my head. "What did he ask?"

"For the time." I grabbed a wet rag off the bar and went to work sopping up the foam from the latest overpour.

Nick glanced in the direction of the patron and then back at me. I held my breath and prayed the man was too drunk to approach the bar. The band swept into another song and the man's focus veered back to the pint in front of him.

Before Nick could ask another question, Stellan O'Connor and Mac Flaherty called to him from their regular spots at the end of the bar. They were old pals of Nick's who never missed a chance to gossip about what was happening at the bridge.

"How's work?" Nick settled pints of dark Irish stout in front of them.

"Closed the roadway gap on the eighteenth. You should have seen the look of pride on everyone's faces when that final piece went in minutes before sundown. They say work is slated to be finished in early spring." Stellan tapped his thick, calloused fingers against the glass. His curly dark hair sprung up and down as he spoke. "There's talk they're going to put on a week-long celebration. Open the bridge to foot traffic at first. Let the whole city get a gander at what we've been building these past several years before they let the cars take over."

"Supposed to be quite a party with marching bands and circus performers," Mac added, his deep voice cutting through the late afternoon revelry. His hair was a shade redder than mine. Men often teased him for his short stature, but whispers said he was the best welder in the city so the ribbing never lasted too long.

Nick scrubbed the bar with a rag. "What are you boys working on now?"

"Setting asphalt over the roadway. Once it's done, painters will add road striping for the lanes," Stellan said. His gaze veered in my direction as I took my spot behind the bar.

"Hear you're about to join the Sisters of the Sacred Spirit. My sister's been there two years now."

"How does she like it?" I asked.

He scrubbed his chin. "Don't know. She's not allowed to come home. Only seen her the one time when she went from being a postulant to a novice. She's still got another full year until she's considered a sister."

Mac took a deep gulp of his beer. Thick brown foam covered his lip. "Don't know how those gals do it. Locked up in that convent. Having to be silent for up to ten hours a day." He shook his head. "I'm a church-going lad, but there's no way I could be that committed."

"Willa will be fine," Nick said. "It's family tradition. She knows this is what's meant to be. Our mam and da talk about it all the time. How she's bringing honor to the family by serving God."

Heat flared in my throat. It was happening again. Nick talked as if I wasn't in the room, much less standing only inches away.

"I *can* speak for myself, thank you very much Nicholas MacCarthy!" The rag trembled beneath my clenched fingers.

"Wilhelmina, that's enough," he grumbled.

Both Stellan and Mac eyed their drinks like they were the key to human survival.

"Had some real excitement at the bridge a few weeks back," Mac said doing his best to interrupt the murderous stares tossed between me and Nick.

"Stellan and me were working near the Marin Tower when we heard a man got hurt bad near the South Tower." He hunched into the bar. Stellan followed his lead. "Rumor is a lady doc took care of him."

Nick glanced in my direction. We hadn't spoken about Paddy's accident since the day it happened. None of us told our parents about Doc Maloy's retirement, or that Doctor Winston was his replacement. It was like if we didn't acknowledge Doctor Winston's help, we could pretend it didn't happen.

Nick swiped Mac's nearly empty glass off the bar. "Want another?"

Mac slid several coins toward Nick in response.

"Wouldn't ever let a woman work on me. Lord knows what she'd get wrong," Stellan grumbled. "Just not right having women tend to men."

"Why not?" I asked. "Don't you think women are as smart as men? Last I heard your mam was doing the books over at Leary's Printing Press. Takes quite a bit of smarts to do that."

He drained the last of his stout and swiped a hand over the lingering foam at his lips.

"Math is one thing, but medicine is different. Women ain't meant to work with blood and organs. Their constitution is too fragile."

I gripped the edge of the bar and measured my words carefully. "Did you know the first woman graduated from the university in 1876? Her name was Doctor Lucy Wanzer. She practiced right here on Geary Street for over thirty years. In fact, she was a prominent member of the San Francisco Medical Society. Many men in this town respected her for her brain. And I can guarantee you, when she was delivering babies and saving lives no one questioned the state of her constitution."

"Willa, stop." Nick's warning only spurred me on.

"Right now over at the college almost five percent of the medical class is women. I'm told once this country digs its way out of this financial crisis that number will only grow!"

My heated tone earned me more than a few stares from the men lining the rest of the bar. "I bet that woman at the bridge, whoever she was, did a lot to help. Maybe her care was even better than a man's."

It killed me that as I spoke all I could think of was the confidence in Sam's eyes as he helped me care for Benny on the bridge. The way he assured me I could take care of his only living family. For weeks I'd been avoiding him at the Hooverville, but I still couldn't wipe the scent of him, or his deep, lyrical voice, from my head.

Stellan and Mac huffed out a laugh and went back to their drinks. My speech rolled off them without any notice. Nick grabbed my elbow and dragged me back near the kitchen.

"What in heaven's name are you doing? Spouting off about lady docs like that? Men come here to enjoy themselves, forget their troubles, not get a lecture from you."

I wrestled out of his grip. "Men, including you, need to open their eyes. The world is changing and so are the women in it."

Nick propped his hands on his hips. "What has gotten into you lately? You never used to be so . . ." His shoulders tightened up around his ears.

"Outspoken? Brazen? Honest?" I said not wilting under his frustrated gaze.

"Rude," he growled. "Those men are paying customers. They work hard out on that bridge and the last thing they want is you shoving your opinions on them."

I laughed in his face. "Nice to see you notice I have opinions." I spun to move back to the waiting customers, but he stepped into my path.

"Listen, I know Mam and Da have put a load of expectations on you." He scratched behind his ear, his mouth softening. "And ever since the accident, it's been tough. But they are depending on you to carry on family tradition. I can't give them that sense of peace. Neither can Paddy or the twins. Please, don't do something that would bring them more pain."

His words were harsher than a slap across the cheek. I was tired of being reminded how my parents' happiness rested on the fact that I become a nun. Why was tradition so important to them? Why was being able to brag about having a daughter who was a nun such an honor? Sure, they could talk about it at future kitchen rackets. Feel like somehow my being a member of the convent earned them some holy recognition. But none of that took into consideration what I wanted for my own life.

"What about your future, Nick?" He curled the rag in-between his fingers. "I've seen you corner Mr. Lofton at the Reilly's parties. Talk his ear off when he comes in for a pint. There's no mistaking the change in your voice when you ask about his work. How many times have you begged him to tell the story about how his boss, Mr. Giannini, over at Bank of America bought six million dollars in bonds allowing the construction of the bridge to get under way? Or the means in which he's trying to help the city out of this depression?"

As the days drew closer to my commitment to the church, the more I felt the noose tighten around my throat. Every Sunday Mass, every trip to Confession, was a slow slog toward a murky future. Even standing here now with Nick, the walls closed in.

I couldn't take the way he stared at me with a mixture of regret and pity. Every ounce of me wanted to tell him about the last month I'd spent with Doctor Winston. How she'd talked to me like a real person. Taught me how to not only fix wounds, but care for all the needs of a patient. How medicine was an art of observing both the seen and unseen. How people's injuries weren't necessarily always on the outside. Working beside her, I'd felt more purpose and joy than I'd ever felt within the walls of St. Monica.

"I'm not the only one struggling to figure out my future, and I'm tired of listening to the lot of you boys tell me how to live my life when none of you seem to be happy with yours."

I didn't realize how much my voice carried in the noisy bar until half the patrons turned to give me a wide-eyed stare.

"I can't stay here," I said tossing the dirty rag onto the bar.

"Willa, you promised to help. The crowd will only get bigger tonight."

"The twins are upstairs. They've been begging to help around here for too long. Go grab them."

Before he could stop me, I pushed through the crowd and out the front door. My feet carried me in a forbidden direction. There was someone else who needed to hear me out, and I wouldn't let this day end without saying what was on my mind.

CHAPTER TWENTY-ONE

Boyle's Boardinghouse
San Francisco, California
November 28, 1936

Three quick breaths slid past my lips before I mustered the courage to knock. Footsteps clicked toward the door. When it swung open I couldn't help but smile at Mrs. Boyle's cheerful face.

"Willa, this is a pleasant surprise. How can I help you this fine Saturday evening?"

I tapped my foot, trying not to shiver at the cold mist coating the air. "Is Sam here?"

A wide grin lifted her lips. "He's here, but I have rules about ladies and gentlemen mingling in the house."

"Oh, I'm sorry."

Heat hit my cheeks and she reached out to pat my hand. "But I can let him know he has a guest waiting outside." She gave me a quick wink. "Have a seat and I'll send him out."

I puddled down onto the first step on the concrete porch. Across the street, Mr. Norris pulled down the shades in the front of the pharmacy. Next door at the dress shop, Mrs. Emerson adjusted the sapphire blue beret sitting atop a mannequin's head. Minutes after she disappeared, the lights dimmed. Five o'clock crept up sooner than I'd noticed.

The breeze had an even colder bite as the sun dipped toward the horizon. I was an idiot. Why had I run out without grabbing my coat? Once the sun was out of sight, the night would plunge its icy talons deeper into my skin.

"Willa, it's not right to see you shiver like that." Sam appeared, removed his coat, and gently placed it over my shoulders. That tick of a smile that once set my heart thumping now made my blood boil.

"Guess you're wondering why I'm here?" I said.

"Not really." He chuckled. "I don't care why you're sitting on the steps in front of where I live because I'm too damn glad to see you. It's been nineteen days since you stood me up. And yes, I was keeping count," he sighed. "I've visited the field hospital and the camp over a dozen times hoping to see you. If I didn't know better, I'd say you've been avoiding me."

He scratched a hand anxiously through his pale hair, loose tufts sticking out around his ears. "Oh." He gulped. "My apologies for cursing, Willa."

I did my best to ignore the familiar hitch in my stomach that happened every time he said my name. I yanked the heavy wool coat off my shoulders and shoved it back at him.

"What's wrong? Is it your brothers? Simon or Maeve?"

"*You* are the problem." It was hard to keep the venom from my voice. The quicker I said he was a louse, the sooner I could be on my way.

"Me?"

"Yes. I may seem like a young girl Mr. Butler, but I do have brains. Did you think you could toy with my feelings? Pretend to enjoy my company and then take off when you'd had enough of me?"

"What on earth are you talking about?"

"Benny came to see me. He told me about your reputation. Wanted to warn me so I wouldn't get hurt."

"Reputation?" he sputtered.

"He said you love to swoop in like a protector and take advantage of a woman's grateful nature. He mentioned a girl in Alaska. How she swooned when you saved her from a fella bothering her in a bar. Well, I'll tell you right now I am no damsel in distress."

I jumped to my feet. "You should be ashamed of your behavior. Treating women in that fashion is plain wrong. And to think, I actually considered you a gentleman."

"Benny," he growled under his breath. "I shoulda known he'd pull something like this."

His hand moved in my direction and then he quickly pulled it back. "Please, give me five minutes to explain. If after I'm done you still don't believe me, I'll never pester you again."

"You have three minutes." I sat back on the step hating myself for losing my resolve so quickly.

"I think I told you I've been on my own since I was fourteen. When my ma passed, I went to Benny's first. He's two years older, and I'd always admired the way he seemed to have the world by the tail. We worked a few jobs that year. We laid brick for new apartments in Baltimore. In Texas, we helped brand cattle. Take care of livestock. He vouched for me saying I was sixteen so they'd hire us both."

He stretched out his long legs pretending the cold didn't bother him even though he shivered every time the wind picked up.

"Over the next years, we zigzagged across the country. At a construction job outside of Indianapolis, a load of lumber fell off a truck and broke Ben's leg. We didn't have a whole lot of money, and

I'm quite sure the doc didn't set his leg right. We got word a short time later that his mother died. The drinking started right after."

The door behind us swung open and two men passed us on the way to the street saying their hellos to Sam. Mrs. Boyle, God love her, hovered close to a nearby window keeping an eye on us.

"No matter what city we go to now, Benny never wants to stay long mostly because he's banned from every bar. With jobs being scarce, I've managed to keep him in San Francisco because of the steady work, but he's always itching to move on." He propped his head in his hand and fixed his steady blue eyes on me. "The story he told you was all about getting me to leave. He's been pushing me for months to get out of California. Head back to Texas. I keep refusing because I want to stay and see the bridge finished. It feels good being part of something so historic."

"Why should I believe you? Benny seemed very sincere."

He scrubbed a hand over his tight mouth. A rough breath escaped his full lips. "I bet a dollar he told you some flimflam about my pa dying in the Great War."

The stunned look on my face made him growl. "That's what he tells the gals in every bar we go to. He calls it the 'sympathy play.' It's a total lie. My pa never went to the war. He left my ma a year after I was born."

I sat up straight and pushed down the hem of my dress. "That's awful. Playing on women's sympathies like that. But that story about the gal in Alaska, did you save her?"

"No, that was our friend, Rory. All he got for his trouble was a punch in the nose from the fella and a snub from the young lady."

"Benny seemed so honest. Like he wanted to help me."

"Don't get me wrong, Ben can be a good man when he wants. The drinking, and the wanderlust, it gets hold of him and he makes poor choices." He inched in closer to me on the step. "Do you believe me?"

My mind still spun with questions, but my heart was lighter. If I was honest, the real reason I'd come here was to look into his eyes and see if I'd been a poor judge of character. If he was really the louse Benny painted him to be. A part of me hoped and prayed it was a lie. Seeing the pain in his eyes, I understood the truth.

"Yes, I believe you."

He glanced at the door and then back at me. Neither of us knew what to say next.

When I left the pub I didn't think twice about what I was doing. I was tired of being afraid. Living a half-life when I should be experiencing everything the world had to offer. If I was going to make the most out of these last months, I wanted to spend that time with Sam. Out of everyone I'd ever met, he seemed to understand the world best. Accept every moment, live every moment, like it was his last. I craved that sort of freedom. Now that I had the truth, I hoped Sam would show me how to have that life.

"It's damn cold out here." His cheeks flushed. "Sorry, there I go cursing again."

"It's all right. I've heard my brothers say much worse."

His shoulders tensed. "Don't suppose by any chance they're hiding behind the trees, or waiting on you down the street? Wouldn't want to cause a scene like that night at the racket."

"No, it's only me. And I'm sorry about that. They are a little overprotective."

"I can understand. If I had a sister as gorgeous as you, I wouldn't let her outta my sight." He sucked in a quick breath. "Um, but I'm sure you do just fine on your own. I've seen it with my own two eyes at the camp."

I let out a strangled laugh. He was even more handsome when he was all flustered.

A streetcar rumbled down the track in front of us. The groan of the motor rang in my ears.

"This is nice," Sam said clasping his hands in front of him. "I could sit here all night."

"Oh, that's too bad. I was hoping you'd be interested in joining me on a little adventure."

His brows twitched up. "What did you have in mind?"

"Why don't you come with me and find out?"

I jumped to my feet and skipped down the last two steps. A lift in my chest like a feather dancing through the air sent me racing down the sidewalk. I had no concept of what I was doing with Sam but was thrilled by the fact that for once in my life the future, or at least the next couple of hours, were mine.

CHAPTER TWENTY-TWO

The Number 2 Clement Streetcar
San Francisco, California
November 28, 1936

Steel lines hummed beneath us as we climbed inside the west-bound streetcar. Once we found a seat, it didn't take long for the car to start rumbling along the track in the direction of Lands End.

Sam offered me his jacket again. Before the goosebumps could become permanent marks on my arms, I slid into the sleeves. I loved being wrapped in its warmth. The smell of him, soap mixed with a tinge of metal, lingered on my skin.

"Are you going to tell me where we're going?"

"Wait and see," I teased.

The heat of him shot through me as his hip pressed against mine. His white shirt pulled against his thick arms. The nicks on his brown leather suspenders showed years of wear. Couples around us filled the car. Women wrapped in their winter finery nuzzled in close to their dapperly-dressed men. Small boys and girls raced down the narrow aisle. Candy cane treats dangled from their small hands. Under their breaths, they sang the same holiday tunes I loved as a child.

A dizzying buzz washed over me. While I wanted to be here with Sam, I worried I'd been too rash. My actions too brazen. Too confident. Words no one would ever use to describe me. I pictured Doctor Winston in the same situation. She'd never be afraid. She'd sit tall with her head held high, conversation easily rolling off her lips. I fixed that image of her in my head, relaxing next to him as if it was the most natural thing to do.

"Feels like ages since I've been on an adventure." Sam's mouth softened as he gazed out into the black night. His shoulders loosened as if lost in some dreamy thought.

"Tell me about all the exciting places you've seen. I've never been out of the city."

He stayed quiet, and I pictured the cogs in his brain churning like he was trying to figure out what to tell me.

"Since I can remember, Ma and I struggled to put food on the table." His fingers tapped in a hurried rhythm along the back of the seat. "A year after she passed, Benny and I were tired of working on farms and construction sites so we headed to Alaska. I was bound and determined to never be poor again, so all I wanted to do was work."

I couldn't help squirming at the mention of Alaska. Quickly, I wiped away all the lying words Benny once used to fill my head.

"We found jobs right away at a cannery. There weren't such things as shifts. You worked until the catch from that day was unloaded. Sometimes I was on my feet for twelve or fourteen hours straight. Only real good thing about it was the pay."

He wasn't much older than the boys I went to school with, but the set of his shoulders and the way he carried himself said he was wise beyond his twenty years.

"We worked all summer long, but we'd heard stories about how cold the winters could be, especially along the coast. One of the older fellas on the line asked if I could ride a horse. When I said I could, he told me and Benny about jobs working a ranch in Arizona. The first night the temperature dropped into the low forties in late September, we agreed to follow him to the Southwest.

After Arizona, Ben and I traveled the country like switchback, picking up odd jobs here and there."

He inched in closer. "When we'd get tired of a place, we'd hop another train and jump off at whatever town seemed interesting. Over the past years, we've shucked oysters in Washington, branded cattle in Montana, learned to pour concrete and weld in California. Figure the more skills we have, the easier it'll be to find work."

"Don't you ever get tired of traveling? Wouldn't it be nice to stay in one place for a while? Sleep in the same bed for more than a few months?" I asked.

"Most of the time I enjoy the rambling. There's lots of this world to see. San Francisco is different. I see how people look at the bridge like it's a monument to the human spirit. For the first time, I see the difference my work will have in a city. Can't help but be proud of that fact. Every job ends though and one day we'll have to move on again."

The fingernail moon slipped out from behind a bank of clouds. Its thin silver light danced across the dark streets like a chorus of ballerinas skipping across a stage. A brief beam of white far out above the darkened sea warned ships they were headed too close to shore. Like the light, our time together would be over in a flash. I understood he'd have to move on. So would I. But at least for tonight we had the hum of the streetcar, our conversation, and the promise of a new adventure.

The streetcar chugged up past Point Lobos Avenue and slid underneath a wooden roof and into a small station resembling an open barn. The scent of cooked hot dogs and freshly brewed coffee wafted out from the small snack bar inside the Market Street Railway depot.

The line slowed and we came to a sharp halt beside another

idling car. Couples swept past us whispering about the cocktails they'd order at the fancy Cliff House restaurant nearby.

Feeling brave, I clasped Sam's hand and pulled him out into the night. The sounds of crashing waves punctured the cold, damp evening. Shops lining the wide thoroughfare spilled out before us. Colorful signs advertised everything from Coca-Cola to souvenir photos. We walked along the street and stopped in front of a large white building with two towers draped in an art deco façade. A bright orange sign nestled between the towers read, "Tropic Beach: Sutro Baths."

Sam's eyes widened at the bold white sign proclaiming "Swimming Inside."

"But it's November," he argued.

I held back a laugh and directed him through the entrance. The enormous warehouse-style building stretched out for what felt like a city block. Overhead, the glass ceiling bloomed with a blanket of early evening stars. Three stories below us the roar of water churned. The air reeked of salt like we were standing at the edge of the bay. Slick, clammy air prickled at my skin and curled the hairs along my forehead.

We walked down a long flight of concrete steps. Each step was flanked with a towering palm tree. At the bottom, Sam insisted on paying our general admission fee at the ticket booth.

I led him toward another flight of stairs. "Wait." His footsteps stuttered. His gaze landed on a row of long glass cases. "Are those Egyptian mummies?"

"Yes. This is the museum level where there are stuffed polar bears and pythons. We'll come back in a minute. I want to take you to the promenade first. It's the best place to see all the pools."

"All the pools?" His head whipped back and forth as he tried to take it all in. The length of the glass ceiling, the rows of swaying palm fronds, the sounds of splashes and cheers lifting toward us.

We descended two more staircases and walked down a long J-shaped terrace until we reached the edge of an observation platform. Fifty feet below, six pools spilled out before us. Swimmers filled the water like tiny ink stains painted against a swath of bright blue.

He leaned down, palms flat against the railing. "What is this place?"

"It's an indoor bathhouse. It was built in the late 1800s by a local entrepreneur named Adolph Sutro. He wanted the people of San Francisco to have a place to socialize that wasn't too expensive. My parents brought me and my brothers here once about ten years ago. They had to drag us off the slides." I pointed to a long hollow tube in the corner of the vast room. Next to it were crumbling concrete and broken steps, which made it impossible to access. "With the poor financial situation of the city, the place has fallen into disrepair. Word is Mr. Sutro's grandson is going to do some renovations next year. They say he's going to demolish two of the pools and turn them into an ice skating rink."

We stood in silence, the splashes and roars of joy wafting up toward us. He tried to be sly, but every once in a while I'd catch him staring in my direction. As soon as my friends were old enough to recognize the admiring gaze of boys, they wanted their companionship. Many couldn't spend more than a week in between beaus. At dances at the KRB, Irish American, and Hibernian, Cara couldn't sit for more than a minute without a fella asking her to dance. I, on the other hand, tapped my foot in the corner not bothering to come out of the shadows. Cara commented more than once that it was my brothers' fault I was timid around men. Their fiery gazes whenever a boy attempted to speak to me was enough to make them run away. I'd never wanted that attention until now.

A display a few steps away caught my eye. I moved toward the glass case filled with dozens of stuffed exotic birds. Their bright feathers, splashed with every color of the rainbow, drew me in for a closer look.

"Have you ever imagined your life being something different than what's been set out in front of you?" I asked. Sam stepped in close, his breath warming the glass. "Let's say your father hadn't left. Would you have stayed near your home? Finished school?"

"I don't know," he said. "I think life is what you make of it. Sure, there's a course set out in front of us, but it's up to us to decide whether we head north or south, east or west. A friend I met in Alaska said he was the captain of his own ship. He could steward his future in whatever direction he wanted."

"But what if you didn't have a choice? That expectations were set up for you in a specific direction that you weren't allowed to change?" The words rolled off my tongue in one quick tumble. I'd never been good about sharing my feelings, but Sam's kindness made it easy to open up and reveal all my troubles and fears.

"We were all given the ability to make choices, Willa. I'm sure that priest of yours has spoken about free will. The ability to do right or wrong. Choosing the direction of your own life is no different. You make a decision and move on."

I sat on a nearby bench and pressed the top of my dress against my legs. The patterns of gold and brown flowers shifted under my fingertips. I couldn't look at him and admit I wasn't allowed to have a choice. That doing anything besides what my parents wanted would cause them pain. I was like one of those stuffed panthers in a nearby display case before they met their final fate. Trapped with nowhere to go.

Sam inched in closer. The heat of him too intense to ignore. "Since the day I met you, you've had this sense of sadness trailing after you wherever you go. Here you are, this bold, beautiful woman but the way you carry yourself says you're almost . . ." his words trailed off as he sank down next to me.

"Finish what you were going to say."

"Haunted. You move through this world like you're living a half-life. A ghost hiding in the shadows. I can't for the life of me figure out why."

All the air left the space around us. The wide-open room became too tight for comfort. He'd barely known me two months but he whispered a truth no one else would voice. Paddy and Cara had hinted at my melancholy. I'd always denied it and promptly plastered a smile on my face to convince them I'd accepted my fate.

"My apologies." A look of regret spilled across his face. "I tend to say whatever comes to mind without thinking about other's feelings."

The height of revelry in the pools below us drew me back to the edge of the railing. Below, children kicked and splashed without a care in the world. Their parents sat in the nearby sand or below thatched-roof houses placed in haphazard spots along the tropical, beach-like shore.

Sam placed his hands next to mine on the railing. "Willa, please talk to me. You won't say the words, but I see your pain. It's apparent in the way you hunch your shoulders as if you want to be smaller, unseen. I've never seen grief embodied in someone so plainly until I met you." He turned me to face him. The edges of his fingers caressed my cheek and I leaned into his warm touch. "Tell me your secrets. Let me carry your burden if only for tonight."

I'd been too terrified to reveal the truth to Doctor Winston, but held within the sphere of Sam's steady gaze the fear faded as quickly as the cheers and hoots in the pools below us. The way he circled me in his protective grip said he trusted me. That he'd protect me. Fight off any of the fierce animals in the display cases if they suddenly came to life.

"I told you about being a nun. It's a promise I made my parents many years ago. My da's older sister decided to join an order back east. His aunt and great aunt both took their vows in Ireland. It's a long-standing MacCarthy family tradition, but there's more to the story."

"Go on," he said.

"By the time I was twelve, my mam was still trying to have children. She had a terrible miscarriage when I was ten. I found her in the bathroom lying in a puddle of blood. A year later, she was pregnant again. She was so happy she practically floated around our apartment. One day when she was eight months along, we had a quarrel about my school lunch. She was sending me with leftovers again. I shot out the apartment door refusing to take the bag. She caught me at the top of the stairs. In a fit of anger, I pushed her away. One minute she was next to me, the next she was crumpled on the floor at the bottom."

I'd told the story only one other time to Cara. That time, too, it was hard to choke through the tears. "She lost the baby. It was a girl. My sister, Margaret. Maggie," I whispered. "Ever since that terrible day, I've promised my parents I'd be the best daughter. I'd never argue. Never speak up."

I shook my head, the pain so real it scratched against my

bones. "You said I was like a ghost. Well, it's practically true in my house. Since that day, my parents have looked at me like I was a stranger."

I took in a slow, deep breath and clutched the smooth wood railing hoping it would keep me upright. "With every fiber of my being I intended to keep that promise, until I discovered my first medical text. Being a doctor is all I can think about. Some nights I even dream about it."

Saying the words was like unthreading a ball of tight yarn lodged in my chest. Each truth unraveled an intricately woven lie. The ache in my always tight jaw loosened as the words spilled out of me.

"After the accident, my father refused to take me to see my mam at the hospital. I went on a hunger strike until he gave in."

"Even at twelve, you were a handful." He brushed a wayward tear from my cheek.

"I don't know about that. All I knew was I missed my mother terribly." The pucker of his lips said he, too, understood that kind of pain.

"Da took me into a tight, narrow room in the hospital. Women filled the fifteen beds jammed into the small space. Each of them were tucked in tight. Sterile white sheets nestled up high on their chests. What struck me most was the keening wails of the babies. The noise louder than a crowd striking pots and pans with thick metal spoons."

The memory made me shiver. "When I found my mother at the farthest end of the room, she was curled up into a ball. Da tried to rouse her, get her to look at me, but she stared right through him as if he wasn't there. I pawed at her, tried to get her to respond, but she barely blinked. A doctor arrived a few minutes later and spoke to Da. He said that with a still-born child the best thing to do for a mother was to get her up and moving. Help her to forget the dead baby by keeping her busy with her other children."

Sam sucked in a quick breath.

"I had that exact reaction. Even as a child, I understood the cruelty of that doctor's remark about her forgetting her deceased child." I smoothed down the edge of my dress trying to calm my trembling hands. "My mother went home the next day. She's never been the same."

Even though the humidity clung to my face, I snuggled deeper into his coat. "The memory of how ill-equipped the doctor was to take care of my grieving mother stayed with me. He was a man. He'd never understand the emotion of becoming a mother. The joy of creating a new soul. The crushing agony of that life being ripped away. Some part of me felt there had to be a better way to treat women who faced such a loss. When I found the medical texts in the trash bins outside the apartment, I started learning about the human condition, both the brain and the body. Inside the pages of those books, I understood what was the key to helping women like my mother. Rest. Conversation. Understanding. I've seen it work with my own eyes as I watch and learn from Doctor Winston. Women caring for women in the most difficult situations."

Even to my own ears I sounded broken. Tormented by the memory of loss.

I was haunted.

Sam pressed a finger to my quivering lips. "Shh," he whispered soft as a cloud. "It'll be all right."

His eyes searched for an answer I couldn't vocalize. I placed my hand over his, hoping he'd understand my reply. He leaned in and the brush of his lips over mine was so soft I couldn't believe it was real. Slowly, he threaded his fingers through the loose braid at my neck, winding me in tighter to his chest.

His heart thrummed in a steady one-two beat, keeping time with mine. I'd been kissed before. Eddie Matthews at the eighth-grade picnic at Golden Gate Park. Thomas Bellows at the kitchen racket the summer before my senior year. But those kisses were nothing like Sam's. His embrace was the weight of a thick blanket wrapped around me on a bitter January day. His kiss warm enough to spark the coldest heart to life.

I sunk into the comfort of his hug wanting to forget all my fears. My brothers were probably searching the city for me. When I did appear at home, the lecture would likely be hours long. I didn't care about any of it.

Sam pressed a gentle kiss to my forehead. "You were talking so fast, and your whole body was shaking. I needed you to stop for a minute and take a breath."

I couldn't hold back a laugh. "And you thought kissing would help? All that did was *steal* away my breath."

He did his best to look indignant until a laugh burst from deep inside him. "Yes, well I probably didn't think that through." He scratched a hand over his hair and before I could reply, he pulled me in for another kiss, this one deeper and stronger. He was the moon pulling me in like a wave. A lighthouse directing me around the crashing rocks until I was safe within his shore.

I'd brought Sam here as a distraction. A way to help me forget my troubles. Not once had I imagined he could be something more until his kiss opened me up to the possibilities of what life had to offer. I didn't want to consider our differences in religion, or that in a few months he'd leave San Francisco. All I craved was more of his touch.

"Willa, you're the smartest girl I've ever met," he sighed against my cheek. "When you took over on that bridge to help Benny, there was no doubt you were meant to be a physician." His fingers caressed the hairs at the back of my neck. "You could have run away after your brothers appeared, but you pressed on. When Ben shoved you away in anger, you could have fought back, but instead you settled him." Anger flashed across his face and then quickly disappeared. "Those women like your mother, they need someone as kind and caring as you to look after them."

The confidence in his eyes almost convinced me there was a glimmer of hope for my future.

"Stepping away from what people expect of you is a terrifying thought," he continued, "but I've traveled the country. Seen my share of horrors. Men stabbing each other for a slice of bread or a bottle of booze. Children with ribs protruding from their chest due to hunger. This world can be a dark place," he huffed. "It needs more healers—not more nuns."

An older man walked past us and cleared his throat. After we unwound ourselves, he tossed a judgmental stare in our direction.

Sam clutched my hand and guided me toward another set of stairs. "Didn't you say something about polar bears?"

His look of childish wonder made me smile. I was done worrying about the future. My fear. My regrets. For tonight, I planned to live in this moment like it was my last.

CHAPTER TWENTY-THREE

Baker Beach
San Francisco, California
December 14, 1936

Over the next two weeks as soon as my shift was over at the field hospital, I'd dash off to the Hooverville. On the weekend, if I could sneak away from my family, Sam would accompany me. It was hard not to laugh as he'd hover close by, being both ghost and bodyguard at the same time. When no one was watching, he'd twine his fingers through mine and press a warm kiss to my cheek. It was hard not to shiver with delight at the memory.

My first order of business this afternoon was to check on Mrs. Cleery. Doctor Winston insisted that I remind her that if she felt any contractions she needed to get to the office immediately. Mrs. Cleery waved me off with a nod and got back to the small work she'd found mending rich people's clothes.

Word spread about me throughout the camp. Each time I arrived, Simon directed me to a new tent. With each patient, I questioned symptoms and areas of pain. I ran down the list Doctor Winston taught me: vitals (pulse and breathing), visual examination, which included signs of discoloration of skin or eyes. Next, overview of symptoms and possible causes. Often the cure could come from a medicine I carried in the bag Doctor Winston gave me. Other times, I would refer the patient to see Doctor Winston for more urgent care. Over and over, I slid her card into their hands hoping it would be used instead of becoming kindling for many of the fires burning around the camp.

Simon trailed behind me to every tent. It was like he could sense the moment I stepped through the low-lying brush and overgrown trees. Trying not to show my hand, I allowed him to walk to a few tents before guiding him back in the direction of his own. His sister's cough still gnawed at me.

Mrs. Cleery sat on an old crate outside the tent. Red, angry blisters covered the tips of her fingers. "How many dresses have you worked on this week?" I knelt beside her and slathered ointment over her ragged skin.

A low hiss slid past her lips. "About twenty. Saving to rent us a room," she said.

"Mam." Simon kicked at a piece of loose stone on the ground and scratched at his head. "I told you I was old enough to work."

"You listen here, son. Once we got a decent place to lay our heads, you're headed back to school. You need to learn to read and write better so one day you can be like those lads we seen on the streetcar with the fancy hats and suits."

He mumbled a quick apology and she shooed him inside. He quickly returned with Maeve. I didn't need to ask if she was feeling better. The purple rings under her eyes and rough exhales told me all I needed to know.

I bent down so we were eye-to-eye. She hugged my doll, Annie, to her chest. "How is the throat today?"

"It prickles like I swallowed a bit of sand," she said.

It was hard not to bundle up Simon and Maeve and carry them home. I understood their mother was doing her best, but no child deserved to live in the same spot with men who stumbled about drunk only inches from where they slept. Broken down tents and overgrown weeds were a poor excuse for a playground.

"Mrs. Cleery, I need you to promise you'll bring Maeve and Simon to see Doctor Winston."

"Yes, Simon's told me your concerns. I'll bring them by soon." Her hesitant words gave me pause, but I slid the medicine into her hands anyway. "This is for Maeve's cough. It's powerful and should only be used before bedtime. Do you understand?"

She clutched the brown-tinted bottle. "What is it?"

"Just know it will help her rest at night." She placed the bottle into the pocket of her coat and went back to mending a dress.

I said my goodbyes and headed for a bank of tents higher up the hill. Before I'd dart inside, Simon would tell me the history of the family and who was sick. I often teased he was a better judge of illness than I was. Said I'd recommend him for a job to Doctor Winston when he was old enough. It was hard not to laugh at the way he puffed out his chest with every compliment.

After our last visit, we rounded the outside of the horse-shoe-shaped camp. A series of angry shouts blasted from over the hill. Simon raced up over the dirt mound and I followed. Five men stood in a circle around a bank of broken tents.

"I know you took the pocket watch, Malone," a thin man with long oily hair growled. A man twice his size with ruddy cheeks and hair to match towered over him. "The whole camp knows you got kicked off the bridge yesterday for lollygagging about. Now you're stealing from me to pay for your drink and women."

"Like I said two times before, I ain't never been in your tent, Simpson," Malone growled.

The two men started shoving. Before I could stop them, fists started flying. Simon gasped and his eyes went wide as Simpson's hand cracked against the red whiskers covering Malone's jaw. His head snapped backward with a sickening crack. He wobbled and then when he got his bearings, Malone used his full body weight to take down Simpson at the waist.

"Simon, do you know anything about that missing watch?" I asked.

"Miss, I swear, I'm done thieving."

The men's fists continued to connect until they fell to the ground, rolling close to our feet.

"Stop! That's enough." I scrambled backward, pushing Simon behind me. The men continued to pummel each other. The scene was a blur of punches, kicks, and cracking bones.

"She said that's enough!" Sam appeared at the top of the hill. He raced toward the men and shoved his way between them.

"Stay out of this, Butler. We're not on the bridge now. You can stop acting all high and mighty like you rule the world." Simpson shoved back his hair and spit blood onto the ground next to Sam's feet. Sam continued to hold him back. "Carlo laid me off last week. Look around, I'm out here living among swine like this louse who steals family heirlooms."

"I said I didn't nick your watch," Malone huffed.

Sam snapped his head to the right and the three other men convinced Malone to take a walk.

"Get out of here, Simpson, before Malone comes back and wants to clobber you again."

The man huffed and took off toward a far copse of trees.

Sam turned to me. A combination of worry and anger carved deep into the lines around his mouth. "I told you this place wasn't safe for you."

I tried not to snap at his tone. He'd broken up a fight, and I knew from years of watching my brothers tussle that I needed to give him a moment to tamp down his temper.

"Did we say we'd meet today?" I asked.

"No. I told Simon we'd go down to the shore and have another one of our talks." He shoved his hands into his pockets doing a poor job of hiding his frustration. "When are you going to listen? You shouldn't be here alone." His tone flared in the same way Nick's did when he didn't get his way.

"Miss Willa," Simon tugged on my skirt.

"Hold on a minute, Simon. Mr. Butler here is under the impression I need saving."

"Willa," Sam grumbled.

The thing I liked about Sam is that he didn't treat me like a precious doll, or a breakable piece of porcelain, but the situation had turned him into the type of brute I didn't like.

"I told you before, I am *not* a damsel in distress. These people need care. Do you think they are going to trust me? Allow me to treat their ailments if you act like I need protection from them? One small fight will not keep me from coming here. That's something you better settle in your head right now."

Simon gave my skirt another firm shake. "Miss!" His voice rose higher. "Those soldiers are back. You gotta leave."

Screams filled the air. Several yards away military policemen mounted the rise above the camp. Simon's lower lip wobbled and he pointed a shaky finger in the direction of tents about fifty feet away. A dozen soldiers swarmed the site. They kicked dirt over fires and wrenched men away from their families. Small children shrieked as the soldiers knocked down tent poles and swiped away skillets warming over fires.

"I can't leave, Simon. There are at least five families I still need to check on."

"You gotta go now," he pleaded.

Families near us scattered. Simon took off in the direction of his own tent. I started to chase after him when Sam grasped my arm. "You can't help him now. This time is different. There are a lot more military police. When they start rousting the place like this, no one is safe."

The soldiers moved in pairs, bulls stalking across the clearing, knocking down anything in their path. Behind them a handful of photographers snapped and clicked their cameras, eager to document the raid.

Sam urged me toward a bank of trees a hundred yards away.

"Sam, let go." I dug my feet into the dirt, tried to shake him off, but his fingers curled tighter around my blouse. "I haven't done anything wrong."

"They don't care, Willa. They aim to make a point. That's why they let the press tag along. What do you think your folks will say if they see your face in the paper? Or worse, if they have to come see you in jail?"

I let him lead me around the tents and past a row of smoking fires. Racing up a nearby hill, he tugged me into a tangle of trees, backpedaling until we were flush against a cypress with low-hanging branches. Our stampede shook up mounds of dead leaves and sent small rabbits and squirrels skittering deeper into the underbrush.

The roar of the pounding sea filled my ears. From our vantage point, we could see the entire camp. A soldier snatched up Maeve. Mrs. Cleery's arms flew up in a frantic fit as she clawed at her daughter. When Simon tried to interfere, another officer grabbed him by the scruff of the neck and dragged him away. Mrs. Cleery chased after both her children, a thick iron pan clutched in her hand. Once she reached the officer carrying Maeve, she struck him across the shoulders. Before she could get in another swing, a second soldier tore the pan from her grip and marched her off toward a waiting truck.

"No!" I tried to break free of Sam's hold but he circled me in tighter.

"You can't help them now."

Together, we sunk down onto the forest floor. "I don't understand. Why are they back? Wasn't last time enough?" I cried.

"Look over there." His soft touch guided my gaze in the direction of the beautiful homes in Sea Cliff. "I'd guess the well-to-do who enjoy this beach may have protested about the camp."

I gulped down the acid churning in my stomach as I imagined Cara's father complaining about good people like the Cleerys and Ms. Bea.

"These folks are suffering," I insisted. "Having them out here is better than having them sleeping on the street in town. It's not like they're harming anyone."

"I overheard a policeman at a pub a few weeks back. He said local politicians think the Hoovervilles make the city look dirty. Guess they don't want that in San Francisco. Plus, they are trespassing on government land."

The sharp screech of a whistle echoed across the clearing. Two men sprinted past the trees with two military policemen not far behind. Sam pulled me further into the shadows. I shouldn't have allowed the heat of his arms to comfort me, but my traitorous body sunk into his embrace.

"Are your folks still upset that you disappeared that evening we went to the Sutro Baths?" He tried to keep his voice calm knowing I needed a distraction.

"Yes. Even though I keep insisting I lost track of time saying the Rosary at St. Monica, my mam keeps quizzing me about where I'd sat in the church. Whether or not I'd seen the new priest while I was there. We still haven't met face-to-face so it was easy to lie."

"That was some good thinking on your part."

"You mean lying. It was some good lying," I whispered.

His lips quirked up into an irresistible grin. "Benny calls lying 'creative storytelling.' You could always think of it that way."

"Speaking of Benny," I said. "Did you talk to him about our encounter?"

His grin faded. "He's lost his job at the bridge and hasn't been back to the boardinghouse. Think he might be on a bender."

"Are you worried about him?"

He scrubbed a hand over his mouth. "No. Ben's done this before. He'll be back in his own time."

The heavy thud of footsteps sounded only feet away. Sam clutched me tighter to his chest. His arms circled my waist, pulling me into a warm ball. I held my breath praying the loud thud of my heart wouldn't give us away.

"Someone back here?"

A deep voice with a tinge of an Irish brogue bounced through the trees. Boots collided with brush. Sam tugged me in closer. His low breaths matched mine. He motioned like he was going to stand and give himself up, drawing attention away from me. I held onto his shirtsleeve and refused to let go. Our eyes warred.

"Fitzgerald," a voice barked out. "Sergeant O'Shea wants you back down the hill. We need help loading the trucks to get these folks out of here."

"Hold on a second, I could have sworn I heard voices back here."

I held my breath and leaned into Sam.

"I don't hear nothin', and I'm not about to get my arse chewed off cause you didn't want to follow orders."

The clomp of their boots receded. Sam leaned his forehead against the back of my neck. Slowly, the tense set of his muscles relaxed into me.

"That was a close one," he whispered. I tried to stand but he held onto me. "We should give it a few minutes. If they're loading the trucks, the soldiers will need time to get back down the hill."

The creaks and moans of the wind in the trees sounded like cries of small children. Or was that the desperate voices of Simon and Maeve being carted away?

"I can't sit here. We have to do something to help them," I said.

"I wish we could. But if we get thrown in jail, there'll be no one on the outside to plead their case."

The thought of little Maeve being scooped up like a criminal and set inside that military truck made my stomach twist.

"I'm sorry about before," he said. "Those men scuffling near you and Simon, it sent me overboard. But still, it's not my right to order you around. I suppose you get enough of that from your brothers."

"True," I said. "But those are the types of things that may occur if I'm a physician treating the injured. You need to understand that."

He dropped his head in acknowledgment. The cries from the camp died down although visions of Mrs. Cleery being dragged along by the soldier, her swollen belly pressing against her threadbare dress, still darkened my head.

"Tell me a secret," I begged. "Something no one knows about you."

His brows pinched together. "A secret?"

"Yes, I'm terrified right now. Tell me something that will push away the horrors spinning though my brain."

"Hmmm." The sound rumbled through his chest and against my back. "A secret I've never told anyone." He clicked his tongue once, then twice more. "When I was about four or five, I used to have terrible nightmares that would rip me from a deep sleep. My mother would have to shake my entire body to wake me. Once my eyes fluttered open, she'd curl me into the crook of her arm and play a game with me called 'Weaver of Wishes and Dreams.'"

His eyes had a sad, far off look like he was having a difficult time picturing the scene in his head. "She loved history and travel. As part of the game, she'd have me pick a place in the world I wanted to visit. Africa to see elephants. Egypt to see the pyramids."

I placed my hand on his cheek. "She sounds wonderful."

He leaned into my touch and whispered, "She was." His breath hitched once before he continued. "We'd come up with these incredible tales of me traveling in a canoe along the Amazon. Or hiking through the snow in the Swiss Alps. It was enough of a distraction to settle me down and get me back to sleep."

"That explains why you love traveling. It keeps you close to your mother."

A flicker of envy went through me. The moment my mam fell down the stairs everything changed between us. She once looked at me like I was a spring flower appearing after a long, damp winter. These days she barely spoke to me. When she did, it was to offer some terse word or ask how penitent I'd been. I couldn't blame her. My presence was a constant reminder of the final child she'd never have.

Sam ran a slow hand over my hair. "Guess you're right about my ma. When I stop in a new place, I often wonder what she'd think of it. I got to see the Grand Canyon once. It was breathtaking. Like the sun, wind, and rain joined forces to paint this beautiful landscape for the whole world to see."

His voice had a light that could have scared away every shadow around us. The tension left his mouth as he went on to tell me more about his mother. The golden color of her hair. The beauty of her hands even though they were worn from all the washing she did for her employer. Although his stories were short, they spoke volumes. They explained why traveling meant so much to him. It made sense why he could never stay tied to one place for too long. On the road, he felt like he was living a dream not only for himself but for his mother too.

"What would you say if my mother was here now and asked about your dreams?"

"A year ago, I would have said it was to make my parents happy. To do what they asked. Go to the convent. Serve God. Bring them respect in our community."

"And now what would you say?"

"You'd think I'd say I wanted to be a doctor, but it's more than that. Being in this camp, seeing the needs of so many, I think my answer would be to use medicine to help those in need. Those who have nothing and are too afraid to seek care unless a doctor comes to them."

He placed a sweet kiss on my cheek. "The more time I spend with you, the more I'm enraptured. This world has become dark since the crash, but you, Willa MacCarthy, are a beacon in the night like that lighthouse not far from shore. You make me believe humanity can do better. That the pain and fear of the world can melt away one caring soul at a time."

The intensity in his stare was almost too much to bear. His eyes held a hunger that if I'd looked in a mirror I was convinced I'd see in my own reflection. He spun a lock of my loose hair around his finger. I couldn't help but hesitate. Time was dwindling. Soon I'd be expected to head to the convent, and Sam had nothing holding him here but the bridge. He'd told me time and again that as soon as the final rivet was driven, he was on the next train out of town.

He was waiting on me to lean in, and despite my fears, I couldn't resist his pull. When we were no more than a breath apart, a rattle in the bushes made me jump away.

"Doctor lady, you back here?" Ms. Bea pushed a knobby hand through the brush. Before she could take another step, she collapsed into my arms. Blood poured from a gash over her left eyebrow.

"Did they strike you?" Sam snarled, helping her to a nearby rock.

"No. I'm an old woman unsteady on her own two feet. When I rushed away from the melee, I tripped and fell."

I lifted the hem of my dress and pressed it to her head.

"Here," Sam tore the edge of his linen shirt and pressed it into my hand.

After dabbing at the wound, the bleeding slowly stopped. "It's a minor cut. You should be all right."

"Looks like the soldiers are headed out." Ms. Bea winced as I pushed the cloth against the wound. "I'm sorry your little friend and his family got swooped up in the raid."

"Do you know where they'll take them?" I asked.

Ms. Bea and Sam swapped a tense look.

"Sam, where will they take them?" I pressed.

"Some they'll drop off at the outskirts of the city. Warn them not to come back. Those who resist, like Mrs. Cleery, may be turned over to the San Francisco Police."

His words were too measured for comfort.

"What aren't you saying?"

Ms. Bea's eyes darkened. "If their mother is arrested, those kids may become wards of the state. They'll put them in an orphanage with other kids who are abandoned or don't have any living kin."

"But they have a father," I protested. "A real family. He's south of here working in the fields."

I'd seen it almost every day since the crash in '29. The homeless, especially immigrants, were looked at as no better than stray dogs on the street if they didn't have a steady job and a roof over their heads.

"I won't let Simon and Maeve be separated from their mother."

The blank look they gave me said my words didn't matter. There had to be a way to help them. I refused to give up until Simon and Maeve were living somewhere safe with their mother.

Charging down the hill, I skidded to a halt in front of their tent. The dress Mrs. Cleery was mending sat in a dirty heap on the ground. Next to it, covered in a thick layer of black ash, lay my old rag doll.

CHAPTER TWENTY-FOUR

Lobby Outside the Dublin Crown
San Francisco, California
December 24, 1936

Every member of the MacCarthy family, except me, worked to-night. Paddy and Nick took their regular positions behind the mahogany counter doing their best to be both barkeep and friend as they listened to men's long tales of woe. Mam made sure the band did its job of keeping the late afternoon crowd entertained. Da happily poured the customers' favorite concoctions with a warning that they'd better drink up because we were closing soon for Midnight Mass.

Sean and Michael moved about the room acting like busboys and bouncers, making sure no lad gulped down too much whiskey and caused a scene. Even though they weren't behind the bar, the spring in their steps said they were all too happy to have a role in the night's festivities.

While Mam and Da ordered me to stay upstairs and tend to the evening's dinner, I couldn't help but come down and watch the revelry from outside the door. I needed something, anything, to take my mind off Maeve and Simon.

When I wasn't working with Doctor Winston, I was at the police station pestering every officer about Maeve and Simon. According to one officer, who was tired of hearing my pleas, the children had been sent to a local orphanage. Mrs. Cleery was held for a day until the soldier she'd struck felt guilty about her condition and refused to bring charges against her.

I pressed the officer about releasing the children into their mother's care. He waved me off and said if I wanted to help them I should go downtown and bother someone in Children's Welfare. So much for the holiday spirit.

The fiddler went on his own riff, his bow dancing across the strings in a frenzy.

"Billy Flynn's band sure has the crowd moving."

I jumped at the trill in Cara's voice. Her tight blonde curls moved in time to the music. Her sweet melodic voice sang along with the chorus. Every time she opened her mouth, goosebumps covered my skin. Her voice was more than beautiful. It was proof God had given her a gift.

"What are you doing here?" I pulled her back to the bottom of the stairs. The sound inside the pub faded as the door closed.

"Can we head up to your apartment?" she asked.

"Sure."

Once we were inside, the scent of roast clung to the air. It was the only time during the year my parents splurged on a nice cut of meat from the local butcher.

Cara stopped in the doorway and took a deep inhale. "Is that your mam's rosemary beef?"

"Yes. Christmas Eve tradition."

"I wish my mam would do that instead of making her great grandmother's stew, which always tastes like a worn old boot."

Cara dragged me to our sofa and plopped down beside me. The edges of her bright red dress flailed out around her.

"So tell me," she dropped her voice to a whisper even though we were alone, "how is it going with the doctor? Are you still getting your hands all bloody?"

Leave it to Cara to go right to the macabre. "No, not a lot of blood, but some." She almost bounced off the cushion as she waved for me to continue. "I didn't get a chance to tell you the night of the racket, but I went up onto the bridge a while back to treat an injured worker."

"What?" Her screech filled the room. "Did your brothers catch you? Did you know what to do? Were you terrified? I know I'd be scared silly."

It was hard to keep track of all her questions. "Shh! I don't want the entire pub to hear you."

She inched in closer and dropped her voice. "I want every detail."

I explained the terrifying height of the bridge. The twin's angry gazes. How Sam was by my side the entire time.

"I knew you weren't telling me everything." She clapped her hands like a child. "Have you spent any more time with him?"

Before the last word was out of her mouth, my cheeks were already ablaze. "We went to Sutro Baths together. Ever since, we've tried to spend a few quiet moments together." Her eyes widened.

"You have a boyfriend. Say it out loud, Will."

"It's not like that," I protested. "He's only . . ."

A smile brighter than the sun lit up Cara's sweetheart-shaped face. "A boyfriend."

"Fine. He's more than a friend," I hissed.

She threw her arms around me. "I knew you'd make the right decision."

I pulled back from her vise-like grip. "What do you mean?"

"With working with the doctor, and now the time you're

spending with a handsome fella, it means you've changed your mind. That you're gonna stand up to your folks. Tell them you're not going to the convent."

"I want to be a doctor more than anything, but . . . "

Cara's shoulders sunk. "None of this has changed your mind," she said.

"When I'm in that office my heart is full. My mind is clear. But, I have to be honest with myself. I'd never be able to afford the schooling, and you've seen my mother's complete devotion to the church. If I refuse to go to the convent, I'll lose my entire family."

"Paddy would never let that happen." She placed her hands on my shoulders, giving them a firm squeeze. "It's your decision, but let me say this last thing. That baby sister of yours, had she lived." Her eyes watered around the edges. "She would have seen the bravery in you. Told you to live your own life." She shifted back and smoothed down the creases in her flared skirt.

"Sadly, I'm your only sister, so I hope you'll listen to this last thing. In fifteen, maybe twenty years, your folks could be gone. Your brothers will be running the pub. Perhaps married with their own families. They may have girls of their own. Do you want them to have to live under the same weight as you? Unable to follow their own dreams because of some ridiculous family tradition? Being the first to step out of line is difficult, but if anyone can do it you can."

She took in a deep huff and reached down for her pocketbook near her feet. After inching open the brass clasp, she pulled out a red foil package. The scent of my favorite lavender soap wafted out from underneath the trimming.

"Thank you. Let me go get your gift."

I rushed back to my room. Her words buzzed in my head. I

never thought about future MacCarthy girls. Did my choice make it impossible for them to have their own lives? Their own dreams?

I pulled Cara's rectangle package from my bedside table and landed back on the couch next to her with a thud.

"My apologies for lecturing you. I know that is the last thing you need right now."

The nervous tap of her foot warned something was off. Was she having second thoughts about New York?

"Open your gift," I said.

She tore back the paper and gasped. With trembling fingers, she slid out a bright blue winter scarf that matched her eyes. It was the only thing I'd bought with the small amount of money I'd earned from Doctor Winston.

"I thought you may need it for Times Square. Heard it can get mighty cold there."

She blinked twice, and I knew if she started crying so would I.

"You all packed?" I asked quickly.

"Yes," she gulped. "Been hiding clothes in a small suitcase in my closet for a week. My mother's been asking about laundry and I keep putting her off." She twiddled her thumbs, unable to look me in the eye.

"Is this what you want, Cara?" I asked.

"That's funny coming from you." A single tear slid down her cheek and plunged off her chin.

I squeezed her hand trying my best to stay strong. "I'm happy you're getting this opportunity. Your voice is a gift people should hear. It's wasted in San Francisco, but on the stage in New York it'll be shared with the world."

She dragged her palm across her cheek. "It's possible I could travel all the way there and never get a job."

"You won't know until you arrive. This is an incredible chance to live your dream." I patted her hand until she looked up at me through her long lashes.

"Maybe one day I'll be able to tell everyone my best friend is a famous stage actress in New York. Bigger than Helen Hayes."

"She's a dramatic actress." Cara sniffled. "Anyway, it'll be a little hard to brag if you're locked away inside a convent."

She was right. Once I became a postulant, the outside world would be gone. For the first six months, I'd be expected to learn all the rules of being a nun. After that, the council would vote on whether I was worthy to become a novice, forever dedicating myself to the Sisters of the Sacred Spirit.

"Let's not think about that now. Tell me about your trip. How long will it take you to get to New York?"

"Four days on the train. I've managed to save enough to book an upper berth on a Pullman car for the first three nights until we reach Chicago. I'll have to change trains there. It will take me another day to get to New York."

A shout of revelry from the pub below wound its way upstairs. "When will you break the news to your parents?"

Her fingers twiddled in her lap again.

"Cara, you have to tell them. You can't disappear into thin air. They'd go out of their minds with worry."

Those wide blue eyes of hers offered a silent plea.

"Oh no! I'm not telling them after you've gone."

"I'm leaving them a note, but you know this is the first place they'll come." She pushed to her feet and started to pace. "Please Willa, you know how they are. If I tell them about New York, they'll argue, coerce, sob until they get their way. I'll be powerless to refuse them. I have to go now or I might never have the courage again."

The tears came in a flood now. She'd always been the stronger one. The one who would shove the boys when they were mean. The one who ended up in the principal's office after speaking up when a nun got overzealous with cracking someone's knuckles under a ruler. But when it came to her parents, Cara had a hard time finding her voice.

"I'll do my best to ease the blow," I said.

She clutched me in a tight embrace. The faint scent of lavender soap filled my nose. It broke my heart to think of her so far away, but she deserved this chance. When the time came, I'd tell her parents where she'd gone and why. Perhaps it would help me find strength to confess my own truth one day soon.

CHAPTER TWENTY-FIVE

MacCarthy Residence
San Francisco, California
December 25, 1936

There was something about Christmas Day that always brought light into our home. I wasn't sure if it was the satisfaction of having made it through another difficult year, or the fact that the pub was closed for the day. Whatever the element of joy was, I reveled in it because when the holiday was over it would be gone.

Mam wore her bright red apron. Her cheeks were pink, and for once her smile didn't seem pressed to her lips because the moment required it. Da tapped his knee in time to the music floating out of the nearby radio.

Once Mam appeared with breakfast, the boys didn't waste any time helping themselves. Sean elbowed Michael out of the way as they both reached for the eggs. Paddy helped himself to a huge slice of Mrs. Boyle's fruitcake that smelled too much like feet for my liking. Nick remained quiet in his seat. Out of everyone at the table, he was the only one who didn't seem infused with holiday cheer.

"Here, Willy." Paddy shoved a plate in my direction. My family could be aggravating and overbearing, but having us all together, safe in our warm home, was a blessing considering what was happening all over the city.

Surrounded by my family, I thought of Sam. Over the last few days after his shift at the bridge, we'd go to the orphanage and try to visit Simon and Maeve. After the headmistress would order us away, he'd hold me and we'd talk about all the ways we could get the children out of that cold, dark place.

He assured me he'd spend today having a warm meal with Mrs. Boyle and the rest of the boardinghouse residents, but the thin line of his mouth warned it would be more about keeping Benny sober.

It was hard not to wish for a time when Sam could sit at this table with his hand slipped between mine. It was an impossible thought, but this special day called for those kinds of dreams.

A child's Christmas carol streamed from the radio and my mind turned to Maeve and Simon again. Today there would be no family, no presents, for them. Acid churned in my stomach and the steaming plate of eggs in front of me lost its appeal.

"Willa, please eat," Mam said. "You're looking too thin, sweetie."

A knot welled in my throat. She hadn't used that affectionate term for me in years. I held onto her look until the shriek of the telephone forced me out of my seat.

"Who is calling us on this holy day?" The joy in Mam's face disappeared.

I'd barely said hello when I took a thick swallow, immediately recognizing the voice on the other end.

"Willa, oh thank goodness. I had to beg the operator to locate your number. Can you come to the office? We have an emergency." Doctor Winston's frantic tone made the tea in my stomach tumble.

I cupped my fingers around the receiver and inched as far from the table as I could. "All of my family is here. I'm not sure I can come right now."

"It's Mrs. Cleery. She's in full labor. There's no time to get her in my car or telephone for an ambulance. I've called on every doctor I know, but because it's Christmas no one can come. Please, I need your help."

A faint cry in the background made my blood run cold. What would happen to Simon and Maeve if their mother didn't make it?

"I'll be there as soon as I can."

"Hurry," she said before the line went dead.

After making up an excuse about wanting to see all of Cara's holiday gifts, I raced out onto Geary with my hat barely on my head. The streets were empty like a western ghost town. I half expected a tumbleweed to cartwheel into my path as I crossed 22nd Avenue.

As a small gift, the fog stayed away today. The sun burned bright yellow overhead. The low melody of Bing Crosby's "Silent Night, Holy Night" wafted out an open apartment window. For once the city felt like it was taking a deep breath. The crush of the Depression disappearing for this one day.

"Willa." My name echoed along the empty street. My feet stuttered to a halt. Nick rushed toward me.

"You forgot your mittens." He gripped the red wool but didn't offer them to me. "Where are you really going?"

"Cara's of course," I gulped.

He placed his hands on his hips. The look of disappointment in his eyes reminded me too much of our mam. "Stop lying," he said. "You know as well as I do that Cara lives in the opposite direction."

I stayed frozen in place. My mind warred over whether or not I could tell him the truth. If he would understand why I'd been lying these past months.

"That argument we had in the bar has been gnawing at me for a while now," he started. "I knew something wasn't right with you. Last week I went out to get more napkins for the pub and decided I'd stop by the soup kitchen and say hello. Imagine my surprise when the fella who took over for Father O'Sullivan said he'd never heard of you or Paddy."

"Nick, I promise I will explain all of this to you later, but I have to go. There's someone who needs my help."

"Is it the lady doc?"

A part of me should have gone cold, but heat burned at my lips instead. I was tired of lying and listening to everyone in my life telling me what to do.

"As a matter of fact, it is. There's a woman in labor. Doctor Winston needs my assistance."

I waited for the long lecture about right and wrong. How deceiving our parents was a sin. Instead, his shoulders crumpled as he held out my mittens.

"You're not going to stop me?" I asked.

"I'm not blind, Willa. I see how these last years have been hard on you. Mam and Da have done their best, but they still carry the pain of Maggie's death. And while they try not to take it out on you, I do see how in certain moments they look at you with . . ." he scratched at the red whiskers on his chin.

"Loathing," I finished for him.

"No," his voice cracked. "It's more like regret. Like if they could go back, they'd do things differently. I think we all feel that way, but it's too late for that now."

"I wish what you said was true, Nick, but nothing will ever stop them from holding me responsible for our sister's death. I was the one on the stairs that day. The one who pushed Mam away."

He nodded and placed the mittens into my icy hands.

"Are you going to tell Mam and Da?" I asked.

"I've thought long and hard about what you said about Mr. Lofton. You're right. I do want more than working every single day in the pub. I've thought about telling Da I want to take business classes at the college. Perhaps open another bar one day." He toed a crack on the sidewalk. "I understand hopes and dreams, Willa."

He let out a long breath. "This job with the doc is your secret to keep. Please, be careful though. Secrets have a way of getting out. I know that drunk fella you had words with in the bar recognized you." He scrubbed a hand through his russet hair. "I can tell your heart is in this work, but the time is coming when you're going to have to tell the truth. You need to be prepared for the consequences. Whether you believe it or not, Mam and Da love you, but their hearts will be broken if you don't go to the convent."

He patted my head in a way that older brothers do and slowly walked back in the direction of home. While I worried about whether Nick would really keep my secret, I had more serious matters waiting on me a few blocks away.

Mrs. Cleery's moans greeted me as I raced inside the exam room. Her brows knotted together in anguish. Sweat soaked her hairline. Doctor Winston took her pulse and reminded her to keep her breaths even.

"She is almost fully dilated. Grab some extra towels from the hutch."

When I went out into the office, Doctor Winston followed. "The baby is breech. I'm going to have to turn the child around before she can deliver." I didn't like the way her mouth drooped as she said the word deliver.

"I can still call for an ambulance," I said.

"No, it's too dangerous to move her now. Grab those towels and let's get started."

For over an hour Doctor Winston spoke in low tones to Mrs. Cleery, checking her progress every few minutes. When the time was right, she went about turning the baby. Mrs. Cleery's screams rattled the walls. It was hard to listen to her wail and not think of my mam. Her curled into a ball at the bottom of the stairs. The hem of her dress covered in blood. I'd replayed that day over in my head a hundred times. If I'd been a good girl and taken the leftovers. If I hadn't raced out the door, my life would be so different. Nick was right. Mam and Da did love me, but it would never erase their grief.

Doctor Winston instructed me to grab a few more towels. Once I placed them underneath Mrs. Cleery, Doctor Winston said, "It's time to push, Louise."

"I can't do it," Mrs. Cleery argued.

No matter how hard I tried, I couldn't erase Mam's anguished face from my mind. How empty and alone she must have felt as she lay in that cold hospital ward with all the crying babies—none of them hers.

"Yes, you can," I insisted. "You have two beautiful children who are waiting on you. Who want to see their baby brother or sister. Do it for them," I said.

"I've failed them," she sobbed. "And now there will be another mouth to feed. How am I going to do it without my husband?"

I grasped her hand, wishing I could have done the same thing for my mam. Been present when my little sister's still body was born. Promised her that everything would turn out all right.

"We won't let anything happen to you. Doctor Winston and I will make sure you deliver this baby easily. Let your body take control and we'll help with the rest."

Doctor Winston instructed me to brace my palms against Mrs. Cleery's back, keeping her upright. She moved to the foot of the exam table. Her gaze fixed on me. She never blinked or looked away. Instead, her eyes shone with confidence and something more like respect.

In the last few months she hadn't been easy on me. When I made a mistake, treated a wound wrong, forgot to wash my hands or sterilize an instrument, she'd let me know. She'd warned time and again that this wouldn't be an easy life. I'd brushed off her words, but with two lives in the balance, now her words took on grave meaning.

In slow measured tones, Doctor Winston instructed Mrs. Cleery to push. It took only twenty minutes before the baby appeared covered in blood, amniotic fluid, and a thick white mucus. Doctor Winston cut the umbilical cord, held the baby by the feet, and patted its bottom. A few heart-pounding seconds ticked by until a small squawk burst from his tiny lips. The little boy squirmed and Doctor Winston quickly wrapped him in a soft white blanket.

My cheeks were wet and my heart heavy. I couldn't help but whisper a small prayer of thanks as I looked at the baby boy cradled in Mrs. Cleery's arms. He blinked his bright blue eyes in my direction. It was as if someone reached inside my chest and squeezed. The smile Doctor Winston gave me was brighter than any of the holiday lights they hung downtown. Together, we'd brought this new life into the world. It was the best Christmas present I'd ever received.

Once both the baby and Mrs. Cleery were resting comfortably, Doctor Winston steered me out into the waiting room. I was glad the office was empty as we both looked like ghouls in our blood-stained clothes and crimson-tinted hands.

"That is always both a thrilling and terrifying event," she said, sinking into a cushion on the worn green couch. The caverns around her eyes edged deeper into her skin as she released a long sigh. "I know I can be a taskmaster. Quite sure I've scared away a nurse or two with my focus, but you, Willa, never seem to be ruffled by my directions. I'm very proud of how far you've come in such a short time."

I wanted to tell her how much she'd changed my life in the past months. How she trusted me. Respected me. To her I wasn't some ghost taking up space in her office. Or the youngest child who was meant to be seen and not heard. To her, I had value.

"Don't worry about Mrs. Cleery." She quickly patted my hand. "We will figure out a way to get her reunited with her children."

Her smile was rich with admiration and trust, and I knew it was time to tell her about my role in Maggie's death. After what we'd accomplished together, she had to understand and forgive my failures.

I did my best to force the words from my mouth, but they clung to my throat like a dry piece of soda bread. When I looked at her with nothing but a wide-eyed stare she leaned forward.

"Say what's in your heart, Willa."

"Thank you," I whispered.

"For what?"

"For believing in me. I didn't realize it until now, but over these last years I've given in to what everyone else wanted for my life. You've made me face a future I never considered."

"You are so much more than a sister or a daughter, Willa. You have a gift for seeing what people need. A sense of how they should be treated. That may serve you well as a nun, but you could also use it to serve this community. I see how you walk about the streets. How the people of the Richmond react to you. Think about what's really in your heart. You could take over for me here one day. You wouldn't have to fight the prejudice as much as I have. These people might bristle at first, but they would come to trust you."

I glanced back at the exam room. Memories of Mam's screams rang in my ears. A terrifying thought sank deep into my bones.

"Something is scaring you. Is it how your family will react if you choose a different life than what they want?"

"It's that and. . . . Do you ever get frightened you'll lose a patient?"

She rubbed a hand over her weary eyes. "Every day. But I can't let that stop me from doing my job. There's always a chance something will go wrong. That's why going to medical school, being forced into uncomfortable situations like cutting open a cadaver splayed in a ungentleman-like manner, is important. No matter what you are confronted with, a cooler head must prevail." She sank deeper into the cushions, her eyes closing. "Unfortunately, many times there's not room in life for being anything but a doctor."

Every element within me was weary, ashamed that once again I couldn't find the strength to tell her the truth. "I saw the way

268

you looked at the baby. Have you considered having a child of your own one day?"

Doctor Winston sat up and scrubbed her face. "It's something I've discussed with my husband at length." The lines around her mouth tightened. "I'm almost too old now, and this practice has become my child in many ways. It needs constant care and attention."

As is if on cue, a little screech erupted from the exam room. Doctor Winston swept inside and reappeared with the little bundle.

"There are sacrifices we all make to do what we love. Those men on the bridge risk their lives every single day to create a monument that will bring joy to the city. Even though they fight wind, rain, and thick fog, they return to it every day insisting it be finished."

The baby squawked again and raised his little hands. "We each work for a purpose. For some of us, it is to help those in need. For others, it is to bring joy, and perhaps escape, like your father and brothers at the bar. None of us thinks of our legacy. What will happen after we're gone. We live in the here and now. Doing our best to make a difference. For some that might not be enough, but every time I look into a child's eyes like this and know that they could be the change in the world, I am satisfied with my choices."

CHAPTER TWENTY-SIX

The Office of Doctor Katherine Winston
San Francisco, California
January 28, 1937

Since Christmas, things had gone downhill with Mam. When I slid in the door late Christmas afternoon, I did my best to act penitent. Bowed my head. Hid my blood-stained sleeves in the pockets of my coat as she lectured about not spending one of the most "holiest of holidays" with the family. Unfortunately after that, matters only got worse. When Cara's parents discovered she was gone, they showed up at our door. Poor Mrs. Reilly's sobs were so loud I was positive the crowd down in the pub could hear her.

Once they left, Mam started on another tirade about impudent children. The fact that our generation was an ungrateful lot. How disrespectful Cara was for taking off without her parents' permission. After the first week, I learned to tune her out at mealtimes.

Thankfully, Nick had kept his promise. Even though he'd stayed quiet about my work with Doctor Winston, it was hard not to burn with guilt every time he looked at me.

My saving grace from the tension at home was the quiet moments I snuck in with Sam, and the consistent frenzy at the office. I'd barely settled my coat on a peg near the door this morning when Doctor Winston called me into the exam room. A middle-aged man with a shock of black hair sat on the exam table. He cradled a thick kitchen towel wrapped around his forearm. The scent of burning flesh coated the air.

"Mr. Cairns received a second-degree burn during a kitchen fire. Let's get to work and see how we can help."

Slowly, she unwrapped the wound. "What do I want to do first, Willa?"

"Make sure the burn has not adhered to the towel."

"If it has?" she quizzed.

"We will need to leave the cloth in place so as not to disturb the blister and excise the area around it to determine the damage."

Mr. Cairns bit into his lip. Doctor Winston inched back the towel to reveal a large deflated blister, slightly larger than a quarter, an inch above his wrist.

Before she could ask, I handed her a sterile gauze covered in tannic acid jelly. The minute she applied it to the skin, a low hiss escaped Mr. Cairns's mouth. Once the gauze was in place, I wrapped more sterile dressings around his arm.

She pretended to busy herself while I worked, but she couldn't hide her proud smile when the man shook my hand amidst a flurry of thanks.

"How are Simon and Maeve?" she asked once we had a noontime break.

"Still very sad. I promised to visit them tomorrow at the orphanage. The hawkish headmistress has only allowed Mrs. Cleery one visit. Simon and Maeve told me they barely had a few minutes with baby George."

"You have a good heart, but you may need to let this go. It's impossible to help every soul in need," she said.

"Yes, I understand, but they shouldn't be in that wretched, cold home. They belong with their mam." I tried to keep my voice calm as frustration boiled in my veins. "There are so many children. Simon tells me he bunks in a different room than Maeve, but he can still hear her cries at night. It's a horrible place. It smells like a toilet and the children have nowhere to play."

She gave me a disappointed frown. "It's not prison."

"It might as well be," I grumbled.

I kept seeing the pure joy on Maeve's face when Sam sweet-talked the headmistress into letting us finally see her. An ache splintered my heart as her tiny fingers clutched the rag doll I returned to her. When the headmistress ordered us away after only a short visit, she had to yank Maeve from my arms. In quieter moments, I could still hear her pitiful cries.

I shook away the thought and pulled out the book Doctor Winston gave me about the heart. Right ventricle. Left ventricle. Like a drill instructor, she quizzed me about blood flow and issues with clogged arteries.

Halfway through her lecture on arrhythmia, Doctor Owens barged through the door. His circular spectacles tilted across his nose like he'd put them on in a hurry.

"Katherine, we have an emergency in Sea Cliff. Can you close the clinic and come with me?"

Doctor Winston rushed to grab her bag. Once her coat was on, she paused near the open door, walked back, and pulled my coat off the peg.

"What are you doing?" Doctor Owens paced in the threshold. "We have no time to waste."

"Willa, let's go." She motioned me to the door.

Doctor Owens's eyes bulged. "No, Kat! You can't bring her. This is too delicate a matter for one so young."

"She and other young women are the future of medicine. I think she could be of help," she argued.

"Between children's vomit and sticking my hands inside a

bloody body, I can't imagine anything else being too overwhelming," I insisted.

"Absolutely not!" Doctor Owens shoved Doctor Winston's red winter scarf in her direction. "Think of the legal ramifications."

She tapped her foot and chewed on her lip. The seconds ticked by. Doctor Owens continued to grumble under his breath.

"He is right," she sighed, returning my coat to the peg. "This is one time you must stay behind, Willa. If more patients arrive, let them know I will return in an hour or two." Without another word, they rushed out to Doctor Owens's car parked at the curb.

I moved around the room trying to busy myself with cleaning. A handful of reasons why I should stay behind, why I should listen, filled my head. Who was I kidding? I needed to know why there was so much secrecy between the two of them. Why racing off to Sea Cliff was so important. I grabbed my coat and hat and raced out the door.

It was a good thing I'd spent half my childhood running around the Sea Cliff neighborhood with Cara. Knowledge of the streets helped me quickly find Doctor Owens's black Chrysler parked outside an exquisite brick home that took up half the block.

I stayed hidden behind a shoulder-high bush. Before climbing several tiled steps, the doctors conferred on a long path covered in expensive red stone outside the home. A maid appeared at the arched mahogany door and waved them inside.

What was so secret about making a house call to a mansion in Sea Cliff?

Stepping into the courtyard, I skirted past a trickling fountain with a copper dolphin spurting water from its mouth. Orange, pink, and yellow rose bushes lined the walkway.

I paced in front of the door for a minute before finding the courage to knock. The same maid appeared in the threshold. "May I help you?" Her brown curls sprung out from under her starched lace headband. The hem of her black uniform dress clung to her knees.

"The physicians who arrived a few minutes ago are expecting me."

Her gaze narrowed and ran down the length of my dress. When I refused to move, she huffed out a breath and waved me inside. The home's large entryway made me gasp. Marble the same shade of the light pink roses outside covered the floor. A chandelier with at least one hundred crystals dangled overhead.

"Follow me, please." The maid mounted a carpeted spiral staircase with an intricately carved bannister. I swore it was just as wide and grand as the one at the Sutro Baths.

Before we reached the final step, the screaming began. The sharp wails were muffled by a door, but it was clearly coming from someone suffering intense pain. The maid's cheeks ticked. She pointed to a long labyrinth of a hallway.

"She's down at the end of the hall." Without another word, she scurried out of sight.

I walked past five elegantly outfitted bedrooms and two baths that were larger than our kitchen and front parlor combined. My knees wobbled. My pulse quickened as I got closer to the source of the screams.

At the end of the hall, I was greeted by a man and woman. The man was dressed in a dark evening suit. Diamond cufflinks glittered on each sleeve. A gorgeous green silk dress floated around the woman. A stunning necklace made of emeralds clung to her throat. There was something familiar about her frame and the way she held her hands.

"Who are you?" The woman barked.

I looked her straight in the eye hoping to convince her I was meant to be here. "I'm the doctors' assistant."

The man looked as if he might jump out of his skin as he paced the carpet in front of the arched door etched with intricate gold scrolls.

"She's locked herself in the bathroom and has been screaming like that for over half an hour. The doctors just went in."

He wrestled with the brass knob until the door sprung open. I rushed inside and closed it behind me. The room, decorated in bright pinks, purples, and greens, resembled a fairyland. A wide lace covering tented the four-poster bed. Leaded glass windows on a far wall let in natural sunlight and provided a grand view of the sea below.

"Willa, what in the devil are you doing here?" Doctor Winston gasped.

"I'm sorry, but you've been so secretive. I had to know what was happening."

"Stupid girl," Doctor Owens spit out. "You'll only make matters worse."

"No, it's right that she's here. She may be able to calm the patient down. They are about the same age."

Doctor Winston rushed forward and examined my hair. "Bobby pin?" she asked.

I scrubbed through my loose knot, located a pin, and dropped it into her outstretched hand. It only took her a minute to work the lock until it sprung open.

The rusty scent of blood hit me first. It covered the lush white tile, the side of the claw-foot bathtub, and the tangle of crisp white towels surrounding a young woman whose translucent skin warned she was near death.

Doctor Owens rolled her onto her back, and I clamped my hand over my lips muffling a gasp.

"What is it Willa? Do you know her?" Doctor Winston asked.

The last time I'd seen Molly she was in the alley with Cyrus. Her cheeks pink with life. Now she lay still as a corpse. Her white nightgown drenched in a horror scene of blood.

"Yes, she was a year ahead of me at school."

"Miss Gallagher." Doctor Owens patted her cheeks. Her eyelashes fluttered open and her mouth opened into another blood-curdling scream.

"Willa, grab as many clean towels as you can carry and bring me my bag."

I did as Doctor Winston ordered and raced around the room doing my best not to step in the growing pools of blood.

"Doctor Owens, come and hold her shoulders while I do the exam." Doctor Winston moved down to Molly's feet. "Willa, lay out the towels around her sides and do your best to try and slide one under her lower back."

The moment my hand touched Molly's legs she bucked in pain.

"It's all right, Miss Gallagher," Doctor Owens said. "We are doctors. There's nothing to worry about now."

Molly's thrashing splashed blood across every surface. Small droplets covered Doctor Owen's jacket. A crimson spray dotted Doctor Winston's chin and cheek. Despite the chaos, Doctor Winston did her best to speak to her quietly. Her voice a gentle comfort amongst the frenzy.

Like I'd seen her do with countless female patients, Doctor Winston examined Molly. With each touch, Molly vacillated between screams and sobs.

"How long ago did you have the procedure?" Doctor Winston pressed her hand over Molly's abdomen, and she arched up in pain.

"No procedure," she cried out.

I didn't like the pained look the doctors swapped.

"Can you tell me what you used?" Doctor Winston asked.

"Knitting needle," Molly breathed out. Her eyes rolled back in her head and she lost consciousness.

"She may be suffering from peritonitis." Doctor Owens's dark whisper made me shiver.

I'd only read briefly about the condition, but I understood it was an injury to the tissue that lines the inner wall of the abdomen. It made sense now why Doctor Owens's skin paled. Injury to this area was serious because it housed most of the abdominal organs. If left untreated, peritonitis could infect the blood and cause major organs to shut down, sometimes causing death.

Doctor Owens jumped up and ran to the phone near the bedside table. In a flurry of words, he called for the ambulance.

"Willa, take her hand. Talk to her while I try to stop the bleeding," Doctor Winston said.

Molly's long, icy fingers slid between mine. I spoke about the day we first met in school. How I marveled at her speed in gym class. The way she could sprint past all the girls while still looking prettier than any film star.

I tried to push the terror from my voice.

Blood.

A knitting needle.

Her boyfriend, Cyrus, nowhere in sight.

I was proud of the way I'd managed to control my fear in the most terrifying of situations, but sitting next to Molly's almost lifeless body I questioned whether or not I was capable of being a physician. Whether I deserved to be a physician.

I let go of Molly's hand and lost the contents of my stomach in the sink. The edges of the room shimmered.

I couldn't be here. Her screams. The blood. It was all too much like that day. Like my mother. I'd betrayed her. Failed her. Stolen all the light from her life with one act. That moment wasn't something I could wash away by working with Doctor Winston. It was a dark mark on my soul no amount of penance could erase.

The roar of sirens approached. I raced for the door and threw it open. Mr. Gallagher rushed into the room and collapsed onto the blood-soaked tile next to his daughter.

Before I could get away, Mrs. Gallagher gripped my hand. "I recognize you now, Willa MacCarthy. You must promise me you won't tell anyone about what's happened here today."

"You have my word, Mrs. Gallagher," I said over the ache in my throat.

She gave me a stiff nod, her need to protect her reputation more consuming than her dying daughter only steps away.

CHAPTER TWENTY-SEVEN

Doctor Owens followed the ambulance to the hospital promising he'd telephone with an update on Molly's condition.

With the ambulance fading in the distance, the full weight of the day swallowed me. My head buzzed. My legs shook as if the earth tilted around me. I crumpled down onto the curb. Mrs. Gallagher's final words, and rigid demeanor, burned into my mind. Her look, so devastated, so broken, shook me. It was what I imagined my mother's face would resemble if she discovered all my lies.

Doctor Winston blew out a harsh breath and sank down next to me.

I opened my mouth several times trying to explain my behavior. Why I'd run away. How recalling the chaos in the bathroom still made it hard to take in a full breath.

"I've never seen so much blood before," I managed to say.

Doctor Winston twisted her red scarf between her hands. Its color eerily close to the crimson stains on her fingers. "It can be shocking to witness the brutality of this job. There is much joy to it. Witnessing a broken bone heal. Seeing a new life be born. There is also much sadness. Seeing someone whose taken their own life or hurt themselves in an unthinkable way."

"Is this what you've been whispering about with Doctor

Owens? And that day in the operating theater with Doctor Briar? I wasn't supposed to be eavesdropping, but I heard something about saloons and blood."

"Yes. There is a small group of doctors who work together to care for women who find themselves unexpectedly in a family way. Too often women like Molly feel such shame they take matters into their own hands." She scrubbed her fingers over her weary brow. "By law we are not allowed to help them. As a result, they turn to men or women who claim they can end the problem. It's usually in some filthy room with dirty instruments. Those bastards end up killing most of the women they treat."

What Molly had done to herself was shocking, but even worse would be what would happen if she died. Her parents would have to confess the truth about what happened today. When they did, the church would never let Molly be buried in a Catholic cemetery.

I glanced back at the house trying not to recall the horror inside. On instinct, I bowed my head and said a short prayer. The word "amen" drifted quietly from my lips.

"I know what is going through your mind, Willa. Seen it before with many families. You're worried about Molly's soul," Doctor Winston said.

"I'm not sure I can do this," I whispered.

"You have to if you want to be a doctor. Care of the patient must take precedence over everything else."

Care of the patient.

Her words burned in my ears. Since the day I'd met her, I'd wanted to confess what happened with my mam. About Maggie. I never understood what kept the words jammed in my throat until now. If the truth slid past my lips, she'd say I wasn't worthy of being a physician.

Yes, religion could be a conflict, but deep down it was more about my guilt. That I had no right to heal the sick when my own act had taken a precious life.

In the room with Mrs. Cleery, I wanted to be brave. Holding onto her, bringing baby George into the world, felt like some kind of divine absolution for what had happened with Maggie. But when the time came to stand up, to help Molly, the blood and heartbreaking screams took me back to being twelve years old and standing helpless at the bottom of the stairs. The terror gripped me, forced me from the scene, and proved once and for all that I had no right to be a physician.

"But what if I can't do that?" I said. It was easier to let her believe religion was the real reason for my cowardice than the truth.

"Enough, Willa! You're stronger than this. Running out on a patient, unable to face their trauma, is not appropriate for a physician." She dragged her hands through her already tousled curls. "This is about more than faith. When we have a patient who is sick or dying, there is no one there but us to care for them. You can pray for strength; many physicians do. Hell, I just did inside the Gallagher's home. But that doesn't mean we ever lose focus on the patient."

Her shoulders crumpled as she shook her weary head. "It's okay to be afraid, to ask for help, but you can't stop working. Can't stop fighting. No matter what religion you subscribe to, in the end it's only you and the patient. You have to trust what you've been taught and put that to work. It's the oath we all abide by when we agree to administer to the sick. You will have to reason out how to integrate your beliefs with your care because there will be another situation like today where you'll have to choose what is more important. The patient. Or your beliefs."

I tugged on the hem of my skirt, trying my best to ignore the ache in my chest that told me what I had to do next.

"Perhaps I should be done with our acquaintance if you cannot accept me for who I am."

Her gazed narrowed. "Willa, I see you for who you really are. Stop trying to be a shadow of yourself. Who your parents or your brothers want you to be. Be strong enough to speak up for what *you* want."

"From the first time we met, I told you I had an obligation to my family. To my church. Perhaps your confidence in me was misguided." Each word was a caustic burn across my lips, but it was better this way. She needed to move on and so did I.

She reached for her bag and shoved it under her arm. "Let's end the day. We can talk again tomorrow. Start fresh."

"No. It's best we end things here," I said, unable to stomach how easily the lies poured from my mouth now. "I made a promise that I'd tell you if this was too difficult for me. I need to go home. That's where I belong."

She did her best to hide her feelings, but it wasn't hard to miss the tick in her cheek. The way her grip tightened around the handle of her bag.

"What are you so afraid of Willa? Running away to the convent won't make your troubles disappear. That passion you feel for medicine is not easily extinguished." She placed a hand to her chest trying to control her breath. "I told you my husband went to find work in the Central Valley, but that's not completely true. We've been arguing for months. He wanted me to settle down. Cut my hours. Think about having a child. I thought it through and finally told him no. My calling is to be a physician, not a mother.

He had a hard time hearing that truth and left to clear his head. I haven't heard from him in weeks."

"Why are you telling me this?"

"For a long time I tried to pretend I was someone else. A teacher. A wife. None of those things ever brought me as much joy as being a physician. I realized one day that if I wanted to be happy, I had to settle into that truth no matter the consequences. I don't want to see you struggle for years like me."

A knot the size of a fist filled my throat. Her steady look said she believed in me. That I was a good and kind soul. It was better to have her angry than to see the true disgust in her eyes once I told her the reason I couldn't stay in the room with Molly. Experiencing that look of betrayal, or utter disappointment like I often saw on my own parents' faces, might be the final thing that broke me.

"I am *not* you." I said steeling myself against the tears threatening to tumble down my cheeks.

"That's true, but I do know one thing. Not until you face your fears will you finally be free. You can tell yourself lies over and over. Convince yourself a family obligation is your only path. But I think we both know that no matter where you are, what you choose to do, deep down you will always have the heart of a physician."

She turned on her heel and stalked down the street. Part of me wanted to chase after her, but what good would it do? Today showed me I'd been a fool to believe I could study medicine. That I had the right to take up anymore of her time.

When Katherine Winston appeared in my life I'd needed her. She'd taught me about medicine. About life. But that was over now. Perhaps she was right. I'd needed to witness the horrors of her world to realize I had no right to be part of it.

CHAPTER TWENTY-EIGHT

The MacCarthy Residence
San Francisco, California
February 11, 1937

Every day for two long weeks I sat in the apartment and played the obedient daughter. Pretended to listen as Mam taught me how to make soda bread and stew. Remained frozen in an uncomfortable wood chair as we read her favorite Bible verses. Even now with a needle clutched between my fingers, it was impossible to keep the clinic from my mind, or how it'd been too long since I'd held Sam's warm hand.

Mam's look of surprise when I quickly attached a button to one of Da's shirts brought a real smile to her face. For me it was a knife to the gut. Without Doctor Winston, I could have never made such meticulous stitches.

Whenever Paddy could get me alone, he urged me to go and talk to Doctor Winston. Today was no different.

"I know she'll take you back if you go and apologize. Tell her the truth about your hopes and fears."

"And who are you to talk about truth?" I snapped. "Where have you been going these past months, Paddy? What have you been doing with your time? Last time I looked, you weren't exactly forthright about your *plans*."

He closed my bedroom door and motioned for me to sit next to him on the bed.

"Let me speak first. After I've finished, you can say anything you want."

His mouth tightened as he scrubbed the three fingers on his hand through his russet hair.

"I've been going to St. Monica after I leave you with the doc. At first, I just went to pray. Sort out my feelings about losing my fingers. Ask for guidance, because deep down I hate working in the pub. Maybe that's why I've pushed you so hard to chase your dream. Someone around here should get what they want."

He waited a minute, expecting me to be shocked by his revelation. Truth was you had to be blind not to see Paddy didn't belong in the pub. I squeezed his hand and nodded for him to continue.

"One day I was praying, and Father Murphy joined me. I like him. Think if we were in school together we'd be mates."

He sucked in a quick breath. "We've been talking for a while about our favorite Bible passages. What the church means to us." His lips thinned. "Like you with the doc, I think I've found what I'm meant to do with my life. Yesterday, I told Father Murphy I'd like to enter the seminary."

My jaw hung open and all thought raced from my brain.

Paddy chuckled and patted my shoulder. "I know it's a shock, me wanting to wear a stiff shirt and white collar for the rest of my life. But, I do look good in black."

"No," I protested over his jokes. "I won't let you do this. It isn't right. You're trying to protect me again. I can't let you throw your life away because you want to shield me from Mam and Da."

He tightened his remaining fingers around mine. "Willa, I want this with all of my heart. A part of me feels whole when I step through the doors at St. Monica. I'm at peace. I suspect that's the same way you feel when you work with the doc, although you're too damn stubborn to admit it."

"When are you going to tell Mam and Da?" I said, ignoring his jab.

"Soon, I promise. I'm supposed to go over final details at the church today with Father Murphy."

"If this is what you want I'm happy for you, but it doesn't change my mind about what I've promised to Mam and Da. Now they get two children serving God."

"Willa," he sighed.

Despite his continued protests, I knew what came next. After giving Paddy a quick embrace, I went to my closet, grabbed the black leather bag hidden behind a mound of clothes, and fled out the door.

I had every intention of going straight to Doctor Winston's office and returning the bag, but my feet carried me in another direction.

There was nothing left of the Hooverville. Tents were gone. Firepits dismantled. No sign of the families that once called the clearing their home. I placed the doctor's bag down next to the burned-out ruins, the black leather sinking into wood remnants and dark gray ash.

What once had been the Cleery's tent was in pieces. Like with Doctor Winston, I'd let them down. I'd promised to help them, and then I'd sat idly by and let the soldiers take away everything. What good could I be as a doctor, even a nun, if I couldn't help one single family?

"Willa?" Sam crushed me into a hug, and I quickly pushed

him away. The joy drained from his face. "Where have you been? Neither you or the doc have been to the field hospital in weeks. I've waited for you outside the home where they have Maeve and Simon, but you've never appeared. I walked down on the beach today after my shift, and when I looked up and saw you, I thought I was imagining things." He moved to embrace me again, but I stepped back. "What's going on? Did I do something wrong?"

"No, you've done nothing wrong. I've needed some time and space to think." I kicked at a patch of scorched ground where a firepit once warmed a family.

"How are you?" he asked.

"I'm well," I lied. "You look . . ."

His brows hitched up. "Dirty?" He nodded to the gray bits of concrete clinging to his arms and face.

"I was going to say worn out."

"Yes, that's true." He pointed to the part of the bridge near the center. We're finishing the last bits of the roadway. Looks like we might be done by late March, early April, providing there's no problems."

In the distance, the net under the working part of the bridge pitched with a sharp burst of wind. "How do you go out there every day and battle the fear? Is it easier to work knowing even if you lose your balance, you won't plunge to your death because of the net?"

He stayed quiet and I didn't like the way he avoided my gaze. "Is there something you're not telling me?" I asked.

The edge of his boot toed at the ground. "That net is a good thing, but sometimes it makes the men a little reckless. They bounce about unhindered now like even if they fall they won't get hurt. It puts the rest of us at risk."

"What kind of risk?" I pushed.

He swiped his cap off his head and scratched at his hair. A faint puff of concrete dust filled the air above his head. "Yesterday, some men were jumping from the platform and they knocked the one I was working on loose. We swung out and I lost my balance." He shoved the cap back on his head. "I hung onto the steel ledge for a minute until another worker pulled me up. The net is supposed to keep us from that cold water, but I've seen a few men bounce into it and still get hurt."

Doctor Winston treated those same men who'd arrived with broken wrists or arms. While she cared for them, they puffed out their chests, crowing about how they'd faced down death and lived to tell the tale.

"You didn't want to be part of the 'Halfway to Hell' club?"

My words were meant to be teasing but they came out hard. Who would brag about almost dying?

I'd seen the fear in Molly's eyes as she squirmed on the ground in pain. Blood pumping out from between her legs. You'd never really seen terror until you'd watched someone's life spill out of their body. Their skin turned thinner than parchment. Their eyes widened in fear. Neighborhood gossip spread quickly in the days after we cared for Molly. Whispers said she'd be hospitalized for weeks but she'd survive.

"I have no interest in that nonsense," Sam grumbled. "My only goal is to do a good job and finish the bridge. Some other fellas though, they don't act smart up there. The foremen try to keep an eye on it, but they can't catch everything." He jammed his hands into the pockets of his work overalls. "It's no matter. Like I said, job will be done soon and I'll be on to other work."

His words stung. Why was I doing this with him? I couldn't

help but look up at that bridge and worry about my brothers dangling high up on those steel lines. Sam moving from platform to platform. In his own words, he'd said how dangerous every moment was. Didn't I have enough to worry about with the mess with Doctor Winston? My mind swirling over what was happening to Simon and Maeve?

"What will you tell Simon? That like his father, you're another man in his life disappearing? Why spend all that time with him only to let him down?"

He blinked like he couldn't believe I would be so cruel. I clutched my bag to my side. The ache slowly growing in my gut moved to my chest. "I need to go."

"Wait. At least let me walk with you," he pleaded.

"No. I think it's best if we didn't see each other again."

He stepped back like I'd slapped him. "Willa, I'm sorry. I didn't mean to frighten you."

"It's more than that. My life is such a mess. I quit working for Doctor Winston."

"Why? What happened?"

"We had a row. She's been keeping secrets and I followed her. What I discovered was something I can't straighten out in my head. A girl I know hurt herself because she didn't want to have a baby. There was so much blood. I couldn't move. Couldn't help Doctor Winston. Once again, I failed someone important in my life."

The words tumbled out of my mouth so fast it felt as though I'd been socked in the stomach. Seeing what happened to Molly should have made me swear off medicine forever, but there was a part of me who ached seeing her near death. A part of me who knew that without Doctor Winston and Doctor Owens's care, she wouldn't be alive.

Life. Death. Church. Sin. It was all too much to consider.

"My life has become much too complicated," I said. "A relationship between us would only end in heartbreak. Our lives are very different. Our beliefs at odds."

"Don't push me away. I don't care about religion. Or what polite rules of society say about how we act. These past months with you have been the best of my life. Every morning I wake up thinking about you. Wondering where you are. If your folks and your brothers are treating you with the love and respect you deserve."

He tried to reach for my hand but I backed away. My heart was splintering into a dozen pieces. If I allowed him to touch me, I'd never let go.

"I see the real Willa MacCarthy." He quickly closed the space between us. "The woman who doesn't shy away from the hard moments in life or its dirty complications. You are the beating heart of this messy body of a city, and I want to be a part of that pulse. Today and every day after."

The knots in my chest tightened. He was so wrong. What he saw was a lie. I wasn't brave. In the bathroom with Molly, I'd proved what a fraud I'd become.

"I've given my word to my parents. What good are we as humans if we can't honor our promises? When I'd agreed to work for Doctor Winston a small part of me understood it would have to come to an end. The same goes for you. I've been avoiding it, but it's time to face the truth."

I clutched my coat around me tighter. The whistle of the wind did its best to gnaw deeper into my skin. I turned away unable to face the pain etched into every line on his beautiful face. "My calling is with the church. In a few weeks, I'll become a postulant. That is my future, Sam."

"No," he argued. "Deep down you know where you belong. It's side-by-side with the doc during the day. Caring for women and children like Simon and Maeve. At night, it's next to me listening to music and dancing under a blanket of stars. Don't turn your back on the life you should have. Be brave enough to open your eyes and see the truth."

I spun back around to face him. "Why does everyone in my life think they know what's best for me? My parents. My brothers. Doctor Winston. Now you. My choices may be limited, but I know what role I must play."

He tore his hands through his pale hair. "Do you hear yourself? What role you have to play? Is that what you plan to do for the rest of your life? Act in a way you believe will please your parents? When are you going to stop lying to yourself? Deep down you know what you are meant to do. I've seen the delight in your eyes when you help the sick and the hungry. You feel your purpose, even if you keep denying it."

"How dare you assume you know what's inside my head," I snapped.

His fists clenched at his sides and he started to pace, kicking up dust around him. "Stop thinking about what everyone in your life wants from you. What do you want, Willa? Will you be satisfied to only teach? When one of those children in your classroom gets hurt, will you be able to step back and let others care for them? Can you picture yourself looking back on your life in twenty years? Will you be proud of what you've become?"

I tried to look everywhere but at the burning fire in Sam's eyes. I wished things could be different. That I could be strong enough to be a doctor. He might be right. In twenty years, I may regret my choices, but I wasn't going to cause my parents any more pain than they'd endured over the years. He may never understand, but it was a sacrifice I was willing to make for them to be happy. To finally forgive me.

I pulled the beautiful stethoscope from my bag and placed it in his hands. "Stay safe up on that bridge."

"Willa, don't."

His pleas faded into the whir of the wind. I didn't dare look back as I raced across the clearing. If I was going to make Sam my past, I had to keep moving toward the Richmond. I had one last stop. Back to Doctor Winston's office where I would leave my bag and any chance of being a physician behind.

CHAPTER TWENTY-NINE

Geary Street
San Francisco, California
February 11, 1937

The sights and sounds of the Richmond District beat around me. I didn't hear any of it. Even though a truck rumbled by, and the butcher and pharmacist continued their same disagreement about FDR and the success of the WPA, I plodded toward my destination.

Sam's arguments filled every element of my body. My head pounded. My fingers twitched. I pushed it all away. Once I arrived at Doctor Winston's, I'd stand as firm as I did with Sam. Like she'd done so many times before, she'd try to talk me out of my decision. She'd wring her hands and arch her brow in her own contemplative way. With all the calm in the world, she'd list the numerous reasons why San Francisco needed another female physician. I'd let her say her piece (I owed her that much) and then retreat home.

A blaze of lights greeted me as I turned the corner. The Geary streetcar hitched at an odd angle on the tracks. Men and women swarmed the empty car. The faint murmur of gasps and cries filled the air. Mothers clutched their children to their sides. Men leaned their heads close together in muffled conversation. The conductor stood a foot away. As he talked to a grim-faced police-man, his arms flailed out to a spot in front of the car I couldn't see.

A creeping chill hiking up my spine warned someone was injured. Clutching my bag, I raced behind the rear of the car and in the direction of the office. A massive crowd made it impossible to reach the entrance. I elbowed past them until the sharp whimpers of a child stopped me. Simon sat on the curb with his legs tucked to his chest. The skin of his kneecaps poked out through the holes in his pants. His focus never veered from the streetcar. I stepped toward the front end and it was hard not to gasp. Laid across the tracks was a body covered in a blood-stained sheet.

Simon's cries rang in my ears.

Maeve? No. What were she and Simon doing here?

As I drew closer, the thrum of my heart slowed. The sheet was too long to cover the body of a child. I turned and called to Simon. He blinked as if seeing me for the first time.

"Miss Willa." He crashed into me with a fierce hug. His entire body quivered. The torrent of his tears soaked my shirt. I pulled back and examined him.

"Are you hurt?"

"No, but she . . . " He broke into a sob again, his words too garbled for me to understand.

A thick-necked police officer approached. "Are you by any chance the boy's sister?"

"No, I'm his friend. Can you tell me what happened here? Is there anyone else hurt? There is a doctor who lives right upstairs. I can fetch her if needed."

His eyes darkened. "Would you mind letting the young man go for a minute so we can talk in private?"

Once I convinced Simon I would return, he let go of me.

The police officer pointed to a spot on the street a few feet away and I followed.

"Miss, I see you're carrying a doctor's bag. Did you work with Doctor Winston?" His eyes flicked to the bloody sheet.

My vision blurred. Blood jackhammered in my ears. My brain couldn't fire quickly enough to process the scene.

The officer continued to ask questions, but I turned and raced up the stairs. My fist pounded against the door over and over. The skin on my knuckles scraped raw as I cried out her name.

"Please answer," I whispered against the door. When I was greeted by nothing but the hushed crowd below, I puddled onto the floor. A sob building deep in my chest dragged its way up my throat and burst from my lips.

A small body crushed on top of me.

"I'm sorry. I'm sorry," Simon cried. "This afternoon the orphanage brought the older kids to the Alexandria Theater over on the next block to see a picture show. It looked familiar and I remembered the lady doc's office was nearby. When the theater went dark, I snuck away from the headmistress. All I wanted was the lady doc to come and see Maeve at the orphanage. Her cough's come back and the doc working there can't fix it. She agreed to come and followed me outside. I raced across the tracks and didn't see the streetcar. She pushed me out of the way, but it was coming too fast."

His sobs thrummed against my chest and together our cries rattled the glass in every window around us.

"Miss." The officer inched up the stairs toward us. "I know this is a shock, but I need you to identify the body before we take her to the morgue."

Simon clung to me. "It's all right. Let me do this and I'll be back."

One by one, I dragged my fingers from his grasp. I made my way onto shaky legs and descended the steps. Two officers met us at the bottom of the stairs and pushed back the crowd.

Men clutched derby hats to their chests in reverence. Ladies twisted their gloved hands. I wanted to scream at them to go away. To go back to their lives where their friends still had a heartbeat, fresh air in their lungs, unlike my mentor and friend who lay still on the ground before me.

The officer who first greeted me nodded to the sheet. "I'll pull it back quickly. All I need from you is a quick yes or no."

This couldn't be happening. It wasn't possible she was gone.

The officer gripped the sheet and tugged it away. Doctor Winston's legs were twisted like a tangled rope. Her left arm bent in an upside down "V." Her voice echoed in my head. "Most likely a left broken tibia and right femur. Deep lacerations to right forearm. Broken collarbone." I forced my gaze to her head. "Fatal blow to right side most likely snapping the neck and causing instant death."

The whole process took fifteen seconds but to me it was like fifteen long days.

Maybe they were wrong. None of them were physicians. They didn't know how to feel for a pulse. Examine for signs of life the way she'd taught me.

Ignoring the blood, I sunk down and laid my head against her chest. I waited for the thrum of her heart against my cheek proving them wrong. I waited one moment and then another. She couldn't be dead. My hands moved over her crushed chest until my fingers rested at the carotid artery. There was no beat under her pale porcelain skin.

The keening cry of a woman rang in my ears. It took me a few seconds to realize the screams of horror were spilling from my own lips.

CHAPTER THIRTY

Geary Street
San Francisco, California
February 11, 1937

My knees gave way and my palms skidded across the ground. Simon threw himself down next to me and his cries shook me to my core. He nestled into the crook of my arm and we rocked back and forth not saying a word.

The officer pulled him away despite my protest. "Sorry, Miss. He's gotta be returned to the orphanage."

Amidst his sobs, I promised I'd come and visit him and Maeve soon.

Simon's cries still rang in my head as I stumbled toward home. The soft-spoken officer from the stairs offered to escort me, but I needed to be alone.

When I walked into the lobby of my building I was hit with the raucous noise of the fiddle tearing across the strings. On the other side of the door, people drank and danced like the world hadn't flipped upside down.

How could they be happy when we'd just lost a precious soul? A fury burned deep inside me. How could God do this? Take away Doctor Winston who only added good to this place? Who'd spent her entire life sacrificing her own needs to help others? It didn't make sense that she was gone when there were so many awful things happening in the world.

My foot hovered over the first step on the stairs. It would be impossible to press a smile to my face and convince everyone I'd been the perfect well-behaved girl they'd expected me to be today. I was no longer that girl. Over the last months, I couldn't see the change, but Sam, Paddy, Doctor Winston, they'd all recognized what I'd refused to acknowledge.

Voices filtered out from the apartment. As my house key untumbled the lock, the door flew open.

"Where have you been Wilhelmina MacCarthy?"

Mam clutched my arm and dragged me inside. If I hadn't been so numb, I might have been frightened by the scene that greeted me.

The twins, still covered in flecks of orange paint from their shift, squished next to each other on the loveseat in the front parlor. Paddy and Nick paced behind them. Da sat in the over-stuffed chair across the room. To his left in a chair pulled from the kitchen table was Father Murphy. He tugged repeatedly at his white clerical collar like the room was too warm for his liking, but I think it had much more to do with Mam's brisk tone.

Ice should have shot through my veins at the sight of him, but I didn't care. I understood what was happening. This was my reckoning for the months of lies I'd told. Father O'Sullivan once lectured that we all paid a price for sin and mine was the death of Doctor Winston.

Some may say I was being overdramatic, but wasn't it the truth? If I hadn't returned to the Hooverville and become friends with Simon and Maeve, urged Simon to bring Maeve in for care, Doctor Winston would still be alive.

Mam pointed to a chair in the center of the room.

So, this was to be an interrogation.

I sunk down onto the seat. Da refused to look at me. My

brothers found the cracks in the ceiling and the stains on the rug very interesting.

Mam blew out an overexaggerated breath and paced in front of me. "Your da and Nick left Stellan O'Connor in charge of the pub because Father Murphy said he needed to speak with us all. Apparently, both you and your brother have been keeping secrets. First, Paddy announces he wants to enter the seminary. When we say we're excited for Father Murphy to talk to you again about the convent, a strange look crosses his face because he tells us he's never met you in person!"

I tried not to flinch as her voice rang higher than the guitar being plucked downstairs.

"I demand to know where you've been going these last months at all hours, because I know now it hasn't been to Mass, Confession, or to work at any soup kitchen. And don't you fib to me, especially with Father Murphy here. There's a special place in hell for people who lie while a priest is in their home."

"Perhaps we shouldn't be so rough on the girl, Mary." Da finally looked in my direction. It wasn't anger or disappointment shining from his eyes, but pity mixed with a tinge of sadness like he could feel my pain. It was the same haunting look that covered his face every day since Paddy's accident. A look too reminiscent of those weeks after Maggie died.

"Brennan Ryan MacCarthy, you will not let our daughter get away with this!"

"Look Mam," Paddy started.

"Patrick, I know you had something to do with this. Making up excuses for her. Escorting her to God knows where! You sit there and be quiet as a church mouse or so help me I'll send all you boys from the room."

The vitriol in Mam's voice even made Father Murphy shift uncomfortably in his seat.

"Now," she tugged down on the edge of her white ruffled apron, "should I make introductions? Father Murphy, this is our daughter, Wilhelmina who I suspect will be spending many hours in Confession soon."

The new priest looked like he'd been caught with his hand in the cookie jar. Although he'd done nothing wrong, Mam's direct tone often made even the strongest men squirm.

"Hello," I managed to say in his direction. He half-arched out of the chair and shook my hand. He stopped mid-pump and all the color left his cheeks.

"Miss, is that blood on your fingers?"

He did a cursory scan of me like he expected to find a wound. He wouldn't find anything broken, at least nothing on the outside.

Mam shouldered her way around him. "Is that blood on your cheek?" she gasped.

I didn't need to check a mirror to know there was a thin sheen of Doctor Winston's blood staining my face where I'd leaned down to check her heart. A heart that had been so open. So driven. A heart that allowed me into her life.

Tears burned the corner of my eyes. I should have screamed. Cried. Cursed God for taking Doctor Winston away. That kind of anger required strength. A strength that no longer filled my empty body.

"Yes, I've frequently had blood on my hands lately," I managed to say. "In fact, I've washed skin, tissue, excrement, as well as blood, off in our bathroom."

Mam stumbled back to a nearby chair like I'd struck her.

"You're right. I've not been going to Mass, Confession, or the soup kitchen. The work I've been doing is much more important."

For months, I'd wanted to tell the truth. Share with my parents, the people who were supposed to love me unconditionally, the important lessons I'd learned from Doctor Winston. But every single time I thought I'd found the courage, they'd mention how important the church was to our family. How my commitment to the Sisters of the Sacred Spirit would seal that bond like every past generation.

"After Paddy cut himself, we took him to Doctor Maloy's office. When we arrived we met Doctor Katherine Winston instead."

Father Murphy's mouth formed into a thin line. "A female?"

"A very competent female." My voice rattled with both anger and pain. "I helped her care for Paddy's wounds. After Nick left us, she offered me a job to assist her at her clinic and at the field hospital set up over near the bridge."

The twins wrung their hands and looked at the ceiling trying, and failing, to make themselves invisible.

"Boys, did you know what your sister was doing?" Mam asked.

"Well," Sean hedged.

"We did," Michael's shoulders snapped back. "You should have seen her at work, Mam. She splinted a bridge man's broken wrist in less than a few minutes."

"It was a sight to behold," Sean added.

"The lot of you have been lying to us then?" Da leaned forward. His narrowed gaze focused on each of the boys.

"You never asked. Is it lying if there wasn't a question?" Michael stopped as soon as Da gave a swift shake of his head.

"Wilhelmina, whose blood is on your cheek?" Mam took a

step closer. She reached out her hand toward my face and then quickly pulled it back.

"It belongs to Doctor Winston. She was hit and killed by a streetcar earlier today." I said the words but they still didn't feel real.

They couldn't be real.

"Willa, no." Paddy sank down beside me. He gripped my fingers, not caring they were covered in someone else's blood. My friend's blood.

"Patrick," Mam's voice wobbled like all the fight drained from her. "What is she saying?"

Nick sank down next to me and nudged Paddy aside. "Tell us exactly what happened."

"She was trying to help a young friend of mine I'd met at the Hooverville near Baker Beach. He darted across the tracks and Doctor Winston pushed him out of the way, but . . ."

My voice shattered like a glass dropped off the ledge of the bar. Nick wound me in close and Paddy followed. Their strong arms were the glue holding together my splintered body.

I'd never be able to close my eyes again and not see the twisted angle of Doctor Winston's legs. The crushing injury to the side of her skull.

Deep sobs rattled in my chest. Even though Paddy and Nick assured me everything would be okay, their words were hollow promises. Nothing would ever be right again. It wasn't just about her death, it was every piece of my life. Medicine. Sam. The people of the shantytown. Nothing in my life made sense anymore. The world had gone mad, and I was quickly following suit.

"Did the lady doctor have a church?" Father Murphy's deep Irish brogue floated across the room. "We are, of course, past last rites but it might be helpful to talk to her close relations. Ease them through the tragedy."

"She didn't attend church," I said. "Medicine was her religion." Mam clucked her tongue but didn't say a word. "She does have a husband, but he's down south working in the Central Valley. I don't know how to reach him."

"Never you mind." Father Murphy's warm smile felt out of place in the cold living room. "I can go down to the morgue and make sure she's looked after until they reach her family." He moved to his feet. "We can have this conversation another time, Mr. and Mrs. MacCarthy. Mother Superior at the convent will understand why you may not want to bring Willa to her now. Considering what has transpired, perhaps she needs another six months of contemplation."

Da shook the Father's hand. "My apologies for my daughter, sir. She is a MacCarthy, and we often have minds of our own." Father Murphy smiled and made his way to the door.

"Wait," I said. "What time was the meeting supposed to take place?"

"Next Tuesday at the convent. Eleven o'clock sharp," he said.

I scrubbed my hands over my face. "I'll be there."

Paddy rested a hand on my shoulder. "It can wait. Give yourself time to mourn."

"No, I made Mam and Da a promise. These last few months I've selfishly chosen my own wants and needs over what was expected of me. Look where that's gotten me. My friend is dead. The best thing to do is keep my word. Perhaps I need a life of quiet reflection to repent for what I've done."

Da shook his head and followed Father Murphy out the door. Mam stood frozen in place. Her gaze never moved from the bloody stain marring my cheek. My parents' look of disappointment cut into me, but what sliced the deepest was the pain in Paddy's eyes. Months ago on the street I'd allowed that look to cloud my judgment, but I knew better now. The only life I deserved was one committed to God. Perhaps my parents had known best all along.

CHAPTER THIRTY-ONE

Convent of the Sisters of the Sacred Spirit
San Francisco, California
February 16, 1937

Late last night I couldn't ignore the knock at the door and quiet whispers. Through a series of inquiries and telegrams, Father Murphy located Doctor Winston's husband. Paddy asked about a burial, but I closed my door, unable to hear the rest of the details.

This morning I walked like I was outside my body. Mam and Da turned down a quiet street and I trailed several steps behind. I did my best to stay invisible these last few days, unable to bear the broken creak in their voices when they had to address me, look at me, acknowledge my lies and months of betrayal.

On the next corner sat a cream-colored building that ran the length of the entire block. To the passerby it may have looked like a grandiose building, but to those in the Irish Catholic community the long narrow building was a place of reverence. A place where young girls went to be brides of Christ. A place where deceptive daughters went to serve out a lifetime of punishment for their lies.

With each step, my breaths sped up. By the time we reached the front door, I was positive my parents could hear my heart knocking against my ribcage.

A nun with a white wimple that covered her entire head and skimmed her shoulders greeted us at the door. The girl, who couldn't have been more than a few years older than me, walked us through a narrow vestibule. Her white dress floated only inches above the floor. Her long pale face reminded me of the angel statues I'd once seen in a cemetery—seemingly content, yet yearning for something more.

When we reached a small seating area, she pointed to a worn upholstered couch and a long bank of high-back chairs. "Please wait here. The Mother Superior is currently with another family. Once she is finished, I will take you in to speak with her." Her voice didn't rise above a faint whisper.

My parents bowed their heads. I couldn't look away as I searched her face for some sign she was happy in this place. That I'd made the right choice. She disappeared around a corner leaving me with too many questions.

Mam and Da kept their heads together. Their whispers were barely loud enough for me to hear.

"Will they want it in an envelope when she arrives? Do we give it to the Mother Superior at the beginning or after they take her away?" Mam asked.

As if my stomach wasn't already in knots, now they had to talk about my dowry. I'd never understood why they had to pay the church when I would be doing their work for free. When I asked about it one day, Mam shooed me off saying it was none of my worry. Cara later told me that without a dowry I would be treated as a charity case within the convent, which was worse than being dirt on the bottom of someone's shoe.

"Willa, please let Da and I do all the talking." Mam's voice wavered in a way I didn't understand. Her face should have bloomed with a smile. Wasn't this what she wanted?

"You need to show the Mother Superior you can be quiet and obedient," she added, clutching her pocketbook between shaky fingers.

Quiet and obedient. Perhaps three months ago I would have described myself that way, but my time at the Hooverville with Sam, and the hours spent with Doctor Winston, taught me to be curious and outspoken. How did I tuck all that back inside me again?

The pin-drop silence of the room gave me my answer. I'd been told by Father O'Sullivan that once I became a postulant I wasn't allowed to question the rules. That my one and only job would be to serve God and the people of the community without hesitation.

Exhaustion wound its way through my bones. I pinched the skin on my arm to stay alert. Every time sleep descended, images of the off-kilter streetcar and Doctor Winston's mangled body flickered across my mind like a silent film. No words, only the slow action of the officer pulling back the sheet. The scream jammed deep down in my throat.

I clutched the corners of the chair and willed back my tears. At least I found solace in the fact that Paddy had gotten word to Doctor Owens about treating Maeve. Before we left the apartment today, he sent word that she had a mild case of bronchitis and would only have to be treated for a short time. All I could hope was that Sam would check up on her and Simon and make sure they were all right.

The door behind us creaked and the young novice appeared again.

"Mother Superior will see you now."

My parents led the way down a tiled corridor. When we reached the end, the novice knocked once and then pushed open the heavy oak door. Seated behind the desk was the Mother Superior. A long dark habit including both the coif and veil covered her entire head and hung down to her shoulders. On a thin cord around her neck hung a simple wood cross. Her black tunic hugged her thick shoulders and swooped down to cover her forearms and hands. Cara's sisters once told me part of the requirement of being a nun was concealing your hands when they weren't in use for work or prayer.

"Come in please." Her voice was quiet like the novice's but had a tinge of only what I could call serenity. Her warm brown eyes held no judgment or preconception. She swept out from around the desk. "Wilhelmina," her eyes narrowed, "or do you prefer Willa?"

"Won't the church give her another name soon?" Mam asked.

"Something about you says, Willa. We'll call you that. For now." Mother Superior's cheeks bunched into a wide, welcoming grin.

I already liked this woman.

She waved to the three simple wood chairs in front of her desk. "Let's get started. Many fine girls to see today."

She began by telling us about the history of the convent and the number of postulants they took in each year. Mam fiddled with the brass clasp on her pocketbook, her gaze glancing my way every few minutes. I sat upright in the chair. The carved wood gnawed into the skin on my back. The walls inched in closer. The books in a nearby shelf seemed to squeeze together. A crucifix on the wall loomed larger by the second. I closed my eyes and tried to settle myself. This place would be my home soon. Mrs. Boyle's sister had learned to love her convent. I hoped I could eventually do the same. At this point, there was no turning back. I had to accept my fate no matter how much my heart ached for Sam, and my mind screamed to get up and run.

"Let's talk about expectations." Mother Superior's voice rose like she knew my mind was somewhere else. "Upon arrival, Willa will bring nothing but a small suitcase. Her street clothes will be turned in immediately and she will be required to wear a postulant dress and habit. Her clothes will be donated to the poor. Once her training begins, she will not venture outside the mother house for six months. You may see her on Visiting Sundays if you wish, but for her first five years of service she will not be allowed to return home. Marriage, birth, death, none will be considered an acceptable reason for her to leave."

Da shifted in his chair. His fingers clenched the worn brown hat in his lap. I couldn't help but shiver at the haunted look in his eyes. The way he sank deeper in the chair as Mother Superior talked about what would happen once they left me here.

Mam took several deep swallows. The more Mother Superior spoke, the stiffer her shoulders became. I was giving my parents what they wanted. Why did they seem so unhappy?

"Her days will be spent in prayer and learning our ways. At night, she will rest in a small sleeping cell. We observe The Grand Silence after chapel in the evening until it concludes the following morning. When she is in the hallways, she will show deference to the other nuns by walking close to the walls."

With each new rule the knots in my chest tightened. I hadn't realized how much freedom I'd had these last few months. Rising at any time I wanted. Walking the streets of the Richmond. Moving about the field hospital as if I belonged there. My mind would have to be trained in a new way. My life would no longer belong to me but to God.

"Please be aware this is not an easy existence," Mother Superior went on. "You will be submitted to exercises and tests designed to root out your faults, curb your passions, and prepare you for the future. If you question any of our practices, you do not belong here."

She held my gaze as if expecting me to flinch, but I refused to look away. The first step was accepting everything she had to say.

"After six months with us, a congregation of our sisters will meet and decide whether Willa has shown willingness to accept the vows of poverty, obedience, and chastity. If they are in agreement, she will become a novice. A year later, she will receive her vocational assignment."

She tented her hands on the desk. "I'm not going to pretend your parents and Father Murphy have not told me what has transpired these past few months." Mam pursed her lips. "I understand times are changing, but within these walls you must submit yourself fully to our rules. Here you will be expected to live a life of sacrifice. It will be a constant struggle to be obedient. You will be asked to detach yourself from everything and everyone in your past. Memories and objects from your prior existence will have no place here."

Mother Superior moved around the desk and stopped at the wooden crucifix hung on the wall. "Most importantly, you will be expected to destroy your love of self. Before you commit, you must ask if you can let go of old wishes and dreams. Only those who can accept these rules are a success within this mother house."

Her eyes fixed on the image of Jesus splayed out on the cross. My mind immediately went to the wounds in his hands. How much damage the nails would have done to his bones, veins, and arteries. I closed my eyes and willed that door of my mind to close. As much as it ached, medicine could no longer be part of my life.

CHAPTER THIRTY-TWO

Geary Street
San Francisco, California
February 16, 1937

My parents walked several steps ahead of me trading tight whispers. Da turned to make sure I was still following. Where was I going to go?

Once he was assured I was there, he locked eyes with me. That same sad look that had crossed his face over the last few weeks shook me. When we arrived at the pub, Da circled me in a tight embrace. Why was he shaking? Before I could react, he released me and marched inside.

I followed Mam through the lobby door and almost crashed into her back when she stopped short. A man sat on the bottom steps. With nimble fingers, he spun a light brown cap in his hand. A thick layer of dirt covered the tips of his shoes. There was something about the set of his mouth that looked familiar.

"Can I help you?" Mam asked.

"Yes." He stood and looked around her at me. "Are you by any chance Willa?"

Mam shuffled back like a protective shield. "What do you want with my daughter?"

"My apologies. I should have introduced myself. My name is Jack Winston."

The picture on Doctor Winston's desk came to mind. I often found her brushing a thumb across his smile.

"I was told Willa spent a lot of time recently with my wife," his voice cracked. "I was wondering if I might have a minute to speak with her?"

Mam's shoulders quickly drooped. I reached for her hand. "Please Mam, I'd like to talk with him."

Instead of arguing, she gave my hand a squeeze and slowly mounted the stairs.

"Would you like to take a walk Mr. Winston? It can get noisy in here with the pub just on the other side of the door."

He scratched a hand through his hair. Doctor Winston was right. It was a shade darker than coal.

"After you, and please call me Jack."

We walked slowly down Geary. The district went about its everyday business. On the corner, Mr. Abner straightened the signs for Lucky Strike cigarettes and Ivory Soap outside the pharmacy. Next door, Mr. Reardon set out fresh loaves of soda bread in the window. A cool February breeze blew in from the ocean. From the looks of it all, it could have been a normal Tuesday, but both of us understood nothing about this day was typical.

"I won't pretend I was a great husband." He thumbed a worn spot on the pocket of his trousers. "Katherine always had her own way." His shoulders hung low as if saying her name was a crushing blow. "That's why I loved her so much. She was an equal to me, but I didn't tell her that enough. I considered us partners, not just a couple. We had plans, you know, to build a little place near Lands End when I came back." He scrubbed a hand over his weary mouth. "When I left to find work, I wasn't the kindest man. She brushed it off though. Told me she loved and believed in me. It's sad how pride often gets in the way of the things that matter most."

We continued down the sidewalk, letting silence fill the space between us. "I know you brought her joy these past months. She'd send me letters, tell me how quickly you were progressing. That the future of medicine looked bright if more girls like you took an interest in it." He kicked at a loose rock in front of us. "I gotta admit I was pretty unhappy at first when she told me about the money she'd set aside for your schooling. How she'd already talked to the dean about securing a spot for you at the college."

My footsteps stuttered and I stumbled into a bench in front of the apothecary.

"Miss Willa, are you all right? You're awfully pale. Should I run inside and fetch you some water?"

"No, I'm fine. I just need a minute," I said, crumpling down onto the bench.

He shook his head and shoved his hands into his pockets. "Something tells me Katherine never said a word about the money or the schooling."

The words jammed into my throat.

No.

Thank you.

She was the finest woman I'd ever known.

None of them fit what I really wanted to say. How she'd shown me more care and kindness than my own mam these past months. How poorly I'd treated her the last time we were together.

"Katherine did have a knack for keeping things close to the chest until she thought it was the right time. She fancied herself to be a bridge across a broken shore. If she saw someone in need, she wanted to be their lifeboat. Their path to safety. That's what she did for me."

He sank down next to me and his shoulders shook in a way I understood.

"I started a job on a building near Masonic in late 1926. One day a riveter missed his shot, and I got hit with a hunk of metal right here." He lifted his cap to reveal a scar a half-inch below his hairline. "My buddies took me to the hospital up near Golden Gate Park. Doc there started stitching me up. Half way through, this gorgeous woman barrels her way around the table and starts asking all these questions. Never quite believed in love at first sight until then." He pulled down the brim of his cap. "After that day, I found every reason possible to walk by that hospital hoping I'd bump into her. Never happened. Thought it wasn't meant to be. Then a few months later, I got myself cut on a piece of steel. Went back to the same hospital and lo and behold who walks in to stitch me up? Katherine."

He rubbed at a thin scar on the pad of his thumb. "Have you ever been so drawn to someone your mind gets jumbled and you can't form sentences? That merely the sight of them yanks the breath right out of your chest?" He shifted back on the bench and kicked out his feet. "Katherine, she sure scrambled my brain." He swiped at his eyes with the back of his hand.

He might as well have been explaining my feelings for Sam word for word.

"I'm sorry for your loss." I sniffled. "If it helps at all, she spoke about you often. Her love for you was clear."

"Thank you," he said. "That's enough about me. I came to find you because I need to see out Katherine's wishes." He pulled an envelope from his jacket pocket. "Found this in the drawer in our room. It gives all the details about the money for your undergraduate schooling and the dean you should speak to at the medical school when the time comes."

My eyes filled with tears, looking at my name written in her clean, neat script on the outside of the envelope.

"I can't take it."

"Why not?"

"Because I'm not going to be a doctor." His brows drooped in confusion. "All along I explained to Doctor Winston that I had an obligation to my family. Next week, I'm joining the Sisters of the Sacred Spirit. Keep the money. Perhaps donate it to another woman who wants to be a physician."

"No, she was very clear it had to be you." He scratched a hand through his hair. "That's what she meant in her last telegram," he mumbled under his breath. He shoved to his feet. "Can you please follow me, Willa. There's something I need to show you."

"I really should head back home."

"Please, there's something important at the office I think Katherine would want you to see."

The sound of her name made my body ache. While I wanted to turn around, head for home, and try to forget my living nightmare, there was no way I could refuse him.

I trailed him for several more blocks and stopped at the corner. The spot where Doctor Winston's body once laid was back to nothing but steel rail lines.

"What is it?" he asked.

"Her body, it was right there. About five feet from the track."

"I know," he said too quietly before directing me inside.

I couldn't handle the silence that greeted us. There should have been a line of patients waiting along the back wall. Doctor

Winston should have been rushing between the two exam rooms, smiling and easing the worries of the people under her care.

"Seems wrong to be here without her," I said.

"I remember how proud she was when she bought this place. How she had all these plans to rent out the extra space to other tenants. Even take on a partner one day."

He yanked open drawers in her desk. When he didn't find what he was looking for he went to the bookcase. Running his fingers along the spines, he stopped at a red leather-bound book. Once it was in his hands, he flipped to the center page. He turned the book to face me. Tucked inside were two pieces of expensive parchment.

"Oh Katherine." He looked to the heavens. "Always the sharpest tack in the room." He handed me the papers. "Go on, read them."

The university insignia covered the tops of the pages. Was this private correspondence? I folded the papers quickly and handed them back to him. "I shouldn't read her personal papers. She wouldn't like it."

He pushed them back at me. "If she was standing here right now, she would tell you it's important."

I sank onto the lumpy sofa and scanned them. Line after line, my stomach twisted. This couldn't be right.

Jack sat down beside me. "I'm the only one she ever told. She couldn't believe with all her smarts and schooling, they turned her down from the medical school. Twice."

"She never said a word."

"Of course not. It was hard enough for women to get into the program. The last thing she wanted to do was let anyone know it'd taken her close to three years to do it."

"Why are you sharing this with me?"

"In her last telegram, she mentioned wanting to show these to you. She believed that if you wanted a dream bad enough, you should stop at nothing to achieve it."

"Even from the grave, she's still trying to convince me my choice is wrong," I said. "But this is different. It's more than wanting a dream. It's generations of tradition. I have no right to change things now." I thrust the papers back in his direction.

"Just like Katherine, you will come across many roadblocks in your life. Learn from her, push back, take what's meant to be yours. Don't wait until it's too late."

He turned back to the desk and rummaged through a drawer. The lines around his mouth tightened.

"What's wrong?" I asked.

"She always had a silver pen on her desk. It was my wedding gift to her."

"Yes, I've seen it. She used it to sign medical papers at the field hospital near the bridge. She was always misplacing it. Perhaps she left it behind on our last visit."

He wasn't listening to me. His gaze swept over the room and stopped at the frame housing her medical degree. He slumped into the chair and crashed his head against his arms.

"She's really gone, isn't she?" His pained voice echoed through the room.

"Yes, again I'm so sorry. Please, let me return to the hospital tomorrow and retrieve her pen. I know she'd want it returned to you."

"Thank you." He faced me with red-rimmed eyes. "If you reconsider Katherine's offer, please let me know. She believed in you, Willa. No matter what happens, never forget that."

Once outside, I leaned back against the door and swallowed down my sobs. That day after Mrs. Cleery gave birth Doctor Winston talked about legacy and the importance of making your mark in the world. I couldn't help but think if she could see the choices I was making, she'd say her belief in me was sorely misplaced.

CHAPTER THIRTY-THREE

Golden Gate Bridge Field Hospital
San Francisco, California
February 17, 1937

Bribery always worked with the twins. Early this morning after Mam went to her sewing circle, and the older boys went to open the pub with Da, I talked Sean and Michael into driving me to the bridge. They ignored my pleas until I told them I'd convince Nick to give them more time behind the bar.

I hunched down in the backseat as they talked their way past the guard at the gate. When we were finally through, they warned I better not get caught. They grumbled on about punishment, and getting an earful of grief from Mam and Da, before they went on their way to work.

Standing at the top of the access road, memories of my first day here filled my head. How the hammering of the heavy equipment rang in my ears. The confidence in Doctor Winston's stride as she guided me down the narrow path, ignoring the catcalls and whispers of the passing workmen.

It still shot a shiver through my bones to see the mammoth structure spanning the Golden Gate. How the bright orange suspension cables wavered in and out of the mist. It was hard not to look at the bridge and wonder if Sam was somewhere close. If he thought about me as endlessly as I dreamed about him.

Once inside the hospital, I tried to ignore the pointed gazes from the nurses and physicians. A few were brave enough to offer their condolences. The rest opted to keep their distance.

A bank of long tables at the rear of the field hospital was crammed with stacks of paperwork. I shuffled through mounds of files searching for Doctor Winston's pen.

Francie walked toward me. "Willa, did you lose something?"

"I'm looking for Doctor Winston's silver pen. Have you seen it?" Her eyes clouded over. "It's not been stolen. I promise."

Looking unconvinced, she followed me to another desk near the back of the hospital. For over an hour, we moved side-by-side, turning over every file and pushing aside chin-high stacks of paperwork.

"I take it you won't be returning to work here?" she said.

"No, I can't, not without . . . "

"Her," she finished. "That's a shame. You both shook up this place."

We continued to move down the bank of tables. "You will continue your studies though. Become a physician like Doctor Winston?"

When I didn't reply, she went quiet. At the final table, I swiped my hand over a stack of books and the pen rolled out from underneath. As I was about to slide it into my pocket, shouts and screams filled the air outside.

Doctors and nurses scrambled out the door. Francie and I weren't far behind. A doctor next to us pointed at pieces of scaffolding crashing into the dark, churning water.

Francie stopped a bridge worker racing by. "What happened?"

"Looks like a stripping scaffold under the roadway deck near the center of the main span gave way. Bunch of men slid off and went into the net. Weight of the scaffold pitched forward and broke off. It toppled onto the men and dragged them and the net down into the water. Not sure there are any survivors."

Scaffold. Net.

I sprinted down the rocky path past the fence separating the bridge from the waiting workmen. At the edge of the wharf, I scanned the water. The roar of the black waves drowned out my screams as I called for Sam. I paced the shore. Sirens filled the air. Ambulances arrived at the hospital. Minutes later the road was filled with policemen and press.

The Coast Guard circled the area where the net went down. This couldn't be happening. The bridge was supposed to be the safest worksite ever created. The net itself had already saved the lives of nineteen men.

I continued to scream for Sam over my sobs. Policemen walked the shore swapping whispers about body count. Flashbulbs sparked in quick succession around me. One reporter approached and began to ask questions. I pushed him out of the way and continued to search the water for signs of life.

Frenzied shouts filled the air as a boat moved into shore. A crab fisherman called for help. Men waded into the water removing two people from the deck. One man they called Slim was still alive. The other worker named Fred was unconscious. Whispers among the men said twelve went into the water.

Twelve men.

I whispered prayers under my breath. Dirt filled my shoes as I stumbled back toward the hospital. Another death. I couldn't breathe. I couldn't think. Sam understood me in a way nobody else in my life could, and I'd pushed him away. I'd never have the chance to tell him how I really felt. That I wished things had been different between us.

My legs gave way and I crumpled onto the rocky ground. Was this more punishment? I wasn't sure how much more I could take.

"Willa?" Sean and Michael raced toward me and circled me in a hug.

"Thank goodness you two are all right. Have you seen Sam? Is he alive?"

"Last time we saw him the foreman was asking him to work on the platform," Sean said. "We're sorry. We think he was one of 'em that went in."

Their embrace tightened around me. My body shook so hard my teeth rattled. Footsteps sounded around us.

"Men, can you tell me what happened out there?"

A reporter stood inches away with a notepad in hand.

"We're not talking," Sean growled.

"Miss, what about you? What are you doing out here?"

"Listen fella," Michael barked. "We told ya, we ain't talking."

The man splayed out his hands in surrender and crept away.

"Are they all dead?" I managed to ask.

"Don't know yet," Sean whispered.

The boys held me tight. Even with their combined heat, the wind off the water bit into my skin.

"Let's get you home," Michael said.

"No. I need to go back to the field hospital. They could use my help."

"Will, but Mam and Da," Sean said.

"I don't care. There are men hurt. Sam could be . . ." my voice trailed off. I couldn't allow myself to fall to pieces. Not here. Not now. In life, I'd disappointed Doctor Winston. I wouldn't do the same in death.

The shouts of the policemen rang in my ears as they gave

orders to search the shore. Pops and cracks from cameras filled the air. I moved toward the hospital unable to think about anything but helping the injured. It was the only thing keeping me from crumpling down onto the ground again.

I took a few more steps. My name lifted on the wind. "Come back," Michael called.

I spun around ready to argue. There was no use in going home. It was nothing but a reminder of everything I'd risked and lost.

A familiar figure walked the shore toward us. Tossing down my coat, I took off. Heavy dirt and wet sand seeped into my shoes and caked the hem of my skirt but I didn't care.

Before he could say a word, I flung myself into Sam's arms. "You're alive!"

He pulled back and searched my face. I didn't need an answer or an explanation. All I wanted was the feel of his lips on mine to prove he was real. My mouth was on his and my bones went to liquid as he returned my kiss. I wanted to drink him in. Feel the beat of his thrumming heart against my chest. Be assured he was not a figment of my troubled imagination but real flesh and blood.

He wound me into his heat and deepened his kiss. His hands tore through my braid until my hair flew out in all directions like a flickering flame. I wasn't sure how it was possible, but I was crying and laughing all at once. The roar of the waves behind us not long ago was a death knell but now it was a reminder of the fragility of life.

His mouth moved to my ear. Sweet reassurances whispered he was all right. That he wasn't down at the bottom of that cold sea but right here with me. I melted deeper into him not wanting to let go.

Behind us there was movement. I was ready to yell at my

brothers when a sharp *pop* sounded behind us. A cameraman and the nosy reporter stood only feet away.

"Word in the hospital is you're a doc too." The reporter continued to scratch at his notepad. "Shouldn't you be up there helping?

"I'm not a doctor. Just a—" I stopped short not sure what I really was.

"Mark my words, she will be a doc one day," Sam replied.

Before the reporter could ask any more questions, Sam guided me toward my brothers. Michael and he exchanged a firm nod. Sean focused on a deep cut on Sam's hand.

"Do I want to know?" I asked.

He simply shook his head.

"Willa, why don't you take him inside? If anyone knows how to fix him up, it's you," Michael said.

I hesitated, not sure I'd heard him right.

"They're sending us home. We'll cover with Mam and Da," Sean added. "Go on. Head back to the hospital. It's where you belong."

I wrapped them both in an embrace, grateful they believed in me.

"Make sure she gets home safe, Butler," Michael said, pulling Sean away. Together, they headed slowly back up the access road.

I wound my hand around Sam's arm and directed him toward the hospital not caring that his blood stained my fingertips. It was a sight I'd gotten used to by now.

CHAPTER THIRTY-FOUR

Golden Gate Bridge Field Hospital
San Francisco, California
February 17, 1937

"First, there was a scream. Then there was a sharp *ping, ping* as the net came apart at the outriggers. Men tried to scale up the side as fast as they could, but the weight of the platform was too much and it dragged them down into the water. Those fellas never had a chance."

Goosebumps covered my skin as a weary bridge man explained the accident to a policeman. The officer's thick hands flew over the pages of his notebook as other workers added their own details about the grisly event.

Pure chaos did not accurately explain the scene inside the hospital. Nurses and doctors rushed about treating workers who were clearly in shock. A thick-necked officer near the door kept out the prying eyes of the press.

"Only one death and now this tragic accident." Doctor Fairchild sighed as he examined the two-inch laceration on Sam's hand. When he caught my eye, he waved me in closer. "Might as well come work. I assume Doctor Winston has shown you how to close a wound like this."

"Yes sir," I replied, but I couldn't force myself to move.

"Well, what are you waiting for? I watched you work with Doctor Winston. I know you're capable."

I swapped a quick glance with Sam. After the way I'd treated him, I'm not sure he wanted me pressing a steel needle through his skin.

A slow smile lifted his lips. "Come on, Willa. I'm bleeding here."

I switched places with Doctor Fairchild and he pointed to where I needed to put the first stitch. Hearing Doctor Winston's voice in my head, encouraging me to keep my hand steady, I went to work. While not perfect, my path of stitches looked clean. Even my mam wouldn't be able to deny the precise detail in each knot. Her hours of lessons paid off in a way I'd never imagined.

"Excellent job," Doctor Fairchild said. "Think Doctor Winston would be proud. Go on and wrap it in a clean dressing." He sucked in a deep breath and his mouth drooped. "I must apologize to you, Miss MacCarthy." His gaze ticked around the row of cots. His staff worked at a furious pace trying to calm the sick and steady the worried frenzy in the small room. "You and Doctor Winston did much good here. I was wrong to have judged you both so harshly." He ran a hand over his mustache. "I hope that even though the doctor is gone, you will still consider a career in medicine."

By the pained expression on his face, I understood that by allowing me to help he was honoring her. He bowed his head and went to check on a nearby patient.

The look of sadness in Sam's eyes was too much, and I rushed to grab some clean dressings. When I returned, I couldn't meet his gaze. Instead, I focused on placing each loop through his fingers. I felt Doctor Winston's presence like she was guiding me, reminding me not to wrap the hand too tight. Even though she was gone, her words would stay with me every single day.

For the next few hours I worked side-by-side with Doctor Fairchild until the last of the workers were treated. Carlo offered Sam and me a ride home. When we reached the entrance to Sea Cliff, Sam asked him to stop.

"Thanks, Carlo. We'll walk from here."

He grabbed my hand and pulled me out onto the street. We moved in silence up 25th Avenue until he let out a low, weary breath.

"The accident happened real quick. One moment I was talking to a few other workers on the deck, the next the stripping scaffold and the net below the roadway were gone. There was one piece of the net I tried to grab a hold of, but a loose nail protruding from a board sliced through my hand, and I had to let go." His shoulders sank and his voice was as brittle as glass. "There was nothing I could do to help those men. In the blink of an eye they were lost to that black, unforgiving water."

Even though we were in the middle of the street in broad daylight, I pulled him into an embrace. I didn't care who saw us. I needed to prove to myself again that he was real.

"I read about Doctor Winston in the paper. Willa, I'm so sorry," he whispered into my hair.

His quiet murmurs splintered my heart. I still couldn't believe she was gone.

When I didn't reply, he pulled back and took a long look at me. "This is not on you any more than your sister's death was your fault. It's like what happened today at the bridge. Some things are out of our hands." He pulled me in close. The steady beat of his heart was a sweet symphony to my ears.

"I've seen people do some pretty selfish things in my life. Take unnecessary risks. Hang off trains as they sped faster than seventy miles an hour. Pick fights with lads twice their size after finishing off a bottle of whiskey. Those are people who take thoughtless risks and suffer the consequences of their choices," he said. "That broken scaffold. Your sister's death. What happened to Doctor Winston. They were all simple twists of fate."

While I appreciated Sam's kind words, I didn't believe him. Although many people tried to convince me I wasn't to blame for my sister's death, it didn't make the pain in my mother's eyes go away every time she looked at me. It didn't erase my father's hesitation before he mounted the stairs to our apartment every night after he closed the pub. The weight of the past heavy on his shoulders as he sidestepped the old blood stain on the floor. A constant and heart-wrenching reminder of that terrible day.

Death left a black mark on those it touched. Whether or not there was blame to be passed around, it didn't remove the sorrow that haunted the edges of everyone's lives. Once Maggie was gone, grief became the eighth member of the MacCarthy clan. Even in the happiest of times, its dark pall hovered over our family.

When we reached the corner before my street, Sam stopped. "No matter what choice you make, the convent or medicine, I want you to know you've changed my life. Before you, I thought I wanted a solitary existence. No attachments. No family. But watching you with your brothers, spending time with Simon and Maeve, it's shown me I want more." He reached for my hand and his steady gaze locked on me. "What you said about me running away, showing Simon I was another person in his life who would disappear, was right. I don't want to be that kind of man." His warm touch tightened around my fingers. "I saw Benny last night. Told him I was staying in San Francisco. That my rambling life was over."

"That could not have gone over well," I said.

He shrugged. "I think he knew it was coming, especially after that stunt he pulled with you."

"Sam, I don't know what to say. I care about you, but I've also made a promise to my family. I feel split in two. My obligation to my parents. My desire to be a doctor. I can't have them both."

"In the church isn't there something like a calling? A sense of what you are supposed to do?"

"That can happen sometimes. I've asked God for a sign. When I was working for Doctor Winston I thought it was a sign that I was doing right. But with her gone, I realize I was wrong."

"Are you sure about that?"

"What do you mean?"

"This sign, is it supposed to be something that hits you all of a sudden like lightning or is it gradual?"

"I don't know."

He inched in closer, his clear blue eyes pinning me in place. "Could it not be that all that's happened—meeting Doctor Winston, working at the field hospital, encountering Simon and Maeve, it's all a way of placing you on the right path?"

The bells in the distance chimed. An eerie reminder that I needed to head home.

I placed my hand to Sam's cheek. "What you say may be true, but I've made my choice. Today, treating those men, the grief and horror on their faces was heartbreaking. After Cara left for New York, I saw that same pain and grief in my mother's eyes. She's already been through so much. Please understand that it would break me if I hurt her again."

"But Willa," he started to protest until I pressed a finger to his lips.

"These past months with you have been wonderful. Your stories have allowed me to travel to places I never imagined: Texas. Arizona. Alaska. Even within the walls of the convent, those will be memories I can cherish always. Thank you for giving me such a beautiful gift."

He tugged me in tighter to his chest. "Stay with me," he begged.

"Goodbye, Sam."

I placed a kiss against his cheek and breathed him in one last time.

CHAPTER THIRTY-FIVE

MacCarthy Residence
San Francisco, California
February 18, 1937

Golden rays of light streamed in through the window. I stayed hidden beneath the covers lost in my thoughts about what transpired yesterday. I closed my eyes hoping sleep would rescue me from seeing the net fall into the water. The shocked men in the hospital. The way Sam insisted Doctor Winston had been my sign. How his body shuddered when I gave him my final kiss goodbye.

Voices in the hallway began as quiet whispers but quickly turned into frenzied shouts. I slid on my robe and slippers and braced myself for whatever was happening in the parlor.

My parents sat in the worn armchairs near the window. All four of my brothers stood behind them assembled like a firing squad. In the center of the room, his face positioned in an ugly glare, was Father O'Sullivan. Father Murphy flanked his side. Cara's parents hovered close by. When I entered the room, Mrs. Reilly grasped Mam's hand.

What was going on?

"Wilhelmina," Father O'Sullivan barked out, scanning my dressing robe.

What did he expect? It was eight o'clock in the morning.

"I returned from the Central Valley last night. Imagine my dismay when I received a frantic phone call at the seminary this morning from your parents."

He pulled a folded-up newspaper out from underneath his arm. "Would you like to explain why your face is splashed all over the cover of the *San Francisco Chronicle*?" He snapped the paper inches from my eyes. In black and white type the headline read "The Girl and the Gate." Below it was a picture of my embrace with Sam.

"That picture is an embarrassment not only for your parents, but for your entire family. I can't imagine the Mother Superior will tolerate this kind of behavior from a young woman who wants to join her convent."

What was he expecting me to say? That I was sorry? I wasn't. I'd grappled all night with the outcome of my actions. Had it been wrong to lie to my parents for months? Yes, but couldn't that be reasoned out with all the good I'd done with Doctor Winston? The treatment and care I'd given to the injured yesterday at the hospital? Didn't God want us to care for our fellow man? Treat him with compassion and kindness in times of sickness?

"Wilhelmina, can you explain this?" Mam's broken voice sliced into me sharper than a scalpel cutting flesh.

Before I could answer, Paddy moved out from behind my parents and stood by my side. Nick, Michael, and Sean followed like dutiful soldiers. Together they stood as a force facing my parents.

"The four of us have spoken at length about this," Paddy started. "We respect you Mam and Da, but we all agree you can't keep doing this to Willa."

"Doing what?" Father O'Sullivan huffed. "Expecting her to act like a respectable young woman?"

"Expecting her to be someone she's not!" Nick's growl sent Father O'Sullivan stumbling back. Father Murphy caught him before he hit the ground.

"Mam. Da. Have you read the article?" Michael shoved his spectacles up the bridge of his nose. "All those doctors and nurses, they talk about how much Willa's helped at the bridge's field hospital. Cuts. Broken bones. You should be proud."

I double-blinked and did my best to stay upright as each of them continued to plead my case. Who were these men and what had they done with my bossy, overbearing brothers? If I wasn't so terrified of what my parents would do next, I would have embraced them all on the spot.

"Proud?" Mam twisted her hands in her lap, avoiding the judgmental gaze of Father O'Sullivan. "No self-respecting woman trots about amongst those kinds of men, all alone with blood and grime. A proper young lady does not lie to her parents every single day about where's she's been. Who she's spending her time with unbeknownst to her family. I will not allow her to become one of those young women in our parish who runs off and ruins their lives."

The words crushed all the light within her, and I wasn't sure I could stand here and watch her crumble.

Mrs. Reilly shook off Mam's hand. "Mary, watch what you're saying. We may have been upset about Cara leaving, but we're proud of her now. She's working in the chorus of a show and loving New York. At first, we hated the thought of her being so far away, but we came to realize she needed to live her own life if she was going to be happy." Mrs. Reilly's soft gaze landed on me. "I'd say the same thing holds true for Willa."

The boys continued to grumble under their breath. Father O'Sullivan tapped his foot impatiently. Like all the other times in my life, people spoke about me like I was a phantom in the room. An apparition floating about with the inability to be seen or heard.

As much as I'd fought it, there was no denying the warmth that filled my soul every time I stepped over the threshold of Doctor Winston's office. How that heat turned icy when I pictured the cold hallways of the convent. How I'd slid Paddy's fingertips into my pocket that day, forcing me to return to the office. The fear and wonder of watching baby George come into the world. Everything led to this moment. To this choice. My future was laid at my feet. All I had to do was take one final step.

I was tired of being invisible.

Tired of being a ghost.

"Stop!"

The priests gasped and the rest of the room went silent as my roar bounced around the walls of our tiny parlor.

"For years, I've sat idly by and let people tell me what my place was in this world. No one ever let me forget I should be a dutiful daughter. A helpful sister. Not once in all my eighteen years has anyone in this family asked me what I want to do with my life."

I knelt in front of my parents. They were the only ones I owed an explanation.

"The day Maggie died I felt your pain, Mam." She shook her head and crumpled against Da. Her sorrow was still so raw it floated off her in a heavy anguished wave. I wrapped her fingers in mine and took a long, strangled breath "Along with you, Da, and the boys, I understood how much having another sibling meant to this family. And when she was gone, I cried too."

Da let out a small sob and I curled his fingers in my free hand. I clung to my parents hoping they'd understand me.

"These past years I've hidden myself away. Tried to find solace in church. Guidance in prayer. But none of it mattered because guilt has stripped me of who I am. Who I want to be. I'm tired

334

of being a shell of a soul. I want to have a voice. To finally come out into the light and be a person who helps this community. A person you can look upon with pride.

"I've been telling myself that I have no right to be a doctor. That the only way I can earn your forgiveness is by going to the convent. But I think we all know I don't have it in me to be obedient. To turn away from this family and my one true calling."

Tears slid down Mam's face. Da's shoulders trembled. A pain I never understood until recently untethered within me.

"I'm sorry about the stairs. The accident. Please understand, working with the sick, being able to fix their wounds, it's filled a hole in me that's been deepening since that dark, terrible day."

I turned to the two priests. Pity spilled from their eyes. "You deliver sermons all the time about God's purpose for us. I often hear you preach that there's a reason why we grace this world. Why can't my reason be medicine?"

The long years of grief haunted my mother. It could be seen in the lines around her mouth, the stoop of her shoulders. The way she often looked at me as if I was a living, breathing reminder of all she'd lost. Those doctors in the hospital advised her to move on with her life, but a child's death was a mark on the soul. A wound so deep even the march of time couldn't erase it. Watching Mam over these last years was like observing a building falling into disrepair. It did not crumble all at once but eroded slowly one brick at a time.

"Please think about it," I begged. "What if there was a woman like you who was losing her child and I could help save the baby? Wouldn't you want me to be that hand of God in this world? And what about women like Molly Gallagher? No matter the circumstances, doesn't she deserve the best care? Not to be thrown away like trash because she made a mistake?"

Father O'Sullivan's stare burned into me. I refused to acknowledge his disdain. He'd never understand the heartbreak women like Molly had to endure.

Mam dropped her head in her hands. Da wrapped an arm around her shoulder and spoke through a strangled voice. "Our daughter speaks the truth, Mary. It's like I was saying after Willa wrapped up Paddy's hand like a real doctor. It's the same thing we talked about after our visit with Mother Superior. She has something special burning within her. As her parents we need to fan that flame, not be the villains who extinguish it." His voice shook as he took her hand. "The Lord has a way of showing us the right path. Perhaps this is his way of telling us Willa needs to make her own choices."

That day in the pub I was sure Da was disgusted with how I'd tended to Paddy's wounds, but I'd been wrong. All those tender looks. Gentle smiles. That dance at Cara's. He'd been trying to tell me he saw the light within me all along.

Mam's head bobbed once before a sob slid past her lips. "The day I found you in your room with that book, I should have listened. When you walked in here covered in the doctor's blood, I should have understood what you were trying to tell me. Fear stopped me both times," she cried. "Since the day we lost Maggie, I've been terrified every waking moment that something might happen to one of my other children. Deep down I realized that if I lost another child, I would not be able to walk this earth another day. The pain. The grief. It almost broke me last time."

She reached for my chin and tilted up my face so we were eye-to-eye. "Your father insisted my determination to send you to the convent had nothing to do with God and everything to do with locking you away some place safe so no harm could ever come to you." Da reached over and lovingly squeezed her arm.

"Watching you stand here on your own two feet, speaking your truth, I realize that while the convent is a good place, it is not the *right* place for you. Your spirit could never be contained there." She placed a hand against my cheek. It was the gentle touch I'd been waiting for these past years. "Please forgive me. The way I've treated you is wrong. I believed if I was firm. Strict. I could keep you from harm, but now I see I was the one causing you pain." Her lower lip wobbled but she pushed on. "It's time to put Maggie to rest and allow you, and all of your brothers, to live your own lives."

The priests bowed their heads and stayed immobile in the corner of the room. I folded Mam into my arms as my brothers and Da crowded around us. Together, we finally mourned the missing member of our family. It wasn't the final suture in a long open wound, but it was the first step in the long process of healing our family.

When I stepped into Doctor Winston's office that day in October I never expected it to lead here. It would take time for my parents to understand how much medicine meant to me, but I was willing to take that long walk if it ended in a place where they'd finally accept me.

EPILOGUE

The Golden Gate Bridge
San Francisco, California
May 27, 1937

Six o'clock in the morning was much too early for a parade. Even the fog seemed displeased with the early hour, grasping and tugging on the bridge with all its mist-driven might.

Men, women, and children packed the long road leading up to the bridge. Sean and Michael arrived before us and stood further up the road doing their best to get a good look at Joseph Strauss, who'd arrived only minutes earlier. They deserved to take their place alongside the Golden Gate's visionary creator and all the other men who'd toiled these past four years on the bridge.

"You should really go stand with the rest of the men." I encouraged Sam to move up the bridge. "After all, you've been here for both the pleasure and pain of seeing this project come to life."

"Why bother when there is a much better view right here." He circled his hands around my waist and planted a sweet kiss against my cheek.

Since that late April day when they'd driven the final rivet, he'd done everything in his power to find work in the city. Last week, through the help of a local union superintendent, he'd secured a job on a new office building being erected downtown.

After my face was splashed across the front of the *San Francisco Chronicle,* I received a final visit from Jack Winston. His face split into a wide grin when I agreed to take the money for college. Days later, my entire family stood by my side as Jack buried Doctor Winston underneath a copse of trees in the Colma cemetery. What felt like the entire medical community crowded in around us. It was a fitting tribute to all she'd done to help the people of San Francisco.

When the service was over, I stayed behind. Standing next to her gravesite, I spoke quietly to Doctor Winston about my plans for the future. I told her the truth about Maggie. How grateful I was that she took a chance on me and pushed me to step out of the shadows. How right she was about me having the heart of a physician. It wouldn't be the last tear I'd shed for Katherine, but deep down I knew wherever she was she'd be pleased I'd finally changed my mind.

Mam appeared at my side and said her own prayer. Her voice was no more than a thin wisp of sound barely heard above the breeze blowing across the cemetery. "Thank you for recognizing all the beauty and intelligence in my child I was too broken to see. While I can never properly show you my gratitude, I hope you know that I will be eternally indebted to you for helping my daughter find her voice."

She squeezed my hand and left me to say my final goodbye. Mam was slowly finding she could speak about Maggie without her entire body shaking. As a family we agreed to no longer hide from her death but remember her as an important part of the MacCarthy line.

"Willa." Paddy tapped my shoulder, pulling me from my thoughts. He pointed to a spot near the bridge's entrance. "Nick and I are going to stay back and wait on Mam and Da."

They were still playing shield for me. Thankfully, with Paddy heading off to the seminary at the end of the summer it'd taken

339

a bit of the attention off my choices. For the first time since the accident, the line of his shoulders weren't tensed. The edges of his mouth frequently softened into a contented smile now. Serving the church was a wonderful calling. Even though it wasn't right for my future, it was the perfect choice for my beloved Paddy.

With prodding from me, and all my brothers, Mam and Da agreed I could attend classes at the University of California, Berkeley in the fall. It was easier to sway them once Nick explained he'd be on campus taking a few finance courses. With Nick gone a few days, and Paddy off to the seminary, Da was forced to give the twins a chance behind the bar. They'd only worked a few shifts, but were quickly proving, much to everyone's surprise, that they were more than capable of running the bar.

The college conversation with my parents was a breeze compared to our talk about my relationship with Sam. About a month ago, after work one evening, Sean and Michael dragged him to the apartment for dinner. Sam quickly won over Da with his tales of rustling cattle in Montana and avoiding alligators in Florida. Mam did her best to be polite, but every chance she could she grumbled under her breath about him being Protestant.

Sam checked his watch. "Only a few more minutes now."

The headlines in the papers called this entire week "The Golden Gate Bridge Fiesta." Today was the beginning of the celebration with what was being termed "The Pedestrian Bridge Walk." From sunup to sundown, the bridge was reserved for the people of San Francisco to stroll along and marvel at its stunning beauty. Tomorrow, Mayor Rossi would arrive at the Marin side of the bridge and cut through a steel chain. Once it was severed, a parade of motorcars would officially open the bridge to traffic.

The crowds moved in closer. In the distance a foghorn blared.

With great revelry, the barriers came down. The ground shook as people clapped their hands and stomped their feet in celebration. Young boys elbowed each other out of the way in a foot race toward midspan. Grown men and women stood in place as if held there by wet concrete. Their jaws hitched down at the marvel promised to them since 1919.

Sam and I walked hand-in-hand along the sidewalk. We stopped every few steps and he pointed out where he'd worked, telling me about the wind, rain, fog, and all the other mishaps that pushed back the men as they did their best to finish this beauty of a project.

When we were close to the center of the bridge, a small hand tugged on my sleeve. Maeve's bright smile lit up the foggy morning. I pulled her up into my arms.

"Where's your family?" She shoved a tiny finger in the direction of a nearby pylon. Simon waved in our direction. Mrs. Cleery chased after him with little George snuggled deep down in a white blanket in her arms.

Thanks to Sam and Mrs. Boyle, Mrs. Cleery was cooking at the boardinghouse. She now shared a room with the children and Mr. Cleery, who traveled back to the city a month ago. Sam used his connections with a local supervisor to get him a union card, which brought him a job and the return of his family.

Simon crushed me in a giant hug. It was the first time in weeks I'd seen him smile. He was still struggling with what happened to Doctor Winston. We both were. Several times I'd caught him on the steps outside the boardinghouse staring into space. It was hard to forget the kind of trauma he'd been through. I understood his guilt and pain and vowed he'd never go through years of torment like I did. With his family back together, I hoped we could all help him heal.

Two girls raced past us on roller skates and Simon pulled Sam along after them. A sweet chirp lighter than a little bird escaped Maeve's mouth when her father whisked her out of my arms and onto his shoulders. He bowed his head in my direction. "Thank you, Miss. I know you and Mr. Butler did a lot for my family. Not sure I can ever repay your kindness."

"Mr. Cleery, I didn't do much."

"Of course you did," he gripped Maeve's tiny hand. "My family was struggling and no one but you wanted to help. People like us, we travel here in pursuit of a better life. I love Ireland, but I understood if I wanted my children to have a future we had to come to America. From the moment we arrived, we walked this city and almost everyone treated us like vermin. That is except for you and the kind lady doc, may God rest her soul."

He gave an adoring glance at his beautiful daughter. "My wife told me you won't be a nun, but I say there's something definitely angelic about you. I'm quite sure the doc would be proud."

I still woke some mornings with a light in my chest. For a blissful minute, I thought I could slide on my shoes and sprint down Geary to ask Doctor Winston about the signs of appendicitis or how to care for a child with croup. When the truth finally hit me, I'd go in search of Paddy and run my fingers over the scars on his hand, remembering that her work, her love for medicine, would live on in every patient she ever touched.

Simon dashed back to us and dragged his family toward a brass band playing a rousing rendition of "God Bless America."

As we strolled along, the wind played a symphony across the suspender ropes my brothers helped to paint International

Orange. Sam and I craned our heads skyward. Dozens of families stood beside us frozen in awe. Below our feet, the bridge swayed. I clutched onto Sam.

"Like I told you before, it's meant to do that. Mr. Strauss and the other engineers knew what they were doing. Hundreds of years from now this bridge will be as solid as it is today."

I'd first seen the towers rising out of the water two years ago. Back then they'd seemed like a dream. A whisper of the future. Over time, cables were spun and the roadway stretched out over the entrance to the bay.

Change was taking place. It was like the day I'd stumbled into Doctor Winston's office clutching Paddy's bloody fingers. Inside I was in pieces and parts like the bridge, but she'd taught me how to connect with the beauty of medicine and what my life was meant to be. She'd made me whole.

I'd never be able to show her my appreciation for all that she'd done for me like the thousands of San Franciscans who walked the bridge today in honor of the brave men's work. All I could do was carry on what she'd taught me. If I could change one girl's life, like she'd changed mine, that would be enough.

AUTHOR'S NOTE

It may sound a little bit odd, but one of the best things you can do as a writer is pay attention when the muse is speaking to you. That muse can come in many forms: song, poem, even a picture. One day I saw a stunning photo of the Golden Gate Bridge and my writer brain went to work. I thought about the extraordinary circumstances that had to align themselves to make people believe they could build a suspension bridge over an enormous body of water. I tried to shake the idea away until another image appeared on social media an hour later that celebrated the life of physician Dr. Lucy Maria Field Wanzer, the first female graduate from the Medical Department of the University of California, San Francisco (then known as Toland Medical College). At that point, I listened to that muse nudging me and the idea for this book was born.

Like any historical writer, you do months, even years, of research to discover details about a setting, but sometimes to capture a city's important details you have to visit it. In late May 2018, I went to San Francisco for the specific purpose of walking the Golden Gate Bridge. I wanted to feel how it moved and swayed under my feet. Some force inside me needed to look at the 220-foot drop from the roadway down into the water and comprehend what those brave, heroic men building the bridge had to endure. On the day I visited, there were high winds and the bridge bucked beneath my feet. I will admit it was a little terrifying, but I worked every single element I experienced that day into this story. While at the bridge I picked up two books: *Building the Golden Gate* published by the Golden Gate National Parks Conservatory and Golden Gate Bridge Highway and Transportation District, as well as *Spanning The Gate: The Golden Gate Bridge* by Stephen Cassady. Both provided an enormous amount of critical information about how the bridge was built.

One other significant thing that happened during my trip was I had the immense pleasure of meeting local historian, and Richmond

District native, John Freeman. We sat in his house in the Richmond District for over three hours as he deliciously detailed the history of the neighborhood. He has been my constant source of information about the area and a thorough reader for me. Any missteps in this novel are on me because John is a consummate pro.

I spent quite a bit of time reading detailed accounts of how the bridge was erected, as well as watching numerous documentaries about the bridge's construction. These documentaries included first-person accounts from the men who worked on the bridge. Many of the details I've included in this book come from real incidents.

Al Zampa did fall into the net on the Marin side of the bridge and broke four vertebrae in his back. Al would become one of nineteen members of what the workers deemed the "Halfway to Hell" club. The first death did come from a derrick arm crushing worker Kermit Moore. The final climactic scene with the net going into the water is a true event. On February 17, 1937, a traveling scaffold broke loose and took part of the safety net and twelve men into the water. Slim Lambert and Fred Dummatzen were both rescued from the water by a local crab fisherman. Slim Lambert sustained multiple injuries but survived along with another worker, Oscar Osberg. Unfortunately, Fred Dummatzen succumbed to his injuries. Ten men in total perished in the accident. If you visit the bridge today, there is a memorial plaque that recognizes all the men who lost their lives.

Much of the details about the workers and the accidents on the bridge were culled from Labor Archives and Research Center's *Golden Gate Oral History Project: The Accident of February 17, 1937* found on YouTube, as well as *Building The Golden Gate: A Workers' Oral History* by Harvey Schwartz. Two television programs, "Golden Gate Bridge," part of *Modern Marvels* on the History Channel and "Golden Gate Bridge" from PBS's *American Experience* helped add color and detail to the story.

Other parts of this book were created via my own imagination. The Hooverville located at Baker Beach was of my own fictional making. I traveled to the beach and walked among its beautiful cypress trees and gorgeous views of the houses in the Sea Cliff area and knew it had to be the location of the camp.

The field hospital at the bridge did indeed exist. It is only briefly mentioned in a few accounts so details were also of my own creation. I also took creative license with Willa being taken up onto the bridge. At that time, even with an injured worker, there would be no way they would have allowed a woman onto the construction site.

On a later visit to San Francisco, I took a long walk through the Richmond District and scouted out locations for where Doctor Winston might have had her office. I also visited the real St. Monica and took a stroll through the Sea Cliff neighborhood. The convent Willa is supposed to enter is another of my fictional creations. I wanted to play with the elements of what a postulant's life would look like so I borrowed from a few sources, thus creating the need for a fictional convent. The structural details of a nun's intake process were taken from several sources, but most helpful was "Discipline, Resistance, Solace and the Body: Catholic Women's Religious Convent Experiences from the Late 1930s to the Late 1960s," a journal article in *Religions* co-authored by Christine Gervais and Amanda Watson.

Other elements of the story, including Willa and Sam's visit to the Sutro Baths, are authentic parts of San Francisco's history. The baths were a real place until a fire in 1966 gutted the entire structure. The remaining concrete ruins are now part of the National Park Service's Golden Gate Recreation Area at Lands End. The majority of the details regarding the baths came from *Sutro's Glass Palace: The Story of the Sutro Baths* written by John A. Martini.

Special thanks to Lisa Borok, Park Interpretive Specialist at the California State Railroad Museum Library, for providing detailed information so I could make Cara's trip from Sacramento to New York historically accurate.

While Dr. Katherine Winston is a fictional character, details of her ambition, kindness, and commitment to the San Francisco community were inspired by Dr. Lucy Wanzer, who did in fact practice on Geary Street up until her death in 1930. Like Katherine, she faced prejudice when she entered the medical college. The account Katherine describes to Willa about her early run-in with Dr. Briar comes partially from the prejudice Wanzer experienced as a student. Dr. Wanzer graduated in 1876 and became the first woman west of the Rocky Mountains to be recognized as a physician. After she graduated, her name was submitted to the San Francisco Medical Society, and she was threatened to be blackballed. She refused to withdraw her name and was later admitted. In 1888, she was elected the first female president of the group. Along with another local, prominent female physician, Dr. Emma Sutro Merritt, she would dedicate her life to caring for both the women and children of San Francisco. A tremendous resource in researching Dr. Wanzer was a biographical paper written by Dr. Robert S. Sherins called, *Dr. Lucy M. Field Wanzer: First Woman Graduate U.C. Medical Department.*

Doctors like Lucy Wanzer and Emma Sutro Merritt broke many barriers and pushed back against those in society who believed they had no right to be physicians. They paved the way for many young women to follow their dreams to study medicine. Both Dr. Wanzer and Dr. Merritt may only be blips in U.S. history, but with this novel I hope to honor their tenacity and elucidate their travails and triumphs through both Willa's and Katherine's stories.

ADDITIONAL RESEARCH MATERIALS

American Red Cross. *First Aid Text-Book*. Philadelphia, PA: The Blakiston Company, 1937.

American Red Cross. *Home Hygiene and the Care of the Sick*. Philadelphia, PA: The Blakiston Company, 1933.

Bowen, Robert W. *Images of America: San Francisco's Presidio*. Charleston, SC: Arcadia Publishing, 2005.

Dietz, David. *Medical Magic*. New York: The New Home Library, 1937.

Fialka, John J. *Sisters: Catholic Nuns and the Making of America*. New York: St. Martin's Press, 2003.

Fitzgerald, Martha Holoubek. *The Courtship of Two Doctors: A 1930s Love Story of Letters, Hope, and Healing*. Shreveport, LA: Little Dove Press, 2012.

Golden Gate Bridge and Highway District. *The Golden Gate Bridge: Report of the Chief Engineer to the Board of Directors of the Golden Gate Bridge and Highway District*. San Francisco, CA: Golden Gate Bridge and Highway District, 1938.

McGuiness, Margaret M. *Called to Serve: A History of Nuns in America*. New York: New York University Press, 2013.

Ungaretti, Lorri. *Images of America: San Francisco's Richmond District*. Charleston, SC: Arcadia Publishing, 2005.

Van Der Zee, John. *The Gate: The True Story of the Design and Construction of the Golden Gate*. Lincoln, NE: iUniverse, 2000 (originally published by Simon & Schuster, 1986).

ACKNOWLEDGMENTS

It takes a writer sitting in a chair for many, many hours to create a story, but it takes an incredible cast of people to make sure that story makes it onto the shelves and into readers' hands. I'm eternally grateful to each person who has taken the time to help me bring this book to life.

First to David. Thank you for that quiet day when you patiently went through all my medical details and kindly pointed out all the places I'd gone astray. I couldn't imagine walking through this life without you. You are an incredible friend and partner. For Ryan, thanks for taking that long walk on the bridge with me and not rolling your eyes too much when I made you stop and take dozens of pictures. That day, while windy and cold, will always be one of my favorite memories. To Olivia, my brave, smart girl. I always think of you when I create these fierce female characters. Every day you teach me what it means to be strong.

For my mom, Joan Price Trueblood, who answered all my questions about the Catholic church pre-Vatican II. Thank you for bringing to light some important details, and not laughing at my silly questions, especially when it came to batting words around about how young women in the 1930s talked about their period. From the beginning, you have believed in my writing dream. I can never tell you how much your support has meant to me. To Jon Grossklaus, you are much more to me than a father-in-law. Thank you for answering my early medical questions. Your knowledge was incredibly helpful.

Truebloods, Welches, Buzzards, and the entire Grossklaus family, thank you for attending my events, telling everyone who would listen about my books, and for being my biggest champions. And for my best friend Tiffany, who lets me talk on and on about the wild world of publishing. I love you all.

John Freeman, historian extraordinaire, who was always open to share his wealth of knowledge about the Richmond District and San

Francisco. This book is infinitely better because of you. Special thanks also go to historian John A. Martini, who sent me detailed emails about his research regarding Fort Point, and for writing the beautiful book about the Sutro Baths, which gave me inspiration for that scene in the novel. Also to Woody LaBounty at Western Neighborhood Projects for connecting me with John Freeman. Jean White Smith walked the bridge on that opening day in May 1937 and was kind enough to spend a long lunch sharing her memories of the city with me. Special thanks to her daughter Kathie McMahon for connecting us.

Big shout-outs to my early readers Megan LaCroix and Michelle Mason. Your notes and detailed comments helped make this story stronger. Kim Chance, who I know is only a text away and is my steady voice of reason. I'm so lucky to have you as a pub sister! Joanna Meyer who early on sat with me during a long lunch and listened to me ramble about a girl and the Golden Gate Bridge. Lydia Kang who answered my questions about early antiseptics. Thank you for your patience and quick replies. The entire AZ YA/MG writing group who continues to astonish me with their talent and insight when it comes to the writing world.

There are really no words to emphasize how grateful I am to the entire team at North Star Editions and Flux. Thank you for continuing to believe in my bold, unflinching girls. Mari Kesselring, you made yet another dream come true when you said "yes" to bringing Willa and her secrets into the world. My editor, Kelsy Thompson, who loved Willa, Sam, and the outrageous MacCarthy boys from the start. Megan Naidl, publicist extraordinaire, who is a fun partner-in-crime at conferences and a calming hand during signings. Sarah Taplin for the beautiful cover design.

Loving appreciation goes to the Electric Eighteens and the Class of 2K18. Your constant support makes it so much easier to navigate the daunting world of publishing.

Finally, to the readers, librarians, bookstagrammers, bloggers, book clubs, and everyone in the reading community who has supported my work. Thank you for loving my fierce girls as much as I do!

ABOUT THE AUTHOR

Amy Trueblood grew up in Southern California only ten minutes from Disneyland, which sparked an early interest in storytelling. As the youngest of five, she spent most of her time trying to find a quiet place to curl up with her favorite books. After graduating with a degree in journalism, she worked in entertainment in Los Angeles before settling into a career in public relations and advertising in Arizona. When she's not writing, Amy's crafting a Spotify playlist for her next book or drinking her favorite iced tea. Her debut novel, *Nothing But Sky*, a Spring 2018 Junior Library Guild selection, is available in bookstores now.

For more on Amy, check out her website
AmyTruebloodAuthor.com.

READ MORE BY
AMY TRUEBLOOD

Seventeen-year-old Grace Lafferty only feels alive when she's dangling 500 feet above ground. As a post-World War I wing walker, Grace is determined to get to the World Aviation Expo, proving her team's worth against flashier competitors and earning a coveted Hollywood contract.

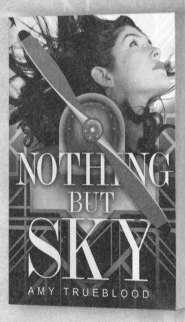

But when a stunt goes wrong, Grace must decide if she's willing to risk everything for one final trick.

A 2018 JUNIOR LIBRARY GUILD SELECTION

"An exhilarating historical novel with a strong feminist core that will appeal to a broad range of readers."
—*Booklist*

flux
®